BEACHGLASS

Wendy Blackburn

BEACHGLASS

ST. MARTIN'S PRESS
New York

www.stmartins.com

Design by Kathryn Parise

LIBRARY OF CONGRESS CATALOGING-IN-PUBLICATION DATA

Blackburn, Wendy.
    Beachglass / Wendy Blackburn.
      p. cm.
    ISBN 0-312-35158-5
    EAN 978-0-312-35158-8
    1. Recovering addicts—Fiction.   2. Substance abuse—Fiction.
  3. West Hollywood (Calif)—Fiction. I. Title.

PS3602.L32529 B43 2006
813'.6—dc22   2006040803

First Edition: May 2006

10 9 8 7 6 5 4 3 2 1

For my family
And for my friend Rick

Note to Readers

While some elements of this novel may have been partly inspired by true events and real people, the author wishes to state that this story is strictly a work of fiction—not a memoir, not an autobiography. For the few characters who were based, quite loosely, on actual living people, their names and other identifying factors have been changed and blended in with traits, demographics, occurrences, and descriptors from the author's imagination, thus creating whole new beings within this fiction narrative.

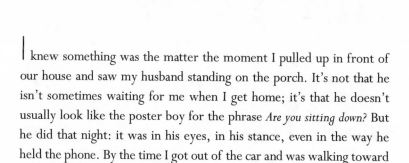

I knew something was the matter the moment I pulled up in front of our house and saw my husband standing on the porch. It's not that he isn't sometimes waiting for me when I get home; it's that he doesn't usually look like the poster boy for the phrase *Are you sitting down?* But he did that night: it was in his eyes, in his stance, even in the way he held the phone. By the time I got out of the car and was walking toward him, I could hardly breathe.

I stopped on the top step. "Simon? What is it?"

"Timothy just called."

"What did he say?"

"To call him back. Tonight."

"How did he sound?"

"Oh, you know Timothy—simply *fab*ulous. I put Clara on the phone, and she sang the teapot song to him. He didn't say why he was calling."

He didn't have to. "Is she asleep?"

"She went down about a half hour ago."

He held the cordless phone out by one end and pointed it at me like the baton in a relay race. I took the other end, and we stood like that for a long moment, our eyes locked. He finally let go of the phone, leaving it in my hand.

"This might take a while," I said.

"I know."

"Wait up for me?"

"Of course."

I wrapped my arms around him in an embrace longer than the usual hi-honey-I'm-home hug. I was recharging my battery, taking a nice, tall drink from the Fountain of Life.

After he went inside, I sat down on the porch swing and looked at the phone in my hand. I pictured Timothy, twelve hundred miles south, holding his phone, too, waiting for my call.

We had always known this would happen someday, but I hadn't imagined what my life would be like when it did, who I would be. My new life was like the egg in the egg-drop project that high school science teachers assign—the one where the students have to use household materials to construct a contraption in which they can nestle an egg, drop it from a second-story window, and have the egg not break. I was the kid who padded her egg effectively, using anything she could find, holding her breath and letting go, watching as her invention bounced and survived, egg intact, seemingly unbreakable—until moments like this came and I wondered if my well-crafted cushioning could withstand one more fall, especially one from this high up.

I had to call him. I had to hear what I already feared was true, and I had to prepare to take the action I had committed to taking years ago. So I hit the *on* button and let go.

When I went back inside, Simon was sitting on the couch. I flopped down next to him and set the phone on the coffee table.

"What did he say?" he asked.

"Exactly what I thought he would say. Remember when we were down there in May and he said everything was fine, but no one believed him? Well, we didn't believe him because it wasn't true. He's not fine at all."

I started to chew one of my cuticles. My mind was racing. I crossed and uncrossed my legs, wiped my hands on my jeans, and walked into Clara's room, kneeling by the side of her bed. I watched her as she slept. I looked at her sweaty curls, her arms flung overhead. I rested my cheek on her, gently, inhaling her scent, feeling her chest rise and fall with every breath. I stood up, watching her, not wanting to go back out to the living room.

Simon came and stood next to me. He put his hands on my shoulders and began to massage the knots that were already forming along either side of my spine. He knew just where they were. "Come on," he said, leading me out of her room and back to the couch.

We sat down.

"This sucks."

"I know." He took my hands in both of his. "But Delia, we've known it would happen someday. What do you want to do?"

"I don't know. I want to go. I mean, I promised him I would be there. But that was before I met you, before we moved to Seattle, before we had Clara. When Timothy and I made the *no matter what* pact, there was no way I could have imagined how far my life would be now from where it was then."

I thought about the two of them. My men. Timothy was my first soul mate—certainly not in a romantic way; he's about as gay as it gets—and Simon is my second. He's not an AA person like us: I had married outside the tribe, and, like a marriage between people from different countries, the love can certainly be passionate and delicious, but there were limits on where the learned language could take me compared to the native tongue. Simon had always understood that Timothy was part of my homeland. And he had never been jealous, though he had watched like an outsider at times. He also understood that when the homeland beckons, you go.

"He needs you."

"So does Clara."

"And so do I," he said, pulling me toward him, his touch softening me as it always has, "but right now, he needs you more."

I searched his eyes and felt mine moisten, with sadness for Timothy and love for Simon. I wiped my face with my sleeve.

"It's Timothy. You have to go." He said it with such confidence and common sense that it actually sounded logical. Of course I would just pick up and leave my family and fly to Los Angeles. Who wouldn't?

I opened my mouth to protest again but stopped, letting his matter-of-fact attitude quell my emotions for a moment. "Do you really think we could make it work?"

"We can make anything work."

"But what about Clara?" I hated leaving her even for a few hours; she was only two years old. I had stopped nursing her just a few months earlier. I had given up my career to stay home with her, and the only people I ever let watch her were Simon and my parents. My leaving might mean day care, and I wasn't willing to put her someplace other than my own home.

"I can take the sabbatical I've been meaning to take," Simon told me. "The timing works out perfectly. Fall quarter isn't even staffed yet. And you *know* your mom and dad would help out—I mean, they moved up here when she was born just to be with her. They'll welcome this as much as I will."

I stared at him. He was seriously willing to do this for me.

"Don't worry—no day care," he said, grinning. "We'll take care of her. Sweetie, I know it's scary, but you can't not go."

I continued to stare at him, letting it sink in. He was right. Either way, I would be guilt ridden. If only a coin toss were appropriate for life-and-death decisions.

I took a deep breath. "Okay," I said. "I'll go. I'm going. Let's get this thing figured out."

At midnight, after about two hours of logistical detangling—going through Clara's very crowded social calendar of playgroups, toddler swim lessons, and birthday parties, calling the airlines, calling my parents, looking at appointments I needed to cancel and bills Simon and I had to pay—we turned off the lights and decided to go to bed.

On the way there, I stopped in Clara's room, again, already feeling my departure as a physical pain deep in my chest. It gripped my heart, shortened my breath. I straightened her blanket and bent over and kissed her on the nose, whispering, "Good night, sweet pea. I love you." My eyes filled with tears. I stood up before they fell on her.

By the time I got to our bedroom, Simon had lit a few candles and opened the French windows, letting the slow winds of that warm August night drift into the house. I took his hand and led him outside. Encircled by ancient cherry trees, our backyard was secluded from the neighbors yet open to the sky. Moonlight came through the leaves and faded our bare skin to a fine pale-white as we removed our clothes and laid them out on the grass. Our kisses were urgent and tender and profound as we dropped first to our knees, then to that makeshift quilt, our bodies intertwined as I held on to his shoulders, buried my face in his neck, pressed my wet cheek against his jaw. We clutched at each other hungrily, frantically, trying to get closer than was humanly possible, as if our lovemaking could create enough heat to span the distance my absence would bring.

I opened my eyes before dawn the next morning. We were back in bed, and Simon was propped up on one elbow alongside me. He had been watching me sleep. I could still smell the earthy, barky scent of last night on him. We lay together until it was light out; then he pulled on his pajama bottoms, tossed me a T-shirt, and said, "I'll be right back. I have a present for you."

He returned with a still-sleeping Clara in his arms and laid her on me, tummy-to-tummy. Her legs dropped off either side of my waist and her arms folded naturally and loosely around my neck. I kissed the top of her head and nuzzled her awake.

"Mama!" She hugged me tighter and then wiggled to a sitting position on me, her hair a wild snarl, her eyes sleepy but bright, her chubby hands tugging at the neck of her footy pajamas. "Off. 'Jamas off." I helped her with the zipper and pulled her arms out. This was how she liked them when it was hot, not off completely but unzipped to the waist with her arms out of the sleeves. Topless. I tied the sleeves in a knot like a bustle in the back, and she giggled.

I tipped my body so she slid down between Simon and me. Somehow we managed to tell her, without too many tears and with the blessing of her unformed concept of time and distance, that I would be away for a little while. We told her I would call home every day, even two, three, four times a day, and that Daddy was taking off work just to be with her. The excitement of that news quashed any separation anxiety she may have had, and she threw herself at him, squealing. Then the two of them rolled over toward me, and she put her little hands on my face. Later that day, I boarded an airplane, my heart still in that bed with the two of them.

"Would you like something to drink?" The flight attendant craned her head and looked at me with manufactured sympathy. It was a look that said she could tell I had been crying but was not going to prod, that her customer service skills only went so far.

Would I like something to drink? I almost laughed out loud. If only she knew. I would like *every*thing to drink. I looked at the beverage cart, at the tiny bottles of wine. And closer, at the tinier bottles of vodka, gin, bourbon, and the wet-cold beers on the bottom rack. They all called my name. Loudly. Being a recovering alcoholic was like being on an obstacle course. Everywhere there was something to dodge, something to keep you on your toes.

"A Sprite, please." This had been my answer for the last dozen years. It came out automatically and before my craving had a chance to get too intense. After she put the Sprite on my tray and disappeared down the aisle, I leaned my head back and closed my eyes. After my ears stopped filling and popping, my mind went back to the night Timothy told me he had tested positive for HIV.

It was in the spring of 1988, during one of our slumber parties. Timothy had gone into his kitchen, humming, and returned with a mug of tea in each hand and a box of Lu cookies tucked under one arm. I remember the way he shuffled in, his green pajamas baggy and crooked, his reading glasses sticking out of his breast pocket. He had walked over to me and leaned forward so I could take the cookie box and he could safely set our tea on the side table. Small motions like this, small partnerships, had all added up to create our rhythm, a rhythm like that of an old married couple or telepathic twins.

We used the open sofa bed as a sort of picnic blanket. On it was his guitar, our boxes of cigarettes, an ashtray, a magazine, incense, a few random pages of sheet music, and now the cookies. I sat Indian-style in the dim light. He folded himself into the same position across from me, grabbed my hand, and said, "I have news."

I thought he was going to say he had gotten a gallery showing or had met someone.

"I got my test results back from Dr. Vincent."

I had looked at him blankly, as if he were speaking in some exotic new dialect.

"My HIV test. It was positive."

I swayed, as if the mattress had shifted under me. Black stars tingled in my peripheral vision. My jaw opened just a crack, like a toad's. My eyes first opened wide, then slammed shut against the dizzying combination of what I'd just heard and the spin of the room. My lips parched. My skin blanched. My ears rang as I tried to rehear what he had just said.

When I was finally able to open my eyes, I knew by the look on his face—brave, apologetic, strong—that I had heard him correctly. I fumbled for words, then just looked down and started to cry. I thought, *No, no, no,* over and over again. I may have even said it out loud; I don't know. Who knows what I did? And why was it easier for him to tell me than for me to hear it? I watched him, him with his wide-open brown eyes and quick hand gestures, as he went on to insist that he would beat the odds, overcome it, be alive for the cure they would no doubt be finding any day now. He said whether it was by a medical breakthrough or a flat-out miracle, he would live to be an old man. I listened patiently and smiled with him, encouraging him, but the voice in my head said he was a dead man. I hated the voice in my head. I would have given anything for his faith, but as always he was the believer and I was the cynic.

So he had lived a long time, compared to what I had figured. That was over eleven years ago, and who knows how long before that he had contracted the virus.

Contracted the virus.

I wished, childlike, that I could go back to the moment when the poison first entered his body. I could change its course maybe, flush it out with . . . what, I couldn't imagine, but I would have worn a red cape or a gas mask, held a wreath of garlic, a mirror, a cross, something. I certainly would have tried.

The pilot announced that we were beginning our descent into Los Angeles. The basin. I opened my eyes. Bright sun. I pressed my forehead against the plastic of the window and looked straight down to see the beaches. Mountains rolled along the coast, black from fire in some places, covered with dry-green sagebrush in others. As we banked left to come in from the east, I saw the *Hollywood* letters scattered dirty-white and crooked against the wrinkled, faded violet hills. Then we turned to the right, circling first a downtown that rose like stalagmites up through the smog, then over the ghettos and toward the airport. I saw the graffitied stucco of boarded-up buildings, the clotheslines and chain-link fences, the strip malls and cheap nail salons. I could hear the voice of the city, a raspy voice speaking Spanish, Vietnamese, Jive, Russian, Pig Latin, Korean. It was a voice that I knew well. My welcoming committee.

Staring out at that giant washed-out landscape covered by five-lane freeways and so much concrete, I realized that I had grown used to the colors of Seattle, the way the constant rainfall kept every plant fertile, lush, and emerald colored; the way moss grew three inches thick on trees and between every crack in the sidewalk; the blue of the lakes; the silver of the bay. Here, brown filth choked the earth and stunted its growth with a film of polluted dust and stillness. Some people said it did the same to its inhabitants.

The plane lowered itself to the runway, found its gate, and was immediately filled with the clatter of seat belts unfastening and overhead compartments opening. People were standing long before they could move, shifting weight from foot to foot and trying to see if those up front were moving yet. They wanted to get to where they were going.

I was not as impatient. I stayed in my seat, continuing to look outside. It was all framed by that little round-rectangle window: my past, my future, and this thing that was about to happen. Would this be the one thing my sobriety couldn't handle? For all the other stuff, I had Timothy to fall back on. *As long as we have each other,* we had always said, *we can get through anything.* Okay, but what if we don't have each other? Then what?

I prayed as I drove from the rental car place to Timothy's house. No— not prayer, really, it was more like rehearsal. I played it in my mind over and over until I thought I could do it: I would pull into the driveway, get my bags from the trunk, and walk up the stairs to find a newly solemn Timothy sitting in dim light. I would be okay. I could do this. *Worse things have happened,* I told myself, knowing it was a lie.

I turned onto his street and nearly laughed aloud at how wrong I had been. Instead of a dim and solemn anything, there was Timothy, leaping across his lawn and waving madly, every skip and prance contradicting the alleged collapse of his body, the losing battle being fought there under his skin where we couldn't see it.

"Hon!" he yelled.

I parked and ran from the car, hugging him so tightly that eventually he had to peel me off like a wet sweater. We stood and looked at each other, then walked inside holding hands and talking a mile a minute about everything but the reason I was there.

My bags stayed in the trunk. We were too absorbed in each other to be bothered, and there was nothing I needed right then that my suitcases could provide anyway. All I wanted to do was look at him and sit next to him and listen to his voice. It was still strong and familiar.

When not talking about his health began to feel obvious, we both grew quiet. I looked away, and he cleared his throat.

"Well then. I guess there's a lot I need to fill you in on . . . my meds and all the what-ifs, and I have a list of doctors' names and phone numbers I should give you. I'm still seeing Dr. Vincent, but now I have a lung guy and a viral guy, and a few others who I think just want to see me because they like me." He winked and tried to laugh, but it came out like the canned laughter of a sitcom sound track, tinny and forced.

I wasn't sure what to say. It was too much to take in. Lung. Viral. Meds. I took a deep breath and said, "Just tell me what you need help with, what you want me to do and not do. I mean, you seem fine, but you're not, or else I wouldn't be here. Right?"

A pause, short but long enough.

"Right, yeah. But it'll be okay—I mean, I've done a lot of work, meditating, closure, all that good stuff. Honestly, I'm at peace with it."

It.

I flinched. We hadn't said the word yet: *Death.* Or the others: *Dead. Gone. Dying. AIDS. Funeral. Never. Good-bye.*

"C'mon, really! I am okay with it. I'm not going to be angry and bitter. That's never been my style; you know that. I'm trying to embrace my death," *there, he said it,* "with the same attitude I embraced life," *past tense, oh God,* "and with the people I love being right here with me. We'll be fine. It isn't really good-bye anyway, toots; we'll hook up in another life just like we always have. So relax. And let me walk you through the technical stuff so we can get on with just being. Let's start with the pills, since I have, like, four million of them. . . ."

We walked into the bathroom. The counter, which had always been decorated with trendy soaps and bath salts, was now covered with orangey-brown plastic pill bottles. I tried to pay attention but was glad he had written it all down for me, because I wasn't hearing his words so much as I was listening to his voice, wanting to capture it and hold it tight in my fist. I wanted to turn it into something visible and stare at it forever.

"I'm going to take a hot bath and then lie down for a while," Timothy called out from the bathroom. "Make yourself at home."

I smiled. It went without saying; his house had been like a second home to me for years. While he was in the bath, I got my things from the car and started to settle into my space, the now-enclosed balcony off of his bedroom that was just big enough for a futon, a dresser, and two little tables. This balcony was separated from his room by a wide doorway and a roll of bamboo shades and from the outside by several giant windows, which I opened right away, feeling the warmth of the tatami mats underfoot and knowing it would be a hot night. Then I opened my suitcase and began unpacking. I shook out a wrinkled linen shirt, decided to dip it in the kitchen sink and hang it over a chair to dry, then took out my glasses, a book, and the photographs of Clara I had brought with me. I sat down on the futon, homesick for my little girl. I needed her, but, I reminded myself, Simon's voice in my ears, Timothy needed me.

He had already slipped out of the bath and under his covers. Within minutes I could hear him snoring in the next room. His breath was ragged and strained and reminded me of one of the sounds my parents' old Volkswagen used to make. I called home and made Simon put Clara on immediately. I felt my eyes wet as I heard her soft, "Mama?" on the line, tentative, still wary of telephones.

"Hi, sweetie. Yes, it's Mama."

"Mama on airpane?"

"I was, but it landed. I'm at Uncle Timothy's house now, in California."

"Unca Tim!" she cried, with a note of excitement: In my mind I saw Clara's eyebrows shoot up. They had met in person only a few times, but I had impressed him upon her as much as I could, telling her stories, showing her pictures and videos, putting her on the phone with him. She loved the paintings of his that hung in our house and the cards he made just for her on holidays. I wanted her to know him. I corrected myself: *I wanted her to have known him.* I would have to practice thinking in that tense. It was an awkward tense to think in. To live in.

"Hey, Clara? I miss you so much."

"Miss you, Mama."

"I love you, sweet pea."

"Love you, Mama."

"So, you're there." It was Simon back on the phone.

I heard Clara's voice trail off as she ran down the hall. I closed my eyes and wished I were there with them, safe in our every-evening routine of dinner, a walk, bath, stories, bedtime.

"Yeah. I'm here."

"How does he look?"

"Um." I wasn't sure how to answer that one. There were none of the trademark purply lesions on his face or neck, but he had dropped several pounds, and the loss was most visible around his shoulders and chest. The emaciation gave his eyes a doelike largeness and made his teeth slightly overprominent, like he was smiling even when he wasn't. The medications had frizzed and dulled his previously shiny brown hair, and it had begun to thin as well. His skin looked thin, too: ashen, fragile, made from a wet tissue. Everything about him was thin. Even his laugh this afternoon was thin. He looked awfully old for forty-seven. He had stubble. With gray in it. I couldn't recall ever seeing him anything but clean shaven.

"He looks . . . okay. I guess. Considering." I cleared the lump from my throat, the lump that had settled in the night before and couldn't seem to leave. "I just wish there was something someone could do to help."

"That's why you're there."

"Right." I took a deep breath. "How's Clara doing without me so far?" I was afraid I was scarring her, giving her the abandonment issues that all the now-adult latchkey kids claim as the cause of their failed relationships.

"Sweetie, you've only been gone five hours."

We laughed, and he assured me she was fine. Although this didn't do a lot to assuage my longing or my worries, I grabbed hold of it and decided to at least pretend to believe it so I could concentrate on what I was here to do.

"God, I miss you guys."

"I know. We miss you, too. But we're doing just fine. And please, you have enough to worry about without worrying about us. Just take care of him. And you. And we'll talk tomorrow. Okay?"

"Okay."

"I love you. Give Timothy my best."

"I will. I love you, too."

I hung up and looked over at Timothy, trying to let my eyes adjust to his bony frame, his pale skin, his sunken cheeks. He had tried to appear so healthy this afternoon, but when he had given me the rundown on all of his medications, the act had dropped away like a cheap Halloween costume. The bells and whistles slowed and then stopped, and I saw so clearly in his eyes that he was afraid and exhausted.

He woke up a few hours later and said he wanted dinner. I took this as a good sign. I still hadn't accepted the fact that there was no such thing as a good sign—appetite or not, humor or not, coughs gone for the day or not, he was not going to get better.

"What are you in the mood for?" I asked him.

"I don't know. There's some stuff in the fridge. We can forage."

We went into the kitchen and turned the lights on. He opened a bag of pretzels and started eating them, then made a face and closed the bag. "Salt. Painful," he said, opening his mouth to show me the white patches there. "Thrush. How about something bland?"

I opened the refrigerator and saw that there were fresh vegetables. I opened the cupboard and took out a can of chicken noodle soup. "I can make us a little soup and salad. Is that bland enough for you?"

"That's perfect. *Chicken Soup for the Guy with AIDS's Soul*—isn't that a book?"

He sat down on the kitchen table while I pulled a head of lettuce from the crisper.

"Can I ask you something?" I said.

"You know you can ask me anything, hon. Except for, like, out on a date."

"I'm serious."

"So am I. You're a girl."

I stared at him until he stopped making the cootie-shot sign with his hands.

"Okay," he said. "Sorry. What's your question?"

"What's your T-cell count?"

"About fifty."

"What?" I was sure I had heard wrong.

"Fifty, five-oh, Roman numeral *L*." He held up his hands, one splayed, five fingers outstretched, the other curled into a little *O*. He looked from one to the other. "Five. Oh."

I just stood there. I don't know what I expected to hear, maybe three hundred, maybe less; maybe I was still in a little denial. But fifty? He could drop at any minute.

"I know. It's low, huh? When Dr. Vincent told me, I was floored. Especially since he had just confirmed that my pesky cough is the start of pneumonia. Again. Hence the antibiotics. He didn't have to tell me that they probably won't work this time, which is why I called you, hon. But you knew that."

I didn't know what to say. I began tearing the lettuce into pieces, dropping them into a big teak bowl, looking down, seeing if I could cry without the tears falling out, without his knowing that I was crying, since that seemed like a skill I'd need to develop, if I was going to be anything other than a drain to the man who needed the strength of my friendship more than he needed the river of tears we both knew we could cry, given the opportunity.

"So," he said, nodding in the direction of the hospital where we had met. "That's where it all started." We were sitting on the balcony after dinner, eating ice cream straight from the containers. "And I'm telling you right now, that's not where it's going to end. I'm staying here, at home, till my fat lady sings."

End, I thought. It had a start, and it will have an end, this era of my life, this friendship, this person. But we were both thinking of the beginning as we looked at the hospital.

"You know it was twelve years ago this month," he said.

"Of course I know that."

"You know that if we hadn't been alcoholics, we might never have met."

"And how boring would that have been?"

"Quite. And I'll let you in on a little secret, hon. When you get to the end, you find out that not only do the things that matter, matter more, but you realize that even the things that seemed awful really weren't. I used to sit in this same chair and look at the hospital and think, knowing they had a drug rehab, wouldn't it just be the pits if I wound up there? And I'd pour myself another gin and tonic, minus the tonic, knowing damn well I needed to get sober but thinking how horrible it would be to quit drinking. And then I did wind up there, and instead of it being the worst thing, it was the best thing. I found you and

AA—and myself. It really takes the fear away, when you stop seeing things as 'good' or 'bad' and start seeing them as equal pieces of the big, beautiful picture that is the human experience."

He dug into his ice cream and came up with a giant spoonful and pointed it at me. "That's why I don't have any regrets, why I'm not fighting it. Sure, I wish I could have some more time here, but my dance card is punched full and I'm going out with a smile on my face."

It took a long time to fall asleep that first night, and when I finally did, I had a series of strange dreams, the last of which featured me, trying to scream, but with nothing coming out except a teeny little whisper. *Great,* I thought, *real handy.* I didn't need to bust out Timothy's dream analysis book to figure out what that one meant.

When I woke up, dawn was diluting the blackness that had covered us in our sleep, a silvery haze at the far base of the sky, stars growing harder to see. The house was quiet except for Timothy, who slept making that strange sound that was louder than breathing but not quite a snore. Things invisible in the dark emerged and took form, first just shades of blue, then regular colors, then details. Timothy's Indian blanket grew from a lump of wool to a brilliant geometric splash, triangles of red and orange, stripes of green and aqua, an ivory fringe at his chin and feet.

I couldn't resist. It was the same feeling I had when I watched Clara sleep. I walked over, curled up next to him on the bed, and watched him. His eyes were so heavily closed, long brown lashes resting on relaxed cheeks. His brow would occasionally and ever so slightly pull into a quick frown, then release. I watched his dreams dart around under his closed lids for a while, and then I fell back asleep, too. I woke up when the sun fell across the bed, the intense light and heat feeling like midday already.

A few moments later he stretched, a drowsy cat arching across the bed, nearly pushing me off, and then pulled up to a sitting position.

This was how he always woke up, first the arch, then the sit, straight from asleep to awake with not much lingering between the two.

"Good morning," I said.

"Morning."

"Shall I put on some water for tea?"

He nodded while yawning and lifted his fists to rub his eyes.

I went to the kitchen and returned with big mugs of herbal tea. We sat up against the headboard together, knees up, four bare feet side by side on the sheets.

I looked out the window. There were a few remaining signs that it was the same city into which I was born: my childhood house, still sitting square on its tiny lot down by the boardwalk; the tall palms bent black against a sky red and full of Malibu-fire ash; the smell of bus fumes and ocean and sage, cigarette smoke and poppies and jet fuel; the brown muck that lay like a blanket over Pasadena and made it impossible to breathe in August, then left by November to reveal giant snow-capped mountains against a sky the color of blue hydrangea. Instead of feeling rooted the way I used to, I felt pulled, a tug-of-war inside. My body may have been lying alongside Timothy's, but my inner compass pointed north to Simon and fixed itself on Clara as she moved in my soul and roamed in my dreams, laughing, her eyes a dark shimmer, her voice a song.

I closed my eyes and let the sun wash over me, wrapping myself around Timothy's arm.

In theory, my recovery—and everything else I had experienced up until that point—had prepared me for this. It had strengthened me, toughened me, and shown me that I could take any leap of faith and land not only unscathed but improved. On that morning, though, holding on to Timothy's skinny little arm and feeling his laborious breathing, I wasn't convinced. I saw myself making that leap and silently slipping through a crack somewhere, never to be seen again.

2

A few days after I arrived, I sat in the chair next to Timothy's Mickey Mouse phone, calling home, as I did nearly every time Timothy took a nap. Simon's voice struck the perfect balance of concern and buoyancy, holding me up like hands laced together in a foothold.

"Did you guys have a good day?" I asked him.

"Yeah. We spent all morning at the lake, and now Clara's napping."

"That sounds so wonderful." I closed my eyes, and I was back on the sand with my daughter on the day before I left. The strings of her soft denim hat were tied in a bow under her chin, her body as sleek and trim as a dachshund's in her wet navy blue suit. She ran back and forth from the water's edge to my towel, bringing me shells, some of which were small cracked pieces, others which were perfectly intact, all of which were treasures to her.

I rubbed my forehead. "We haven't even left the house since I got here."

"Aw, sweetie. You should get out, while he's still up for it."

"Yeah. I really should. Maybe I'll take Timothy out for dinner tonight. We can hit the Dresden Room afterward, see if that old piano player's still there."

But as those words came from my lips, words like *Timothy* and *dinner,* I pulled James's phone number from my photographic memory.

"Great idea. Just don't start smoking again." I heard the grin in his voice. He knew that I used to love to sit in the big red leather corner booth and chain-smoke.

"Don't worry. It's the last thing on my mind."

"Are you doing okay . . . otherwise?" Simon rarely worried about me drinking again, and when he did, he didn't quite know how to ask. "I mean, this is a really hard thing you're going through. It would be understandable if you wanted to drink."

"I know, but I'm fine, really. I'm good. I'm going to go to some meetings while I'm here, and just concentrate on being there for Timothy. I can't do that if I relapse, now, can I?" I didn't mention how tempting that drink cart on the airplane looked. Or that I was about to call James. And I couldn't believe I was concealing potential weapons from Simon. It wasn't like me at all. At least, not anymore.

"No, I suppose that could get pretty ugly. Just take care of yourself, okay?"

"Of course," I said, not sure if I was assuring him or myself.

"All right. I'll let you get going. I love you."

"I love you, too. I'll call you in the morning, when Clara's up and about."

"Okay."

I pushed Mickey's puffy white-gloved hand down to hang up. I looked through the doorway to the bedroom where Timothy slept, his chest rising and falling slowly. In my hand was the shiny yellow receiver, which I jiggled up and down, small tosses that ticked off seconds as I thought about what to do. There was no way Timothy was going anywhere. When he had gone to bed at five, he told me not to wake him till morning. I looked at the numbers arranged in a neat square by Mickey's feet. I extended my index finger and began to push the buttons, each making a different *beep,* each bringing me closer to James's voice.

It rang four times, and then he breathlessly answered just as I was about to hang up. Worried that I was going to pause too long, that I had been struck mute, I forced out a hopefully nonchalant, "Hey, James, it's Delia. Is this a bad time?"

"Hey! My God, girl! How are you?" He was surprised and animated. It had been at least a year since we'd spoken over the phone. "What's up?"

I could hear his smile.

"I'm in town, staying with Timothy. Thought I'd give you a call."

"I'm so glad you did. I just got home from work, just. Literally. I am taking my shoes off as we speak. It's got to be a hundred degrees in here. Again, literally. Can you hang on while I open some windows and turn on the air?"

I smiled. He was never one for energy conservation. Everything in excess.

He came back to the phone. "You busy tonight?"

"Not yet."

"I have a dinner date, but do you want to meet at DuPar's for dessert? They still have the best lemon meringue pie in the city, you know. How's nine-ish?"

He had always spoken as if he had been wound to the point of breaking a spring. I smiled wider. "Sounds good. I'll get us a table if I get there first. Will I recognize you?"

"I'll be the one wearing the red carnation."

"There's a look."

"See you in a bit. Hey, Dill?"

"Hmm?"

"I'm glad you called. It's been too long."

I smiled some more. "See you there."

As soon as we hung up, my smile started to fade. That conversation was so familiar, so like a million others we'd had—the cadence and the rhythm, the way he had called me by the shortened version of my name that only a few people ever use, the ease, the connection, the shorthand, the unimportance of time or space. A swarm of fireflies began to move and take flight deep in my gut when I thought about the lightness in our voices and how the light betrayed the darkness of all the things that lay underneath.

Taking off my shoes, showering, dressing, writing a note for Timothy in the unlikely event he should wake up and find me gone—it all seemed mechanical, one-dimensional. I took the towel off my head and combed my straight ashy blond hair, letting it wet my shirt across the shoulders and marveling at how quickly it dried in the heat. Between the cold and the rain in Seattle, it seemed my hair was damp more often than not.

I decided to walk up to DuPar's. It was at least a mile away, but tension had knotted my calves into fists that only a walk could relax. I strongly craved the noisy solitude that comes from walking alone in the city, how the sound of your own thoughts slips under the hiss of buses and the howl of sirens. As I left Timothy's small street, I was instantly drowned out and swallowed up, hypnotized by the hard rhythm of feet on concrete, left, right, left, right, marching, a worker ant steadfastly moving through sidewalk cracks. Without thinking, I held my key chain in my palm so one key stuck out from between each knuckle of my fist, a fan of metal points poised just in case. It was a growing-up-in-LA habit. The sun had set an hour before, leaving a long summer twilight and tall city streetlamps in its place. Jacaranda trees dripped purple petals along Beverly Boulevard, littering wilted blossoms into the gutters.

I thought about Simon as I walked and what an idiot I was for tempting fate and laying myself at James's feet. Though, I told myself, that wasn't at all what I was doing. I wasn't tempting fate, and there was no lying at anyone's feet. I was simply meeting an old friend. For pie. Not a problem. I kept walking.

I passed Jan's Coffee Shop. There was a new sign, and they had added a new awning and outdoor seating to make it appear to be a bistro, a café, when its original appeal had been the fact that it was just a glorified Denny's, and not even all that glorified. At least the orange Naugahyde booths were still there, divided along their tops by small partitions of urine-colored frosted glass. The waitresses still wore their orange-white-and-brown polyester maid's dresses, looking as sour and surly as ever.

My feet continued east. I worried whether what I had put on was the right choice: a slim black skirt, not too short or clingy but definitely not frumpy, either, and the white linen shirt. Lip gloss, but no other makeup. Sandals, silver necklace, small earrings. Wedding ring. It seemed simple and clean, neutral, not looking like I wanted him to notice me. Which maybe I did; I wasn't sure. I didn't think I did, but who knows. Always the anxiety over what I looked like when I saw James. *Like it matters,* I told myself, *like I care.*

Already at Crescent Heights. Standing at the crosswalk, waiting for the flashing red hand to change to a white figure walking, I told myself that the slight windedness I felt was just because I'm a fast walker with long strides who doesn't do enough cardio. That's all. Certainly not nervousness. The light turned, and I stepped into the crosswalk, walking slower and breathing fully into my whole body the way my yoga instructor had shown me, pushing my abdomen out, pulling air deep into my lungs and holding it. Then I felt a jumping palpitation like a cattle prod when I thought I spotted his car rounding a corner, up a block. But it wasn't him. I let out my breath in relief, yet my feet were almost numb as I inched my way up the sidewalk.

They say that before a tornado hits you can feel the air change. The pressure shifts; the sky bruises a sickly blue-yellow and goes dead silent. Firefighters say the same thing about a backdraft. They open doors to quiet rooms only to have rolling flames rush and envelop them in an instant. They never see it coming, but they always talk later about the calm that preceded it.

I felt that shift in pressure as I pushed open the glass door to the diner and spotted him, halfway down the aisle at a window booth. My vision tunneled until he was all there was, and then it was like the air was sucked away, gone. I rocked on my heels for a moment, regaining my balance. He didn't look up from his menu, didn't even notice I'd walked in until I was standing at the edge of the table.

"Can I take your order, sir?"

"Um, sure. We'll have—" He looked up then and let his menu fall to the table. He grinned. He started to slide out of his side of the booth, but I slid into mine before he could get up and hug me. I wasn't ready to see how quickly we could flip the breaker switch back on.

"So. How are you?" I asked him. My voice was wavy, unsure of itself.

"I'm in the mood for dessert. I was hoping you really were the waitress; I was going to order for us."

"Sorry to disappoint you."

"Oh, no disappointment, trust me," he said, and then we looked at each other a split second too long. My stomach went soft, dropping, as if in an elevator. I hadn't had enough time to convince myself that he had stopped having this effect on me years ago. He cleared his throat and turned toward the window, and I studied his profile. His looks had hardly been altered by the passing of time. He had the same early crow's-feet in the corners of his eyes that I did, but where mine were the kind that suggested sleepless nights and the beginnings of age, his were the kind borne only out of years of academic concentration, cigarettes, and hard laughter. He was still beautiful. His cobalt eyes, the arc of his brow, the pout of his lips, the fine bone structure. I remembered what a talented poet he was, the way he worshipped Pablo Neruda and Hemingway and Faulkner, how he preferred subtitled films over mainstream movies. His white oxford shirt was unbuttoned enough so that the hollow place at the base of his neck was exposed, and his sleeves were rolled up to just below the elbows. He turned back to me as the waitress arrived with two glasses of ice water.

As James and I ate and talked, I disappeared into his eyes, his voice, into the meringue of the pie, eggy and dense with sugar. I plucked the tiny burnt points off the top and licked the velvety lemon filling from my spoon. With each bite I slipped further into another time, another place, another life. We were eighteen, at an AA meeting, in his car, in his bed. I recalled his smell, his kisses, the golden skin on his neck, his hands, his back—the memories came at me sharply, more persistent as I tried to keep them down. By the time we finished, I was completely absorbed in alternately denying, fighting off, and surrendering to them.

He paid the bill and asked if I wanted a ride back to Timothy's. I accepted, because I still hadn't told James the reason for my being there. It had been so easy to fill him in on my life and listen to him talk about his that I had put off telling him about Timothy.

As we walked to James's car, I felt the dryness in the air and knew without having to see a weather report that the Santa Ana winds would come next week. I also knew that when the air is like that, James and I should not be alone together. But there we were anyway.

"Let me get the door for you."

"Thanks."

I watched him as he walked around the front of the car. He opened his door and slid down into the driver's seat, moving the way he always has: like a cat, or like mercury. I felt the hair on my arms and across my neck rise and then fall. *God damn the energy between us,* I thought. Our past. Puppy love. With rabies.

He had parked illegally in an alley a block over from DuPar's. I looked at the brightly colored stucco garages and the weeds growing up through the cracks in the smashed-glass-strewn asphalt and listened to the steady hum of traffic over on Fairfax. I knew that regardless of where I should ever physically live, I was always here, on these streets that were as known to me as my own signature, their curves etched like wrinkles into my soul. Cut me open and, instead of arteries or even tree rings, you'll find a map of Los Angeles, long boulevards running the length of my legs, clover-leafed freeways crossing my chest. I was born in a hospital in a Spanish barrio on Alvarado Street, I was raised on the canals of Venice, and I could still hear the Pacific beating on

Santa Monica's cliffs if I closed my eyes and thought long enough about the smell of salt and wood and beer.

When I had felt its pulse from the airplane, its hundred foreign languages, its neon and vandalism, the grid of buildings and freeways fanning out to the horizon under the olive-drab haze, my heart had fallen into its rhythm. I loved LA's size, its grime, its crassness. When Simon's job took us to the Northwest, the part of me that wanted a nice little house and a nice little baby and quiet hours spent reading and drinking hot *chai* tea by the fireplace—that part of me was thrilled. But the other part of me was not, having been thrust beyond the 213 area code, living in a land that had snow, seasons, lakes, ferries, clean water. There was always this tough little Mexican-accented lady in the back of my head—my inner *chola*—who snickered at me, laughed at my new life. She wanted me in the streets of Venice or the hills above Los Feliz. Sometimes she called me a traitor. My lungs missed the smog.

As I sat in James's car that night, it was that smog and the heat that lured me back not to the friendship part of our connection but to the other part, the quick physical part. My body felt electric, as if just being in the city itself had transformed me from the now-me to the then-me. Which I loved. And which disturbed me. I was a mother, a wife, almost thirty years old. I had become conservative in Seattle. I had grown pale and traditional under layers of sweaters and flannel and fog and politically correct conversation. I had Grown Up. I now Behaved Myself.

I was snapped back into reality with the realization that he was talking. Talking and driving. I hadn't even noticed he had started the car, and we were already a mile from the alley, driving west on Melrose.

"I'm sorry, what?"

"Where were you?"

"Oh, nowhere. What were you saying?"

He lit a cigarette, and I saw that he still used a Zippo lighter. Its gassy smell and the *clink* as he flipped the lid shut put me right back in his arms. I had to shake my head like an Etch-A-Sketch to clear the thoughts.

"I asked you how Timothy is doing."

I turned away from him and looked out the window at the loitering teenagers, drag queens, bikers, and nighttime shoppers that filled the sidewalks, and then my eyes glazed over and took me beyond the horizon, focused on a point he couldn't see, nobody could see. He was waiting for an answer, but I was silent. I wanted to hold on to the pretense for another few minutes. I wanted for him to have not asked at all. But of course he had, and even if he hadn't, I would have told him—it was just hard to make the words come out.

"Um. Not great." *Damn!* I did not want to cry. It took a second to successfully blink back the tears and clear my throat.

"Actually, James—why don't you pull over. This might take a minute."

There was nothing I could say to make it sound like less than it was.

James had parked the car and I had turned to face him, leaning against the door. He looked up at the night sky through the sunroof, quiet for a long time.

"So you're taking care of him?"

"Yeah." I was tempted to yank one of his Camels out of its crumpled pack, they lay on the console so pleadingly, begging me to touch them.

"And you'll be here . . . indefinitely?" He didn't know how to say it. I didn't know how to answer it. I looked down instead.

"Will you call me if there's anything I can do?"

"Of course. And I'm sure he'd love to see you. If the lights are on when you drop me off, come upstairs with me. Otherwise, we'll let him sleep, and you can come by another time. I think he'll still be around for another . . . while. At least."

I attempted a laugh, but it came out just like Timothy's had that first afternoon, strange and awkward. Thin.

. . .

Timothy didn't ask about my evening with James until a couple of days later. Part of me wanted to keep quiet, because it felt more exciting to me that way; it felt secret and dark and sinful if I held it to my chest— and powerful, like a good hand of cards. Telling Timothy would put it up on the rack, as we used to say, where he might say something that would break the spell. It would also open the doors to the whole dis- cussion about friends coming over, coming to say good-bye, to clasp my hand sympathetically in both of theirs and hug Timothy and cry, laughing through their tears as Timothy fell into his clown role. He would cheer them up, and they would leave feeling happy and sad at the same time, and we would talk about them after they left. They would start saying *Can I bring anything?*—and once people started to bring things, it would start to feel like death, like a wake, church ladies bring- ing casseroles to the neighborhood widower. They would bring flowers (dyed carnations, I'm sure), pies, magazines, candy, books, bread, muffins, crossword puzzles, candles. Things with angels on them. It would start looking like a swap meet in here if people "brought things."

The subject of visitors frightened me, but I was looking further and, as usual, with more worry than Timothy was. He wanted to have fun, see as many people as he could, keep his eyes as wide open as they would go. And we had to start somewhere.

"James wants to come over."

"Great. Hey, you didn't say much about your dinner with him the other night."

"Not dinner. Pie. And there wasn't much to tell. He's the same. He still works at that advertising agency; he's still single; he smokes a lot, talks a lot. He's, you know . . . the same."

"Hmm. 'The same' as in the way you two always seem to wind up doing things you shouldn't, or 'the same' as in good friends behaving themselves?"

" 'The same' as in good friends behaving themselves. I am married, did you forget?"

"No, but there was a time—"

I cut him off. "That was years ago. And that was different." I thought back to my wedding to Simon at the courthouse in Seattle—the way I had held our newborn Clara in my arms like a bouquet, a white-chenille-blanketed bouquet, and how we had honeymooned afterward, the three of us on a foggy island in the middle of Puget Sound—and then to my other wedding, the one to which Timothy was referring, the one where I had stood at an altar with another man, thinking of James and the way we couldn't stay away from each other even while I was engaged to someone else. Clearly, James hadn't been the only one with an aversion to commitment—we were both dogs back then—but I had changed. My marriage with Simon was real, honest, nothing like that first run. "No. You can't even compare the two. They're like night and day," I said, and looked at Timothy, at the way he watched me with his eyes that missed nothing.

"Okay, but don't try to tell me it didn't cross your mind. I'm sure being alone, in his car, a hot night . . . how could it have not crossed your mind?"

"Crossing my mind is not the same as committing adultery. It was just good to hang out with him. You know we've kept our hands to ourselves for years now."

"But it did cross your mind."

"Okay, for a second, fine, maybe, but no. No! Not really. At least not like it used to."

He stared at me, unconvinced. "And he wants to come over."

"That's what he said."

"Well then, yeah, whenever—it would be nice to see him. I haven't seen him since the last time you saw him. I mean, except for the other night. Did you tell him?"

"About you?"

He gave me the *duh* eyebrow and I laughed. Like, *About what else?*

"Right. Yes, I did. He was surprised, but not. I mean, he's a smart boy; he knew it was only a matter of time. But you've been so healthy for so long, it was easy for everyone to forget that you would get sick someday. Do you want to call him or do you want me to?"

Timothy thought for a minute, then said, "I will."

He left a message that James returned an hour later. He'd be over after work.

That feeling returned to the pit of my stomach, the one that was all excitement and nerves, the one that kids get when they sneak into their parents' bedrooms and search the drawers for secret strange adult things. I don't know if it was pleasant or unpleasant, but it was strong, and though I tried to keep it below Timothy's radar, I felt as if it came out of me like a vapor. A thick vapor with a scent and a color that I could never possibly hide from anyone. Of course I was still attracted to James—he was attractive. But it was more than that: from the first time we met and the very air between us ignited, there was always the potential for our pheromones to throw us into a blind intoxication, a sudden lust that would knock us both to our knees, left afterward to wonder what had come over us and swear it would never happen again. So, as always, I prayed I would be strong enough to resist the pull.

Timothy and I set the table with the real silver and linens and calla lilies cut from the yard. Then we showered and got ready as if we were going out, Timothy with his citrusy cologne, me in a thin-strapped dress with my hair pulled back.

There was an awkwardness between us when James arrived—his not knowing what to say to Timothy, Timothy's watching the two of us for signs of anything other than friendship. By the time we sat down at the table, we were as we had been before James and I went haywire or after we had figured ourselves out or before Timothy even tested positive.

After dinner, we all sat on the balcony facing the hospital. The hospital that had been the site of so many strange and wonderful events, the hospital I had arrived at on the fourth day of a sweltering August not unlike the present one, with its intense light and permanent smog, the sirens howling, my mind blurring all over the place. I looked at the helipad and remembered the nights I spent listening to the medevacs come and go, bringing new traumas in and leaving to get more. I had huddled in the fluorescent light of the tiny bathroom with the door locked, afraid of the loud blades slicing the air with their giant sweeping circles and the throbbing noise as the propeller gained speed and blew dirt off the roof and made the paramedics run all squat and slanty. I was afraid of it all, the sound and the motion and the movement, the creepy shadow as the helicopter hovered, then swung and veered into the night.

I watched one lift off now, tiny lights blinking on the tail and the tips of its skis, looking like a big electric insect with a bulbous glass head, the windshield its eye, the pilot its brain.

"You hated those things."

I looked over at Timothy, watching me watch the helicopter. "Mind reader."

We stayed out there talking well after James left, until it got to be late and I reminded Timothy that he should get some rest. It came naturally, this nurselike, motherlike, coachlike voice. I had assumed that after all Timothy had taught me and done for me, it would feel backward, but instead it felt like a reimbursement, a calibrating. Even-Steven.

As Timothy got ready for bed, my mind drifted again to when I was seventeen—back to the hospital food and strange roommates of that summer; the ride to the hospital in the backseat of my parents' car, my lying fetal and their whispering nervously about visiting hours and medical insurance; the way I had felt my life shift, as if correcting itself, when Timothy arrived, as if a missing puzzle piece had been dropped in, changing and completing both of us. It was my rock bottom, vomiting, scratching, crying, rocking myself as I curled into a ball, unable to blink or speak. As I uncurled, there he was. And for him, as he came to, there I was. And that was when we first knew. We would be fine as long as we had each other.

3

Late in the summer of 1987, while my high school classmates were going off to college, I went off to the drug and alcohol rehabilitation unit of the local hospital. I had been using one chemical or another since I was eleven years old, so the fact that I would bottom out at an age when most people were just getting started was not surprising.

The day I arrived, I was examined and questioned by a doctor who smiled a lot and tilted his head when he looked at me as if he were about to tweak my nose and say, *You are quite a specimen!* But he never did. He didn't have to. His look said it all, in a condescending, amused sort of way.

He watched the nurse as she slid the smaller weight on the upright scale all the way left to zero, then stopped, frowned, and moved the bigger weight from one hundred over to fifty and tapped the smaller one back to the right. I was nearly six feet tall and weighed eighty-nine pounds. I did not care. The nurse took my blood pressure, 70/45, which got another frown, this one from the doctor, as did my resting pulse of 104 and my pathetic temperature, 96.5. After she left, he looked at me with grave concern.

"You're seriously underweight."

I just stared at him. I did not blink. What was I supposed to say—*oh?*

"What's your normal weight?"

Like I knew. Like I cared. "Uh, more than it is now? I don't know, maybe one-twenty?"

He wrote that down. I could see he made his "2" with a little loop at the bottom. Cute. I wondered if he dotted his "*i*"s with circles and what kind of quack doctor would write like that.

I could see him puzzling over my Dachau spine, my stick legs. I wore a paper robe, and my hip bones jabbed out like boomerangs. My elbows were pointy white weapons. Lately, when I got out of the shower, water pooled in the hollows above my clavicles. I had bruises on the inside of each bony knee because of the way they clunked together when I walked and rubbed when I slept. If I slept. My skin was dull and rubbery. My hair was a yellow snarl.

I remember thinking I looked good compared to some of the other patients. I did not look good. I was seventeen years old, and I looked dead.

He wanted to hear my lungs and my heart and tap my knees for reflexes. He wanted to look in my nose and ears and eyes and down my throat. My expression was passive and docile, bored even, as he prodded my stomach and felt organs that were probably rotting. I wasn't sure if I should tell him about the muscle cramps or the bleeding gums or the hair that came out by the handful. *Nah,* I thought. *I'll wait to see if he asks me first.*

"Hmmm," he said, looking up my right nostril with a cold metal cone. "What?"

"You have a deviated septum."

I looked at him blankly until he explained. "It's when the cartilage that divides the nasal passage breaks down, erodes." He was using his hands to illustrate this, the way doctors do. "It was caused, in your case, by excessive intranasal cocaine use."

"I blew a hole in my nose?"

He smiled. "Yes, basically, you blew a hole in your nose. Have you been having nosebleeds?"

Honey, I thought, *you don't know the half of it.*

"Yes."

I had been having them so bad that I'd have to switch to smoking crack every few weeks just to give my poor nose a rest. Too much snorting made blood come out of my nose, down the straw, and onto the cocaine, and the few people I still used with didn't accept this easily. They thought it was "gross." And there was always the risk of ruining the coke by bleeding on it. Plus it really hurt. It burned like mace. I remembered sneezing once and a solid piece of something came out. I wanted to ask him if that could have been cartilage, but I kept that to myself, too.

"Can it be fixed?"

"Actually, yes, and sometimes it corrects itself; it just grows back together. We'll reassess it before you leave. If you do need surgery, that's definitely an option. But let's wait a few weeks and see if it heals on its own." He smiled again.

Boy! That sounds like great fun! I'll bring the popcorn!

"O-kay," he said. We were shifting gears. He looked at his notes. "I'm going to ask you some questions about your drug history."

I was hoping I didn't come out sounding like an addict. I wanted to answer "no" to a lot of the questions, be released back into the wild with a big red stamp on my forehead: *Not An Addict. Social User. Normal.*

"So, let me know if you have used any of the following drugs. Starting with . . . alcohol?"

I had to work real hard not to say *Duh.* When your dad is an alcoholic, you grow up with easy access to booze and an abundance of reasons to drink it. I cleared my throat and looked at my hand. It bled, too, from three cuticles and a big ragged spot right behind my knuckles. I held it up the way rich ladies admire their manicures. I vaguely remembered scratching it raw the other day. I sighed loudly. "Yes."

I could see him check off a box on his form. The alcohol box.

"How much do you drink?"

"As much as I can. I don't know. I don't sit around measuring it."

"But roughly. Do you drink every day?"

"Yes."

"Hard liquor, beer, or wine?"

"Yes."

"No, I mean, which of the three? Or all of them?" He looked at me. "All of them?"

"Sure."

"Would you say alcohol is your drug of choice, or cocaine?"

Drug of choice, I thought. If I had a choice in the matter, I wouldn't even be having this conversation. My drug of choice: *what are you in for?* Like in prison movies.

"Well." I contemplated his question. "Alcohol was first, but cocaine was definitely the more destructive of the two. And the more expensive. But I only did cocaine so I could stay up and drink longer. But if I had to pick one? I guess alcohol."

"Okay. Thanks. How about marijuana?"

"Yeah."

"Cocaine?" He smiled. "Well, we know intranasal; what about intravenous?"

"No! God no. I've never used a needle in my life." *Ha, there's one!*

"Crack, freebase?"

"Yes."

"What about the amphetamines—crystal meth, diet pills?"

"Not really."

"Meaning?"

"Meaning not really. Not on purpose. But who knows what's cut with what?"

"Gotcha. LSD?"

"Once."

"PCP?"

"Yes." I looked down. I was failing miserably.

"Any other hallucinogens—peyote, mescaline?"

I looked back up at him. "Right. Like, where would I get those? What am I, a shaman?"

"So that's a no?"

"That's a no."

"Pills?"

"Sometimes."

"Which ones? Do you remember?"

Do I remember? Glad he had a sense of humor. Asshole. I tapped my chin and looked up at the ceiling, sarcasm that was lost on him. "Let me see. . . . Vicodin for sure. Percodan, Percocet, Darvon, and Darvocet. Valium when I can get it."

I stared at the overhead lights to make my eyes hurt on purpose and wondered if everyone didn't sometimes rummage through other people's medicine cabinets and take anything that promised drowsiness and advised against the use of heavy machinery.

"So—opiates and benzos." He checked two more boxes. "Anything else?"

My head snapped back down, my eyes away from the light and on him. "Quaaludes. Real ones. From Europe." I loved them for their sinky, dreamy feeling, my head elevating and growing lighter like a big helium balloon, and the softness of everything, the way I used to laugh so hard but so quietly, just floating on my dealer's water bed, smiling for hours, then sleeping.

The doctor was saying something.

"Huh?"

"I asked if you ever tried heroin."

"No. Never." I looked at him with dismay and sat up straighter.

"Hash?"

"Mmm." I was smiling. I stopped. "I mean, yes." I would miss hash, the way I used to keep it in a wad in a little film canister in my backpack. I would miss my hiding places, my pipes, my roach clips and containers. Sometimes I think I loved the ritual and paraphernalia more than the high. Not quite, but almost.

By the time we were done, he had in his notes a girl who drank every day and was able to, and frequently did, consume a fifth of peppermint schnapps in one night; a girl who smoked pot like other people smoke cigarettes, with a constant joint resting casually between her index and middle fingers as she held a beer and chatted away, inhaling and exhaling lungfuls of smoke as if nothing were the matter; a girl who had started looking for things to snort and swallow and smoke before she was even all the way out of elementary school, who had worked her way up to an eighth ounce of cocaine a day plus as much of whatever else she could get her hands on. Four trips to the emergency room for overdoses, three times packed in ice in hotel bathtubs, and now this nose thing.

So maybe I wasn't a social user after all. I was sounding a lot like the old junkies who lived under the pier with the barnacles and shot up with the rusty needles they found in the pockets (or arms) of their unconscious friends. Maybe not as desperate or as salty, but still, I didn't think social users smoked PCP in the mornings before class, stole cocaine from their dealer's condo while he was on vacation (climbing through his unlocked third-floor window and opening the safe, having peered over his shoulder once to memorize the combination, just in case), got taken to the hospital after the prom, or lifted some cash now and then from their parents and friends and the register at their after-school job. Social users could stop. I couldn't.

He asked more questions about my life, my habits, my deviations, looking to see how my disease operated, how far in the mud I was being dragged.

And God knows how or why, but I managed to answer him honestly. I rolled my eyes, I was snotty and sullen and sulky, but I told the truth. Yes, I dealt to support my addiction. Yes, I went to school loaded; who didn't? Yes, I was losing friends. Yes, I drove in blackouts. Yes, I hid my using. Yes, I lied, cheated, stole. Yes, I had exchanged sex for drugs, and no, that certainly was *not* the same as prostitution, thank you very much. No, I had no control over it. No, I couldn't remember a day in the recent past when I hadn't been high on something. No, I couldn't stop. Yes, I had withdrawals if I went too long without anything. Yes, I suppose I had paranoid delusions, if that's what you call the people in the shadows. Yes, I heard things. Yes, my period stopped six months ago. Yes, I had tried to kill myself, but just the one time, really. Yes, I hate myself. Yes, my stomach hurts and my skin hurts. Yes, I guess I'm an addict, and yes, fine, I want help. Okay? Christ. Leave me alone already.

It was hot. There are a few summers that stand out in my mind as being just horribly, grossly hot, and this was one of them. I was in the part of the hospital treatment center called Detox, and most days I felt like I was dying of heatstroke, even in its cool air-conditioned rooms. Outdoors was painful, and I fainted once at the morning AA meeting. I panted. I soaked through shirts. I was miserable. I looked around to see if anyone else was as hot, but they all sat around easily in nice shorts and airy tops made of linen and silk and gauzy cotton, while I pulled and tugged at my own skin, my eyes darting around nervously, my mouth opening and closing like that of a dying fish, trying to find better air. I felt as if I had been bound in a swath of wet, scratchy wool. At one point I was showering three times a day in cold water just to get comfortable. I wondered if I could just go ahead and make myself die. I was convinced nothing good could ever come of this suffering. It would melt first.

By the time Timothy checked in, I was feeling better. He came out of the elevator doors one Friday night in a heap and was wheeled down the hall to his bed, where he stayed for three days in an Ativan-induced stupor. His room smelled like the whiskey that was working its way out of his system through his pores. We didn't officially meet until he was moved to the other end of the hall—called Rehab, where the awake-people were, those of us who were well enough to participate in all the group activities: lectures, educational films, community meals, art therapy, group therapy, recreational therapy. When Timothy and I did meet, we fell for each other instantly, the friend equivalent of love at first sight. We sat next to each other in every meeting and walked together on outings and stayed up late talking, the whole time clamped together like children at a scary movie.

I stared, transfixed, at the dust that hung in the little sunbeams that cut in through the open door of the morning AA meeting. It spun lazily, its glitter twirling in the light. The once-ivory linoleum floor was a nasty shade of coffee-spill grime, and the folding metal chairs looked like crippled praying mantises. A fan in the front of the room attempted to push the cigarette smoke out the door and blew the hair of those near it into unwanted wings. The microphone crackled as some middle-aged man at the lectern told us about his descent into the depths of alcoholism. I can't say he interested me. A fly buzzed in, landed on a Louis Vuitton purse, and was shooed out, which, for some reason, made me laugh. This was the 7:30 A.M. Log Cabin meeting, located in an actual log cabin, a building as misplaced on West Hollywood's trendy Robertson Boulevard as its occupants were in life. Fifty or so regulars every morning, plus us, the Rehab People. The Unit, as we called it, was just a few blocks away, and the staff walked us over here every single morning. And every single morning, Timothy and I sat in the back row, the drone of the speaker's drunkalogue ignored like Muzak as we whispered to each other and laughed into our hands. We were always locked into our own intensely private conversations, which frustrated the staff, because we were supposed to be forming a support system—but we suspected that we were probably the only two people in our whole group who would actually get better, so we really didn't care what the staff wanted us to do. We knew. "Fuck 'em," he would say, and I would smile and agree. Fuck 'em all.

I may have been a mere teenager then, but I felt ancient. The first time someone told me I was an old soul I knew that they were right and answered only by staring at them, through them, past them, with my disturbingly level eyes. Timothy was thirty-five, younger in many ways than his peers, so carefree and exuberant, like a child or a puppy, but also wiser and more experienced than most of them. He was fluent in Mandarin Chinese, a locally renowned artist, and a survivor of the California prison system thanks to a sizable hippie drug bust in the seventies. He could read tarot cards. He knew show tunes. And he was pleased to find someone who could keep up with the speed of his conversations, the obscurity of his references, and the inanity of his sense of humor. He was probably surprised at first to find it in me, a girl who only days earlier had been drinking stale bong water in some stranger's apartment down by the boardwalk, but the one thing he had always believed the strongest is that life is a constant surprise and you just never know.

One morning, though we sat in the back as usual, I had found something up front that finally interested me. I leaned over and nudged Timothy.

"Hey, question."

"What?"

"See the guy in the front corner, on the bench? What's the deal?"

Timothy looked up to see a young guy in a suit, smoking a Camel, looking bored and cool, lighting his cigarettes with a Zippo. At first glance he was just another good-looking California boy: light brown hair beach-striped with platinum, teeth that screamed *My parents have money,* and startling cornflower blue eyes. But there was something in the way he moved, the way he looked around the room, even the way he smoked, that was brilliant, different. When Timothy put his head down I knew he was doing his third-eye thing, trying to pick up psychic messages from where we sat. He did this a lot. He looked back up with a frown, then leaned over and whispered to me that I would only wind up getting hurt. I told him that sounded so soap opera and asked him if he was sure or if maybe I couldn't just have the guy for a little while and then give him back. I smiled, but it didn't work. Timothy held my elbow, firm, as if to keep my body tethered since my head was floating around someplace else.

"Don't you start, missy."

During one of our first conversations, we had decided that boys were off-limits for both of us, at least during this fragile-crazy early-stage recovery. "At least for a little while. For like, a minute, maybe? We *are* in a hospital," he had said, and we had laughed, but it was true. I needed to deal with the mess my life had become instead of creating new messes. Boys for me were always messes.

"But . . ."

He shook his head no.

I sighed. I bit my thumbnail, tearing off a small crescent, flicked it away, and went back to pretending to pay attention to the meeting. The other inmates sat slumped in the chairs around us, but beyond that it was a room full of strangers who looked blissful and radiant, their eyes twinkly even at this early hour, their bodies hopping up with glee to hold hands and say the Serenity Prayer at the end of every meeting. This puzzled and annoyed me to no end. My bones hurt; the with-drawals and the heat nauseated me—and as if any one of those things wasn't enough to make me irritable, the militant staff woke us up at dawn. I couldn't even sleep through the pain. I thought about the junkies under the pier, how they'd still be sleeping and I was stuck in an AA meeting. I wondered if I envied them their ruin. I may have.

My gaze traveled again to the front of the room. All I wanted to do was look at him. . . . *I'll go to these meetings just to look at him!* I thought, and smiled to myself. He was truly stunning, chiseled to perfection by the hands of a decidedly female God. I tried to listen to the speaker and Stay in the Now, as they told us. I tried not to look at him, up there be-ing so beautiful. He blew a stream of smoke from his mouth, and I felt my stomach dip as I watched his lips under the blue screen of smoke. I wanted to touch them.

Focus, I told myself. *Focus on what you have and not on whatever it is your warped mind may think you want.*

What I did have, unquestionably, was Timothy. Looking over at him, I smiled at how mismatched we probably looked to outsiders: he in a rainbow-striped cardigan and moccasins, hair conservatively cut, and me in torn Levi's, an oversize inside-out black sweatshirt, and Doc Martens, finally getting up near a hundred pounds. But who says soul mates have to look alike?

A reverse role-modeling took place on the Unit, one in which other people's fuckups revealed, by process of elimination, what I did not want to become. Over the next two weeks their actions confirmed my decision to stay clean. As each day passed, I felt equal parts more afraid and more confident, as if moving farther out on a ledge, letting go of familiar handholds, and telling myself that I could do this. And don't look down.

When I found another patient freebasing in the bathroom, looking surprised as he inhaled while holding his lighter to a stinky white rock on the end of a rolled-up piece of foil that had once been the top of an orange juice container, I told the staff. He was discharged on the spot.

The three heroin addicts who were there when I first checked in had already left and started using again, and one of them had died. There had been two fistfights. Matt, the only other teenage patient besides me, had gone AWOL earlier that week and hadn't been heard from since.

My favorite person in there besides Timothy was Reggie, a football player in on a last chance from the NFL. He was beautiful. Big and black and muscle-bound, built like a tank and with a broad smile, nostrils that flared when he was about to cry, and a hug like a boa constrictor's. He was terrified of leaving the hospital, afraid he would relapse and lose everything. He wanted to stay there forever, he told me. "Sweet fancy Moses," he would say, shaking his head, hanging it low, "save me from myself." Then he'd roll his eyes and smile that smile that was so white against his skin.

I was starting to feel the same way. And I was beginning to wonder which was more crazy, life in here or life out there. It seemed there was always another tragedy, new problems to hash out at the half-hour meeting we had every day after lunch, the one where we "processed community issues" and appointed our officers: hall monitor, time-keeper, wake-up person. We were left among ourselves for this half hour a day, in order to practice things like decision making, being a part of society, asserting ourselves. The song "The Lunatics Have Taken over the Asylum" played in my head during those meetings. I mostly stayed within my self-imposed silence, looking down and picking at my sock, only occasionally making suggestions or defusing arguments. I noticed that people listened when I talked, looking at me funny, like, why was this teenage drunk so on the ball? I didn't feel "on the ball"; I just wanted everyone to get along. I wanted this to be a safe place and not just another weird group of people who would self-destruct, the way they tend to do when they're composed of strong-minded, emotionally brittle people, like lab rats when there are too many of them in one cage and they start eating their own offspring. I had seen it in school, around my dealer's house, in my own family, and I didn't want it to happen here.

Every Wednesday night was family group, the most excruciating two hours of the week, because either you had family—hurt, angry family who asked too many questions and shamed you with every word they said or did not say—or you didn't, which spoke volumes to the words *burned bridges*. My dad came undetectably drunk to every session. My mom and I were the only ones who knew, but we would never tell, having long since been silenced by alcoholism's illogical loyalties.

"Codependency," the family therapist began, "is as much a part of the disease as the alcoholism itself is. This is a family disease, and, like any system, each part is directly impacted by the others. Like a mobile—when one moves, the others move." She stopped and looked at the group. There were about forty of us, and we all looked shell-shocked. "Every one of you has been affected by addiction, not just the addicts. And tonight, I'd like to spend some time with each family." She looked around the circle again. *No,* I thought, *not us; don't pick us first, anyone but us.* I looked down, tried to go invisible. It didn't work.

"Delia, how about you and your parents bring your chairs to the center of the room?"

I would rather have chewed tinfoil than bring my chair to the center of the room.

My dad glared at me—just in case I wasn't clear that this was all my fault, an embarrassment to the family, and an inconvenience for him—while my mom picked up her chair and obediently moved it to the exact center of the circle. It took my dad and me a moment to disengage from our silent standoff, and then we moved our chairs, too. I could feel the eyes of everyone in the room on us as we waited for the therapist to say something. The silence seemed to last an eternity.

"So," the therapist finally began, "why don't we start with you, Delia? Why don't you tell your parents how you think your addiction may have affected them?"

Was she kidding? Why was there no preparation for this, no warning? I froze.

"Do you need some help?"

"Uh, yeah."

"I want you to—first, I want you to look up. Delia? There. Thank you. Okay, first I want you to look at your parents and try to remember all the times you may have worried, or angered, or scared them. I want you to think of the last few months of your addiction and imagine seeing it from their perspective."

My mom reached for the Kleenex box.

"Okay," I ventured. "Um . . . when I wouldn't come home at night, I imagine you guys were really scared. And the time we went to the ER when I overdosed, and I lied and told you someone must have slipped something into the punch." I was on a roll. I looked at my mom. This was the most real we'd been for months, years. Tears streamed down her cheeks. "And the money I took from your purse."

"And the dent in the car? I suppose your 'someone must have hit it in the parking lot' story was a lie," my dad interjected.

I looked down.

"We didn't know what to do," my mom said, sobbing. "We knew something was wrong, but we didn't ever suspect it was . . . drugs. You've always been so smart, so together. You got good grades; you had good friends. We gave you everything. I don't know what I did wrong. . . ." Her words trailed off as she got more Kleenex and buried her face in her hands.

"Mom. Stop. It's not your fault. You're a wonderful mom. Probably too wonderful. I took advantage of your trust in me."

The therapist interrupted, "Remember, addiction is a disease, and it's no one's fault. Even the genetic piece of it," she looked at my dad when she said this, "isn't about assigning blame. Bottom line, we're not here to blame or shame, just to start to get things out in the open and begin the healing process." She looked at me. "Back to your good grades and your good friends for a moment, because I think this is an important piece to your denial, the family's denial. How do you think those things tie in with your addiction?" she asked me.

This I had the answer to. This we had already covered in group. "Well, just for the record, I lost all my friends. I don't have anyone left. Either I screwed them over or they just got disgusted with me. And that job I told you I've had all summer at the library? No job. I just needed an excuse to be out of the house all day." I paused, letting them digest that for a minute. "But back to the grades-and-denial question. My straight A's are my protection. If I can look good on paper, people leave me alone. They don't suspect I have a problem. It can be my own little secret, and I can avoid having to face the truth, or at least doing something about it."

What I couldn't say out loud was that I had learned this trick from my dad. He didn't look like an alcoholic, whatever that means. He looked like an athletic guy in his late thirties, hardly even a gray hair, with a beautiful wife, three cars, a great career, a big 401(k)—he was not slumped in front of a Salvation Army building smelling of cheap wine with ten teeth left in his head, wearing baggy jeans stiff with dirt and pee. That would have certainly not been keeping up with appearances, as was important in our family—look good on the outside, fall apart on the inside. My dad's success had, like mine, enabled him to keep drinking: *See, look, I'm fine; now go away.* Apple doesn't fall too far from the tree.

"If your grades had slipped, do you think someone would have confronted you—your parents, teachers, the school counselors?"

"Well, yeah. I mean, isn't that always first on the 'Is Your Child on Drugs?' questionnaire? Grades slipping, red eyes, a change in attitude?"

"So—it was so important to you to keep using that you went to great lengths to hide it."

"Great lengths. Altoids, Visine, gum, perfume, makeup, buying test answers, putting on the fake smile, making up stories, living a double life, lying, whatever it took."

The therapist asked me, quietly, "Isn't it exhausting?" And she said it with so much compassion that even I got tears in my eyes.

"Yeah, it is."

"And you're ready for it to be over."

I nodded. She turned to my parents and said, "She's ready to do the work. She's doing what we call in the program 'surrendering.' This is a major shift, but in order to stay there, she's going to need a lot of support from you."

"We haven't supported her enough already?" my dad asked, a hard edge to his voice.

"I don't mean financially; I mean emotionally."

"You're telling me that we don't love our daughter?"

"No, I'm telling you that people early in recovery need support. They need to form a support system, and, even though that may include the family, AA will likely be a bigger part of the addict's recovery than the family itself. In a family such as yours, where the addict is the child, and a child still living at home, you'll need to talk about what this will look like. She will need to attend meetings regularly, and she will be connecting with a lot of other addicts, people who understand her and can help her. Yet, as parents, and as parents whose trust has been shattered, you'll need to put some boundaries on that and look at your own fears and misgivings. Like I said, addiction impacts each of you. So does recovery."

With that, she was done with our family and ready for the next one, and we moved our chairs back to the outer circle. My mom clasped her Kleenex tight in her hand, my dad clenched and unclenched his jaw, and I folded myself up in my chair and began scratching a deep raw groove into the skin above my ankle, one that would leave another sickening carved-out scar that nobody would notice.

A few long days later, I walked past the nurses' station just in time to overhear one of the counselors talking to Reggie on the phone. He had completed his twenty-eight days and left; then on the way home he had pawned his Superbowl ring and was doing cocaine at a friend's house in Compton when his manager called him in for a random drug test.

The counselor looked up to see me pretending to read the posted schedule, knew I was eavesdropping, and put Reggie on hold.

"What is it, Delia?"

"Nothing," I muttered, and turned back toward the kitchen. As I walked away, I heard the counselor repeat Reggie's name a few times. He had hung up while on hold, off and running, no one there to save him from himself.

It was around this time that I first saw Timothy's evil side, thanks to Stevie, an annoying little cocaine addict from Chicago who considered himself "hip," even though he was anything but, with his toupee and his slinky shirts unbuttoned to reveal black chest hair and a gold chain. A leftover-from-when-*Miami-Vice*-was-cool stubble beard neatly framed the lower half of his miniature face like an adolescent sideburn. When Timothy and I first saw him, we almost laughed out loud. When Timothy said, "The only thing missing here is an Italian horn and a disco ball," I had to leave the room.

I hated Stevie. Early on I had dropped him to the floor with a swift kick to the balls after he'd tried to hug me under the guise of "offering support." Even the guys didn't like him. I wondered if the staff didn't like him, either. A pinworm of a man, he fit in nowhere. Especially not on the Unit. We may have been crazy or toxic or damaged, but at least we were cool.

All I can figure is that his lipping off to Timothy and trying to act mean, or whatever, was some form of short man's complex. It didn't work, though, and Stevie never learned. He never learned to keep his mouth shut; he never learned that he couldn't handle the fights he started; he never figured out that he was a poor judge of character, that my one kick would drop him to the floor and Timothy would humiliate him beyond words. He didn't know enough to know that if he called Timothy a faggot, he would react. Stevie thought Timothy was an easy target. He was wrong. And one afternoon as we walked down the hall to our rooms after group, he said it, he called Timothy that name, and we both froze, then turned. I stood stock-still as Timothy whipped an arm out and picked Stevie up by the neck, pinning him to the nearest wall.

"Excuse me?"

"Uh, n-nothing. I'm s-sorry; I was just k-kidding," Stevie stammered.

"Sorry, my ass, you little bitty freak." Timothy's jaw clenched, and his normally relaxed good looks hardened, threatening. He held Stevie there, dangling, until Stevie's tiny bearded face darkened to a beet red, until sweat formed on his forehead, until he could no longer see or breathe. Timothy gave Stevie's throat one last hard push and let him drop to the floor gasping for air, coughing, probably seeing stars.

I was standing a few feet away, ready to kick him again if I had to, but obviously I didn't have to. I didn't move until Stevie caught his breath, struggled to his feet, and scampered down the hall. Then I high-fived Timothy, grinning. I was impressed, proud. We hooked elbows and started walking.

"That was excellent."

"Thanks, toots, but that was only Part One. I'm thinking he deserves a Part Two."

"What do you have in mind?"

Timothy smiled. "I'm not sure, but I'll know it when I see it," and he squeezed my arm so we could break apart and race each other to his room. We laughed the whole way, out of breath as we fell against his door at the same time.

And so that evening, when Stevie asked if he could borrow someone's hair dryer, all I saw was him standing out in the hallway with a towel around his waist like a hairy wet child, but Timothy saw opportunity. He smiled, reached into the drawer for his dryer, and tossed it out to Stevie. We resumed our nightly game of gin rummy.

I studied Timothy's grin. "What?"

"That was Part Two."

"What was?"

"Just wait. Listen. And keep playing. Don't move a muscle."

Not a minute later we heard an almost feminine shriek, followed by swearing from the shower room down the hall. As the other patients ran to see what was going on, Timothy looked at me and put his cards over his mouth. We sat and stared, and finally Timothy leaned in and told me that his hair dryer had some kind of nasty electrical problem and he hadn't used it since it had thrown a spark at him last week. Stevie's bad toupee had melted like Styrofoam into a small black patty right there on his head.

The shower room door remained locked until after lights-out; then Stevie scurried back to his room with a towel around his head, reappearing shiny-bald and reinvented in the morning, declaring, "I'm a free man! This is the real me!" The staff actually thought he had had a breakthrough, but as far as Timothy and I were concerned, the victory was ours.

That afternoon, Stevie made a leash out of twine and put the remains of his hairpiece on it, walking it behind him like a dog. He called it Harry, and it sat next to him at dinner. I questioned what I was learning here. I questioned everything but Timothy. Him I swallowed up whole.

I sat in my room pulling strings from around the hole in the knee of my jeans and gazing absentmindedly at the yellow Cadillac that was spiked headlong into the roof of the Hard Rock Cafe across the street. It was after dinner, free time, a typical Friday night on the seventh floor.

I had spent the first week looking longingly out this very window, but now, due to be released in less than a week, I was afraid to leave. Everyone around me was relapsing as soon as they left. Was sobriety even a realistic goal for us? I thought about Reggie, how badly he wanted his sobriety and how quickly and easily he had thrown it away.

Save me from myself.

It had been my decision to check in, ultimately—I wasn't forced in by a probation officer or a parent or a boss. In fact, I probably could have gone on turning my life to crap before my family's eyes indefinitely, our denial ran that deep. I looked like hell, I stole alcohol from my dad and money from my mom, I rarely slept, and when I did, it wasn't at home, but between them not wanting to believe there was a problem and my skilled manipulations, everything was "fine." Fine, except that once I saw the look on my mom's face the day I walked in the door after being gone for two days and said, "Mom, I have a problem," I couldn't unsee it, and my heart had broken when I saw the fear and sadness in her eyes. It may as well have fallen out of my shirt and onto the floor, splintering like red glass. As my hallucinogenic mind watched the pieces mingling on the floor and I heard my own voice saying the words, "Help me," over and over again, I sank down to sit by her feet, hugging her legs.

My mom cried herself to sleep that night, after my dad and I had a screaming fight, after I swallowed three Vicodin and stumbled off to bed, knowing I'd be in a rehab the next time my head hit a pillow, knowing things would never be the same again, but not knowing if that was good or bad. I wanted to get better, and I didn't. I was Siamese twins in a bad argument. The only thing I had ever been sure of was that the dam would eventually break, that something was bound to give, but I'd always assumed that the thing that would give was my body—my bleeding nose, my aching sides, my cocaine-weak, palpitating heart—not my self-destructiveness. The divine timing of this rare appearance by my survival instinct surprised me.

Part of me was dying. Not the whole part, just the addict part. This took a while to understand, and because I'd never really anticipated an ending other than death, I wasn't sure I was ready for anything else. It made me think of the bumper sticker on our neighbor's VW Bug that said: *If I had known I was going to live this long, I'd have taken better care of myself.*

Continuing to pick at the growing hole in my jeans, I started to cry. I couldn't stop the tears. They raged from my eyes salty with fear, pain, and anger. I wiped them with the back of my hand, but they just came harder, as if to disobey me.

The fear was an all-purpose dread stretching over the wide, empty space of my future. I was afraid of waking up every day without putting something into my body to numb my oversensitive nerves. I was afraid of being clean, and I was afraid of going back to the way I was. What if I did relapse and Timothy wasn't my friend anymore? What if he relapsed? What if we both did? If it weren't for the sound of our laughter in that place, I know that the voices inside my head and the silences at night would have driven me insane.

The pain was the kind that makes you want to curl up in a corner taking turns between catatonia and hysteria. It came from the things I

had done and the things that had been done to me. It came from secrets.
It was a pain that was rooted so far deep inside, from so long ago, that I
couldn't even see or remember its origin anymore. It's not as if my
childhood had been tragic or newsworthy. I was not an orphan. I was
not abused. We did not live in our car, heating nightly cans of Spam
over the engine. The exterior of my life would bore the average day-
time talk-show host. But inside, there was an ugliness, an ignored hurt,
a constant grief that, coupled with a biting self-hatred, had eventually
led to my never-discussed half-assed suicide attempt at fourteen, the
feel of which I could still recall: the sharp of the razor as it slid coolly
into my skinny left wrist—horizontally, though, and not even deep
enough to really scar; apparently I wasn't all that serious—leaving red
lines where other people would wear a bracelet, blotting outward like
ink on porous paper into the tiny crosshatchings of my skin.

My little wrist-slitting event may have been a literal manifestation
of my feeling like I wanted to die, but all that had come before and after it had had a suicidal bent to it, too. I had dared death to take me over
and over, with reckless drunk driving, potentially lethal overdoses, and
forays into the darkest, nastiest parts of Venice. I felt ill as I remembered the alleys, the cars, the favors exchanged, and the way I would
later cut or scratch or cigarette-burn myself just to feel something predictable, something I could control.

The anger was that I had drunk and used myself into such a state
that I was now being told I have a disease, a condition tamed only with
complete abstinence: *alcoholism, addiction*—they said those words were
interchangeable, that we could call it whatever we wanted to when we
stood up at meetings and introduced ourselves, but it was all the same
disease. I would get the scarlet letter either way. Unlike Hester
Prynne, though, I got to pick what my *A* stood for. I decided *addict*
sounded the cooler of the two, but I was an alcoholic from the gate. I
had a built-in tolerance to the stuff, thanks to genetics, and it had
worked as emotional anesthesia from the first time my young hands
twisted the lid off of a bottle of Jack Daniel's. I had found pills and

marijuana shortly thereafter, by the time I was twelve, and cocaine, PCP, et cetera, had just been the icing on my deranged, dysfunctional cake. And now I was being told: no more. I hadn't known relief and terror could live in the same person, at the same time, but admitting I was an addict brought me both, equally.

It wasn't all bad, though—hiding in there among all the negativity and chaos was a little bit of hope, bursting and floating and taking flight inside my aching chest cavity like dandelion puffs, childhood-memory-like and spreading. The girl who had flatly watched her own blood make red polka dots on the white bathroom rug seemed so far away. I definitely was not her anymore, but I wasn't yet the girl with the "hope," either. It felt cheesy and fake, like the smiles of the people my parents used to call Moonies or how my parents' friends looked after an EST encounter weekend. I had grown so hard, so devious and bitter and fragile and calloused all at once, that I was apt to spit at, roll my eyes at, anything positive or kind. I rejected things that were good for me by nature. It was called sabotage, I had learned in group that morning.

I looked over my shoulder at the clock. Time to meet Timothy two doors down. I twisted farther and looked out at the hall.

Matt sat in the doorway of his room, flipping cards. He did this a lot. I watched as black or red and white spirals hit the trash-can bag with a crinkle if they made it in or landed silently on the carpet if they did not. He had only been back a day or two and was sulking. He didn't want to be here. He almost didn't fit in, except for the addiction part. He was a good kid, soft skin, a head full of sandy curls, and a great amount of charm. I got up and walked over to him, asked if he wanted to bring his cards into Timothy's room and join our rummy game. That brought a smile to Matt's face, and he followed me, then sat down next to me on the floor by Timothy's bed. Matt performed a few card tricks while we watched, amused and impressed as the cards fluttered between his swift hands and circus-announcer voice. He became our mascot, so charismatic we could forgive him his lack of brains.

. . .

Monday morning I sat in one of the counseling offices with my parents, who were joining me for my final individual session. Discharge Planning, they called it. Plotting my new-and-improved life. The counselor started talking as soon as she closed her door.

"So. We're looking at discharging Delia at the end of this week, and we need to get clear on what that will look like. Her daily schedule, her aftercare plan, how the family will adjust to her reentry." She looked at me and said, "Let's start with you telling them what you've learned since you've been here."

"Well." I wasn't about to tell them everything. "I learned that addiction is not a weakness or a moral problem, that it's a disease. I learned that I have a lot of work to do and that I have to go to AA meetings for the entire rest of my life. I learned that I'm not alone and that I can get better." And then, to get on their good side, "I learned that I have a lot of amends to make and that I need to start taking more responsibility for my actions."

"Nice job. Can you tell them what your recovery plan looks like?"

"Well, I'm going to go to AA, at least one meeting a day, probably sometimes two. I've signed up for the Thursday night Aftercare here, and I have to find an AA sponsor. I'm—"

"What's a sponsor?" my mom asked.

"Like a coach, or a mentor. Someone in AA who will take me through the Twelve Steps."

"Oh. Okay. That sounds like a good idea," she said, but I could sense some hesitance there, like she wasn't sure about one of those people helping her little girl.

"Have you two thought about what guidelines, or conditions, you guys would like to see in order for Delia to keep living at home?" the counselor asked. "Some families come up with a written contract; others just use verbal agreements. Either way, it's important to have clear expectations, along with clear consequences, that everyone understands and is willing to follow."

My dad looked at my mom, who brought a folded-up sheet of paper out of her purse. "We wrote a few things down," she said. "Here." She tried to hand it to the counselor.

"Why don't you go ahead and read it."

My mom reached for the Kleenex box and looked at me. "I'm sorry, sweetie. I hope this isn't too much. But they told us to, and—" She started to cry.

The counselor cut in. "You're the parent. Remember that. You need to set boundaries. The family is rebuilding trust, and Delia's recovery will benefit—not just from your love and encouragement, but also from having some parameters and some ultimatums. She needs to hear what you will do if she uses again. It will help her. And you. So—let's hear what you have."

My mom blew her nose and took a deep breath. She unfolded the paper. "Well, no drinking or drugs. And you have to be either in school or working full-time."

I nodded. "Okay. What else?"

"Going to AA meetings and Aftercare."

"I said I was going to do that."

"I know. I'm just reading—"

"What else?"

"A midnight curfew. Dinner at the house, with us, four nights a week. Doing your own laundry, helping with the dishes, the trash, and the lawn. And we need to know where you're going to be at all times, with phone numbers where we can reach you if possible."

"Is that all?" I was trying to not be sarcastic, but I was getting mad.

"No. There's one more. We want to be able to have you do a drug test, if we suspect that, you know, anything has happened."

I started to yell. "You want me to pee in a cup? Can't you just ask me if I've relapsed? You're going to make me pee in a cup is how much you don't believe me? You have to drug test me?"

My mom looked at the counselor for help. The counselor looked at me. "Delia, based on your history with lying and getting away with it, and with putting up a very, very convincing front, it is completely within reason for your parents to want physical proof that you're still clean and sober. I understand your anger. But you need to look at it from their side. They want to believe you so much that it almost killed you. Having random drug tests can help your recovery, give you the extra support you might need when you are tempted to use."

"Oh, now they're random? I thought they were only with cause. Which is it?"

"Well, I think both." She looked at my parents, who nodded, passively agreeing.

"Great. Fine. Drug tests are fine. Back to this school-or-work thing." I asked, "You said 'either in school or working.' If I'm in school full-time, how will the money thing work?"

"We're willing to continue to pay for gas, car insurance, your phone, and little extras. Nothing extravagant, but if you're in school, under our roof, and not drinking or taking drugs, you won't have to worry about money. You just focus on your sobriety and your education. We'll handle the rest."

I considered that. Not a bad deal. "Okay. That works for me. Thanks."

"And Delia, there was something you were going to ask of them?"

I looked at her like, *Do I have to?* We had talked about this in group, and the staff and all the other patients agreed that having alcohol in the house was a setup for me to relapse and that I should ask my parents to remove it. I knew it would piss my dad off, but they said I had to ask.

"I need for there to be no alcohol in the house when I come home."

My mom looked away, and my dad looked at me in a way that made my blood run cold. I immediately regretted having said anything. The pause that followed was too long to be considered awkward.

"You mean my house?" my dad asked. "You're telling me what I can and cannot have in my own house? That's rich. That's really rich. Miss Liar Drug Addict telling me what to do."

I looked at the counselor, hoping she'd bail me out. Nothing.

"It would just make it easier for me, to not have it there," I told him, in a small voice.

"Easier." He laughed. "You want me to make it easier for you? It's not my job to make it easier for you. Did you make it easy for us? Did your deceitful, defiant attitude—"

My mom put her hand on my dad's knee and started, "Honey—"

He cut her off. "Don't. I don't want to hear you coddling her anymore. It's not helping." He turned to me. "You know what? If you can't handle it, you can move out."

"Dad! Jesus! I'm not even eighteen yet."

"So? You can get your own place."

"How would I pay for that?"

"How about with all the money you stole from us?"

His words had the same effect as a slap across the face. I looked down, silenced and shocked, my eyes hot with tears, my cheeks burning.

The counselor spoke, calmly and slowly. Educationally. "In the beginning, recovering people need as few triggers as possible. If Delia can live in a sober household, that's one less trigger for her. If this is something you are unwilling to provide for her, that's up to you. But I would encourage you, all of you, to take a look at what that means for your family." She looked at my dad. "Is alcohol more important to you than your daughter's recovery?" *Brave woman,* I thought. She held up her hand. "Don't answer that now. Just think about it. Are you so invested in your family's dysfunction that you will do anything to keep it that way, including standing in the way of Delia's recovery efforts? She is trying to get better. I want to encourage the two of you to do the same. And I want to remind you that this is a family disease. For this to really and truly work, she can't be the only one changing."

I didn't look at my dad for the rest of the session, and I didn't hear much of anything else that was said. I signed the paper my mom had brought, and when they left, I went back to my room and stared out the window, my head spinning, waiting for Timothy to get out of group.

. . .

They released me that Friday. I had made that transition the staff loved so much, the one where the "before" and "after" pictures were like two entirely different people. I was completely detoxed; I had gained twenty much-needed pounds; I had taken the vitamins they had given me in a little cup every morning. I had signed up for Aftercare and promised I would keep going to AA meetings. It had been a fight; this whole thing had been a fight, eating hospital food and spending hours in back-to-back therapy sessions, not being able to reach for a pipe or a bottle, no pills at nighttime, no speed in the morning, with only Timothy and cigarettes and the occasional contraband swig of coffee to keep me sane. But I hadn't given up. I wouldn't give up. I wanted to keep this life. My old one was like a dried and partially shed snakeskin, dead, connected only by a few cells.

One of the last things they told me to do before I left was find an AA sponsor. I knew who I wanted to ask, and I knew that obeying would help that husk fall off faster and provide some assurance that I would be okay, long-term.

I saw her at the morning meeting every day. She glowed conspicuously even among that perky bunch. She dressed entirely in white gauzy fabrics, always with silver Birkenstocks. She had an angel-white pageboy haircut, but her pale, sage green eyes and golden freckles suggested she had once upon a time been a redhead. Her lips and nails were as glossy-bright as maraschino cherries. She carried herself like royalty, flowing more than walking, chin held high. I approached her on the porch outside afterward, nervous, intrigued.

"Do you . . . sponsor?" I asked.

"Well, yes, I do. My name is Joan. And you are . . . ?"

I was flustered. I tried to swallow, couldn't, spoke anyway. "Oh, sorry. I'm Delia. I'm in the Unit over at the hospital. I get out tomorrow. They told me to get a sponsor, and I saw you, and thought—"

"Here's my card." She smiled as if we already shared a delicious se-

cret, her eyes moving from side to side like an elegant cat. I felt my
heart swell, as if she already loved me. She lowered her voice to a whisper. "Call me this afternoon. We'll talk."

When I called her later, she said that she would be delighted to
sponsor me. She had a way of speaking that was almost formal, something that hinted of an era long since trampled over by today's slang.
She called the people close to her "darling" or "my sweet" and never
forgot to say "please" and "thank you." She often threw winks at her
friends from across the room, magical polished pennies cast for luck.

As I stacked my suitcases by the elevator and looked around one last
time, my fear was so strong I was sure everyone could smell it. The
other patients were writing short messages and their phone numbers
on the inside flap of my AA book, like a yearbook for the dysfunctional. No one wrote "Don't ever change," though. There's a saying in
AA: "You only have to change one thing if you want to stay sober, and
that's everything."

The elevator bell dinged, signaling the official end of my stay and
the start of my life at home without drugs. The very idea made me feel
sick. I hugged Timothy again, then Matt and the counselors, and
stepped into the elevator. I think I was holding my breath. It was like
skydiving: the fear, the leap, the faith.

The three of us got into the car, me again in the backseat but this
time upright and hyperalert. The harsh light drilled through the windshield, and no one spoke a word. As we drove west into Venice, approaching the house, things began to look surreal. In the past
twenty-eight days, I had been outdoors only for the AA meetings near
the Unit and the weekly field trips they took us on. This was my out-
of-the-cocoon greeting: the liquor stores that I knew sold to underage
kids; my dealer's street; my old high school, from which I'd graduated
just two short months earlier, in a blackout and with honors, as was my
dichotomous style.

The smells and sensations of my childhood flooded me as we pulled into the driveway. Lake Castaic on weekends with the metallic-clean-algae taste of lake water mixed with the scent of Coppertone Sea & Ski. Marijuana smoke spiraling from ceramic pipes. The warm, soft hands and long ponytails of my parents, tan California hippies, with me along for every outdoor concert, peace rally, campout, and beach party. I could almost feel my childhood in my fingertips, draped in fabrics that were tie-dyed and fringed, velvet and batik. Everywhere the smell of patchouli and sea salt. Venice in the early seventies.

I walked flanked by my parents up the same walkway I'd known as a toddler, feeling disconnected from my body. As I went back toward my bedroom, my mind flashed back to the nights I'd spent holed up in there, paranoid from too much crack, and I realized I hadn't cleaned it out before I left. There were drugs in there. Drugs I might use, if I found them. My mind was suddenly drained of all the recovery stuff and filled with the knowledge that I was likely within five feet of a pretty decent stash. I stood frozen in the hall, peering in as if over a velvet rope into a fake room in a museum. When my phone rang, I literally jumped, shattered first by the sound itself and then by the realization that I was not ready to talk to anyone from my old life, at least not now, not yet.

I reached into my room and picked up the phone on the third ring even though I wanted to jerk the cord out of the wall instead. "Hello?"

"Hello, my sweet angel-baby, it's Joan. I figured you'd be arriving home about now. How are you?"

"I don't know. I just realized my room is full of—you know. Stuff." I nibbled at a hangnail until I could peel it all the way back, the blood sweet on my lips. "What should I do?"

"Why don't I come over and get rid of it with you?"

I wondered if any sponsor would have known exactly what I needed before I could ask, before I even knew it was what I needed, or just Joan. I decided the latter.

"Go sit outside, take some deep breaths, and send a little prayer up to you-know-who. Give me directions to your house, and I'll be there before you know it."

Twenty minutes later she was in our living room.

"Mom, Dad, this is Joan. Joan, my parents, Carol and Dean."

"It is lovely to meet you both," she said as she shook their hands and smiled that winning smile of hers. "Your daughter and I are going to do some cleaning up."

She followed me to my room and pulled out my desk chair. She sat down, crossed her legs, and said, "Okay. What do we have here? Get it out where we can look at it."

I started with the dresser and found a glass pipe wrapped in a sock within a sock within a sock in the far back of the drawer, a bottle of assorted pills, and a half-empty pint of peppermint schnapps. I set it all on my desk next to Joan. I opened my closet and brought out about two ounces of the marijuana I'd been selling all summer. It was in the form of sticky-green eighth ounces pressed tight against clear Baggies. I dropped them on my bed.

"What about all this?" I asked her.

She made a flushing motion with her hand.

"You're kidding. It'll clog the plumbing. Can't I sell it? I can sell it without smoking it."

She smiled. "Where's the little girls' room?" She wasn't kidding.

I gathered it up in my arms and she followed me down the hall. She closed the door behind us.

"Okay, ready?"

I opened the first Baggie and my mouth watered, smelling that wonderful skunky smell. "Just drop it in?"

"Just drop it in."

I sighed, overturned the Baggie, and flushed. It felt sacrilegious to my addict self, watching perfectly good drugs go literally down the toilet. By the fifth or sixth bag I got the hang of it, though, I got really into it, and Joan and I started laughing.

My dad knocked on the door. "You two all right in there?"

"Yeah. We're fine, Dad." I looked at Joan. "Never better."

I finished flushing the marijuana, and she handed me the pill bottle. I poured them into the toilet, and she handed me the schnapps bottle. I unscrewed the cap and paused for a second, sniffing. The smell of alcohol, instead of enticing me, sickened me. I turned the bottle upside down, holding my breath.

"This is what my stomach used to look like," I said to her, looking down at all the different-colored pills, catching another powerful whiff of the schnapps. I flushed one final time.

She put the Baggies, the bottles, and the pipe in a plastic bag. "Shall we take a walk? Take out the trash?"

"Sounds good," I said.

"I'm proud of you. I know how hard that was."

We walked toward the front door. "We're going for a walk," I told my parents. "We'll be back in a little while."

"Did you take care of . . . whatever you needed to take care of?" my mom asked.

I realized I actually felt lighter. I stood up straighter. "Yeah. Yeah, we did."

Joan and I dropped the bag into a Dumpster in the alley as we walked the short distance down to the beach. When we got there we sat in the sand, sand that was still warm from the day, and I made patterns and curves in it, raking my fingers through it. This was my spot, the place I came to think, my hands always moving, sifting. Ever since I was a child I would comb this beach looking for those little pieces of opaque glass that tumbled up onto shore, because I related to them: broken pieces, out of their element, not fitting in with the shells and rocks around them. Washed up.

A million miles to the west the sun was lowering itself into the water, fiery orange and blurred like a Vaseline mirage, and next to me Joan was talking. I listened to her voice with my whole body. Smooth like an old jazz singer's, it had a precision and depth that fascinated me.

I stared at her lit gold by the sky and thought that's what angels must look like.

She said all I had to do was breathe in and out, not drink, and keep putting one foot in front of the other. We talked about change, about hope, about faith. Faith in rebuilding the spirit. Faith in all the things that you can't see or touch but that are stronger than the things you can.

4

The day after I left the Unit, another teenage girl checked in. She had eyes dark as ink, milky brown coffee skin, and black ringlet-hair cropped to within an inch of her scalp. With her pierced nose and jangly silver gypsy bracelets, she appeared, at first glance, somehow tribal, spiritual—until she opened her mouth and a stream of profanity came out of her like a middle finger, a way for her to simultaneously get up in your face and keep you at arm's length. She was foul, but she was also incredibly smart and had a wicked sense of humor. Timothy called me immediately.

"Are you coming to the meeting here tonight?"

I said I was and asked why.

"I think we've found the latest addition to our club."

Her name was Zodiac, and we became friends against my better judgment. Timothy's call had me excited and curious and ready to meet her, but as soon as she walked in the room, my antenna went up— something about her was off. I pulled Timothy aside and told him this, and he said she was fabulous and I hadn't given her a chance. As he walked away, I realized I was jealous, threatened—she had an aura about her that made me think of the Maya Angelou poem with the line about the men falling down on their knees. Even Timothy was taken by Zodiac. And I should give her a chance. Fine. I agreed to put my antenna aside and get to know her.

As we talked, we discovered similarities as numerous and striking as our differences. We even looked like negatives of each other, she with the cinnamon skin and blackest eyes, me with golden hair and changeable blue-green eyes. She had grown up in New York, me in Los Angeles. Dark-light, east-west. She had half and step- and unknown brothers and sisters too many to count; I was an only child. She left home at fifteen; I lived with my parents. Blue Cross had paid for my treatment; welfare for hers. We had the same birthday. We each had tattoos of the moon, hers a three-quarter moon on her shoulder blade; mine a crescent on my hip. Though our bodies were nearly identical, I usually kept mine safe under big shirts and old jeans, and she flaunted hers and used it to get whatever she needed. We were two sides of a coin, opposite yet the same.

"Next!"

My mom and I stepped forward and I handed the woman at the community college late-admissions window my registration form.

She flipped through the pages and stamped and signed something. "ID please."

I handed her my driver's license. She made a copy of it and handed it back to me. "Your total is four hundred eighty dollars."

My mom got out her checkbook and wrote a check. She had said she wanted to come with me to keep me company and take me to lunch afterward, but I suspected it was to keep me from having to handle the money. After the registration fees, there would be books to buy, and, trust-building or not, who wants to give a newly clean addict a credit card, a blank check, or six hundred dollars cash? Certainly not my parents.

"Classes start tomorrow," the woman was saying. "The campus bookstore has all the syllabuses posted, and those will tell you what materials you need."

"Is that it?" I asked.

"That's it. Next!"

My mom and I turned and walked back through the crowd, headed for the bookstore. I prayed I didn't see anyone from my high school. I wasn't ready for that. I wasn't ready to explain why I was at a community college and not a university, where I had been all summer, or why I was hanging out with my mom.

"Okay, college student." My mom put her arm around me. "Where should we go for lunch?" She was smiling, but I was looking down. *Classes start tomorrow,* the woman had said. Books. Desks. Teachers. Questions. Tests. Other kids. Kids who drink. Kids who use drugs. Kids who drink and use drugs like normal kids, not like me, not in ways that almost kill them.

"Home," I told her. "I want to go home for lunch."

"Are you okay?"

"It's just too much. I don't know if I can do this."

"Oh, you'll be fine. Maybe they have AA meetings on campus. We could call the school later and ask. I bet they do."

"Why, so I can meet the other freaks?"

"You seem to feel better after you go."

"I don't know if I want anyone here to know."

"I'll look on the bulletin board while you get your books," she offered.

I remembered what we had learned about enabling in family group and how much my mom always does for other people. Things they should be doing themselves. Things she does to make herself feel needed. "No, I'll look for myself."

"Oh, right." I guess she remembered, too. "I'll wait over here."

I wondered if it was always going to be this complicated. All I had done was quit drinking and using, but it felt like I'd stepped into a whole new skin, one that didn't quite fit, no matter how much I tried to make it mine.

Joan was a firm believer in using self-nurturing to heal spiritual wounds and form a brace against the growing pains of life. When I would want to cry and chain-smoke and talk in circles, blaming and ranting, she would have me out getting a Reiki massage and a manicure. When I would complain to her about feeling different from everyone else at school and consumed by perfectionism with my grades, she would tell me to take a hot bubble bath. She was big on baths. For everything.

I called her one Saturday afternoon, because my dad had been drinking since he woke up, not a usual habit of his. He usually started in the early evening. I was convinced he was taunting me, doing it just to see how I would react, to test me.

"Joan, he's drunk, and I don't know how to deal with it."

"I want you to draw a nice deep bath and call me in an hour."

"I don't think you heard me," I said. "My problem is my dad. Not body odor."

I could hear the smile in her voice as she repeated herself and added, "Light some candles. Pour in some scented oil or bath salts. Lavender is very soothing."

I did as she said, and damned if I wasn't relaxed when I called her back.

"Okay," she said. "Now. Where is a good place for you? Where do you feel comfortable, and free, and serene?"

"Me? Serene? Like, nowhere."

"No, think about it. I've seen it. I've seen its effect on you."

"The beach?"

"The beach, exactly. Go down there now and just be. And call me later."

I spent the next two hours down there, first sitting in the sand, sifting and swirling, watching the grains fall from the webs of my dusty hands and then walking down by the water, collecting those little pieces of beachglass. There were more of them than I thought. They were surprisingly strong. I tried to snap one in half to see if the inside was still shiny and clear like regular glass, but it wouldn't break. Its scuffy exterior was like scar tissue.

I thought about that as I sat back down, drawing circles in the sand.

I realized later that in those moments I was getting to know myself, this person who had, until then, been living a hundred-mile-an-hour addict life, trying to outrun my thoughts and feelings, trying to stay numb. I was sitting still long enough to listen to myself, I was re-forming, and I was doing it in a place that was safe to me, all fogged in, with waves roaring and crashing at perfect intervals in the distance and lonely seagull laughter piercing the sky.

When I got home, I went to my room and closed the door. I did this as much as possible in those infant days of recovery, trying to create a buffer between myself and my home life. I may have been physically separated by only a wall from my drunk father and careworn mother, but I was somewhere else entirely as I practiced the breathing exercises and prayers Joan had written out for me, as I closed my eyes and nursed chamomile tea or listened to the meditation tape Timothy had given me: anything to keep feeling the sanity I got while I was at the meetings, because now that I was conscious, the house was almost unbearable. I could feel the unrest from the curb. Sometimes I wondered if the stray dogs that walked around on the beach at night could sense it, the way they smelled fear. I pictured them trotting along the boardwalk like skinny coyotes, yellow eyes moving hopefully up our street as they hunted for scraps, then looking at each other as they passed our house, like, *What's the deal there?*

I called Joan back and told her the bath had worked, the beach had worked, and the solitude of my room was working.

"But I'm a little worried. I'm supposed to eat dinner with them before I go to the meeting tonight, which will ruin all of that, I'm sure."

"Or the work has strengthened you, made it possible to tolerate difficult situations. Remember to breathe, say a prayer before you sit down to dinner, and know that you can talk about it when you get to the meeting. With people who understand. And know that you are strong, and you can do this. Are doing this."

I took a deep breath. "Okay."

I sat down at the dinner table. I felt like a raw nerve as my dad looked over his tumbler at me with a flat stare and my mom tried awkwardly and obviously to do everything right. *No wonder I drank,* I thought, knowing he was about to begin one of his nightly picking sessions, which were as predictable to me as if we were going by a script. He would start with a minor flaw, a nothing of a thing, and escalate it into a screaming match. He knew where my weakest spots were and would go there immediately, smug and nasty. Direct hits. He did this almost every night and had for as long as I could recall.

"Going to your meeting tonight, kiddo?" he asked with a condescending sneer.

I looked at my mom first, an *I told you so* mixed with an *Oh great, here we go again,* then at my dad, who was slowly rolling the ice in his glass (*tink tink*).

I thought about what Joan said and tried to remember the Serenity Prayer. *God, grant me the serenity to accept the things I cannot change . . .*

"Yes, I am," I said. Calm. Not defensive.

"Well, good. Glad to see you've joined a cult."

"Dad. Come on. It's not a cult, and I don't want to get into it tonight. Please?"

Turning his attention to my mom, he mimicked in a high voice, "*I don't want to get into it tonight.* Give me a break. Did you hear her? Did you?" He stared at her, and she looked down at her plate, sad that yet another dinner would be ruined. "Answer me."

Her reply was barely audible. "Yes."

"Speak up!"

"Dad, just stop it, okay?" I threw my napkin down and pushed my chair back.

"You're not leaving."

I tried a new tactic: bravery. "Yes, I am."

"No, you're not." His shark-eyed glower was intimidating enough that I dropped back down, bravery gone, my eyes narrow burning slits, adrenaline pumping hard and fast through my veins. I couldn't remember the words to the rest of the prayer, and I couldn't remember anything else Joan had told me. Fear had taken over. I watched him in profile, staring at his jaw muscle as it clenched and released, clenched and released. I've heard it's the strongest muscle in the human body.

He was silent for a good five minutes, then he started in on me again, my mom begged him to stop, he told her to shut up, I told him to leave her alone, he yelled at me, she cried, he glared, and around and around and around we went. Finally he turned to me and hissed, "Go on; get out of here." He was like a kid burning ants under a magnifying glass. Unfortunately, we were the ants.

My mom and I scurried into the kitchen. He returned to his recliner and his martinis. While we cleaned up, we talked about how if I didn't upset him so much everything would be okay. I took more than my share of blame, because I didn't know what else to do. As far as I knew, it was all my fault.

That night wasn't much different from most other nights in my family, except that when it was over, I chose my recovery over sulking, drinking, or stuffing my anger. I knew I didn't have to stay and protect my mom—he would be out cold for hours, and besides, he never took his anger out on her unless I was involved. Alone, they were fine. He might snap at her or silence her occasionally, but she had never been a target for his fury—he saved that for me. So, knowing that she would be fine, I went and got my keys and came back into the kitchen.

"Mom? I'm going to catch the end of the meeting, maybe have coffee with some people afterward or swing by the Unit. Do you mind?"

"Of course I don't mind. You do what you need to do. I'm sorry about . . . him." We looked at each other for a long moment; then I hugged her and left. She waved good-bye from the window, her eyes full of envy. I had a place to go to really take care of myself, but she only had her kitchen and her hobbies with which to busy herself and keep her mind off the situation.

I started the car and pulled away, already feeling the relief. Except as I drove, my recovering self grew quiet and my addict self came out in full force, reminding me that I knew every liquor store within a ten-mile radius that sold to minors and I had some leftover gas money in my wallet. I imagined the way a pint would feel slipping warm and numb down my throat. As if on autopilot, I pulled into the parking lot of one of those liquor stores and got out of the car. When I went to lock the door, my AA key chain caught my eye. *Thirty Days,* it said. *Honesty, open-mindedness, and willingness.* I froze. In a rush, Joan and Timothy and the log cabin and the prayers and even those tough little pieces of beachglass came into my mind, reminding me that the point is to endure, not to break. I got back in the car and drove to the AA meeting. I sat down in the back row and closed my eyes, letting the voices of all those recovering alcoholics wash over me, washing away the close call, the fear, and the notion that I couldn't do this.

After the meeting, I stopped by the Unit. I said hi to the night staff and asked if I could see Timothy and Zodiac for a minute. It was well past regular visiting hours, but they let me go, knowing that sometimes the only thing that could help an addict was another addict.

I walked down the hall and knocked on the doorjamb. "Yoo-hoo?"

Timothy was sitting on his bed and Zodiac was in some weird yoga position on the floor. She smiled, and Timothy looked at his watch and asked how I got past the guards. I told him I had outrun the dogs and scaled the walls. I sat next to him and pulled out a cigarette.

"My dad is being a royal pain in the ass," I said, exhaling smoke.

"What happened?" Zodiac asked.

"He was drunk all day, and when we sat down and tried to have dinner, he called AA a cult, told my mom to shut up, and wasn't going to let me leave the house. No one even ate. And then, when I did leave, my car drove straight to the liquor store. I'm glad I made it to the meeting. I'm glad I'm not drunk right now."

The pressure left my head as I talked to them. I was starting to understand that the more you talked about something the less it hurt, each telling deflating it a little bit more. That was why we had to say it out loud at the beginning of every meeting: *My name is Delia and I'm an addict.* It was so we could stop flinching and just live with it.

"Well, at least you got through it," Zodiac said. "That's cool. And fuck whatever your dad says. He'd be happy if you relapsed, 'cause then he could pick on you, feel better about himself, and say AA doesn't work. You've got to prove his shit wrong."

Timothy nodded. "He's scared. Your sobriety is a threat. I remember when a few of my friends joined AA, and all I could think was that they knew I should be next. I stopped hanging out with them, because they were right. I was an alcoholic, and there's no bigger buzzkill to an alcoholic than a recovering alcoholic. Your dad isn't ready yet. You are. Hence the tension."

I left at lights-out and drove home feeling full and loved, knowing that Joan was right: *I could do this. I am doing this.*

My dad was still unconscious when I got home, as I knew he would be. My mom was needlepointing furiously in the spare bedroom, faster as I told her about my conversation with Timothy and Zodiac. We talked until close to midnight, then went off to our bedrooms, leaving my dad in his chair, inebriated and alone, with the television mindlessly displaying its late-night shows to an unseeing, unhearing audience.

A week later Timothy was released. I drove him home, to a house that was far larger and far better than anything one could reasonably own without having inherited it. It had been redone in the sixties by a local architect who was clearly into taking design risks: round windows and leaf-shaped doors, high ceilings, grooved cement walls, and mosaic-tile floors. I asked Timothy, "Lottery or trust fund?" and he smiled and said it had been his grandmother's. We were both three generations deep in Los Angeles, our roots going down into a time long before the entertainment industry, skyscrapers, and developers took over—a time of orange groves and Mexicans, dirt roads and swamps, hills that had yet to be carved out and plastered with stucco boxes that had panoramic views of the miles of buildings that lay where the orange groves used to.

The way Timothy decorated his house, the way he lived, made it feel like a cross between a museum and a hippie crash pad, with antiques and beanbag chairs right next to each other. Every inch of his bedroom was taken up by his rock collection, small statues, African masks, artwork, walls and walls of books and low tables covered with glass turtles, small boxes, and dolphins carved from wood and crystal and ivory. The bathrooms were all cedar and skylights.

We put his suitcases down next to his guitar and music books and sat on a tapestry couch with giant pillows. I tried not to look as stunned as I was. It was an incredible home. The whole north side of the upstairs was glass, directly facing the hills, the quiet gray Hollywood Hills that sat patiently while the city went crazy at their feet.

The Unit staff had always warned us against isolation, so Timothy and I planned to spend the entire day together, then AA at night followed by a late dinner with people from the meeting. The staff had also warned against idle time, so to keep busy and kill a couple of hours, we walked over to the Rexall drugstore around the corner. We bought lollipops in every color of the rainbow and Xeroxed our faces a dozen times, a nickel for every smeared black-and-white reproduction, each with a different expression that made us laugh harder and harder until we had to sit down. We filled a shopping cart with paperback books, cigarettes, magazines. Things to Do While Not Drinking. We could barely carry it all home.

Back at his house, with the shadows long and the sun weak, we sat in the hammock on the balcony with the magazines and cigarettes and talked about our fears and hopes and dreams. Timothy put on some tea, and we spoke aloud all the questions and worries and what-ifs we had been quiet about while in treatment. And when it got dark we left for the meeting.

"Look who's here." I nudged Timothy. We were standing by the coffeemaker in a room of strangers, two wallflowers swayed easily by the bustle of all the strong, socially adept people rushing about. He looked over to see suit-boy from the morning meeting, out of uniform in Levi's and a T-shirt. "Let's find out his name," I said.

"You go ahead. I'll watch."

"No, I can't! You do it."

The gavel thumped the podium as the leader started the meeting, saving Timothy and me from having to flip a coin to determine who was going to approach him. We took our seats, but like a rhinestone Kit-Kat clock, my eyes returned to him every few seconds, back and forth, back and forth, back and forth.

The next morning I arrived early to the Log Cabin meeting and spotted him again, this time chatting with a nurse from the Unit. As soon as he walked away, I wandered over, sat down next to the nurse, and small-talked my way into finding out that his name was James and he'd been in the Unit briefly earlier that year but had been transferred over to Psych 2, courtesy of his ceaseless acid-dropping and subsequent hallucinations during therapy sessions. "He's doing great now, though, got six months sober and a good program. You should talk to him. He's about your age, and it's good for you young people to stick together. As a matter of fact—James! Hey, James!" She waved him over from across the room. My chest tightened; my mouth went dry. I suddenly felt how very hot it was in there, how stifling. And here he was. "James, I'd like you to meet Delia. She just got out a couple of weeks ago."

Producing a weak smile, I nodded hello to him and longed either to disappear or to become someone else. I hadn't showered that morning and was wearing cut-off 501s and my dad's tank top, the light blue one with the flowers across the chest that said "Hawaii" and was at least ten years old. It was unraveling at the seams. So was I.

James looked at me with eyes full of energy, full of life, bright deep blue with glints like chipped glass, and then he shook my hand, inviting me to come sit up in the front corner with him and his friends. Throughout the meeting he pointed out different people around the room and whispered interesting tidbits about each one—who was sleeping together, who had been sober for how long, who worked the best program, who to stay away from. I hung on his every word. I felt like I glowed in his presence. A few times I almost got the sense that he was flirting with me, but I brushed it off, knowing he wouldn't be interested in someone like me, a mere mortal.

Timothy arrived ten minutes late and spotted us immediately. I wiggled my fingers at him in a wave, and he rolled his eyes and hid a grin, exasperated.

Halfway through the meeting, James said he had to leave for work but gave me his phone number first. "I'll save you a seat tomorrow, too, if you like it up here in the peanut gallery." He flashed that smile, full of those teeth. Amazing.

I had to kick myself to answer. "That'd be great."

He walked out, and I waited a minute before slipping back to where Timothy was sitting. I sat down close to him, looked around, then showed him the scrap of paper with James's phone number written in red ink.

"I think he likes you, hon."

"Really?"

"God, will you stop? Yes, really. But can you watch your step for once? I mean, no offense, but you might not be in the healthiest frame of mind right now, and Lord knows what you're attracting."

"Oh, whatever. Do you really think he likes me?

He sighed. "Well, yes, Dill, but—"

I cut him off with a smile and returned to my seat, oblivious to anything but the thought that James might actually like me, leaving Timothy to pray that I didn't get involved with him.

Come September, I was going to at least one AA meeting every day. The two days a week that I didn't have classes, Timothy and I spent together—we shopped, we ate, we went to movies, or I brought my

schoolbooks over and studied while he painted. Every Saturday night
we went to two meetings, one at ten, one at midnight (a candlelit gathering on the Unit), and I stayed over at his place afterward. We did
tarot readings; he played guitar; I braided my hair; we conducted ama-
teur séances and told ghost stories. We talked nonstop until we fell
asleep, if we fell asleep, and then we got up, did the Sunday *Times*
crossword puzzle, and went to Jan's Coffee Shop for breakfast.

Sometimes Zodiac or Matt would join us during the day, but Saturday nights were ours, and it was during those nights and early mornings
that Timothy and I told each other things we'd withheld in treatment.
He never knew who his real father was; his mother was a missionary
who lived in Africa and hadn't spoken to him in years; his last lover,
Paul, had died of AIDS a year to the day before Timothy had checked
into the Unit. I told him most of my secrets, too.

During these nights and early mornings we discovered we both
knew all the words to David Bowie's *Hunky Dory* album and loved Trivial Pursuit. We drank a ton of tea. We had fun. But when I think about
it now, I realize that those nights and early mornings were our womb,
the time and place we became inextricably welded together, one being
that just happened to take up two bodies.

I finally looked at the bulletin board at school and found that there were
indeed AA meetings on campus, daily at lunchtime. A month had
passed since school had started, and I was not warming up to the experience at all. The academic stuff was fine, but I was always more comfortable in my head than I was in social situations. I could bury myself
in books and assignments and pull down a 4.0 GPA no problem. I just
didn't want to let anyone get to know me while I was doing it.

But I decided to give the AA meeting a chance. Maybe I'd find some
like-minded people there, some other students who were as uncomfortable here as I was, who had found their kinfolk in the rooms of AA
and not in the classrooms, who found the majority of the students to be

as dissimilar to them as I did to me. No such luck. When I walked in, there were only three other kids there, all court referred, all boys, all completely not into it. I stayed for twenty minutes and then made some feeble excuse about having to be somewhere else. They took that as a good reason to end the meeting early, signing one another's meeting verification slips and walking off in separate directions.

I spent the rest of the afternoon at the library, safe among the books and silence, looking forward to that night, when I could go to a real meeting and talk about how much I felt like I was on my own planet at school. Not that anyone had promised that getting sober was going to be easy, but no one had warned me how much harder it would be doing it as a teenager. I looked up from my paper long enough to notice that the guy across from me wore a Corona beer T-shirt, and was drawing pot leaves in the margins of his notebook. I gathered up my books and drove to Timothy's house.

When I got there, ready to talk about my crappy experience at the on-campus meeting, Timothy was on the phone with Joan. She had called to tell us that she had just talked to Matt's parents—seems Matt had taken off for a couple days on a coke run and come home to find his bags packed. His parents sent him to a rehab in Arizona, where he would be for the next three months. Timothy hung up and we just stared at each other. We didn't have to say it—*don't you dare leave me in this alone*—we knew. People we had been in treatment with were relapsing left and right, I was feeling like a leper, and Timothy was struggling with his own isolation and displacement, since much of the gay community's socializing was done in bars and nightclubs. So we did what we always did: linked elbows, walked to the meeting, and sat down together, our bond that much stronger, our commitment to our recovery that much more passionate.

A week later, Zodiac sat next to me at a meeting on the night we were to take our AA chips, me for sixty days, her for thirty. "Chips" were poker-chip-looking key chains that marked time, different colors for each increment. That night I would get a green one and she would get a white one. They were so you could recognize the accomplishment for yourself and so others would know how long you had been clean. Everyone clapped, and you got to make a little speech; then you had this plastic disk to hang from your keys. Important stuff to the newly sober.

As the leader called, "Anyone for thirty days?" Zodiac leaned over to me and whispered, "Don't say nothing, but I smoked a joint at lunch," then got up and smiled, accepting her chip, thanking the group for their love and support. The whole room clapped, except me. I just sat there with my mouth hanging open. I almost missed my own turn at the podium, still reeling from her blatant dishonesty and the ease with which she could lie and charm a room full of people sincerely struggling for recovery. Myself included. I didn't know what to do. I wanted to announce it from the stage, but I had never seen anyone else do that. Plus, no one likes a snitch. I wanted to yell at her, but I wasn't sure why. I wanted to help her, but I didn't know how. I watched at the break as she mingled with everyone, the people who hugged her as she smiled and held up her chip, and I wondered if she ever felt guilt, if she ever felt anything for other people.

One morning I followed James out of the meeting. I just wanted to watch him walk, and I wanted to see which car was his. I was growing more fascinated by him. I stopped at the doorway, leaning there, and watched as he crossed the street, unalarmed and unlocked an old olive green Saab, slid in, sat for a minute, then pulled away. I knew by the obsessive quality with which I had followed him and watched him that I had crossed over some invisible line of sanity.

I looked down at the cement steps, at the hard pink-gray disks of old gum and cigarette butts. I had fainted on this porch at my third meeting. I had asked Joan to be my sponsor right exactly here. Funny the way so many turning-point moments would occur in the same places. I thought of the phrase *if these walls could talk* and knew that for me, *these walls* were Timothy's house, this little log cabin, and Jan's ugly orange booths. They held my story in their hands.

5

Those early days of my recovery returned to me often when I was back in Los Angeles taking care of Timothy. Probably because the places hadn't changed much: Timothy lived in the same house, the Log Cabin meeting was still going strong, and, despite the makeover, Jan's was still Jan's.

Some mornings, I walked over to the meeting, and at first, Timothy came with me. Many of the old regulars were still there, and they wanted to hear about Seattle AA. They were pleased that I had experienced the total conversion that comes with long-term recovery. That I was someone they could hold up as proof: the program really does change lives. Timothy got some spiritual strength from going to the meeting, but it would zap him physically for the rest of the day. When he did go, he would go back to sleep as soon as we got home. I would read in bed next to him, the two of us returned to our shape of old married couple nestled on the foldout.

James still went to that meeting, too. He hadn't mentioned that the night we met at the diner or the night he came over to Timothy's right after I had arrived, but one morning I walked in and there he was, sitting in his usual seat in the front corner, smoking, gorgeous. It was such an iconic image from back then that, for a moment, I felt I was in a dream, a déjà vu, some sort of time warp. It was only when he waved me over that I saw he was a little older, realized I didn't know every person in the room, and remembered that it was present-day.

He slid over and patted the bench next to him.

I whispered, "There's not enough room."

He slid over another fraction of an inch. "Here. Squeeze in."

I wedged myself between him and the overweight older woman next to him, and James and I sat with our bodies pressed together like that for the rest of the hour, even when she got up and left, leaving us plenty of room to spread out.

I was getting used to the routine of the pills. Half of the pills counteracted the side effects of the other half of the pills; then there were pills to help Timothy's body absorb those pills. CD4, DDI, AZT: the triple-cocktail protease inhibitor. Amoxicillin, Acyclovir. Timothy's bathroom counter looked like a pharmacy: rainbow colors of gel caps and tiny footballs, horse pills and beads and buttons. None of which could keep him alive.

I was also getting used to the quiet voice in the back of my head that reminded me that there were painkillers somewhere in the rows of pill bottles, toward the back because Timothy didn't want to take them until he really needed them. The voice was persistent and one that would be with me no matter how many years I was clean, no matter how many meetings I went to. It would talk in my ear during a crisis the same as it would in the middle of a regular old Tuesday afternoon. They told us in AA not to ignore it but to talk back to it.

No one would know, it whispered as I gathered up Timothy's next dose. I unscrewed the cap and told the voice that I would know. It was right there with a reply: *So what? It's been twelve years. You can take one pill. Plus, if ever there was a time to numb out, this is it.* Clever. Part of me agreed. Anesthesia would be lovely, but if there was ever a time to be present, this was it. I don't want to miss a thing, painful as it may be. I told the voice to go away, and, for the time being, it did.

Sometimes that was all it took, just telling it to go away, but sometimes I had to go to a meeting and talk about it, about the voice, the little cartoon devil that still sat on my shoulder opposite the cartoon angel, poking me with its pitchfork and waiting for a moment of weakness.

I had been there about a week when Timothy handed me a folder with all the legal stuff, his will, the deed to the house, bank statements, health insurance, car registration—it was endless. The folder was bulging and held together by a giant rubber band. I flipped through it until I found what he wanted me to read.

It was several handwritten pages containing every detail about the funeral, down to the flowers (callas), his suit (the Perry Ellis), and the music (acoustic guitar). I read page after page of his instructions, then frowned at him with my only question.

"What?"

"Well, it's the music."

"What about the music?"

" 'Soul Man'?"

"Yeah? So?"

"So? Are you nuts? You can't play 'Soul Man' at a funeral. Especially on an acoustic guitar."

"You can at mine, hon. It's a great song. And I thought I could have anything I wanted."

"Timothy. Think of your guests. After you're gone, nobody is going to want to dance for a long time. You know that. We're going to need something a little more subdued."

He sat for a minute, thinking.

"Fine. You're right."

"Thank you. Did you have another song in mind?"

"I'll come up with something."

"That's what worries me. Next it'll be 'Ride My Seesaw.' "

He toasted me with his iced tea and swallowed. "Another one of my favorites."

"Timothy!"

After a long pause, a look came over his face, spreading slowly the way some people blush. What Joan had called the cosmic aha.

"I don't know how I didn't see it before. I mean, hello? I know the song."

"Want me to change it in here?" I held up a pen, along with the pages.

"No, I'll write it down when we're done, and I don't want you to look at it. I want it to be a surprise. Don't worry—you'll be pleased."

I looked at him sideways. He held up two fingers and said, "Scout's honor, babycakes. Oh, and there's one other thing—the car."

I looked at him, puzzled.

"Did you see in the will that it's yours? We'll take your rental back tomorrow and use mine from now on."

I imagined myself trying, later, to drive the shiny little navy blue '69 Volvo as if I weren't in his seat. I tried to see myself crawling over the steep hills of Seattle in the rain, not thinking of him, my hands on the leather steering wheel cover, the leather that was shaped with his handprints. Then I realized it didn't matter if I was in my car, his car, any car; I would always think of him; I would always feel the vacancy, no matter where I sat. I knew no friend, no lover, no car, no home, no job, no book or laugh or long walk would ever replace him or distract me or numb the shock of loss, and in a way that comforted me. He would always be right here with me, in his absence.

And how I hated that paradox.

"Have you talked to Zodiac lately?" I asked Timothy, later that day.

"Yeah, the other night after I called you, I called her. She said she's going to try to come out, too, as soon as things at work slow down. We can call her later."

"What about Matt?"

"I called him a few months ago, but he didn't return my calls. I left another message last week, but I don't think it was his number. It wasn't his voice on the answering machine."

"Hmm. Do you still have Hap's number? If not, I brought it with me." I held up my old address book.

"Wow. I don't know about that; I'll have to think about it. Actually, you know what, no. Don't call him yet. He's so far away and everything, and I don't want to bug him. We haven't talked for so long anyway. Like five years? Six?"

"I think he'd want to know what's going on."

"I've no doubt he would, but let's just wait, okay?"

I didn't figure it out until later, that if people started flocking in from all over the globe, Timothy would feel the enormity of it. That once it became Pilgrimage to Timothy, it was all over, but that with just me here, maybe we could pretend, if just for a week or a month, that the end wasn't quite as close as it really was.

6

Not long after he got out of treatment, Timothy threw himself a party. He was turning thirty-six and said that no self-respecting homo would let a birthday pass without a dinner party.

I had taken my best (only) dress to the dry cleaner's for the occasion. It was black and narrow, with vintage mother-of-pearl buttons down the back. My hair was pulled into a low knot and I had even borrowed my mom's perfume and put on some mascara and lipstick. It was my first time getting dressed up in months, and I had been nervous driving over that night to Timothy's. The last time I'd gotten dressed up was for my prom, three months before I'd checked into the Unit, and that had been a complete alcoholic disaster—one shoe missing, a mystery hickey, the whole bit. But this was different. I was in the company of my closest (only) friends, I was sober, and I was vertical. I closed my eyes and said a silent thank-you, as Joan had taught me to do. I opened them just as she was walking in the door.

On her arm was Hap, a man from the morning meeting. My first thought was, *The Queen and Her Gnome.* She was magnificent in her silky snow white skirts; he wore an ill-fitting blazer and his hair was a crazy staticky wisp hovering about his head. We had all seen him at the meeting, but nobody besides Joan had gotten to know him. She had asked Timothy if she could bring Hap to the party, to cheer him up and get him socializing, and she watched him all night as if he were her own discovery, which he sort of was. But he quickly became ours. Throughout dinner my feeling that he was a piece of our puzzle grew with every off-the-wall comment and fantastic tale that tumbled from his lips. He was full of surprises—I had figured he was just an old drunk, but it turned out he was a junkie from way back, shooting heroin in the quiet back streets and brown velvet front lobbies of a 1940s Los Angeles, a John Fante Los Angeles that is slipping away with every minimall but that you can still catch a glimpse of with a drive east on Wilshire Boulevard to the Ambassador Hotel or with a ride up Angel's Flight. Hap saved the good stuff for later—he let it unfurl slow and heavy over the next several years, always one more story up his sleeve, always told with a grin on his face and a sparkle in his eye.

Zodiac wore a backless dress and a pair of heels she had borrowed from a stripper friend of hers. She was a chameleon, adapting to any situation: what she lacked in authenticity she made up for with invention—which was how that night, even in those trashy stilettos, she could manage to seem elegant. Anyone else would have wound up looking like a prostitute or a drag queen, but not her.

Joan was the overseer, though it wasn't her party. She just commanded that sort of respect, her chair the head of the table even though the table was round. You knew not to interrupt her. When she spoke, we listened like small children to a fairy tale.

We sat in the mostly-glass-walled dining room, silent traffic below, wind rustling the bamboo on the balcony. There were five of us, plus two of Timothy's "other" friends (by then, everything and everyone not connected to AA was "other"), Ian and Bill. We had heard a lot about one another, but this was our first meeting.

Timothy had met Ian and Bill when he lived in San Francisco in the early seventies. Even with the Sexual Revolution in full blaze around them, even as society went from gay bashing to Gay Pride and from promiscuity to AIDS, Ian and Bill had remained a monogamous, devoted couple. Timothy told me that he'd always admired what they had, even during his amoral barhopping youth. He had almost captured that kind of love with Paul, but it had slipped through his fingers with Paul's death.

Ian was the younger and taller of the two, a sculptor whose body of work focused on the Holocaust. First impressions would have him doing watercolors or tender pastels, he was so willowy and shy, like a boy, but his art was as strong as he was soft.

Bill was a rounded attorney with slate-colored hair and cheeks that were pink with a permanent, affectionate blush. He was quick to laugh, which made his tie jiggle atop his chambray-clad belly. He had kissed my hand when we'd been introduced. I couldn't help smiling. He was probably the only person I'd ever met to so completely fit the word *jolly*. I watched the intimacy between Ian and Bill from across the table, my attention rapt.

After dinner, the caterer brought out little cups of espresso and then disappeared back to the kitchen. We were talking loudly, laughing, standing up, telling stories with a confidence we had only imagined possible with the aid of chemicals. After a little while, the caterer dimmed the lights and brought out a glossy fruit torte spiked with tall candles. We sang, and Timothy made a wish, extinguishing the candles in one sweeping blow.

Then the air changed.

The Santa Ana winds that had gusted hot and dry all day suddenly picked up momentum and began to slap power lines against the building like double-Dutch jump ropes. We watched in silence as a transformer popped not forty feet away on a thick, dark telephone pole. First a hot-blue flash, then white, then a bouquet of sparks showered onto the sidewalk below, spilling glowing orange streamers of electricity like the Fourth of July sparklers that tickle and prick your hand, figure eights against a backyard sky.

We looked back at one another for an instant before the lamps strobed, then died, smiling excitedly, with wonder.

Then it went dark.

"How excellent!" Timothy was the first to speak. He took his presents into the living room and began to light the giant candles that sat in big blue and white plates on the end tables.

"Ming Dynasty," he told me as he pulled a matchbook out from under one of them.

After he opened his presents illuminated by the fluttery, eerie candlelight, Ian and Bill went home and the caterer cleaned up and left. We were sitting in a loose circle, me on the floor, Zodiac on the couch, Hap and Timothy on either side of me on the rug, and Joan on the ottoman. It was story time.

Hap started talking first. Throughout dinner he had told a few tales of the time he spent working as a bookie, and I had looked over at Timothy and we had both nodded, once for yes. But now the mood was different. Hap looked on the verge of crying, but then he blinked and began talking in a light, easy manner through a mild grin with half-mast lids, reminding me of the lion in *The Wizard of Oz*. Behind his glasses, his eyes darkened as he said his wife's name.

Timothy and I jerked to attention, looking first at each other, then at Hap.

"Dot was your wife?" I asked, incredulous, surprising Hap, pulling him out from under his momentary black cloud—that was what he called it, his grief. I clearly remembered the night the Unit staff had called us all into the group room to inform us of the death of the recently discharged heroin-addicted Dot, and I had tried to pair up the image of the tender, sweet, late-fifties homemaker with the words *fatal overdose,* tried to see her with a needle blaring out of her pulseless arm. I remembered someone saying that it was no wonder, what with her husband not coming to family group and still using in the house, oblivious to her efforts to get clean.

Hap looked at me with a sorrowful combination of guilt and defeat, sighed, and looked down. He realized then that we knew who she (and therefore he) was and that he had been neglectful in his role as Supportive Family Member. He kind of snorted, scoffing at his own selfishness, his own hand in her relapse, his hatred for the addiction. Then he sighed.

"Yeah. Yeah, she was. My 'old lady' . . . Oh, she couldn't stand me calling her that! Used to just burn her up." A sad smile. "We were married for twenty-four years. She finally decides to get clean, and then she's dead! Poof!" He waved his hands in twin arcs, wide rough palms flat, fingers splayed. "She's gone." Then he snapped his fingers, the sound like the pop of a match lighting. "Just like that."

Hap said his decision to get clean came when they pulled the sheet over her face.

My mind started to wander to my own grief, to my twin brother, who had died before we were even born. I had no memory of him as a person, but the shape that had been him ached like an amputee's lost limb and created a pain that even drugs hadn't been able to numb. Yet I said nothing. I had neatly avoided bringing it up in treatment, and I still hadn't told Timothy. Even during the most intense of our Saturday night sleepovers, with secrets flying left and right, I had held on to this one. Joan had no idea, and I half-dreaded, half-craved the work I'd have to do around it once I told her. I knew that once I did, there would be no turning back, on a million levels, and that I'd better do it tonight, while I felt this safe.

I took a deep breath, gathering courage. I opened my mouth.

And Zodiac started talking. I closed my mouth and let my courage shrink back into its cave.

"I've been getting high again every day," she started. "For about the past week. Few weeks. Maybe more like a month." She looked at me. "I'm sorry about dumping it on you on our chip night; that wasn't cool."

I shrugged. I was glad she was getting honest, but I was still mad at her. As she started giving a string of excuses, in my head I could hear the announcer: *And the Oscar goes to——*

"I want to get clean, I do, but it's really hard for me to work and not get loaded—"

Hap interrupted her with, "Sorry to butt in, what do you do?"

"I'm naked."

"Excuse me?"

"For a living? You asked what I do. I'm naked for a living. I'm an exotic dancer. I dance to stupid fucking disco songs around a pole while a bunch of fat horny white men throw money at my sorry ass. Is what I do. All right?"

She went mute for a moment, eyes distant, blinking large into the darkness. Then she continued on about wanting to change, wanting to get honest, wanting someone to help her. She even cried. It was a great performance, but I seemed to be the only one who was thinking how hard it is to believe a liar when she is confessing to being a liar. Liars think it'll win them trust. The irony is lost on them.

After another long pause, I shifted around in my spot on the floor and went for it.

"Okay. My turn then." I reached for my pack of cigarettes and lit one, wondering what it would be like to say it aloud. "I killed my twin brother."

Maybe that wasn't the way to have said it. Too abrupt.

Timothy turned toward me with deep question marks frowned into his forehead, an unsaid *excuse me?* Zodiac raised her eyebrows; Hap looked at me with interest and softness, Joan with a face filled with unconditional love. All eight eyes on me were too many, and I looked down, so I could just keep talking and get it out.

"No, I'm sorry, I don't mean like recently. Let me back up. My parents always wanted a boy and a girl. Rather, my dad wanted a boy and my mom wanted a girl. So when the doctor first told them that we were twins, they were surprised, but happy, and they went out and bought two of everything and hoped that we would be the girl and boy that they had dreamed of."

I put out my barely smoked cigarette and tried to imagine, as I always did when I thought about it, my parents as twenty-year-old flower children, preparing for my (our) arrival. I tried to imagine what it was like for them and how, how on earth, they have forgiven me. I thought about my birthdays before I knew, with their undefined melancholy, my mom crying alone and pretending not to, my dad drunk and trying to act like he wasn't. I thought about my birthdays since I was told and how unable I was to celebrate.

"This is from what I've heard, and trust me, we don't talk about it, so I'm mostly going from old memories of a story told a long time ago. But this part I remember clear as a bell," I said firmly, lighting another cigarette, taking a long drag, and blowing it out, talking around the smoke.

"They said I came out first, holding his umbilical cord in my fist. Not like, oh, hey, here's this thing lying near or even in my hand, but really gripping it, squeezing it. Enough so that when he was born just minutes later, he was dead. The doctors said he had been fine hours before, they had heard two strong heartbeats on the monitor, but I killed him before he had a chance to live."

I looked down.

"They told me when I was about nine. I had been having nightmares. I would wake up screaming, run down the hall to their room, and fall asleep between them. The three of us, in a double bed. For months. Finally, I guess thinking it would help, and with a child psychologist there, they told me. That I had strangled him. In utero."

I looked up at my friends, hoping they weren't going to try to comfort me by shushing me, telling me it wasn't my fault. Invalidating me. But they didn't; of course they didn't. They just watched me, listening with unwavering focus, which was exactly what I needed.

"I know you're probably thinking it wasn't my fault. And I'll agree that it's not, you know, something I'd do now or anything. I mean, I know it's not literally my fault. But it was me who killed him. I was just very . . . small. And even my parents—they have never remotely implied that I was to blame. Ever. But that didn't matter. I felt guilty anyway. And I have always had the feeling that my dad was disappointed he'd lost the boy and not me. He wanted a son so badly, and I single-handedly ruined that, no pun intended."

I stubbed my cigarette in the ashtray as both Timothy and Zodiac lit new ones.

"So that's what I drank over sometimes; that's the big question in my life: How do you resolve that? How do you accept it, accept yourself, when every day you look down at your hands and see them squeezing the life out of your twin brother, the boy that could now be your best friend, your father's pride and joy, your other half?

"It's not all the time; I mean, I don't just sit around feeling like a murderer. But I know it's affected who I am. I know it's a part of me. And I know it's time for me to deal with it."

After a long silence, Zodiac said, "Damn, girl. That's a lot of shit for you to be carrying around. I don't even know what to say about all that."

Hap said, "Me, either."

I waved my hand, dismissing them. "You guys don't have to say anything. I just wanted to get it out. There'll be time to talk about it later, I'm sure." I looked at Joan.

"You know," Joan said, "it reminds me of something my sponsor tells me: 'God never gives us a problem without providing us the tools to find the solution.' If you're ready to work on this, and it sounds like you are, we'll find you some peace."

I stood on unsure legs to sit next to her. Just as she put her arm around my shoulders, the power surged to life, the neighborhood whirring back on, lamps dawning, clocks blinking 12:00.

We squinted and rubbed our eyes like little moles.

"Wow, it's after three," Timothy said, looking at his watch.

We milled around, not wanting the night to be over but knowing it was. One by one, we said good-bye to each other and happy birthday to Timothy, fully aware that we had gone somewhere that night, somewhere deep and personal and sacred, a place from which we were reluctant to leave. We loved the feeling too much. It was safety. It was home.

7

As Timothy slept restlessly next to me, my eyes scanned his room, aimless and lazy, staring at some things and darting away from others. I was sitting in the old leather wingback chair by his desk. I watched him sleep and I thought about that year, the year of that party and our trip to Yosemite and me turning eighteen, the year we all became so close, close enough that it really was like finding a whole new family. Timothy and I were always the closest in that family, and now here I sat, next to him as always, in this room where so much of my life had happened, with him breathing slowly and strenuously, the weight dropping from his bones.

During that winter of power outages and confessions and road trips, he was healthy and I was hopeful, and we had simply turned up the radio and sung together. I felt more attached to him with every mile we drove, every day that passed, months before he tested positive, years before he got sick. We had a sense of invincibility usually reserved for the very young or the very dumb. We were sure that we would always have each other. We were sure that nothing could ever go wrong.

"Hey, check this out," Timothy had said, showing me a flyer for an AA convention in Yosemite. Even though it sounded lame, we figured if we went together, we could make it fun.

We sat in one of Jan's sticky orange booths, remains of blintzes on the table between us.

I handed the flyer back to him. "Should we invite anyone else?"

"Like who?"

"Well, certainly not Zodiac." She wasn't showing up at the meetings like she had promised she would. We were worried, but Timothy said she'd make her way back. He was not critical. In fact, he was damn near confident when it came to her. Hopeful. He believed every word she said and trusted her completely. My expectations were much lower. Like next to nothing. I suspected that she was the type of person whose greatest blessing and most deadly curse was the way people forgave her and allowed her chance after chance, the way she could rob you blind and you'd ask her if there was anything else you could give her.

"And Matt's still in Arizona. What about Hap?"

"Hmm. I don't know. Who else?"

"Joan?" Timothy offered, but we decided we might not feel as loose with her there, like she would be watching us, poised to offer her wisdom, while we wanted to be silly, free, possibly even downright irreverent for the weekend: certainly not sponsor-friendly behavior.

"Well, then I guess it's just the two of us," I said.

Timothy grinned. "That's very Bill Withers of you."

"I try. So we'll leave Friday morning after the meeting?"

"Sounds perfect."

My parents didn't know what to make of my new life. I think they thought it was stranger than my old one. I think they had hoped I would make friends at school, "normal" friends my own age, who didn't have the torrid pasts and questionable presents of my AA friends. What my parents didn't understand was that I didn't relate to anyone at school. Those people partied like regular college kids and talked about their drunken weekends all day on Monday. They were superficial, bland; they had nothing to offer me. And what if I were to open up to them about who I was? Some of my stories would shock your average eighteen-year-olds, probably even alienate them. It was better for me to make school simply a place where my classes were, not a place to socialize.

When I first started staying over at Timothy's house, my parents wondered, *Is he really gay? Or are they having an affair?* And when I talked to my parents about going to the convention, there was a moment's pause, during which I could almost see their one-word thought, mutual and disbelieving: *Yosemite?* It was a strange request, I know. I didn't usually ask to go to national parks, most teenagers didn't, but they said yes. Who knows what they thought of me going off to John Muir country with the likes of Timothy?

We packed Timothy's car full of duffel bags, AA literature, cartons of smokes, snacks, and tapes and got on the freeway with the windows down and the music loud.

We were in the middle of nowhere for a long time. We had put in a James Taylor tape about a hundred miles back, and it was still going, side A side B side A side B, over and over because neither of us wanted to stop it. It seemed to fit.

When "Fire and Rain" came on for the second time, Timothy glanced away from the road to look sideways at me. "He wrote this when he was in rehab. This friend of his died of an overdose, and he wrote this song for her."

I listened to the words more carefully after that, having this new information, and then we burst into song together for the chorus. We sang with lumps in our throats as we thought of our tenuous grip on our recovery, on each other. I watched him in profile as he drove.

We attended only one meeting the whole weekend. The name-tag idea didn't appeal to us, and the rooms were too warm and filled with middle-aged polyester-wearing fat men who just lived for this kind of thing. They were old-timey AA, all slogans and tobacco-teeth. They gave us the creeps the way they eyed Timothy with their homophobic lookaway-eyes and me with a flat oppressed hunger. It was clear that not all AA was as hip as West Hollywood AA. Some of them had AA pins on their lapels. "Shoot me if I ever fit in with this demographic," I told Timothy, and he said the same went for him. We even shook on it.

So instead we went ice-skating outdoors on an oval of ice illuminated by hundreds of tiny white Christmas lights; we drove around; we had a picnic; we sat up late talking, ordering room service, and watching movies on the bolted-down television.

On Sunday, we took our time driving back home, stopping way more often than was necessary. We stretched a six-hour drive into ten. Drank about a pot of coffee each. Bought a dozen doughnuts. As he drove and we sang, I knew that just being with him had helped me more than any of the meetings we could have gone to that weekend. I pictured us trying to skate on wobbly ankles, falling down, pulling each other back up again, stronger each time, doing better the tighter we held on to each other, symbolism that was not lost on us.

We pulled into Timothy's driveway close to midnight with only four doughnuts left and the ashtray completely full, and I gathered up my stuff and drove home. Alone in my car, I flipped through the stations restlessly, then stopped upon hearing the too-familiar-by-now voice singing "Sweet Baby James." I remembered Timothy telling me that was his all-time favorite song, and I smiled. It felt like him. I would never again hear it without thinking of him and that trip and the beginning of our friendship: ten miles behind us and ten thousand more to go.

I got home, dropped my bags, and fell into a deep sleep. I dreamed about a young boy running alongside a multicolored river, laughing.

As I watched Timothy's eyes move around behind his lids, I wondered if that was him in my dream, though at the time I'd just figured it was one of those fictional dream characters. I wondered what Timothy was dreaming about, if there was a boy on a riverbank watching the water go by like paint in long liquid ribbons of color or if his dreams were fading as he prepared to leave this life. I watched his lips for any sign of a smile, but nothing. I walked over and touched his forehead. Hot. I dabbed it with a cool rag and turned the fan up, pointing it toward him, hoping he was not too uncomfortable. Then I took a picture down from his bookshelf and settled back into the chair. The picture was one of me that Timothy had kept right there in a frame all these years, taken that same winter, at my birthday party.

I turned eighteen the weekend after the trip to Yosemite.

Timothy wanted to have a party for me and he wanted to make it extra-special, not just because eighteen was a landmark year but also because it would be my first birthday in recovery.

"I'll pick you up at three on Saturday," Timothy said. "And don't wear anything fancy."

"Like I was going to. I only have one dress and I just wore it to your party."

"Well, I'm just letting you know. Think rustic."

"How rustic? If there are Porta Potties, I'm not going."

"Don't worry, toots. There are queers involved. We don't do tacky."

He picked me up at three on the dot and drove an hour out of town, out toward Tujunga, up a winding mountain road, through canyons, and finally to a little dirt parking lot. *Switzer Falls, 1 mile,* the carved wooden sign said. He got a few grocery bags out of the trunk and we started to walk along a river, big old oaks on either side of us, the sun in full November glory, the sky a deep cobalt blue, the leaves against it in shades of dry yellow and craft-paper brown.

We came around a bend in the path and there they were, like a moment from *This Is Your Life:* Joan, Hap, Zodiac, my parents, and Ian and Bill. Behind them was a picnic table piled high with presents. A cheesecake. Sandwiches. A wheel of Brie, fresh fruit, and Pellegrino.

I turned to Timothy and started to stammer, wanting to thank him, but he cut me off: "Don't get all sentimental on me, missy." He turned to Ian. "Maestro?"

Ian pushed a button on the boom box and Motown started playing. Timothy grabbed my mom's hands and started dancing. The others joined in. I watched my dad watching us, dancing to Wilson Pickett, up in the mountains, next to a river. I couldn't read the look on his face, and I would have paid money to know what he was thinking.

Zodiac danced over to me and gave me a tight hug.

"I've got thirty days," she said. "For real this time."

I must have looked like I didn't believe her, because she grabbed my shoulders and went on. "I'm serious. Do you think I'd be up in the freaking woods with a bunch of old people and a wheel of freaking Brie if I was using?"

"No, but I haven't seen you at any meetings. Where have you been?"

"After Timothy's birthday party I went on a massive binge, and I was picked up for prostitution. Which was bullshit. But anyway, I was in Sybil Brand for a month."

Great. Prison. "So that's why you were clean, you were locked up?"

"No. I'm clean because I want to be. I could have gotten high in there, but I didn't want to. I want this," she said, waving her hand at the whole little scene. "I really want this."

My mom came over and put her arm around me. "Happy birthday, baby girl. I love you."

"I love you, too."

"I hope you don't mind us crashing your party. Actually, Timothy invited us, but I was worried that you wouldn't want us here."

"No, I'm glad you came. You can get to know my friends a little better." I looked around at this very mismatched group of people. "I know they're funny looking, but they're saving my life."

After a while, Timothy insisted I open my presents, handing me his first: a small box wrapped in paper he had painted himself. Inside it was a necklace, a long silver chain with small colored-glass beads, strips of metal, and a single piece of beachglass that hung from a half circle of greening copper that said "dream" in uneven black letters. I held it up in front of me, letting the glass twirl in the dappled light.

"It's beachglass," I said, thinking of all the times I spent in the sand by my house, collecting these little bits of tumbled glass, and the jar of it that I had on my windowsill.

"I know you collect it, so it reminded me of you. Then I got to thinking about how cool it was that something that could have just as easily been trash is jewelry instead, and it reminded me of us drunks: not only are we salvageable; we're completely fabulous! We're art-work, dammit. And how many people step right over us looking for the perfect seashell? Bor-ing! That glass is the real treasure, as far as I'm concerned. It's like us. We took a lickin', and kept on tickin', hon!"

He laughed and tossed me another box to open, but I was still deep in thought about what he had just said. What a fine line we walked, how close destruction and creation are, and how much of each a recovering alcoholic has. Is.

After the presents, Timothy announced that he would like everyone to stand up for a special ceremony. He handed us each an unlit candle as we rose and formed a circle around the table. He explained that each person would make a wish, then would light their candle from the previous person's candle, put it in the cake, and return to the circle, joining hands with the person next to them. The result would be one very bright cake, an unbroken ring of friends, and eight wishes in addition to my own.

It started with Joan, who quietly closed her eyes in prayer and lit her candle from the one on the cake, which was tall and spindly like a broom whisker. Hap paused, lit his from hers. And so on. The process reminded me of the Olympic torch, the eternal flame, even though I knew it had begun only moments earlier, with Zodiac's Bic lighter. But still.

When the candles were all lit, we stood in silence, in a sort of cluster meditation, hands firmly pressed together, almost swaying. My parents were on either side of me and my friends—*my tribe,* I thought—were all around me. Energy passed from hand to hand to hand like a live beam of light. The circle was charged. Sacred. I could feel tears springing up behind my closed eyelids and chills on my arms. I was relieved when Timothy told me to go ahead and blow out the candles—it was such a thick, precious moment that, though I did not want it to be over, I couldn't bear the weighty pleasure of it for another second.

I leaned toward the cake and turned to look around me. I felt a surge of pure love like a wave swelling past me, raising my body, then settling me back down.

I closed my eyes and held my hands over my heart, in a prayer, a thank-you. I inhaled, made my wish, and bent to blow out the candles. I'll never know if it was the hair spray or what, but instead of feeling a serene release of breath and hearing the patter of applause, I had an entirely different experience.

I felt, rather than saw, the flame lick over the left side of my head.

It made a windy sound and was bright and warm but not painful, and I reached up, calm and unalarmed, and patted it out the way some women fluff their curls. Strangely enough, my hair sustained only minor, nearly undetectable damage, just a light singe that was easily brushed away. Everyone gaped, frozen in various states of fear and wonder, obviously not having spent as much time around crack smokers as I had. It was as if they were playing charades and had been told to act out the phrase *oh my God*.

I turned toward them with my hand over my mouth. They looked to me for a reaction, a clue (burns? tears? embarrassment?), but I was already laughing a sudden, pure, infectious laugh, a laugh that was shiny and clean and fast like Mylar confetti thrown in front of a fan.

Joan was the first to join me, her nose crinkling and her shoulders bouncing. Timothy was the loudest; he couldn't stop. Hap went silent and had to wipe tears from his eyes, and I had never seen Zodiac look so kidlike in the whole time I'd known her. My mom had started to rush to my side but started laughing, too, when she saw I was okay. My dad even cracked a smile.

Once we'd settled down, I turned to extinguish the candles for real this time, making a point of pulling my hair far back from my face, which garnered a few more laughs. After I'd made my wish and blown out each candle, I turned back toward everyone, a dazzling wink of a smile on my face. It was precisely that moment that Timothy captured with his camera, frozen with an old-fashioned flashcube *pah*: an eighteen-year-old me smiling at him, thirty-six and healthy, another lifetime ago. That picture contained everything in a neat rectangle— the magic we shared that year, the strangeness of it, the awe. It said it all. It said, *Even when your hair's on fire, we'll be laughing. Even when your hair's on fire, you'll still have me, hon.*

I put the picture back on the shelf.

Something about this move, about the way the picture had taken me to that winter so quickly and the way I had put it back, reminded me of getting lost in an old scrapbook. Like in movies where the scene freezes and turns sepia and the camera pans back and the big leather cover closes shut. End of chapter. Commercial break. How awful that we wouldn't have any more birthday parties. How awful that nothing was the way we thought it would be, except that we were together. At least we were that. For now.

I heard Timothy moving around. He arched and sat up, rubbing his eyes, yawning, pulling off his shirt. He seemed smaller than he was even two weeks ago—and not only in a weight-loss sort of way, though I would have guessed he had lost close to ten pounds, but in stature as well, as if his former six-two frame was collapsing, shrinking.

"Hey," I said, trying not to sound sad.

He blinked and then focused on me. He could tell I had been thinking about something.

"What is it?" he asked.

"Remember my birthday party?" I picked up the picture again, held it up to show him. I knew my smile was weak, especially compared to the shining girl in the picture.

"God. What a day."

"One of my all-time favorites."

He frowned. "Was James there?"

"No, no, not yet. All that started just before Christmas. It seems like he would have been, though. He should have been."

"Do you remember the first time he came to the Candlelight meeting?" he asked me.

"Of course I do." I laughed. "Do you remember the last time?"

Timothy shook his head. "You guys were amazing. Absolutely incorrigible."

8

James came to the Candlelight meeting on the Unit a few weeks after I had invited him. Four patients attended, primarily out of insomnia
and boredom, and Timothy and I were there, as usual. There was a
lumpy couch on the far wall, a big brown item with enough cigarette
burns to make a polka-dot pattern in the velour. I always sat curled in
its corner. Timothy sat in the neighboring armchair. The patients were
scattered on the floor, and a single candle burned in a glass cube on the
table next to our cups of hospital-cafeteria coffee.

We talked about drugs and no drugs, about the things we used to do
and the things we did now to avoid doing those things. The patients
asked questions, and we responded to them as if we had the answers.
At some point, James threw his arm over the back of the couch and let
it slide down on my shoulder, giving me a sideways questioning look, a
look that was so playful and so perfect that I thought I must have been
seeing things in the dark. The hair on my arms and neck went up as if
I'd been waiting my whole life for this even though (a) I'd known him
for only four months and (b) I had been telling myself there was no way
he would ever like me. But here he was, and when I leaned into the
field of electricity coming off his body I inhaled slowly, like sipping
through a straw, feeling his energy get all mixed up with my own,
down in my lungs and fingertips. By the time the meeting ended we
were one big accidental slouch, breaking apart as the lamp was
switched on, squinting at its sudden brightness.

We walked to the parking lot together, to his car, where we settled for a minute, leaning, me pretending to look for Timothy, him studying me.

"Was that all right, what happened in there?"

It took a second to find my thoughts, my voice. Hiding somewhere. Finally, when they came, I tried not to scream. I managed a quiet, "God, yes, of course."

"Do you have plans right now?"

"James, it's two in the morning. What 'plans' would I have?"

"Meet me in the parking lot of Tail of the Pup. You can follow me from there."

Timothy walked over as James drove away, and I told him that he had invited me somewhere and I was going.

"Nice human pretzel during the meeting."

I swatted him. "I thought it was too dark to see anything in there!"

"Hardly."

"Was it that obvious?"

"Does Rose Kennedy have a black dress? I thought I was going to have to turn the hose on you two. Are you going back to his place?"

"I don't know where we're going."

"But I shouldn't wait up for you?"

"I doubt it. But I'll be back in time for breakfast. I think."

We got into my car, and I started it with a shaky hand. I dropped Timothy off at his house and drove to the parking lot of the hot-dog stand. I rolled my window down and pulled up next to James's car. He was waiting for me, a reggae station on the radio, its rhythms already calling me, rocking me. "C'mon," he said, and I nodded as if hypnotized and followed him north to the hills.

We wound our way through Laurel Canyon, a very small caravan.

Unlocking the front door carefully, he whispered that his parents were asleep down the hall. I followed him up a narrow staircase and into his room. He lit some incense and turned the stereo on. Crosby, Stills & Nash sang quietly in the background as he offered me a Coke from the small fridge tucked under his desk. We popped the cans open, seemingly loud enough to wake his parents, and muffled our laughter. We sat like that for a few minutes, Cokes, cigarettes, muted conversation, the overlapping guitar riffs of "Wooden Ships" swaying us as we filled up time, stalling so we wouldn't seem too hungry or anxious, trying to let the music calm us.

That was about all we could handle, a few minutes, before we stopped hearing the music and let the wave break, the one that had been cresting all night, all month, ever since I first saw him. At some point, my clothes came off, although I don't recall its happening. They very well could have melted under his hands for all I know. We hardly even kissed; it was more primal than that. He held the back of my neck, under my hair, and we trembled as if freezing. Our eyes locked, our bodies knotted together, and for a split second I questioned why he was still wearing his T-shirt. I thought, *A nasty scar? Has girlfriend, worried I'll leave fingernail marks?* Then I thought, *Stop thinking.* I didn't care. Rather, I didn't want to care. I wanted him to like me; I wanted him to be decent. And I didn't want to know anything that would change either of those things.

We tore each other apart over and over, until our fists clenched and dropped open for the last time, limp, depleted. We had rug burns, damp hair. We were out of breath and sweaty, and his bedroom windows had fogged. We stood and started to get dressed but then did it again once more, just because we couldn't help ourselves. My legs shook. I was sore. I hadn't known I could feel this intoxicated and still be sober.

We eventually got dressed with our eyes to the floor, afraid if we even looked at each other we'd go another round. Then we smoked lying on his bed, watching the sun come up, and when he said, "It's getting early out," I thought, *I love him.*

Driving back to Timothy's house, I tapped my steering wheel to the song on the radio, smiled, and rolled the window down. It was 6:00 A.M. and the temperature was approaching seventy degrees. December, but a heat wave. I could smell him on my hands and in my hair, and at every red light I held my palms to my nose, closed my eyes, and breathed him in.

Over the next week James and I spent every night in bed together. We sat next to each other at meetings. We talked on the phone. He took long lunches and I ditched classes, and we met in a booth in the back of a quiet Chinese restaurant downtown. It was during one of those afternoons that he gave me a small gift-wrapped box: a Zippo of my very own that would always remind me of him (*clink*), even long after I'd quit smoking. We left meetings early to do it in the car—or in any dark, semisecluded spot we could find that was good enough, if we couldn't wait the fifteen minutes it would take to speed back to his house. If we were able to be patient, we would drive those twisting roads back into the Hollywood Hills, but still fast, dangerously fast, just to taste it one more time, like children with stolen candy, like, well— addicts. What happened between us was a flash flood, sudden, over- powering, gone as quickly as it had appeared. We drowned and flailed in it, trying to catch our breath. The whole time I moved in a daze, of- ten just staring at him in disbelief that he was giving himself to me, wondering when the other shoe would drop, wondering if this was my reward for staying clean, wondering if it was possible that this was re- ally happening, wondering if Timothy's intuition could be wrong about James being bad for me.

"Are you sure your third eye is never just a wee bit off?" I asked Timothy one morning after the meeting. I had been with James until late the night before, and I still felt like someone had shot me full of opiates, all sleepy and high and indestructible.

"Well, I'm no Jeane Dixon, but I'm damn good."

"And you think it's stupid that I'm doing this."

He paused at my deadpan stare and looked away, then back. "We'll see, my dear; we'll see. I'm not going to try to stop you. Of course I worry. But I know you'll be fine. Plus, you'll always have me to come crawling back to after he's chewed you up and spit you out!" He said the last part melodramatically, with big hand gestures. I grinned and told him to shut the hell up. That I knew what I was doing. Really. Swear to God, I told him.

Then Timothy told me he was going out of town for the weekend and said I could use his house while he was gone; it would be like having my own place, a parent-free getaway. Living with someone who continued to drink was a constant test of my sobriety, to say the least—I could use the break. Plus, what eighteen-year-old wouldn't be thrilled? I called James and he met me there ten minutes after Timothy drove away.

"You've never been here before, have you?" I said. "Let me give you the grand tour."

We made it only halfway around the house before we found our-selves standing too close, trying to seem civilized but starting to breathe fast and each not hearing what the other was saying. I felt as if I was underwater. We were in the living room, surrounded by Timothy's eclectic possessions—sculptures with no arms, mirrors framed in or-nate gold, a bubbling aquarium with bright coral and even brighter fish, a lava lamp. When James touched my arm, my eyes closed and I asked if he would like to see the second floor.

He set his hand lightly on the small of my back as he followed me up the stairs. We sat on the edge of Timothy's bed, but before we had a chance to fall backward, James took both of my hands in his and looked at me seriously. He began to talk.

"Look, I'm really enjoying this . . . whatever we have . . . but . . ."

My mouth went dry, and I looked down, feeling my eyes water. I waited for him to say we should stop, for him to reject me. Real rela-tionships had thus far eluded me, so I had stuck to one-night stands, and bad ones at that, always attracting the most emotionally unhealthy guys and letting the respectable ones go by invisible. I still hadn't been able to shake the feeling that James was unattainable to me, even as he told me over and over, in and out of bed, verbally and otherwise, the opposite. I had also been allowing myself to have daydreams about James being "my boyfriend," to the point where I had let my mind wander off to things like anniversaries and moving in together, and I had written my first name with his last in my notebook like a silly girl. I was a silly girl. I felt foolish. Of course he would come to his senses. This was the other shoe I was waiting for. What had I been thinking, anyway? Silly, silly girl.

What he said next, though, and was still stammering on, was that he was enjoying this. That he wanted it to continue.

He did? *Prayers have been answered,* I thought.

"Even though I'm not ready to get into a relationship per se right now, I want to keep seeing you. No expectations, no commitment, or anything, but I was thinking . . . if we could be friends and still . . ." He reached under my hair and touched the nape of my neck, searching my eyes for an answer, for the end of his sentence.

I stared back at him.

This was no answered prayer; it was a goddamn test. If I said no, that would be the end of it. If I said yes, we'd be nothing more than friends who sleep together for a while until he finds a real girlfriend. Either way, my fantasy of the Actual Relationship would not be happening.

For once, I figured out what I was feeling. It was what the counselors had called A Lack of Self-Worth, because I didn't think I could ever be a "real girlfriend," because I didn't think I rated. Okay, so fine, if I level the playing field and come at this like we're equals, is that all right? If we used each other, was that such a bad thing? It's not like I needed the pressure and confusion of a serious relationship, either. I couldn't deal with the responsibility. I wanted to be mad at him for confusing me, but I couldn't. In my unformed and foggy mind, he was perfect, faultless, ideal. I couldn't be mad and I couldn't say no, so I would rationalize this any way I had to to make it not-over. I wasn't ready to let him go. Besides, maybe if I said yes, someday it could turn into more. I could hold on to that. It would give me something to look forward to.

In that moment, I blew things out of proportion in the way only a teenage girl can, feeling as if my whole life depended on my answer.

We sat in silence for a full minute. Then I allowed my lips to turn upward in a small smile and slowly nodded yes. We stayed in bed for the rest of the day. When we had finally worn ourselves out, we lay next to each other, smoking my cigarettes, no strings attached.

After James left, I called Joan. Suddenly I was mad and hurt and bewildered, feeling like a child in an adult world.

For the past few weeks, she had been watching and listening, and though she didn't ban me from getting into relationships as some sponsors do, she did let me know it would bring up issues. She had told me, *I hope you're ready to do some work. Don't run from the feelings—they'll be useful to us. You should probably call me more often and go to more meetings, too. The tendency can be to hide out, which is bad. As we know. Right? Good.*

She answered on the second ring.

I told her about our mostly one-sided brief conversation and said I felt like an idiot as I repeated it back.

"Why's that, dear?"

"I feel used. I feel like I'm giving in to him and ignoring what I want. I feel like everyone else knows how to do this except me, like I'm the unwitting customer with the slimy used-car salesman, winding up in debt as he walks away with a grin and a big fat commission."

I lit a cigarette with the Zippo, looked at it with contempt, threw it onto the still-rumpled bed, and inhaled and exhaled sharply, giving the evil eye to Timothy's Mickey Mouse phone, too, so cheery, so not meant for these kinds of phone calls.

Joan was excited. She loved picking through the rubble of life to find what was salvageable, smiling as she brushed off the muck and polished the original item with her cuff. I knew she would hold this up to the light after she was done with it, looking at me with anticipation, waiting for me to get it, to catch up with her joy. Her voice was strong and eager.

"Oh, my sweet! We could spend hours on your analogies. I love the whole used-car-salesman thing. There's so much there. Do you realize that you have all the answers within you? Why don't you come over, we'll have dinner and dig this one up. It'll be good."

Dig. That's why Hap had called her the archaeologist. When he was first attending meetings and couldn't remember anything, he made notes in the margins of his phone book, nicknames to remind him who was who. Next to Joan's name he had written *archaeologist*.

I drove over to her little bungalow. Flowers poured from three terra-cotta pots on her front porch and the door was open as always. I walked into the kitchen and hugged her. We sat down at the small round table to eat and work. To dig.

After we ate, I sat on the front porch smoking. She had quit again a few months before but didn't mind if other people still smoked, as long as there was a lot of fresh air and open spaces. A minute into my third cigarette, as I took a break from thinking aloud about James and sat looking intently at my Marlboro's orange cherry, Joan said to me, "It's because I had lung cancer that I quit. In 1983. They even had to remove one of my lungs. And nicotine is every bit as cunning as any other drug, let me tell you. You'd think I'd have got it when the Big Guy said, 'Okay, Joanie, we're taking a lung, you hear me: a lung?' But I didn't. Me and my one lung smoked for another four years before I finally," she paused to knock the wood of the front door, "stopped."

I had stubbed my cigarette out as soon as she'd said the word *cancer*.

I went inside and washed my hands, suddenly self-conscious about the smell even though she never said anything about it, and we sat at the table and talked about James.

"You gave your power away," Joan told me.

She said that I owed it to myself to speak up and not just agree with him, that I needed to stand up for myself. I told her that in other areas of my life I was determined, outspoken. I had even been called ballsy. I could, as they said, Hold My Own.

"Yes, but out of the need to be loved, you give your power away. You have all this spirit and insight and strength, but since you don't see it, you think you need to get your validation from outside yourself."

I give my power away. The phrase hit me between the eyes with its rightness. That was why I'd felt defenseless when he asked his question today, why I had thought I could derive some sort of pleasure from waiting, why I had thought it would give me something to look forward to. It would give me nothing. Nothing.

Joan and I went over what I would say to him. She wanted no stumbling, no caving in. We rehearsed until I felt confident about telling James that what we were doing felt too familiar, too like my old days, and that I enjoyed having him as my friend, but I couldn't sleep with anyone unless I was in a committed relationship, and I wasn't ready for one of those.

Then she told me to read the chapters in the AA book on Step One and Step Two and we would talk about it the next time we got together. I had done Step One in the Unit. How you could spend twenty-eight days in a medically monitored treatment facility and not get that you are powerless over chemicals is beyond me. I might not have embraced the idea at first, but I certainly didn't argue with it. I opened her book and looked at Step Two: *Came to believe that a power greater than ourselves could restore us to sanity.*

"Restore?" I asked, offended. "Implying that I am not sane?"

"Well," she smiled, "the implication is certainly there, but that's not what it's saying, so much as it's saying that parts of us need to be rebuilt, and we might need some help with that."

That I could swallow. I wanted to rebuild; I wanted to get better. I doubted I could do that if I wasn't sober, and they say you can't stay sober for very long or very well if you don't work the steps.

Completely without my knowledge, though, in the very back of my mind, behind all the talk about what I deserved, about self-esteem and healthy choices, was the word *someday*. About James, about drinking. The thought sat back there secret and predatory, waiting and laughing a sinister laugh while making itself comfortable behind the thick green of the new growth.

I left a message on James's machine the next day.

He didn't call that day or the next, nor was he at the morning meeting. I was starting to wonder, but then I came home to find my machine blinking its red light and when I hit *play* I heard his voice, low and sweet, telling me he had gone on a family vacation a few days earlier than planned. He blamed it on his parents, gave a shrug of laughter, and said he'd call me when he got home, sometime after the holidays.

At least I didn't have to talk to him just yet. The relief was nice. It gave me time to gather more courage and think about things. Even though his voice alone made me want to ignore everything Joan and I had agreed on.

I closed my curtains, put on a meditation tape, and fell into a coma-like nap that lasted two hours and left me melty and dazed.

I spent Christmas day at my grandparents' house, not getting high with my cousins for the first time in years and not knowing how to interpret the way the family watched me. The effort it took them to steer conversations away from anything that might lead us to talk about my trip to rehab was almost as great as the effort it took me to not unveil it just to watch them squirm. Like most modern American families, mine was adept at keeping their skeletons locked up tight behind closet doors. We knew how to keep the outsides pretty while the insides got ugly.

My eyes followed the wine wherever it went. First it was on the dining room table; then my aunt corralled it over by her chair. She had three glasses before my cousin disappeared with that bottle and replaced it with a new one. I knew he'd polished the first off in the bathroom. We had been doing that since we were kids. All afternoon I watched the wine move around, get emptied and replaced, and I counted who had how many drinks. When we sat down to dinner, everyone was poured a glass for a toast (everyone but me, who was conspicuously given sparkling apple cider) and I could smell its sweet fermented smell. That voice started up in the back of my head, the one about how much better I would feel if I just had one sip. *Just a little bit,* it told me. *It will help you forget what a dork you look like with your stupid prosthetic glass of cider. It'll take the edge off.*

I left dinner early and went to an AA meeting, where a lot of other people were debriefing from having spent the day with their families. I remembered the part in the AA book where it says: "The feeling of having shared in a common peril is but one element in the powerful cement which binds us." Apparently, feeling like a freak among your blood relatives is another element in the powerful cement which binds us.

Then I spent New Year's Eve with Timothy, Zodiac, Joan, and Hap at a huge AA party that was held inside a local auditorium. We welcomed 1988 standing in a circle, hundreds of alcoholics holding hands, saying the Serenity Prayer:

> *"God grant me the serenity to accept the things I cannot change,*
> *The courage to change the things I can,*
> *And the wisdom to know the difference."*

When I got home that night, there was another message from James, saying he'd be home in a few days. This time his voice sounded strange to me. I figured it was just from being around the noise of the crowds and the music that my ears were ringing, that he sounded far away and hollow. Before I fell asleep, I said that prayer again, even though I had no idea how badly I was going to need all three of those things when he got back.

. . .

On the day James was supposed to return, after a week of hard naps and a clear intuitive jab, I sat in my bathroom holding the pregnancy test box, reading the directions over and over. Like it took a genius to pee on a stick and wait five minutes. I prayed. I made sure the door was locked fourteen times, even though my parents had driven up to see some friends in Ventura and would be gone all day.

With the awkward delicacy of a child peeling her own sunburn, I quietly removed the cellophane wrapper.

Peed on the stick.

Waited five minutes.

During this longest five minutes of my life, I bargained with God, I played games with myself (*if I don't look at it, it will be negative*), I paced. I crossed my fingers. And my toes. I broke into a cold sweat and told myself over and over that the nausea I was feeling was just nervousness and in a few minutes it would vanish and be replaced with the relief of seeing one red line.

I read the box again. Right, we're looking for *one* red line, *one*. I turned it into a chant.

One red line one red line one red line one red line one red line . . .

Two more minutes.

Maybe if I held my breath and looked away, it would come out right. Maybe if I counted backward the number of seconds left and looked away and held my breath, that would clinch it, especially with all the fingers and toes crossed.

Sixty-four, sixty-three, sixty-two, sixty-one, sixty . . .

Still not breathing. Or looking.

Thirty-one, thirty, twenty-nine, twenty-eight, twenty-seven, twenty-six . . .

Now I was walking in a small circle, staring at my thin (*not pregnant, oh please not pregnant*) feet, walking on crossed toes. Finally, *zero!*

I turned around with my eyes closed. I uncrossed my fingers and let my held breath out in a burst, then carefully lifted the stick from the edge of the sink up to my face. I opened my eyes.

What?

Two red lines stared back at me like snake eyes, like blood, like a big "fuck you," and I just stood there, dumbstruck, trying not to cry but then noticing my eyes were bone-dry anyway, dry and hot and darkening into a flat awful gray the color of charcoal and hate.

We faced each other in the puke-orange Naugahyde booth over oily coffee.

I hadn't even called Joan. I had decided to do this myself, but I realized almost immediately that I should have consulted with her first, that I was in way over my head. I hadn't called Timothy, either. I had simply dialed James's number an hour before and said, *Meet me at Jan's; we need to talk,* and he had answered that yes, we did. I had wondered all the way there what news he had that could possibly be more interesting than mine.

I never got the chance to have the conversation with him that Joan and I had practiced. He had been out of town the whole time, and now everything was so completely different.

Behind us the grill sizzled and smelled like that morning's bacon, and not in a good way. I felt vaguely nauseated and a little seasick.

I lit a cigarette and looked at him flatly. "I'm pregnant."

He looked at me as if I had shot him with a tranquilizer dart.

"Oh, Jesus. Are——"

He was cut off by the drill of my stare, knew not to dare ask. Yes, I was sure, and yes, it was his. I continued to stare at him as I blew a plume of smoke his way. He looked down.

A waitress snapped her gum and tapped her pen and took the order of the only other customer, a pale, chubby man at the counter. The wind outside was bitter and dry, and the street on the other side of the cold glass was deserted.

I had decided not to cry.

By this time, James had lit a Camel, and we sat in a stillness polluted as much by our smoke as by the situation facing us. When we finally did speak, we talked not so much about our options—because there really was only one, not much to discuss there—but about how stupid we had been and how quickly we could take care of it. He said he would pay for the whole thing and come with me to the appointment. How very nice of him. He assured me that "everything will be okay," and I wondered how in the fuck he had the audacity to even say that, but I just smiled in reply. Smiled mouth-only. My eyes stayed fixed. They didn't smile at all. I was sure they were the weird metallic color they got when I was boiling underneath my calm surface, but he didn't notice. He didn't even know me well enough then to know my eyes spoke more than my words ever could—and yet for the time being, my body was the home of his short-lived child.

"And you said you had something to tell me?"

I saw his momentary confusion give way to a silent dawning aha and saw his eyes flash toward the door. It seemed he had forgotten what he was going to tell me, and when it came back around to him, he realized his timing couldn't possibly be worse.

He swallowed and stubbed his fourth cigarette in the filling ashtray.

With flickering eyes and a head that bowed in some strange sort of wounded apology, he told me about his girlfriend, his near-weekly visits to her college, and how he had just spent the last several days up north with her, not at all on a family vacation.

I searched for the least emotional response I could give.

"Oh."

He would get nothing else from me, nothing more than he'd already taken.

I was livid, but it wasn't him I wanted to throttle; it was myself for even thinking there was a chance. Why would I even think this was real? Why would he be any different from the rest of them? I could feel gates slamming shut inside me, the same gates that had finally begun to creak open in the past few months. I could feel the bars coming down to lock them back in place. I heard keys turn and get tossed far away.

I should have known. I must have known. My mind returned to his T-shirt-wearing the first time we had been in bed together and how the thought had almost come in but had been swatted away by my wanting to believe everything he said or didn't say. I could never let him know that I had hoped, that I had daydreamed, ever. It would be crucial for me to be blasé. Showing him any feelings would only humiliate me further. I would strive for apathy.

"It's fine, really," I said with a forced smile. "Don't worry about it." I touched his arm, then remembered my need to show him pure indifference and pulled my hand back under the table. He reached for me a second too late, his fingers closing on air, and said he was sorry, he was so sorry. I stared at him and his beautiful eyes with their thousand useless apologies.

"Uh-huh," I said. Still I would not cry.

We paid the bill and walked to the parking lot. Standing in the cold with his long expensive wool coat snapping at his calves and my hair whipping my cheeks, we each held our keys and fumbled for a good-bye suitable for these circumstances. There was none. I secretly, desperately, wanted him to hold me, but I would not lower myself to ask. I also wanted to backhand him. I'm sure all he wanted was to get into his car. We eventually stuttered out a few meaningless words about being able to forgive and forget. About how we would go back to normal everyday life. If you can do that. Personally, I doubted you could.

I turned and walked away from him and heard his alarm chirp behind me. I unlocked my car, and then after I sat down and made sure he was gone, I finally, quietly, began to cry.

I drove straight to Timothy's house. He was painting in his studio, his overalls caked with inch-thick paint in every hue and a cigarette lying lit but unsmoked in the ashtray. He stood ten feet back from his painting, one eye shut, hands on hips, brush in mouth.

I sat in the swivel chair and put my feet on his table.

"So?" he asked.

"So guess what?"

"Um, you're pregnant?"

"What!" He hadn't even looked away from his canvas. "How did you know?"

"Mr. Third Eye." He turned to me and tapped his forehead. "I'd actually gotten the vibe a couple days ago, but I didn't want to freak you out. Not that you're not freaked out now, but you needed to find out your own way, not from your magic-eight-ball of a friend."

"Well. Thank you for that. I just did the test this afternoon. And just had a lovely chat with James, who forgot to mention he has a fucking girlfriend in fucking Berkeley. So I guess between that and this, our little . . . fling is over."

Timothy paused, still squinting in dissection of his work. Then he sat down next to me.

"And that's bad? I mean, as much as I wanted to like him, did like him, he's clearly not someone you'd want to be too much more involved with than you have been already. Consider this a blessing in disguise, hon."

I narrowed my eyes. "Nice disguise." I sighed. "He was cute, too."

"Yes, very."

"And smart."

"Quite."

"And a total bastard."

"Apparently."

We sat for a second not saying anything.

"I really liked him."

"I know you did, hon."

He stood back up. I watched him paint, colors not seen in nature spread out on the canvas in a dazzling manifestation of his intense creativity. His visions were from somewhere far beyond this life, this world.

After a while he took a break to put on some tea. We talked about what was going to happen in the next few days. I was scared. My parents could never find out. It would break my mom's heart, and my dad would have my head on a stick. Timothy knew this and agreed to cover for me. The day of the appointment I would tell them that Timothy and I were going hiking, then to dinner and the Aftercare meeting at the Unit. "And I'll prop you up on the couch and make us hot chocolate and read to you, hon."

It would give me less than twelve hours to look like I hadn't aborted a child. Was that possible? I asked him, and he said it was. He said I was strong and brave, and he told me he'd do anything he could to help me. Though I was not big on trust in those days, I took what he said as real. I was brave, because he believed in me, not because I believed in myself. I leaned on him and cried, getting paint in my hair, on my clothes, violet and red and periwinkle specks of paint like stars and planets against the black sky of my shirt.

James had made the doctor's appointment for Thursday, which left me with three days of the worst feelings I'd ever had. We could hardly look at each other at meetings, let alone sit together or talk. He didn't call me; he didn't acknowledge me in any way. I actually had morning sickness. I could feel my jeans tighten in the waist. Or maybe that was just my imagination.

Every Monday afternoon since I'd gotten out of the Unit, I had gone over to Joan's house and we walked around her neighborhood together, talking. It was during our walk the day after I told James and Timothy that I told Joan I was pregnant. She stopped on the sidewalk, wrapped me in her arms, wiped my tears with an old white handkerchief, and we sat down on the curb and stayed there for over an hour, talking about sending the little soul back to Heaven, saying, *Thank you, but it's not time yet,* and letting him go.

My anger was close to the surface but silent. Joan helped me to give it a voice: she told me to write a letter to James and read it to her, then we would burn it and say a prayer for my anger to be taken away. I was also supposed to write a letter to the little one inside my belly, asking forgiveness for sending him away and telling him why it really was the best thing to do. Then I was supposed to write about my fears, my resentments, and my remorse. Joan drove a hard bargain, but I was glad I had her to push me through to the other side.

Driving home I felt a little better but still deeply, painfully sad. And scared. All I could think about was my twin, my first victim. Was this going to be a habit of mine? A theme? Babies, death, and guilt? After dinner I closed the door to my room and curled into a ball on my bed and cried. I turned my radio on to cover any sounds that might escape, and I retraced my steps, my nights in James's room, my carelessness, how it made sense now that I had taken so many naps lately and felt nauseated since New Year's Eve.

I just wanted it to be Thursday so it would all be over.

My sleep was deep that night, deep and long cave-like. Until I woke up near dawn in a cold sweat and ran to the bathroom to throw up and cry.

Thursday morning after the meeting James drove us, in silence, to the doctor's office. As soon as we walked into the lobby, I could feel the floor start to give way, black approaching from my periphery. I sat down suddenly and waved him on to announce our arrival. He came back, sat next to me, and started to say it would only be a few minutes when the nurse poked her head out and matter-of-factly said my name. I looked at his face for the first time that day. I held his eyes tight, a perfect mixture of love and hate bubbling up behind my heart. He took both of my hands in his and said everything would be okay, and I closed my eyes and counted to ten and wondered why he felt compelled to keep saying that when everything was so clearly not okay. I wanted to smack him. I bit back more tears and nodded, then got up.

On weak legs I followed the nurse to a small exam room, put on my gown when she left, then lay down on the table propped up on my el-bows. I looked down at the stirrups. They looked like animal traps. I felt as if I were crawling into the electric chair. I couldn't begin to imagine what this was going to feel like. I looked to my right. There was a metal tray, upon which was a blue paper towel folded into a neat square and a fat glass canister with finger-thick, yellowy rubber tubing plugged into its silver lid. I looked away.

The doctor entered a few minutes later. He was exactly what you picture when someone says "Beverly Hills doctor"—handsome like a soap opera star and wearing Prada shoes, pressed khakis, and a fabulous hand-painted silk tie. I wondered if he worried about bloodstains. He explained the procedure to my deaf ears, washed his hands, snapped on his gloves, and asked me to lie back.

He said he was going to administer 10cc's of liquid Valium "to relax me" (right), which I refused, explaining that I was a recovering addict, then feeling embarrassed, as if I'd said too much. As if I had just given him more proof that I was a total loser. I told him I'd be just fine with Novocain. He sort of cringed at that and asked if I was sure, then nod-ded and proceeded with a long pinchy needle as far up as it could go. I thought, *If you say, "You're going to feel a little prick," I'll say, "That's what got me here in the first place." Or even better, "He's in your waiting room."* I laughed aloud, then saw the nurse looking at me and stopped.

I closed my eyes. After a few minutes a machine came on, then I heard these weird suctiony slurpie sounds coming from my body and felt a pressure and pulling at my insides, as if they were sucking all my organs out, from my womb all the way up to my heart. I wanted to scream, to tell them to stop, to ask them just to knock me out altogether. I knew my intestines were coming out, my kidneys, both lungs; all my breath and life were being pulled out and shot down a tube. My eyes closed tightly against all the wrenching and severing. The nurse held my hand and kept letting me know how much longer, which was all I cared about.

It really hurt. Had the Novocain even kicked in yet? I probably should have gone with the Valium. I tried not to think about how it must feel to the baby, if this was how bad it was for me.

"Two more minutes."

My eyes were squeezed shut so tightly now that I could almost distract myself with the swirling geometric dots of color behind my lids. Agonizing pain. I thought about James, probably outside smoking and looking at his watch. Fucker.

"Thirty seconds. Almost over."

Tears streamed past my temples into my ears and hair, and all I could think was, *I want my mom.*

The machine whirred to an end just as I was wondering if I was going to faint.

The nurse said it was over and to take as much time as I needed to rest and relax. She put a pillow under my head and told me she'd check on me in a bit. I asked if she would mind getting James for me. I felt closer to the edge than I had in months.

A few minutes later, he opened the door tentatively and approached me. I must have looked as bad as I felt, tear streaked and pale, dry lips gray against chattering teeth. He looked as if he had no idea what to say. I assumed that if he had any guilt and sadness, it was overshadowed by relief, if not something more celebratory. But I was simply drained. I was tired, punchy, far past relief to a place he would never understand. My eyes were suddenly very old and very dead.

Then I looked over and saw it. Why they didn't have the decency to remove it or cover it was beyond me, but I decided I should probably use it, since it was so handy.

"So," I said. "Check it out." I tipped my chin toward it, making him look at it: the canister, now inch-deep with pulpy red. I leaned toward him and asked in a quiet voice, exaggeratedly sweet, "Which one of us do you think he looks like?" Then I laughed like a crazy person, and James excused himself, backing away, saying something about my needing some time alone and that it would be best for him to just go. Weak, cowardly words, a waste of breath. He moved away from me as if I was on fire. Which I may have been, who knows. He turned to get out the door, tripping a little, glancing at me with about as much fear in his eyes as I must have had rage and shock in mine.

As he walked out, I flopped back on the pillow, turning away from the door. I looked instead at the wall, hating. Hating him, myself, the doctor, God, my body, lust, sex, timing, the laws of nature, the baby, everyone, everything, but mostly James. Eventually I got dressed and out of there and found him outside smoking, like I knew he would be. I walked past him to his car, and he followed me. I took one of his Camels when we sat down. It was stronger than a Marlboro but still not strong enough. That 10cc's of Valium the doctor offered might have been strong enough. *No, a drink! A big drink! Now* that *would be strong enough,* I thought, and for a moment I actually felt the warmth of a big slug of whiskey making its way down the back of my throat. Top it off with a fat joint, and I could be nice and wasted in no time. I started to plan it in my head, realized what I was doing, and caught myself. I told myself that even as bad as I felt, relapsing was not an option. That was an AA thing: "It's not an option."

While James drove I continued to talk myself out of the craving; I tried to breathe. And I tried to find it in me to stop hating him for something that was as much, if not more, my fault as it was his. What's done is done, and no good would come from me getting drunk or being a sarcastic little bitch. So I smoked one Camel after the next until I felt good and sick, thinking about what Joan had said, that James was probably hurting, too, but didn't know how to tell me. I tried to keep that in mind as we got to Timothy's house and sat on his couch in the fading sunlight. I was grateful for the way it softened the ugly reality of the present moment. I couldn't believe what I'd done, and I felt like someone else—trash. My chest hurt; my empty bleeding womb hurt; my whole body hurt; my eyes and my head and my hands were sore.

At some point I finally let him see me cry. I fell forward onto his shoulder, and he held me, stroking my hair and whispering, "I am so sorry," until I believed him. When we pulled away from each other, I saw that he had been crying, too, his beautiful Chagall-blue eyes rimmed with shiny tears. Even after all this, I wanted to kiss them, taste the sweet salt on his eyelashes. The urge was so strong I felt like a thirsty man seeing a mirage, tasting the water, and closing my eyes and lips around nothing but false hope.

We sat there for a long time, smoking and talking, looking out at streetlights ringed by dewy gold halos. Timothy eventually came upstairs and turned on some lamps, and the three of us played Trivial Pursuit and ordered a pizza. I could tell they were trying their hardest to amuse and distract me, and I adored them for it.

After James left, Timothy tried to play me some songs on his guitar, but they just made me cry. Finally, as he played "Sweet Baby James" without singing, I was able to relax, soothed by the lullaby notes. You'd think that even the hint of the words *baby* and *James* would have made it worse, but oddly enough that song made it easier. Sadder, but easier.

Later, Timothy and I drank tea and looked up at the stars from the balcony, lumped together in the hammock like children.

The abortion changed me in ways I didn't understand, ways that wouldn't become clear to me until I delivered my daughter nearly ten years later—until I felt her sticky-warm pink skin, held her pliable body like a Baggie of scallops, saw her very small blinky eyes looking back at me. I wouldn't fully grasp my sadness until I heard the soft mewl of that baby and brought her tenderly to my breast, and even then, as I felt the new milk being drunk out of me, my grief was diluted by the joy and awe I felt as I stared at my miracle of a daughter. I just stared at her, her daddy down in the cafeteria, my parents gone home, me curled up in bed at twilight with my sleeping newborn. Nestled in the pocket formed by the crescent shape of my swollen, tired body, Clara stirred, all tiny fists stretching out and lowercase-*o* yawns. I traced her tiny features with one finger, held her sparrow hands and puppy feet and watched her fontanel for a pulse. Tears carved rivers down my cheeks as I spread my palm across her fragile miniature rib cage and thought of that first pregnancy, my almost-baby, the baby who would come to my thoughts every January, the anniversary of when I sent him back, and every mid-September, which would have been his birthday. He had so frequented my thoughts while I was pregnant with Clara that I often felt haunted by the other spirit, as if I were inhabited by an embryo ghost. But this was no ghost, I thought, holding my daughter, this was so real I could almost see the other one's face, and I cried for forgiveness and mercy, feeling the rush of guilt and sorrow that I had thought I was long finished with.

But during that long-ago January and the months following it, the eighteen-year-old me did not understand how to do grief. I did not process the sorrow; I did not purge the guilt. Instead, I had packed all the feelings down tight and shut the lid on them quickly, making a jack-in-the-box out of my mind, one that would fly open at random, releasing drug cravings, crying jags, sarcasm, and thoughts of suicide. Sometimes I couldn't sleep for what seemed like days, or if I did sleep, I had nightmares and awoke with a scream stuck in my lungs. My mom was worried about me and asked in her tiptoeing way if I needed more help than AA could provide, if I needed to see someone privately. "No," I told her, "I'm fine," not entirely sure that was the truth. What was the truth was that I wanted to be numb and I wanted everything to be different, like it was before the whole James mess. I wanted a distraction. And I found one.

Shane had been coming to the morning meeting for a few months now. He was an inch shorter than me and built like a wire, a whip, with ropy arms, a crooked smile, and a ready laugh. Barely a week after Hap introduced us, we found ourselves the last ones to leave the big booth at Jan's one morning. Then we found ourselves on our way back to Shane's apartment, the first of many times I would follow him, speeding east on Third Street into the Korean-ghetto-and-struggling-actor

area of mid-Wilshire that was littered with stately old apartment buildings and wide lawns of Bermuda grass.

In the time it took me to find a parking space, he would have already run upstairs and would answer the door naked. At first it
caught me by surprise and made me blush, but I adjusted. Actually, I
loved it. He was so bold and honest about who he was and what we
were doing, so clear about it, standing there in the doorway with no
clothes on.

He was like an acrobat in bed. I wondered why he had never been a
gymnast and looked around for the trapeze.

The first few times I experienced it all as if I were watching myself
from across the room: I saw my eyes turned away as I thought about
James, about his hands, about the scar between us, the enormous damage, as Shane performed whatever tricks he was into on that particular
day. I closed my eyes and let my soul leave the room. I wondered if he
could tell, if it was like necrophilia, if I was so absent I was only a body,
and if he cared about that or not.

He has no idea, I thought. *No idea what I've gone through.* Though how
can I expect him to know? It's not like they left little graffiti, the in-
struments and the doctor, and even as often as Shane and I see each
other, there's still no need to talk about it with him. That's not his job.
His job, as I saw it, was to distract me. Make me feel good. Make me
forget. That was all. The other thing was, this was the late eighties, the
era of HIV. If I told him about the abortion, he'd know that I'd had un-
protected sex and find me incredibly stupid and possibly contagious.

When I told Timothy what I'd been doing, he thought I had completely lost my marbles. We were at his house, sitting facing each other
in full lotus on his rug. When I moved away years later, I craved the
days of sitting on that rug with him, our legs folded under us like two
skinny white Buddhas. It's where we did our best talking. There and in
the hammock.

"You have been doing what? What about all your work with Joan,

the grief and independence and empowerment? I hate to be the one to
deliver this news bulletin, toots, but you are far from being over James.
Besides, doesn't it hurt . . . I mean, aren't you still healing? I had a
friend who had hemorrhoid surgery, and he couldn't—"

I cut him off. "I really don't want to hear what he could and could
not do. No, I'm fine. Don't worry. It's nothing. And I'm enjoying it."

He gave me the eyebrow.

"I just mean, it's insignificant."

"Insignificant? Oh, hon." He frowned deeply.

"It *is!* This is nothing like it was with James. I'm so over that."

I felt Timothy's third eye like a laser beam trained first on my fa-
cade, then deeper, into my wishes, my fantasy world. I knew he knew
I thought of James while I was with Shane.

"Oh my God. You are so chock-full-o'-shit." He held up one finger
as I started to open my mouth. "No. Don't even try to defend yourself
on this one. Over? James? You're holding on to him tighter than you're
holding on to your own sanity. You say that you have this whole guy
thing under control, but you don't see you the way I see you: you're
losing yourself again. And you've come too far to do that. Shane is just
a stepping-stone back to James. What did Joan say about giving away
your power? You are not a victim. You are a strong, recovering woman,
and you need to start acting like one.

"And you know what else, hon? I will outlast every man in your life.
You watch. And you remember that the next time you think you need to
sleep with a man to know what love is. You don't. It's right here. I'm
right here. I'm real. And I love you unconditionally."

I just stared at him, smiling with tears in my eyes, the way the re-
tarded kid in my fourth-grade class had watched the movie about birds,
then went out to the soccer field and tried to fly.

When I got home I called Joan. I told her about Shane and about the
things Timothy had said and about holding on to the notion of someday

being with James again. I told her that my mom was worried about me and asked if I needed to see a shrink.

Joan said that if I continued being led by my wants, I would drink again. That my wants are not appropriate. That I am still innately self-destructive, underneath my wanting to get well. She said that she didn't think I needed to go into therapy, but that we obviously had a lot more work to do around my "men issues." Obviously.

Then she told me with a smile in her voice that the phrase *my body is a temple* does not refer to the All Are Welcome aspect of a place of worship. And then, without the smile, she told me it was time for me to move on to Step Three.

"Isn't that the one about turning our lives over to God?" I asked.

"Yes, it is. Which will make it difficult for you to just do any old thing your head wants you to do. You'll have a God to answer to, to listen to, to get direction from. You'll have to give up your self-will. Which is what?"

"Destructive?" I guessed.

"Yes!" She smiled and actually let out a little flutter of applause. Then she gave me a list of pages to read and some written assignments and said I needed to tell Shane it was over.

So the next morning when Shane looked at me with that sideways look that was his invitation home, I shook my head no and told him why. I said that if it weren't for this damn attempt at self-realization, I'd be on my way to his place right now, waiting for him to answer the door naked. We laughed. Then he confessed, with his crooked grin, that his sponsor had told him the same thing a few weeks ago but that he was ignoring him.

I spent the following week working on the next assignment Joan had given me. It was a big one. Step Four: *Made a searching and fearless moral inventory of ourselves.* I filled dozens of pages with lists of feelings, fears, regrets, and resentments. When I had finished reading it to Joan, she took off her glasses and looked across the table at me.

"Do you realize you've been looking for him your whole life?"

"Who?"

"Your twin brother. Your other half."

Click. I felt it inside. That was it. My emptiness, my search. I didn't say a word, but she could see the realization in my eyes, in my slightly dropped-open mouth. She winked and pushed her sleeves up and reached for my pen. She began to draw lines on the pages, connecting my brother's death to my feeling like I'd disappointed my dad, to my wanting acceptance from men, to the abortion, and right back to my baby twin. My head spun. But I got it. And I was starting to get that physical sobriety is the means, not the end. Working through all Twelve Steps would give me cosmic ahas like this on a daily basis and the strength to live the life I would finally have the courage to create.

9

It was in April of 1988, not even a month later, that Timothy tested positive and we made the pact. If (when) he died, I would be there. No matter what. He had no family to speak of, at least not locally, and none that would be around for something like that—they had all rejected him the moment he had made his grand exit from the closet—so we decided that whenever it was, it would be me who would be with him. We didn't know how long it would be, of course. According to Timothy, it was never. They had given him two years, but back then they gave everyone two years, and he wasn't having any of that. I went to Dr. Vincent's office with Timothy once and asked him myself: *How long?* The doctor just sort of pressed his lips together into a line and shook his head in apology for his lack of answers. The disease was even more stealthy back then. Not that they've got it figured out now, but the eighties were a time when no one really understood the virus and all of its masks and tricks.

It was also a time when the whole world—or at least the West Coast—had New Age Fever. It was a time when celebrities had yoga instructors and channelers and fought for Tibet's freedom on awards shows. Richard Bach was back in vogue; we read *The Road Less Traveled* till the covers fell off; we listened to tapes of Shakti Gawain; we went to hear Lynn Andrews lecture at the Whole Life Expo, a sort of metaphysical county fair. A Course in Miracles and EST and Lifespring were as hip as any nightclub (so was anything Twelve Step, for that matter), and everyone wore crystals and meditated and did affirmations and in-sisted that everything happened for a reason. The upper classes of Los Angeles chanted for Porsches and thought they were becoming enlight-ened simply by wearing loose cotton clothes and quartz pendants or by sitting in a lotus position saying, "Om," in their Beverly Hills gardens. They did herbs; they drank spirulina and wheatgrass; they became ve-gan; they drank Evian water, not noticing that *Evian* spelled backward is *naive*. It was a miniature late-sixties, but with more money, more plastic surgery, and not as many hallucinogens.

So by virtue of the times and our environment, when Timothy tested positive, the only natural thing for us to do was head to the Bodhi Tree Bookstore. The Bodhi Tree sat on the west end of trendy Melrose Avenue among interior design showrooms, couture boutiques, and coffeehouses. As retailer of all things metaphysical it had every book, tape, crystal, candle, essential oil, stone, statue, or manual you could ever hope for to bring you closer to your higher power, your higher Self, your inner child, the collective consciousness, the universe, God, Goddess, Zen, the Is, Prana, whatever.

The Bodhi Tree smelled of the patchouli of my childhood and old books, two smells I loved more than anything. Incense cones burned all day between the two cash registers and the staff wore beads and scarves and harem pants, their all-natural hair and skin looking exotic in a town like Los Angeles. They served green tea and stayed open late and never questioned you if you stayed there for hours, reading as comfortably and unhurriedly as if you were at home.

On our first trip there after he told me, I sat on the floor in one of the smaller rooms in front of a display of Chinese prayer bowls, read-ing Ram Dass. Timothy was roaming the store, hunting for books that would provide answers and instructions. Answers for questions we were still too raw to ask, instructions for a life that would never be the same as it was even a week ago. Some time later, he walked breathless into the room like he always did, glasses in his pocket, one moccasin untied, a stack of books in his arms, and an excited look on his face. He set down the books and said like a child, "Look what I found!" Watching him, I understood what the word *bittersweet* meant.

He spread out three paperbacks in front of us, written by T. Lobsang Rampa, Emmet Fox, and Dan Millman, then two by Louise Hay, called *You Can Heal Your Life* and *Heal Your Body*. Those had heart-shaped rainbows across the cover and looked cheery and promising. I smiled weakly. Timothy looked so confident and hopeful that he would find in their pages the answers to all those unspoken questions. He looked like he believed that the books could suck the virus out of his body and send his T-cell count skyrocketing. He looked innocent and certain.

I was afraid and suspicious. Then again, I could afford to be.

I watched his brown eyes scanning the words, back and forth, hunting for a secret potion, and felt mine fill with hot tears. I knew then that I would always hold the fear for both of us, just as he would always hold the optimism for both of us.

I also knew that he was too close in to feel his own mortality, but that I was just far enough back to see it and could see it well enough to be absolutely terrified. He couldn't think about dying and I couldn't get the idea of losing him out of my mind.

And now, barely three weeks after I had come back to take care of him, Timothy's silly childlike hope was gone. It had been gone for years really, but now there was no trace of it. He was tired. He had lost another few pounds and tried to joke that it made his cheekbones look fabulous ("Heroin chic for the recovering addict"), but it did not.

Timothy sat next to me reading, and I felt a lump form in my throat as I thought back to that day at the Bodhi Tree and the thousand other times we had shopped for books together. We book-shopped in the same way, first prowling, then setting up camp on the floor somewhere out of the way with a stack, reading first and second and third chapters, stopping only when the other would announce that we'd been there for three hours and we'd better go soon.

I remembered the first time he came to see me in Seattle and I took him to the Elliott Bay bookstore in Pioneer Square, on a typical March morning, foggy, wet, almost dark, us shaking like dogs when we finally got under the overhang, laughing at the way we had run all the way from the car as if we could dodge the raindrops. I had pulled the door open for him, and as we stepped in, he looked up and around, in awe, smiling at the large first room with its exposed-brick walls, cedar shelves, high ceilings, and thick tables, then behind that, the allusion to all the other rooms that went far back like catacombs. After we spent an hour in the store, we went downstairs to the underground café, where I had a latte and he had a hot chocolate and he looked around and said, *I see why you moved here.* Because we both knew that if a city had a bookstore like this—the kind that made you want to hide at closing time and get locked in overnight—it was worth living in.

I did not want to go book-shopping with anyone else, ever again.

"Let's go," I said.

"Go where?" He looked at his wrist, though he hadn't worn his watch for two weeks now, since even on its smallest hole, the strap was too big.

"Books."

"Now?"

"Now."

"Isn't it too late?"

I looked at my watch, told him I could think of three bookstores that were still open—two normal ones and the Bodhi Tree. He smiled. "For old time's sake?"

"Sure. Walk or drive?"

"Let's walk."

"Are you okay to walk?"

"It's three blocks, hon—I think I can manage."

It was dusk, cooling off, and we held hands as we walked, swinging them between us. We stopped a few times to look in the windows of the interior design shops so he could catch his breath.

We walked up Melrose, cars rushing past us on the left, showrooms and boutiques on our right, window boxes spilling flowers onto the sidewalk. The trees were starting to yellow a little, but Southern California doesn't do autumn the way the Northwest does. I told Timothy about our neighbor's maple tree, the one that turns bright red and orange, and the row of golden birches that lines the lake.

"We do seasons up there," I explained.

"We do fire and wind and earthquakes down here."

"And sometimes I miss all three of those things. Well, we get wind, but it's cool and coastal. Clean. Boring. We don't get anything like the Santa Anas."

"Nobody does. Well, Morocco does."

That night we spent two hours walking around the store, reading and pointing. We bought matching bracelets as we had done once many years ago, the woven Rastafarian threads that people call friendship bracelets. They were rainbow colored and thin. *Like Timothy,* I thought, *just like Timothy.* We tied them onto each other's wrists, each of us making a wish as the knot was tightened. I don't know what Timothy wished for. I remember my wish, and I guess it doesn't matter anymore if I say it out loud or not, because it never did come true.

The next morning at Timothy's checkup, I understood how quickly my wish would be coming not-true.

Dr. Vincent was one of the top AIDS specialists still in private practice who hadn't joined the ranks of research. His strength was his rapport with his patients, his compassion, his bedside manner. I was so glad he wasn't wasting that on a petri dish somewhere. He talked with Timothy as I sat on the edge of the extra chair, looking back and forth at their faces, the way they were able to speak all lightly and casually as if life hadn't just gone irrevocably wrong. Dr. Vincent brought his stethoscope to his ears and listened to Timothy's lungs and frowned, then looked in Timothy's mouth at the thrush and in his throat at the nickel-sized bleeding ulcers.

Dr. Vincent's brows pulled together as he wheeled his stool to the middle of the room so he could talk to both of us. He said there were sounds in Timothy's lungs that he didn't like. Sounds that meant fluid was building.

"I want you to rest as much as possible. Like all the time. I'm going to give you more amoxicillin, and some albuterol for your nebulizer. . . ."

His voice left my ears. I was trying to pay attention, but all I could think was, *He's going to die; he's going to die; he's going to die,* and I started to imagine, I think for the first time, really, what it would be like without him. I didn't want to. It seemed an impossibility. I saw the doctor's lips moving, then Timothy's, asking a question. I saw them both frown as Dr. Vincent lifted Timothy's shirt and pressed against his side.

"What?" I asked. "I'm sorry."

The doctor briefly smiled. "Kidneys. Timothy said he noticed a little pain in his side. They feel okay, but I'm going to order a renal panel along with the blood work. It'll require an extra needle, but you don't mind, do you?"

He half-winked at Timothy, who said, "Who, me? The human pincushion?"

And they both laughed. I stared at them. Laughter? Now?

Timothy rolled up his sleeve. The inside of his arm was a dappled watercolor of blues and yellows, bruises in various stages of healing from all the blood draws and injections. They had him on three different non-FDA-approved drugs that we didn't have at home in the cabinet, pills and shots for which he had to come to the office. I noticed before Timothy did that the doctor hadn't gotten them out, and asked why.

The doctor paused for a long moment, not sure how to say it, that it didn't make a difference anymore, they weren't working anyway. Somehow I was comforted by watching him struggle, seeing that even for an expert, none of this got easier. I didn't want it to "get easier," afraid that "easy" would make Timothy's absence final and thinking that I could hold on to him as long as I hurt really, really bad.

"Well. The side effects seem to be outweighing the benefits." He looked at Timothy, who had this great expression on his face, one he wore frequently, of openness and confusion. It was innocent, willing. "Frankly, what that means is, we're not going to keep putting you through it. We want you to be comfortable, so we want to focus on alleviating your symptoms and minimizing your pain. The DDI and CD4 aren't working. Neither are the protease inhibitors, really, except for giving you nasty side effects." He stopped and looked carefully at Timothy, who nodded in understanding. I couldn't breathe.

I wasn't sure what would come out, words or a scream, but I wanted to try. "Do you mean . . . it doesn't matter? He's getting. Worse. Anyway?" I didn't know how to say it. I was stammering; my mind had taken off. I couldn't even look at Timothy.

"Well. Yes. We have reached that point. The drugs that suspend time, like AZT, wouldn't be effective, and even though we can fight the infections with antibiotics, it's like bailing out a sinking ship with a Dixie cup." He looked from me to Timothy. "Last week's T-cell count was thirty-six. That's with the medications; it's gone down fourteen since . . . ," he flipped through Timothy's chart, ". . . three weeks before that."

The room spun. Since I'd been there, fourteen T cells had left? When? Was it while we sat on the balcony or drank tea in bed? Was it the night James came for dinner or the afternoon Ian and Bill came, bringing homemade cookies and a movie? Was I there? Did Timothy feel them going away? They were his little soldiers, his body's only way to fight infection and bacteria, and they were retreating, guns down at their sides, faces long. They were going home, leaving the Pneumocystis pneumonia to win. *Screw this,* they had said, as the virus marched in, littering fluid and germs, making itself right at home. It wasn't going anywhere. It would be with us, as James had said, indefinitely. For the duration.

So the doctor and his nurses would take more blood and see how many were left now. They would plunge a needle deep into Timothy's kidney, mining for bad news. They would send us home with morphine and a Ventolin inhaler and more of the medicated rinse Timothy used for his throat. They would send us home with three slips of paper, slips of paper that I would take to Rexall and exchange for drugs that might or might not help anything. They would smile as we left, the receptionists whose job it was to watch dying people come and go, to call them about their next appointment, sometimes getting the "disconnected" recording that meant there would be no next appointment. They would smile as we left, the nurses with the heavy-duty latex gloves and the sad eyes above sterile masks. Dr. Vincent said he would start doing home visits next week. The four-mile trip to his office was too much for Timothy, even with me driving.

We walked to the car with me as close as I could get to him without throwing us off-balance. I laced my arm through his and held his hand, careful of his inner elbow with the cotton ball under the Band-Aid. Careful of his side, with the same bandage, careful to keep my eyes open and not bounce too much, balancing my tears until they dried a little and I could blink, absorbing them back into my system.

We didn't say much on the way home, and when we got there I tucked him into bed and then crawled in next to him myself. Not so much to sleep, since it was only four in the afternoon, but we needed the protection and safety that comes from blankets and pillows. I didn't know how to comfort him. He didn't know how to comfort me. Finally we spoke.

"Timothy?"

"Hmm?"

"Are you afraid?"

"No, not really. Not afraid to die, not the part after I'm gone. I think that part will be really cool, actually." He smiled and closed his eyes. "But there are too many things that I wanted to do. I wanted to have more time with you. I wanted to watch Clara grow up. I wanted to teach her to paint. I wanted——"

He was working hard to not cry, with his eyes still closed, his mouth trembling. Finally a tear slipped out from his closed lids. I wiped it away with my thumb.

"God, I hate this," I said.

"I know."

After that we just held each other and looked at the ceiling.

I didn't realize we had dozed off until the phone rang and I jumped. It was almost dark outside, and I turned on the lamp next to Mickey. It was Simon, with a very anxious Clara in the background, clamoring for me. Tears ran down my cheeks as I listened to her and told Simon what the doctor had said. I talked to them until Timothy woke up, and then he got on the phone and did funny voices for Clara. When we hung up, I looked at him, puzzled, wondering how he could still want to make children laugh when he was dying. He looked at me, knowing what I was thinking, and said, "Because, my dear, as the Hokey Pokey says, that's what it's all about."

10

The clarity that comes with retrospection has its own brand of exasperation, often expressed through words like *if only* and *should have*. Words like this came to me as my mind took me back to the spring and summer of our first year of sobriety. I was aware even then that Timothy and I were the core, the foundation, of this crazy little family we had built within AA. We watched as the people around us spun while we stuck flat to the earth, lying down, our arms spread wide, our fingers stretched, our calves pressed to the dirt, so we wouldn't get sucked out into orbit. We looked up into the stars and at the moon, it flat and white with its craters perfectly outlined like a peeling sunburn, Timothy pointing out constellations, and I made wishes on falling stars. We talked about everything we could think of. We must have felt the clock ticking even then, heard it counting down the seconds to where we are now.

Timothy called me sometime that spring with the news that Zodiac had been picked up on the corner of Wilcox and Yucca, offering an undercover cop a ten-dollar blow job. She didn't have anyone left to help her, Timothy said, so he had posted bail and driven her back to his place. For the past few weeks, she had been staying on friends' couches or up all night in crack houses and motels, wandering La Brea Boulevard until dawn. He had fed her and put her to bed on his foldout. He said she looked tired but was otherwise fine.

I bit my tongue on an I-told-you-so and heard a phrase in my head, one I'd heard at a meeting but hadn't understood until now: *There but for the grace of God go I.*

When we got off the phone, I picked up my journal and wrote that down. Joan had me in the habit of writing, and I wrote whether she gave me formal assignments or not. When I was done, I called her and told her about Zodiac.

"She had put together some time, too, I thought," I said. "The last time I saw her she had a couple months. Or maybe she didn't. I don't even know anymore with her; I can't keep track. But I suppose the point is to focus on myself and my own recovery, and not let her drama get in my way, right? I should be grateful it's not me, right?"

"Bingo. You take care of you. You're making progress, darling. Strides. Great strides!"

I laughed. "I don't feel like I'm making progress. I mean, what about the whole guy thing? And my parents. I feel like I'm just avoiding that whole issue, and there's so much I need to do to make it right with them."

"You'll get there when you're ready. It's only been eight months. You three didn't get this way overnight, and you won't heal overnight, either. Look at all the other work you've done. You are a clean and sober addict and alcoholic, and that in itself is a big deal. Plus, you're doing great in school, you're forming healthy friendships, and you're developing some integrity. Of course you're making progress!" Then she compared the work we did to the peeling of an onion: "It takes a long time, and we peel the layers slowly, incrementally, transparent layers, around and around, peeling until we get to the core," then she smiled, "and there are always tears." Sometimes I couldn't decide whether Joan's analogies were brilliant or stupid as hell.

She told me to keep writing. After my journal filled up, I bought another one. As I wrote and read my entries to Joan, I felt myself metamorphosing. My growth was like the tide, coming in waves, retracting out of reach, coming back. Sometimes undercurrents came, pulling at my feet, sucking the sand out from under them. I dug my toes in hard and closed my eyes and managed to stay mostly upright, but those riptides came anyway, guided by the same moon that looked so benevolent, so white and happy against the indigo sky, so serene and fat and innocent, so far away.

A few days later I was sitting on the couch doing homework, my mom knitting, my dad passed out. I was writing a paper for my abnormal-psychology class, hoping the teacher wouldn't be able to tell that my information was experiential, not researched. If it weren't for him requiring a bibliography, I could have written the whole thing based on my senior year of high school: delusions, paranoia, depression, mania, self-destruction—it was all there. But we had to cite references, so I had a pile of books next to me, telling me things I already knew.

I looked up from my writing and saw that my mom had stopped knitting. She was watching my dad, his mouth open, his breathing slow. She was very still, and her brow was pulled tight.

"What are you thinking about?" I asked her.

She looked at me, our roles reversing for the moment. "I'm just tired of it."

"Should we do something about it?"

"Oh, Delia. You know I can't. Not now."

"When, then?"

She looked away, not answering me. If even the thought of giving him an ultimatum was too bold for her, the idea of doing it was completely out of the question.

Still we dreamed of him quitting drinking. We imagined him not being so controlling and arrogant; we imagined him asking for help, listening to other people. But that was taking the dream too far. He would rather die than admit he didn't have all the answers.

As her knitting needles started clicking away again, I went back to my paper, ironically opening the book to the chapter on narcissistic personality disorders.

. . .

James had returned to his cool, cultured self after the abortion, and I was determined to match that coolness with a blasé distance of my own. We joked around at the morning meeting, and he often joined Timothy and me and the rest of the group afterward for breakfast. James seemed to think it was great that I was a sport about all this, a real champ, one of the guys. Joan thought my okayness with him was a result of my journal entries and our step work, Timothy thought it meant I had lost my craving for James, and I wasn't sure if I had really let go or if I was just acting like I was in order to keep my foot in his door.

Then he showed up at the Candlelight meeting one Saturday in June, a place he hadn't been since December. Timothy and I gave each other the eyebrow, our interest piqued. James did nothing by accident. I knew as soon as I heard his footsteps on the carpet and looked up into those liar-eyes what was going to happen.

He slid onto the couch next to me like he owned the place.

"Hey," he said.

A hundred emotions swirled up inside me, and I lost any poise I may have had. *I've developed a stutter,* I thought. *I just know it.* I looked at him and smiled what I thought was an offhand, possibly even cavalier smile, then looked urgently at Timothy, who turned off the lamp and said, "Let's get started." I relaxed a little in the dark. But mostly I was tense and electric and jumpy. I crossed and uncrossed my legs. Repeatedly. *Hey,* he had said. *Hey! Just like that!*

A thousand question marks sizzled in my brain, just behind my eyes, making me feel a little like I was on bad acid. When I spoke, my own voice sounded as if it were coming from somewhere far away, over a ship-to-shore radio, with static and high-pitched vowely sounds in my ears. When he spoke, I hung on his every word, fascinated by the effect he had on me and convinced I was insane for even entertaining the thought of him touching me. I waited for the signs he had given me before, starting with the arm along the back of the couch with the hand accidentally-on-purpose brushing my shoulder, then sinking closer to me.

And sure enough, there in the dark room where it had begun it started up again, slow and warped like a record on a turntable being pushed and pulled and finally released to spin firm under the needle. I felt his body shift slightly toward me, and my mind fast-forwarded to the afterglow cigarettes we would share in a few hours as the sun came to pale the sky that was now a deep dark blue. A chill went through my back, raising hairs, weakening me, but I was not surprised. Each time his hand brushed my knee or bumped mine as we reached for our cof-fee on the table, each time I felt his eyes on my neck, I was not sur-prised. I was anxious, curious, wired, even sad in some quiet way, but there had never been any doubt for me that our magnet-bodies would eventually pull back together. I hadn't known how or when and I hadn't imagined it happening so soon, but I had known it would happen. I no longer cared about all the work I'd done. I wanted to undo it. In that moment I no longer cared what Joan would say or what was at stake or how being with him again would affect me. I cared only about the meeting ending and getting into my car and following him to his house, to the ends of the earth, to anyplace he was inclined to take me, as long as we could be alone and at least partially unclad, doing all those things I had tried so hard not to think about for the past several months.

When the lights came back on an hour later, we turned and faced each other directly, something we hadn't done for months. Our eyes were serious and unwavering, each asking the same wordless question. He finally verbalized it in a "Shall we?" that could have been translated into an invitation to simply get off the couch and leave, if I had ques-tioned what he meant. He was clever that way, more practiced. His ar-mor was stronger. Of course, I didn't challenge him. He could have asked me anything in that moment, and I would have fallen to my knees like a slave, throwing Joan's wisdom to the wind. My desire was his whip, and I easily, gratefully, gave him my power. *Here it is,* I thought.

Use it against me. So I just looked harder and harder into his eyes until we both felt the pull; then I quietly said, "Yes, I suppose we shall."

I had slowed down my walk so that I was practically standing still when we got to his car. My vision blurred and then sharpened as my eyes moistened. When I was a child my eyes would water when I was scared or excited, on roller coasters or during scary movies or if someone startled me. This was all of those feelings at once. I looked around for Timothy and realized he wasn't in the parking lot, that he had walked home, giving James and me the time to work out the last of it by ourselves. It was 2:00 A.M., there was no breeze, and somewhere nearby a flowering shrub sent a sweet smell into the muggy night air, making me feel queasy.

He unlocked the car, and we got in. We sat in total silence for at least a full minute, an excruciatingly long time when all you have to do is listen to your own heart beating and wonder. I could hear his breath and it was shaky.

"How've you been?" he finally asked.

I laughed aloud at this formality, bowing my head. "Fine, yourself?"

"Myself has been fine." He smiled.

"Been a while."

"We saw each other yesterday morning."

I was embarrassed, like I'd given away too much, like I had been caught at a failed attempt to be demure. I opened my mouth to backpedal, but before I could, he said, "But yes, it has been a while since we've seen each other so . . . close up."

When I raised my head, I saw that he had moved to sit facing me, his beautiful sculpted cheek against the headrest.

"Yes," I said.

"Yes, indeed."

We looked at each other, feeling the force of the energy between us, as it made our blood race and our lungs swell with held breath and gave us the urge to devour each other.

But on the outside we stayed perfectly still.

I was the first to blink; then James swallowed.

Going through my mind at the time was a mixture of *Oh my God,* and *I love him,* and *I will hate myself for this,* and *Is this really happening?* I felt lucky and awful at the same time. It was a blur of happiness and disbelief and preregret.

We locked eyes. We stayed silent until I whispered, "What are we doing?"

"I have no idea," was his answer, quite probably the most honest thing he had ever said to me. Then he asked, "But can I . . . just . . . right here . . . ?"

He leaned slowly and sweetly toward me and kissed the corner of my mouth very, very lightly. It felt like a whisper, a butterfly alighting for a wing beat or two, then darting away.

It left me with my eyes neither open nor shut, my lips trembling.

I allowed him to pull me onto his lap, and it was there between the steering wheel and his body that I released it, all of it, the months of indecision and hard work and secret wants. I let all my strength go; I let my resolve drain away. Any determination to get over him was gone. All I could feel was his hands on my waist and a push against my thigh, which I reached for and held on to as he nodded an almost imperceptible *yes.*

When it was over, we peeled apart, panting, floored. We could hardly look at each other. I was thankful that my hair was long so I could hide behind it, a curtain of sweaty blond strings that kept sticking to the side of my face as I hid.

He leaned back, his head on the soft leather, his eyes closed, his hands folded neatly across his middle, fingers laced together. I lit us each a cigarette and rolled the steamed windows down to let the smoke out, and as I did, the warm night air came in. I could still smell that sickly sweet flower. Was it honeysuckle? Night-blooming jasmine? It mingled nauseatingly with the tobacco, and I felt drunk for having had him once again.

I was the first to suggest that we were crazy as the only plausible explanation.

"Could have been the heat," he said.

"Oh, good, yes. It was the heat, thanks." I paused. "Unless there's a full moon."

He stuck his head out the window and looked up, then said, "There is. So I guess we have several excuses."

"Great," I said. "Which one should I use when I tell Joan?"

He looked at me incredulously, squinting. We laughed nervously, still wanting to blame the heat and the moon but knowing we couldn't get away with that. We talked about not telling anyone, but Timothy would know, the way he Knew Things, and he would make me tell Joan. And even if he didn't, I would make me tell Joan. I would have to own up to it, without the heat, without the moon.

I whispered to James as I got out of the car that it was worth it; however many hours I'd have to spend with Joan and however many pages I'd have to write, however far this set me back, I didn't care, *it was so goddamn worth it.*

A few weeks later I met Rafael, a tall and lanky Mexican boy with bony shoulders and slippery black hair who had just checked into the Unit, but with all the other stuff going on in my life, he hardly registered in my consciousness.

What was going on in my life was that when I confessed to Joan what had happened with James she told me that, in a nutshell, I would die if I kept this up—it was all part of the same addict mechanism, and if I didn't practice the art of abstaining from things I thought I wanted, I would not learn to live in recovery, I would fall prey to my self-destructive whims. She had me make lists: *How to say no, Why listening to my head is a bad thing, Similarities between James and crack,* and *How my obsessing will kill me.*

I tried to ignore James, but so much of my energy was focused on ignoring him that it was like quitting smoking or being on a new diet, where you just walk around counting every second that you're not doing whatever it is you're trying to not do. It was rare if a whole few minutes passed without me thinking about him, but eventually, from the corner of my eye, came another boy, one in a white ribbed tank top, an old man's undershirt like a million other *vatos,* with a very long ponytail, a tiny amethyst on a silver chain, and a tattoo of an angel on a bicep that was as brown as Tijuana dirt.

When Rafael got out of the Unit he had no car, no job, no nothing. So like good AAs, we all did our part. Timothy had given Rafael some money, Hap was letting him tag along on some work he was doing, and an old friend was letting him stay on his couch. I had been appointed chauffeur. I thought nothing of it, of Rafael, but when he—as is *de rigueur* in West Hollywood, in AA—gave me a quick peck bye on the cheek, it was as if Cupid had let fly his arrow straight into my heart. I called Joan when I got home and asked her if maybe we should just lock me up. She asked me why.

"My newcomer friend kissed me on the cheek tonight, and I think I love him."

She agreed that incarceration might help, but it would have to be solitary or I'd fall in love with my cellmates. I pointed out that there were always the guards.

She laughed, but then she reminded me of everything she had told me when I relapsed on James. She asked if maybe I wasn't switching addictions from drugs to men.

"I don't think so," I told her. "This feels different."

"And darling, it might be different, but he is a newcomer, and you still have a long way to go in the relationship area. If you're going to do this—and I have learned that I can't stop you from trying—I'm going to give you some ground rules. You are not to give up your power this time. He is not to be a distraction from what you really need to do. You have work to do with your parents, you have your schoolwork to focus on, and you and I are not all the way through the Twelve Steps. He may very well be your knight in shining armor, but you must take it slow, and you must not use him as a drug. Do you understand?" I could almost hear her double-blink over the phone, over the top of her reading glasses.

"I do," I said. I wanted to curl up in her lap and stay there forever. I wanted to be her. She was raising me, cultivating me, molding me into a far better version of me than I could have ever dreamed up, let alone lived out, on my own.

But Rafael's kiss stayed with me even as I slept. It was like a brand seared into my cheek.

Zodiac showed up at my house late one afternoon, completely unannounced and completely disheveled. Her hair had grown into small spiky dreadlocks and she was clearly braless under her undersize T-shirt. She put her cigarette out in the plant next to our front door.

"I need your help," she said.

"How did you even find my house?"

"Phone book. Not the point. I can't do this shit anymore. Are you still clean? Of course you are; look at you. Can I come in?"

My mom was already walking to the front door. She had met Zodiac when I had first left the Unit and at my birthday party, but I could see that it took a second to register that that was the same person now on our doorstep.

"Mom, you remember Zodiac."

"Of course. How are you?"

I started to answer for her, to steer us away from the door, but Zodiac jumped in. "Crappy," she answered. "I came to see if Delia could take me to a meeting. I got arrested, again, and I've been living on the streets."

"Oh, you poor thing. Come on in. We'll fix you something to eat."

They were already inside, headed for the kitchen. "What would you like?"

I closed the front door and followed them. I watched Zodiac carefully and tried not to judge her, because she was a mirror for me; I could just as easily be the one turning tricks on Sepulveda and sleeping in unlocked cars. Sometimes I thought I was lucky, although it wasn't luck—I was working for what I had just as hard as she was working to avoid whatever it was she was trying to avoid. I leaned in the doorway and thought about my initial reaction the first day I met her, how clear my intuition was and how easily I ignored it. In a rare victory, my gut beat Timothy's third eye. She wound up getting Matt to sleep with her when he came back from Arizona, which sent him into another brief relapse, and she had taken some cash out of Timothy's wallet the night she stayed at his house after he'd bailed her out of jail. And now she sat at our dining room table, my mom absorbed and sympathetic as Zodiac told her tales of woe between bites of a sandwich and sips of iced tea.

"So you want to go to a meeting with me?" I asked her.

She nodded, her mouth full.

"Well. I usually go to the seven o'clock on Melrose, in the old church. You can borrow some of my clothes and stay here tonight." I looked at my mom. "Is that okay, if she stays here for one night?"

"It's okay with me, but I don't know what your father would say."

Zodiac looked at me. "Is he still drinking?" she asked.

I nodded.

"Is he still an asshole?"

My mom stifled a laugh.

"It'll be fine," I told her. "If we come home late enough, he won't even know."

While Zodiac took a shower I called Joan. "So," I asked her, "back to the whole 'you take care of you' thing. Is it okay that I'm taking her to a meeting?"

"As long as you don't put your recovery at risk. Is she high right now?"

"I don't think so. But she's so slick I doubt I would be able to tell."

"What's your gut saying?"

"That's why I called you. My gut is rather confused."

"Well, then, you'll just have to see what happens. A lot of this is trial and error. And faith. Plus, even if she is pulling the wool over your eyes, you still get to be of service, get out of yourself for a night, and plant some seeds. You get to be an example of the program and show what you know. Whether it helps her or not really isn't even the point, is it? It's helping you."

Zodiac was out of the shower and going through my closet. I said good-bye to Joan and told her we'd see her at the meeting.

Zodiac held up my favorite shirt. "Can I wear this?"

"No. Here." I tossed her some of my less-favorite clothes, just in case I never saw them again. My mom collected Zodiac's clothes. She'd do laundry while we were gone and have it done by the time we got back. I hugged her, Zodiac thanked her, and we left.

Joan and Hap greeted us out on the sidewalk in front of the meeting, and we all walked in together. James sat off to the side, but I didn't allow myself to look at him for very long. Nor, I noticed with surprise, did I really want to. My work with Joan had actually worked. I waved and he waved back, and that was all. Timothy arrived with Rafael a few minutes later. There I let my eyes linger. Rafael really was adorable. Maybe not as scorching-hot handsome as James but definitely worth looking at. Timothy came up to me while Joan was talking with Zodiac.

"You're the one who brought her?"

"Well, yeah. She showed up at my house and said she wanted to go to a meeting."

"I'm surprised that Miss Cynical would do such a thing."

"Maybe you're rubbing off on me," I joked. "I even offered that she could stay at my house tonight."

"Really? What's next, some kind of animal rescue program?"

The meeting started, so we took our seats. The topic that night was compassion. While a man across the room talked about how grateful he was to the person who took him to his first meeting after a relapse, Zodiac reached over and grabbed my hand. Joan beamed, Timothy pretended to wipe tears from his eyes, and I, for that moment, bought it, hook, line, and sinker. All of it.

The next morning I sat on the edge of my bed, holding the note Zodiac had scribbled out: *Had to run. Thanks for everything. Love you, Z.*

I knew without having to look that my favorite shirt would be gone, but I went to my closet anyway. There were about five empty hangers and she had helped herself to a pair of shoes as well. *Compassion my ass,* I thought. *I really should listen to my gut.*

I've tried to dissect, later, what my gut was telling me when I started dating Rafael, but all I remember is that I felt like I finally had a shot at a normal relationship and I was going to take it. And I liked the knight in shining armor idea. I liked that he could whisk me away from my tower and my evil captor. I liked that I didn't have to chase him.

On the Fourth of July, he and I went to a party that some AA people were having. AA parties often resembled day care, the way the host would serve copious amounts of nonalcoholic refreshments, like if our thirst wasn't properly satisfied we would escape into the firework-lit night, looting the town for alcohol. We were supposed to pretend it was a real party and we were real people. I felt like a participant in the Special Olympics.

Afterward, I drove him back to where he was staying, and we sat talking out in the courtyard for over two hours.

As we got to know each other, slowly like that, over the course of months, not days, I came to understand that he was On the Ship, as Timothy used to say. Being On the Ship was his explanation for why certain people were in our lives—even if they weren't exactly wonderful, like Zodiac, and even if we didn't see them very often, like Matt— but especially how we had found each other and Joan and why James was such a recurring dream of a person. Timothy said there were just those people who, when it all came down to that final moment and you were leaving Earth on a spaceship that could fit only so many people, got On the Ship with you. They were familiar. Part of you. Necessary, for various reasons.

Firecrackers exploded all over the city, slowing for a while and then coming back in a stutter of tiny gunshots. Some were real gunshots, as the ghetto celebrated by firing into the sky. Rafael and I could see the last of the Rose Bowl show as a faint eastern light that pulsed and changed, a borealis of sulfur and carbon and lithium. We sat close to each other, our bare legs touching, his smooth and dark against my ivory skin. I touched a birthmark on the side of his knee that looked like a chocolate stain, and shivered as he traced the lines of my palm.

AA is big on celebrating, giving recognition and applause freely for what might seem to an outsider like things to be taken for granted—having a job, paying bills, not being drunk. It's necessary. People in AA get as addicted to the attention as they had been to their chemicals, and birthdays get the most hoo-ha. Once you obtain a full year of sobriety, you stand up as the whole meeting sings to you, then you blow out a candle and give a little speech, and sometimes people give minitributes to you about how much you've changed since they first saw you at your first meeting, the one where you fell off your seat or threw up in your coffee cup, then they beam and say how lovely you are now. Everyone gathers afterward to eat cake. The elders of the tribe look at you differently, as if you passed initiation.

I remember blowing out my first candle at the Log Cabin meeting, and they were right. As much as I may have wanted to downplay it, it truly was magical. It made me feel like a miracle.

As I stood there and looked out at the room, I felt what people must feel when they win Oscars. My lifetime achievement award was a room full of drunks singing "Happy Birthday" first thing in the morning, making a racket that sounded like an Irish pub at closing time, it was so flat and loud and warped, except these drunks were sober, and they were happy because the girl they sang to had not been shitfaced for one whole year.

I looked at Timothy, my partner in all this, who stood a few feet away, smiling. Joan and Hap sat in the front row holding hands, looking as shiny-eyed-proud as if they had given birth to me themselves, which I suppose in many ways they had. The counselor from the Unit looked as if he had suddenly remembered why he had gotten into such a low-paying and seemingly thankless career. James was still grinning and shaking his head, because we had been kidding around about something or other just before they called me up. Now that I had Rafael to play with, James and I could be friends and not worry about accidentally sleeping together.

I spotted Zodiac about halfway back, giving me a thumbs-up. She looked awful again. But she had remembered the date and taken a bus all morning to come here for me, to give me that thumbs-up, risking the gossip and judgment that she knew would follow. She had "crack whore" written all over her, in dirty shin-length leggings trimmed with lace, a tube top, and a men's leather jacket. But her smile was real and not cheap.

Matt was backlit in the doorway, his curly hair like a halo in the sun. He held up the Power to the People fist, cheering, hooting like a true sports fan. After the meeting he told me he had decided to move to Arizona. LA was too slippery, he said. Impossible for him to stay clean here. He'd met a lot of people in the treatment center out there and knew he would be better off if he didn't come back, at least not for a while. We hugged and promised to keep in touch.

Rafael stood next to Timothy, looking at us in awe. He was not quite three months clean yet, and to him a year seemed impossible. I had begun to think of him as my birthday present. He was so gentle and mild, so malleable. He watched Timothy and me carefully; he listened to Joan; he paid attention to the speakers at meetings and to his sponsor. The word was *earnest*. He was afraid of winding up the way he was before, all wasted and sleazy and homeless. He felt to me like an innocent, though God knows he wasn't. He was damaged goods on the mend.

I realized, as I blew out the candle and the room erupted into a roar as powerful as if I'd just scored the winning goal in World Cup soccer, that I was repairing, too, that I was not who I had been this time last year, that I had cried and sweated and yelled and hung on, that I had worked my ass off, and that the sweet smell of victory they talked about was the gunpowder smell of a candle being blown out, of wax dripping onto the icing of an AA cake, of smoke trailing up from a wick and into the air of a stuffy little log cabin on Robertson Boulevard.

Timothy was doing his Louise Hay books diligently. He had the paperbacks, a workbook, and a *Heal Your Body* tape that led him through every body part, praying for each one. It had been six months since he tested positive, and everything seemed exactly the way it had before, just with an invisible guest now sitting inside Timothy, waiting patiently, thinking, deciding. We tried to ignore him, but it was hard, even though he was, technically, not there, because Timothy was asymptomatic. Along with the tapes and books, he also did vitamins and herbs, had quit smoking, and calculated an impeccable diet. His T-cell count was hovering steadily at well over a thousand—about the same as someone without HIV who is getting over a cold. Nothing to worry about, Dr. Vincent assured us. Holding firm. Keep up the good work.

So Timothy talked to his body.

I was early one night picking him up for a meeting, sitting in his big wingback chair and flipping through a magazine while he finished getting ready.

"You're just in time for the rundown." He held up the *Heal Your Body* book. "Want to join in, or just watch?"

"Uh, I'll just watch, thanks."

"Okay, but don't laugh."

"Why would I laugh?" But him telling me not to put us both in a laughing mood.

"Well, it might seem a little . . . different from the affirmations you're used to."

"That's okay."

He propped the book up on the bathroom counter and stood centered in the mirror. He adjusted his shoulders and looked himself in the eye. He was so handsome then, in an intellectual sort of way—the intensely focused brown eyes, smooth skin, squared jaw. He was as slim as a model, and that was with twenty more pounds on him than he had at the end. He wore faded jeans and a red corduroy shirt, a braided leather belt around his waist, and a bronze and copper bracelet on his wrist.

He took a deep breath and looked down at the open book, then at the mirror.

"I love my head," he said. I just squinted at him like, *huh?* but said nothing. He looked back down to the book, then again to his reflection.

"I love my throat," he said, and I bit my lip to not laugh. He kept going.

"I love my lungs.

"I love my diaphragm."

I let a small stifled laugh come out but disguised it as a clearing of my throat. He was deep in concentration, closing his eyes between each one and then opening them and really seeing himself. It was actually difficult work to do, because it was so hard to take seriously and do un-self-consciously. Affirmations were another standard of that era: "I attract all that is good," "I am a loving person," "I walk in the light; my higher self is my guide," et cetera. If I was in that laughing mood, I couldn't force myself to say them with a straight face. If I was folded up in anger and cynicism, nothing was going to make me say anything to myself in the mirror, let alone anything nice. I admired the way Timothy said each one, his eyes focused, his concentration steady, and I watched him quietly and respectfully. Until he got to, "I love my spleen." When he said that, it caught me off-guard, and I snorted a laugh out my nose. He spun around and looked at me, and he began to laugh, too. Finally, he begged, "Stop," through the laughter and tried to muster his seriousness again.

"Really!" He was still smiling and trying not to. "This is important. C'mon."

"Okay. I'm sorry. It was just the word *spleen* that got me. It's a funny word. Please, go on. I'll be quiet. Swear."

He closed his eyes, took a breath, looked down at the book and back at himself, and said, without either of us laughing a bit, "I love my heart."

Oh, hon, I thought, *so do I.*

"I love my kidneys.

"I love my liver.

"I love my intestines, small and large."

I was feeling giggly again, all those organs being loved all out in the open.

I saw him look at his book and then quickly glance over at me. I made eye contact with his reflection and looked down, not wanting to break his concentration. He stayed still for longer this time, then said quietly, "I love my rectum?"

We laughed until our sides hurt. Until all that was left to come out was gasps.

After a while I managed to squeak out, "Does it really say that?"

He handed me the book and pointed to it, and there it was, in calligraphy, *I love my rectum.* I wiped my eyes and turned the page, laughing even harder as I gave it back to Timothy: *I love my anus.* Also in calligraphy. "Is this really helping? Do you have to love your rectum? Must you?"

"Hey, you heard me; it's not just my rectum that I love; it's my blood, my feet, my pancreas . . . it's my hair and my arms and my navel. Who knows if it's helping, but it can't hurt. Usually I don't laugh, though. That's your fault, missy. But you know what, I do think that loving my body will be an important part of this process, either of getting better or of being comfortable with not getting better. It's all about acceptance. And, apparently, rectums."

"Apparently."

He finished up with some reading that was much less a target for our humor, then a few quick silent prayers and a mouthful of vitamins. He rubbed lotion into his hands and arms and patted his face and we left.

Today was his first AA birthday, tonight his turn to feel the rush brought by the single candle and off-key voices. I smiled as he stood in front of the meeting, knowing he felt the same way I had felt, seeing the same look of wonder on his face that I knew had been on mine.

Zodiac walked in as he was thanking the group. She slid into his vacant seat, next to me.

"Here," she whispered. "I'm sorry."

I looked down. She sat a brown paper bag full of my clothes at my feet.

"I've been clean since your birthday meeting. That's two fucking weeks! Can you believe it? And I've been going to meetings every day. Out in the Valley." I looked at her. Her skin was clear, her eyes bright. She wore a simple tank top and skirt, more Meg Ryan than Foxy Brown. I put my arm around her shoulders and gave her a squeeze. Timothy finished his speech, and the room sprang alive with applause, everyone smiling.

After the meeting, we stayed out late with a group of people at Jan's Coffee Shop, filling the big booth in the corner. Joan broke the news that Hap was moving in with her. Here we had thought that they were simply best friends, but they had fallen in love—a stable, mature love that I couldn't begin to comprehend though I knew I wanted for myself someday. Rafael and I sat close together and listened, as if studying for a test. James sat on my other side, looking beautiful. For the first time in weeks, I was thrown into a trance by the knots of his cheekbones, the toothpaste-commercial row of teeth, the cobalt eyes. Timothy spotted it and kicked me under the table to break my stupor. And when Timothy's food arrived, Zodiac led us in another round of "Happy Birthday," holding up her lighter for him to blow out.

As Timothy and I walked back to his house, we recapped the time since we'd met.

"I can't believe it's been a whole year," I said to Timothy, thinking back to the Unit.

"I can't imagine this year without you."

We joined hands and swung them between us. "I can't imagine this year without you, either. You and all your body parts."

Zodiac called Timothy's house a few weeks later, and since Timothy was busy changing a guitar string, lucky me, I picked up the phone. It was well after midnight. She was talking in hushed tones, panicky, as if she were being chased.

"You've got to come get me," she hissed.

"Where are you?" I asked, and Timothy frowned as I listened, nodded, said we'd be right there, and hung up.

"It was Zodiac. You ready for this one? Her boss at the strip club in the Valley beat her up after she refused to have sex with him, and now he won't let her leave. He's got her locked in the dressing room. She wants us to go get her."

My eyes showed how torn I was. One part of me wanted to let her suffer, thought she deserved it. The other part of me was already reaching for my keys and telling Timothy to put the guitar down and get his shoes on. He did and grabbed my backpack and a couple of Cokes and locked the door behind us. I had already started the car and was thinking of the quickest way to North Hollywood. I wasn't thinking much else. I was acting on instinct. I didn't consider the danger we could be in or how late it was or the fact that she only ever called when she needed to be rescued from some horrible drama. I didn't think that I'd rather be asleep or relaxing at Timothy's house, and I didn't tell her to try someone else. We were soldiers in the bunkers together, commando-crawling to save one of our own, even if it was always her and never us. It was always Zodiac who knowingly ran out into the minefield, ego driven enough to believe she was exempt from having her legs blown off. But a comrade is a comrade, even a foolish, destructive one. She was On the Ship. So we drove, and fast, to help her.

I took Fountain Avenue to Vine to Yucca, curling past the Capitol Records building and pointing out John Lennon's star in the sidewalk, then left on Argyle and right on Franklin. Timothy said he liked my shortcuts, and I told him that it's all just one big grid; you could right-left-right your way anywhere across this city. I was just glad to move us swiftly out of this part of town. I knew the smell of the sticky glittery sidewalks inlaid with stars—it was that of thrift shop clothes and urine, sugary melted ice cream and cigarette butts, bus fumes and BO—and I knew the look of the crazy women pushing their shopping carts piled sky-high with their worldly possessions; they all had the same lost haunted eyes, bleached white-blue like those of Alaskan sled dogs and searching under dirt-caked lids like the useless eyes of the blind.

The Cahuenga Pass took us away from all that and swept us up over the hills, paralleling the freeway, headlights and taillights down and to our right, flowing north–south like a big vein, red and white blood sparkling in the darkness.

I turned right on Lankershim when Cahuenga flattened out and became Ventura Boulevard. *Welcome to Universal City* read a brushed-metal sign that was supposed to look like an uncurling film reel. It was surrounded by tiny palm trees and white and green garden lights, and someone had spray-painted the word *sucks* across it.

We pulled up to Octopussy's Garden ten minutes from when we left Timothy's house. Possibly a record. But we hadn't talked about a plan. We would wing it, Timothy said. He told me not to worry, and I reminded him that we were saving our damsel-in-constant-distress from a steroid rapist who most likely had guns or bats or worse and all we had in defense was my expired canister of Mace and a few happy positive thoughts from Mr. I-love-my-rectum. Tell me not to worry, *ha*.

There were only three cars in the parking lot, one of which was a red Firebird with big tailpipes. We saw it at the same time and said in unison, "That must be his." We stereotyped people easily, and to us, those who drove Firebirds or Camaros automatically had tiny fuzzy molester-mustaches and wore sleeveless T-shirts. They had mullets. They were hockey fans. They had scruffy backs and shopped at Kmart and still listened to Blue Oyster Cult. They had way more testosterone than they knew what to do with. They were not a bright people. That one would run a strip club, especially out here in the eastern dregs of the San Fernando Valley, was no surprise to either of us.

It was Timothy who spotted the low, barred windows that ran along the back of the building and got out of the car first. I asked him what he was doing, as he walked toward the windows, and he told me to follow him. I did. This felt like when I was using, I said, and he reminded me that we were here to help Zodiac and not to pass judgment. I rolled my eyes.

We edged along the building until we found what we figured was the dressing room window. It was open a little bit and there was a dim light coming from inside. I crouched down and looked in, and there was Zodiac, curled in the corner smoking, hiding. She was almost naked and had very clearly been beaten. I could see from there that one of her beautiful eyes was swollen shut and bleeding and her lip hung funny. I made sure she was alone and gave her a quick *pssst*. She looked up, scared, then saw it was us and got up and tried to smile, but her smile looked awful, with all the swelling and blood. It was crooked, as if she'd had a stroke, and smeared, as if she were melting. I felt my eyes wet just a touch. The part of her that made us want to bring her in out of the rain shone through the brightest when she was wounded.

The window only opened about a foot, and it was covered with white decorative burglar bars, all scrolls and soft spikes. The only interior door led to the club itself, where the boss no doubt sat laughing and drinking and snorting speed, playing poker with his friends. We entertained the idea of one of us distracting them while the other ran her out the front door, but that was stupid. He would kill us. Timothy had his arm through the bars and was trying to clean Zodiac's face with a

Kleenex. As they tried to figure out ways to get her past the boss, I saw that the bars were one piece like a grill and screwed on in eight places with regular screws. I told them I'd be right back and ran to my car.

I came back with a screwdriver.

They both looked at me, and I explained that my dad always made sure I had in my car a jack, a towel, a can of gasoline, a spare tire, a quarter—and a screwdriver.

"Of course," I muttered, talking mostly to myself as I loosened the second screw, "he probably didn't think I'd be using them to rescue my little crack whore friend from her big bad rapist boss at a strip club in the Valley, but hey, at least he knew I'd need them someday, for something. Right?" I smiled tightly. "Do you have any clothes?" I looked at the still-topless Zodiac, wearing only an ice blue sequined thong.

"He took them."

"Of course he did." I was on the fifth screw. "Timothy, would you go to the car and see if I have a shirt or something out there?"

I turned to her again as he ran off. "You've got to stop doing this shit. You know that, don't you?"

"I'm still clean."

"No, I mean this life. This whole thing. Don't you think maybe it's why you keep relapsing? Can you live like this and feel good about yourself?"

She hung her head. "It's been a really good job. Up until now."

The room she was in was almost like a daylight basement, which meant that to me, the window was right on the ground, but to her, it was up by the ceiling. I was low on my knees and she stood on an old piano bench. Timothy came over with a big wrinkled sweatshirt he'd found in my trunk, just as I got the last screw out and pulled the bars off. They weren't even that heavy. Kmart bars. Zodiac stood on her tiptoes on the dirty red velvet of the bench and got her hands on the windowsill, then pushed her head and shoulders out. Her face was pulpy, and I could see that her front tooth was broken, chipped almost halfway up, more than enough to ruin her smile. Her legs kicked behind her above the dressing room like she was swimming, and we helped pull her the rest of the way out. I handed her the sweatshirt and she dropped it on over her head.

Then the light came on in the dressing room.

We heard a male voice and scrambled to get to our feet; then we took off running and didn't look back. We ran, leaving the screwdriver next to the bars and screws, next to Timothy's bloody Kleenex. We ran to my car and got in, and I pulled away as Timothy closed the passenger door and Zodiac climbed over his seat and into the back, the boss now out of the club and running toward us, yelling and looking exactly as I'd pictured him. He yelled like a big strong remedial kid who'd been tricked. I sped, even though he was on foot, onto Lankershim and toward home. Nobody said a word, and none of us exhaled until we were on Cahuenga, safe in the darkness of the hills that rose on both sides like big arms to hold us, to protect us.

Back at Timothy's, Zodiac took a shower and put on a pair of his pajamas, and we sat up talking and peroxiding and icing her wounds until the sun came up. Then we fell asleep in the foldout bed, all three of us with Timothy in the middle, tangled like triplets in an orphanage.

"Good morning, sleepyhead."

It was Rafael. He called me every morning, whether I was at home or at Timothy's. I smiled and rolled over. We mumbled and purred to each other until Timothy woke up and started teasing me.

"I can hear the natives are restless. I'll let you go."

"Okay," I said. "I love you." I hung up before I realized I'd said it. I looked at Timothy, and he looked back at me, both of us wide-eyed.

"Did you just tell Rafael—"

The phone rang. I answered it before it could even get through one whole ring.

"Me, too," Rafael said.

I laughed. "Really?"

Zodiac had woken up, and she and Timothy were looking at me.

"I'm on my way over. I want to tell you in person," Rafael said, and hung up.

I ran downstairs when he got to Timothy's. He hugged me and lifted me till my feet came off the ground, his forearms strong like straps across my back. We laughed and kissed and spun, and then he set me back down. He leaned in close, and I could smell his sandalwood-like scent. I looked into his eyes, so dark I couldn't decipher the pupils. They were wet with tears, and I saw in them friendship, stability, and loyalty.

We went upstairs for a while and let Zodiac and Timothy tease us for being so sappy; then the four of us walked over to Jan's for breakfast.

I was confused, having actually taken it slow for once, having done the right thing. It had been almost three months since Rafael and I had met, and by the time we exchanged those "I love yous," we actually knew each other. Though I had fallen in love with him, I did not fall facedown; it was not from a great height; it was not a clumsy slip, not painful. It was not my prior definition of *love,* either—this was not obsessive or hungry. It was tame; it was civilized; it was cute. It was what I'd always wanted: normal.

About a week later I decided to take the plunge. My parents had never met the boys I was involved with, partly because there had never been one significant enough to rock the boat over but also because I was never quite sure what my dad would say to them, what scene would erupt, or how he would humiliate me later. But I had a feeling Rafael would be around for a while, so I was willing to risk it. I prepped him on the way to my house.

"Remember, my dad is an alcoholic, and an egotistical, controlling one at that. He'll look put together, but he'll be well over the legal limit. Mom will bend over backward to make you happy and comfortable. Dad will stare at you. We'll make it quick, I promise, and then we'll go to dinner. You okay?"

"I'm fine. Are you okay?"

"Yeah. No prob." I smiled at him and parked the car.

He reached for my hand and held it in both of his and said, "It'll be fine. I'll be right there next to you. There's nothing they can do that will change that. Let's go."

My mom opened the door before we could even knock. I hugged her, and Rafael and I walked in. My dad was standing right behind her.

"Mom, Dad, this is Rafael."

My dad extended his hand. "It's nice to meet you, Rafael."

"You, too, sir," Rafael said as they shook hands.

Sir? I thought. I mouthed it to Rafael as we walked into the living room, and he shrugged, smiling, like he didn't know where that had come from, either.

"So. Where are you two going tonight?" Coming from my mom and not my dad, it was a conversation starter, not an interrogation.

"The new seafood place down on the pier," I told her. "Then to the eight o'clock meeting. Timothy is the main speaker tonight."

"Oh, that's right." My dad looked at Rafael. "You go to those meetings, too."

"Yes, sir. That's how we met."

"So you had a drug problem?"

"Well, alcohol. But yes, it was a problem. Since I got sober, my life has really improved."

"And how long has that been?"

"Almost four months."

"Really." My dad stared at him, unimpressed.

Rafael looked like he was getting uncomfortable. I stood up.

"So! We have reservations. At the restaurant. I wish we could stay longer, but I'd hate to lose our table."

We said our good-byes and got back in the car. We waved at my mom as we pulled away, and I looked over at Rafael. "Are you okay?"

"Yeah, but I see what you mean. I thought he was going to start asking the big questions—you know, do you have a job, a house, a car? You have to admit, he wouldn't have liked my answers."

"He doesn't like anyone's answers. About anything. That's what gives him his unique charm. But we got out in one piece. Next time, I'll bring you over when it's just my mom. We'll work up to Dad. It may take a while."

"Do you think he'll like me? Eventually, I mean."

I rolled my eyes. "Does he even like me? After nineteen years of be-ing his only child, I can't answer that question. I don't think him liking us is the point. I think getting through being around him is the point. Which we did. Oh, look—we're here."

I parked the car, and we walked to the restaurant. It was out at the end of the pier, and as we ate, I watched the waves crashing and thought about the erosion, the turning of rock into sand, and how long it takes to see any difference in the coastline even though it's constantly being worked on.

12

"I need to get out of here for a while and get my shit together," Zodiac said. We were sitting on Timothy's balcony one winter night before a meeting. "This is the longest I've been clean—almost five months— and I don't want to blow it. Again. There's a halfway house down in Redondo that has an opening. I'm going. They get you jobs and everything."

"Jobs with clothes?" I asked.

"Yes, jobs with clothes. And they'll even get me my tooth fixed. And I get food stamps."

"Well, it doesn't get much better than that," I said.

Timothy swatted me. "She's trying to get her feet on the ground; you could at least pretend to be supportive."

"Fine," I said. "I guess having your feet on the ground beats having your legs in the air."

"You know that's right, girlfriend," Zodiac said, flicking her cigarette off the balcony.

Rafael got a job at a hardware store in January and his own place in March. It was a small apartment in a big building not far from Timothy's house. Rafael was so proud to have a home. We lay on his futon or sprawled on the new-smelling Berber carpet, and I would drive home with my radio blasting. I never listened to current music—it was always the oldies station, my parents' tapes, music from the era that I always thought I should have grown up in. Axl Rose was a poor substitute for Janis Joplin's gut-wrenching bluesy scream in "Piece of My Heart," I couldn't stomach Vanilla Ice, and Paula Abdul just didn't quite go with my faded jeans and long blond braids the way Joni Mitchell did. As I drove home from Rafael's house, later each night, I began to layer him in over those songs that had played in the background of my life through the years, steady and constant.

There are still songs I can't hear without smelling Rafael's sweet scent or feeling his long, slippery jet-black hair between my fingers. Just like I can't hear James Taylor and not think of Timothy. My radio is so full of memories, so full of people living in the notes and the silences between them. When Janis inhales to gather her steam and the electric guitar hangs echoing in the distance like a cry—that moment of silence is where Rafael lives. Sometimes now I just leave the radio off, for fear of all the people who will come to visit, of the grief and longing I would feel should I flip a station and find Crosby, Stills & Nash combining their harmony of sad voices to sing about wooden ships or Cat Stevens reminding us that we're only dancing on this earth for a short time. I understand why old people listen to talk radio: no sandalwood, no white pageboy haircuts, no paint-caked overalls or blue eyes in doctor's offices to come out of the music and make you live it all over again whether you want to or not.

"So when is this Rafael person coming over for more than a few minutes here and there? If you're going to be spending all your time with him, we'd like to know who he is," my dad said, staring at me.

"You know who he is," I tried.

"No, we really don't. You breeze him in and out of here too fast. I want him over here more, or I want you over there less."

"Fine," I muttered.

"Fine what?"

"Fine I'll bring him over more. But you have to promise to not drink in front of him."

My dad looked at me, but it wasn't the usual daggers; it was softer. Butter knives. "Is that why you don't bring him over?"

"It's why I don't bring anyone over. Notice Timothy's never been here. Or when I was a kid, did my friends come here on weekends, or did I go to their houses? I don't want to argue about it, or make you mad, but yeah, it makes things a little unpredictable."

"Because I can be a real jerk when I'm drinking, is that it?"

Trick question. I didn't say anything.

"And it's becoming a problem."

I about fell over. I was so stunned I didn't even correct the "becoming" part.

"Maybe the next time you and Rafael go to a meeting, I could go with you. That way I can get to know him, and see what your little cult is all about."

I still couldn't talk, I just nodded, and I was still nodding when he got up and walked away. My dad, asking to go to AA. I looked up and mouthed the words *thank you* to whoever or whatever had answered all those prayers I had said since I was a scared little girl who wanted nothing more than a dad who didn't drink.

That weekend, Rafael and I took my dad to the Saturday night meeting on Ohio Avenue. It was a meeting that had been around forever, and a lot of my-dad-like men went there, those of us they call functioning alcoholics, the ones who have things like jobs and cars and families. No control over alcohol, no happiness, no soul, but they have everything else. Plus, it was a speaker meeting, which meant that one person told his story for the whole hour and the rest of us were just the audience, so there was no chance that we would be called on to talk. We could just listen. Seemed like a safe thing for my dad's first meeting.

"Can I get you some coffee or anything?" Rafael asked him, trying to keep it light.

My dad turned and looked at the table. Three giant decanters of coffee and towers of Styrofoam cups were lined up next to a plate of store-bought cookies.

"Just like in the movies," my dad said. "No, I don't drink coffee. Thanks, though."

He looked around the room. I wondered what he was thinking but didn't dare ask. Joan had told me not to push him at all, just to let him check it out. The meeting started with a reading of the Twelve Steps and a few business announcements. Then the speaker was introduced, and everyone clapped. Everyone but my dad, who muttered the word *lemmings* under his breath.

Well, so maybe he wouldn't fall in love with AA like I did, but that night when I was falling asleep, I realized that, to the best of my knowledge, he hadn't had a drink all day.

As much as I wanted to keep taking my dad to meetings and foist AA literature on him, Joan was insistent that I let go and follow his lead. So I turned all my extra energy to school. Finals were coming up and I was having my first case of test anxiety, plus I was finishing my second year at the community college and looking at transferring to a university.

"I don't even get this," I said to my mom. I was at the dining room table, completely overwhelmed by a stack of admissions paperwork: financial aid, essay questions, transcripts.

"Here, let me take a look," she offered, and began organizing forms. "You're applying for financial aid?"

"Well, yeah. Classes at the university will cost, like, a zillion times more than at the college, and I've been living off you guys for two years. Well, for more than that, for my whole life, really, but I mean, it's been two years since we made the agreement, and I feel like I'm wearing out my welcome. But I don't think I can handle my program, school, a boyfriend, and a job. So I thought I'd apply for a scholarship and see what happens. My grades are good enough."

She was flipping through grant applications. "Get this. There's a fund for people 'coming back into mainstream society after overcoming addiction, domestic violence, or mental illness.'"

"Nice crowd. But two years later, do you think I'd qualify? I'm sort of already 'back into mainstream society,' aren't I?"

"Can't hurt to try."

I started to fill out the application. My mom continued stacking and sorting. She always organized when she was nervous. I stopped writing. "What is it?"

She stopped stacking. "What is what?" She smiled.

"You. What's going on?"

She looked out the window. "It's your father. I think that AA meeting really got to him. He's still drinking, of course, but there's something at work in there. I can't put my finger on it, but something is changing. And he feels like a stranger to me."

"And that's a bad thing? I'd take a stranger over him any day."

She looked wounded. "Don't make jokes; I'm serious."

"And so am I. He needs to undergo a major change, and if he does it right, he will feel like a stranger to you. Is that what you're afraid of? That he'll quit drinking and change so much that you'll have to get to know each other all over again, and our family will have to find its footing again?"

"Maybe. Fear of the unknown."

"But it's not totally unknown. We did it with me, and we can do it with him. Joan told me just the other day, 'Faith is knowing that one of two things will happen. Either there will be solid ground to stand on, or you will be taught to fly.'"

. . .

A few weeks later Joan said that I should ask them, that it was time. I was almost two years sober and had built enough of a foundation that I could handle it, she said. I had written enough, let go enough, was strong enough to ask my parents more about my brother. She told me to write a letter to him and go sit on his grave, if there was one, and read it to him. She assured me that this would not make me drink or go crazy or get thrown out of the house. I told her maybe next year. She smiled her Cheshire cat smile and said I needed to do it soon, that it would be important for me, for my relationship with my parents, and for him.

"For him." It wasn't quite a question but almost.

"For his little baby spirit. He needs to hear from you."

If that came from anyone but her, I would have hightailed it in the other direction. But with her it was okay. It was as if she had a direct line to the spiritual realm, as if she were an ambassador delivering messages to us earthlings.

"But my dad is at a turning point with his drinking. He's thinking about quitting. He even went to an AA meeting on his own. This might send him over the edge," I tried.

"It might. Or it might bring him closer to you and to his own healing. You never know."

So the following Saturday, I was out in the living room early, waiting.

"I need to talk to you guys."

"Is everything all right?" My mom, jumping to worst-case scenarios.

"Everything is fine. But Joan told me I need to talk to you guys about something. Something really important. Can we do it now?"

"Well, of course," my mom said.

We all sat down.

"Okay. I don't know how to say this, but I need to know more about my . . . brother. About what happened—" I looked up. The look on their faces was probably similar to the look on mine when Joan had told me what was next on my personal-growth agenda, except with reversed pain-to-fear ratios.

My mom's eyes fogged over and began to fill, and my dad lowered his head.

"I'm sorry. Joan said it was necessary for my recovery to have some closure." She had also said that grief was like an endless mosaic, always with another tile to place somewhere and a greater pattern emerging beautiful from the broken pieces, the pieces that alone didn't look like much, but I didn't think my dad was in a place to hear about tiles and patterns. He wouldn't even look at me. And my mom was already getting up and going to the hall closet.

She returned with two old Kodachrome prints, tiny two-by-two-inch white-bordered photographs that I had never seen before. She held them out in her palm the way you offer your scent to a strange dog, extended, vulnerable, saying with her wet eyes, *It's okay . . . here . . . go ahead; take a look.*

I picked them up by their edges, carefully, as if they were glass microscope slides, and held them in front of me. One was of two newborns side by side on a blanket. One baby was howling, with a wrinkled, mad face like a small Winston Churchill, and the other was still and peaceful, a sleeping Cupid. I swallowed and looked at the second picture, a close-up of the sleeping one's face. Except he wasn't sleeping. He looked relaxed, with tiny eyebrows tilted up, almost a smile on his lips.

"I don't even know what his name was."

"Gabriel," my mom said, her voice cracking.

They had named him Gabriel, after the angel with the gold trumpet, the one whose job it was to herald good news, and me Delia, after my great-grandmother, whose name was Cordelia, which means "daughter of the sea." I asked my parents if they had noticed that the angel had become an angel and the person, a person. They had not.

"I have to ask you something else."

They waited.

"Was it my fault? I mean, do you blame me? Do you hate me?"

My mom gathered me up in her arms and held me as if I were still that little baby in the picture. She could only get out, "No," and a few other words and then started to cry.

My dad reached over and put a hand on my shoulder. We looked at each other for a long moment, and he said, "Now, I want you to listen to me. No, it's not your fault, and no, we've never held you responsible. Not at all."

They told me there had not been a funeral, but he was buried in the cemetery over on Pico Boulevard along with a few other relatives. They said they'd never taken me there because they didn't want to force it on me. They never knew when the right time was or how to start the conversation or if they should wait for me to ask.

In those few sentences, I understood that they believed I would come to them one day and ask these questions but had also hoped I never would. Don't ask; don't tell. I never mentioned that I didn't think I could go to them, that I knew our family had secrets just like everyone else's, and just as you don't announce over lunch that you were molested by the priest, you don't start asking about your dead twin brother nobody mentions, especially when you've always felt like you were the one who killed him. I mean, I hadn't even known what his name was. Let alone that he had a grave, a tiny headstone, not five miles away. My parents really believed they were doing the right thing by keeping quiet.

And now we had talked about it, and we were still intact. My dad didn't get mad. My mom didn't have a breakdown. And I was not only okay, I was ready to meet my twin brother.

A few days later, I went to the cemetery. I found the family plot near the far fence under a gathering of oak trees. My grandfather was there, as were his parents, and then off to the right was a tiny white cross, no more than a foot high. I walked closer, knowing it was his, and read the slab that lay in front of it. *Gabriel Oliver Dorsey, November 18, 1969.* And then smaller, underneath that, *Son and Brother.*

It disoriented me. "Brother." I said it aloud. And then I sat down next to the baby cross, because I could feel my knees buckling. I traced the letters carved in the marble over and over as I recalled the picture of that newborn boy sleeping so sweetly in his death, next to me.

It was so hard to imagine that the casket underneath me was only about two feet long, that the tiny body inside was wrapped in hand-crocheted blankets trimmed with satin and embroidered with his name and weighed only four pounds at burial. That the skeleton that was now swaddled in those heirloom blankets—that I had matching ones of— looked more like a bird skeleton than the skeleton of a person who should be in a grave. That his skull was hardly bigger than an apple, his finger bones already turned to dust, his newborn legs like drumsticks. I thought of the impossible frailness of his rib cage and the way it never got to rise and fall with breath.

I traced his name, then his initials, and then I realized what they were. A string of goose bumps trilled up my spine and my eyes watered with an eerie joy: *G.O.D.* His initials spelled *God.* I actually let out a small sharp laugh and turned around, as if looking for someone to share this with, *Hey, check this out!* But I saw only a family walking along the path, wearing all black and huddled together, and figured they wouldn't be as amused as I was. Did my parents know? Of course they did! Had they done it on purpose after he died, maybe changed his middle name? Maybe he was going to be Gabriel Something-else until they saw him so serene and powerful in his tiny lifeless body, so awe inspiring that they had to change it. Maybe he was God. I couldn't wait to tell Joan. *Talk about having your own guardian angel! You have your own little God!* she would say. She would be pleased.

I sat tracing the letters, tracing our birthday, trying to remember that far back, but of course I couldn't. I had often wondered if I underwent hypnosis, would I find him deep in the wrinkles of my brain? Is he in there, in my soul somewhere, peeking out, swimming in my double helixes? I let my mind run around for a while. A friend of mine said that dogs and kids were great as long as you let them run around and tire themselves out. My mind was the same way.

When my mind was done running around, I took the letter from my backpack and unfolded it. I had written it just last night, but the words seemed foreign and old to me. Had I really written them? I looked around to see if there was anyone watching or within earshot. The family in black was gone, and the morning fog lay low over the cemetery like waist-high grass, thick and wavy. The beach was just a few blocks west, and I could feel the salt water in the air. *Daughter of the sea.* They had been right. I was. Safely alone, I started to read my letter. "Dear Gabriel," I began.

And in those two words came the release Joan had promised. I read the letter through my tears and stayed for another hour, just talking to him, telling him about our family and the house we live in. I told him about our vacations up the coast and dressing up as Geronimo the Halloween I was five. I told him about the bums on Venice Beach. I told him about Timothy and about being a teenager in AA.

I talked to him like he was my oldest friend.

I didn't want to go. I told him I would be back soon, that we'd do this more often. Next to my backpack was the spray of flowers I had brought for his grave, and as I knelt to get up, I set them in front of the cross. They looked like snow falling or a little burst of stars, all white and soft. They were two stems of baby's breath.

AA had become my anchor. It's funny to think that my life was saved by total strangers, but it was. Someone whose name or face I wouldn't even remember later would say the one thing that would keep me sober for another day, and those days turned into months and then into years. It was very simple, though not always easy, and it was all about repetition. I went to the same meetings and saw the same people in the same seats, and every meeting had the same schedule of readings and speakers and prayers. Sometimes I grew bored with the repetition, but I knew that without it I'd be lost. I had to say my name and that I was an alcoholic every day. I had to start each morning in that log cabin, with its bad coffee, and go to Jan's afterward and hear the same stories over and over and know entire chapters of the AA book by heart. All of this was my map. It told me, *You Are Here* with a big red arrow, so I'd know that I existed.

I found out that I'd gotten the scholarship money—not the "back into mainstream society" grant, I had been clean too long for that, but a regular scholarship based on my grades—and started classes at UCLA in the fall of 1989, right after my second AA birthday.

Either I spent every evening at Rafael's apartment or he came over to our house. I went to at least nine meetings a week, one in the morning before school and a bunch on the weekends. Timothy and I had our sleepovers every Saturday night, and Joan and I had Monday nights reserved for step work. I left myself very little time to think. Very little time to mess up my new life. I just moved through it, swift and blind, intuitively and sometimes haphazardly, swishing my tail and pushing upstream with the force of all the other people in the program around me, with Joan and Timothy guiding, Rafael and James and Hap pushing, and behind me my parents and the voices of my Unit counselors cheering. Sometimes even Matt and Zodiac were there, but their voices were growing distant. I heard the small cry of Gabriel, and I felt the warmth of someone's hands on my shoulders, balancing me, holding me up. Sometimes I felt like I was running from somewhere, but other times I felt like I was running to somewhere.

Just before the holidays, my dad came home from his annual physical and made us all sit down at the table. I was doing homework while

Rafael watched television. My mom was in the kitchen but came out immediately when she heard my dad's voice.

"What is it?" she asked, drying her hands on a towel.

"Sit down," he said. He saw Rafael's hesitation. "You, too. All of you."

My stomach churned. I had never seen my dad nervous before, but his face looked sweaty and red and his hands were shaking. I hadn't noticed until then the yellow cast to his skin. It was subtle, but definitely there and definitely not normal. He waited until we were all at the table and silent before he started talking.

"First of all, I don't want to hear an I-told-you-so from any of you. I don't want hugs or secret handshakes or any kind of big deal made out of this. But I have made a decision about my drinking." He held his hand up. "The doctor says I have fatty liver disease, the beginnings of cirrhosis, and if I don't quit now, I'm looking at permanent damage and a transplant. Not that the doctors know anything. But that's what he said."

We all stared at him. I wanted to jump up and clap, I'm sure we all did, but since he had forbidden us from reacting, we didn't. We just sat there.

"I've been trying to stop on my own for the past few weeks, and quite frankly, it's not working. I even went to another AA meeting, but that didn't help. So I've asked for a month off and I'm going to go to one of those—whatever you people went to, a clinic, a rehab."

We still hadn't been given permission to speak, so I kept my questions and comments to myself. It was my mom who broke the silence. "When do you check in?"

"Tomorrow. And I'm not going to the same hospital you went to." He looked at me. "I'm going out to the desert."

"Dad, I'm—"

He held his hand up again. "Not yet. Not now. This is my problem, and I'll deal with it myself. You can come visit me on weekends. But don't make a big fuss about it."

. . .

As my mom drove, I leaned my head against the window and watched the landscape fly by in a beige blur. We had passed the outlet malls and waterslide parks, and now all that lay before us was miles of highway and hot sand punctuated by yucca trees and faded cacti. I put my feet up on the dashboard and turned to look at her. The lines around her mouth and eyes were less pronounced. Since my dad had left four days ago, she had slept well. She had not worried. She had finally been able to relax, after two decades of being the wife of an alcoholic. But I noticed her knuckles were white as she held the wheel. I turned the radio down.

"Are you nervous?" I asked her.

She loosened her grip and glanced over at me, almost smiling. "I guess a little bit."

"Are you happy?"

And then she did smile. "Yes. I am."

"Is it easier the second time around?"

"Well, I'm not in the denial I was in when you went into the hospital. I think I spent the first three weeks you were there just trying to get my mind around the fact that you were an addict."

"You and me both," I said.

"So that's one less thing we have to do this time. We know what he is. No denial there."

"Nope."

"But being the wife is different from being the mom. There are still the worries and the what-ifs this time, but with you there was more pain. Sweetie, your addiction tore me up. All those nights I didn't know where you were, all the thinking it was my fault, wondering what was wrong with you, where you had gone—I mean, inside, your spirit, it was gone. And that was the hardest thing I've ever been through. This is hard, too, but the pain doesn't even come close."

I tried to imagine seeing the me I was then through the eyes I have now, and I shivered.

"Well," I said, "one down, one to go, right?"

"Right. God, I hope he gets it the way you have. I keep telling my-self that he will. Do you think he will?"

I didn't know how to answer. I wanted to give her hope, but I wanted to be realistic. And the reality with addiction and recovery is you really never know. It's sort of a crapshoot.

I made myself smile and said, "Hey, if I can do it, he can do it. Plus, you know what? You'll be okay whether he does or not. Do you re-member what I told you Joan said about faith?"

"That either there will be solid ground to stand on or I will be taught to fly."

"Exactly. And there's our off-ramp."

When we walked into the main room, my mom squeezed my arm and slowed her pace for a second. My dad was sitting by the window, and he looked like I had, like Timothy had, like Rafael had—like all of us had, those first few days of sobriety when everything has been stripped away and not yet replaced, like a wet cat or a neglected child, all wide eyes and shaking hands, madly looking around for something to hold on to. When you're that new, there's nothing your alcoholic pride will let you reach for; you still want to hold up the mask and pretend every-thing's fine. It's the ultimate rock and hard place to be between.

I approached him slowly, not sure if he was going to recoil or lash out or simply silence me. To my surprise, he stood up, opened his arms, and embraced me. I looked over his shoulder at my mom, who was as shocked as I was. I couldn't remember the last time he had hugged me. I had to have been a child, but if he had done it then, I had no memory of it. This was brand-new.

"I'm sorry," he said. He pulled my mom over and hugged her, too, then let us both go. "I am so sorry. I've really messed up a lot, for a long time."

"It's okay," I told him. "I did, too. We both did."

"Can you forgive me?"

"Maybe," I laughed. "If you can forgive me."

"You still owe us a hundred and fifty bucks," he said.

"She does not," my mom interrupted, before she realized that he was kidding, and he and I were smiling at each other, now members of the same club. Our disease had both torn us apart and brought us together.

The weekend was full of moments like that. It was like we were running marathons, emotionally speaking. The ground we covered, the distance from where we started out to where we ended up. It exhausted me. But each visit got easier, and by the second weekend I was actually looking forward to the third. My favorite part was the informal evening group around the campfire that was like some ancient Indian ritual or sleepaway camp or something prehistoric and sacred. The fire blazed within its circle of river rocks, and we sat around it in the cold desert night, families huddled together in clumps of two or three or five, kids and parents and siblings and spouses; alcoholics, junkies; bankers, musicians, housewives; young, old, rich, poor—in that circle it didn't matter; we were all the same. The sky was so dark and large out there, a deep black sky dotted silver from the stars and orange from the sparks that spiraled up from the crackling fire. We were surrounded by lizards and rabbits eavesdropping in the distance on the cooling sand and watched over by the big brown mountain that loomed over us like a sage and chaparral tidal wave. I spent the night of my twentieth birthday in that meeting.

A week later, my mom and I brought Rafael with us, and the four of us sat with all those other families at long tables with paper tablecloths in the mess hall of a dining room. It was a traditional Thanksgiving dinner, depending on how loosely the word *traditional* was defined. Afterward, we went around the room, and everyone had to name one thing they were thankful for. I remembered being asked that one Thanksgiving when I was a teenager, a hormonal teenager in active addiction fighting off a nasty hangover, and I had had no answer. *Nothing,* I had said, *I am thankful for nothing,* my bangs and my scowl and my tone ending the conversation. But on that evening, sitting between my sober dad and my real boyfriend and looking over at my mom, I couldn't decide. One thing I was thankful for? One? Well, of course, them. But then there was Timothy, Joan, AA, love, family, friends, healing, my recovery, my dad's recovery, my youth, my health, laughter, music, God . . .

When it was my turn, then, I said that's what I was thankful for: that I had so much to be thankful for that I couldn't narrow it down to just one thing.

I closed my eyes, briquette smell in my nose, the December sunshine warm on my face. I heard my mom open and close the screen door and give my dad the big squeezy bottle of Heinz 57 before she came to sit next to me on the bench. Rafael sat on my other side, playing with my hair and humming along to the radio. My dad had been home from treatment about a week, and he stood at the grill, flipping burgers, drinking a Coke. I opened my eyes and saw us in all our Norman Rockwell-ness and laughed out loud. My mom looked at me curiously. I nodded to my dad, like, *Look at him,* and, *Look at us.* She got it and smiled back. I closed my eyes again and rested my head on Rafael's shoulder.

In the spring, Rafael proposed to me, properly, traditionally, complete with the solitaire diamond and the down on one knee. I said yes through my tears, and we drove first to Timothy's house to tell him, then to my house to tell my parents, then to a cottage in Santa Barbara for the weekend.

When we got back, I entered into the manic world of wedding planning.

Over the weekend, we had come up with a tentative guest list that was already close to two hundred, with all our AA friends, my parents' friends, relatives, Rafael's work crew. It grew out of control, a beast on its own, collecting people in its wake.

My mom jumped right in, booking the bakery, the wedding coordinator, and the florist. Rafael and I found the photographer. A friend would videotape. I made a list of bridal boutiques and spent five Saturdays trying on dresses. This was An Event. We found a DJ, a harpist for the procession. A caterer, a limousine, a location, a jeweler, a stylist.

It wasn't until the third Saturday of gowns that my mom could look at me without crying. The first two, every time I came out of the dressing room she wept with her mother's mix of joy and disbelief at the passing of time. When I found The One, she cried again, both of us did, and then hugged until the woman gently pulled us away from the beaded tulle she said I wouldn't want to ruin. I looked like a princess. I was Cinderella at the ball, a puff of air swirling in tiny pearls and netting and a bone-tight bodice. I was white froth. I was meringue. I was magic.

Joan had a shower for me on a hot late-summer day in her tiny bungalow, the women of AA spilling out through her French doors, onto the patio, drinking iced tea and Pellegrino, and I opened box after box of lingerie, laughing and blushing with each scrap of lace and silk and string, each one skimpier than the next.

The box from Joan was tiny, sky blue, with freesia tied into its sheer ribbon bow. I opened it and pulled from it a strand of pearls. I held them up; they were frail. Joan took both my hands in hers, curling the pearls into my fist, curling my fist into hers, and told me that her mother had given them to her on the morning of her first wedding and she had worn them back then and when she and Hap had eloped, and she wanted me to wear them for my wedding, too. So come November, I would loop them three times around my skinny wrist and they would hang down onto my hand, out from under my sleeve.

I hugged her tightly and thanked her and closed my eyes, inhaling her scent that was raw emeralds and vanilla and skin cream, clothesline laundry dried in the sun, love and pure white angel-wing feathers.

. . .

It was one of the hottest summers we'd had in years. The temperatures inland were over a hundred for more than two weeks. The driver's side window of my car was stuck in the up position, it had no air-conditioning, and I seemed to spend all my time on the freeways. I kept a bottle of ice water with me, both to drink from and to flick onto my forehead. I came to understand those stupid five-inch battery-operated fans people stuck to their dashboards, though I never did break down and get one. At night, I flipped my pillow over and over again. I did not sleep in that kind of heat, the heat that fogged the windows with its breath and stifled my dreams.

"Earthquake weather," Rafael called it. We were sitting outside his apartment, sweating. "When it's hot and still like this," he said, "that means an earthquake is coming."

"No, it doesn't, silly," I told him. "The tectonic plates and magma and all that stuff are so far underneath the surface that the weather up here doesn't make any difference at all."

"Yes, it does."

"No, it doesn't. It's an old wives' tale."

"No, it's true."

"Oh, really? So what about earthquakes in Alaska, or in San Francisco in the winter, or at night? There's no heat then, no stillness. Explain that."

He was silent for a moment. Then he looked out at the sky, like he was sniffing at it, and said, as if it supported his argument, "Earthquake weather."

A little while later we went back upstairs and took a nice, cool shower together with the lights off and only a candle to illuminate the wet outlines of our bodies. As he kissed my neck and ran the washcloth over my back, I was aware of how not turned on I was. Sure, it felt good. Rather, it felt good enough. I told myself that husband sex was supposed to be different from boyfriend sex and certainly different from one-night-stand sex and that it was okay, even necessary, to trade lust for love, excitement for stability. And that it was acceptable to have a nonorgasmic marriage. I remembered the way James and I had tried to be so aloof with each other, the phony game we played: who could outblasé the other. With Rafael, there was none of that. I also remembered the uncontrollable passion by which James and I were often consumed. With Rafael, there was none of that, either, but I thought that was a good thing.

Sacrifice and compromise were part of growing up, and I really wanted to be grown-up. I wanted to be as far away from my addict life as I could get. I wanted to show Joan and my parents that I could do it, that I was a model citizen, an AA success story. There was no reason amazing sex had to be a part of all that.

I went down to the beach the next morning and collected more beachglass, brown and clearish white, and wondered if any of it was from broken beer bottles or vodka bottles. I thought about my dad and me both quitting drinking and how I never found whole bottles, just destroyed ones, pieces of them, like God himself had shattered them right here by our house, as if to say: *No more!*

I brought my take home, emptying my pockets on the front porch. My mom came out and sat on the step next to me.

"Whatcha got?"

"More beachglass."

She moved the pieces around, making designs, while I shook sand out of my shoes.

"You've always loved this stuff," she told me. "Even when you were a little girl, you used to add it to the top of your sand castles. You even wrote a story about it called *'The Poor Girl's Diamonds'* in second grade. Do you remember that? It was about a little girl who was too poor to have real diamonds, so she went to the beach and took the free ones, 'the ones the waves made.' When she grew up she got a real diamond, but she always loved beachglass more. 'All diamonds look alike,' you wrote, 'but all beachglass is unique.' You were quite precocious. And speaking of diamonds—"

She reached for my hand and held it up inches from her nose to look at my ring.

"How does it feel?"

"What? The ring?"

"No, being engaged. Does it feel different?"

"I don't know," I said. I felt like I was being put on the spot. Was it supposed to feel different? Different good or different bad? I was afraid to say that there was a feeling buried deep under all the happy feelings that was like resignation. I figured that the voice telling me that I was twenty years old and my life was over, that I was off the market and Rafael was the last stop, was a relative of the one that sometimes suggested I have a drink. Intuition, addiction, fear, the cartoon angel and devil—sometimes they all sounded alike to me. "Different how?"

"Well," she tried, "does it feel right?"

"Of course it does," I said, not sure if I was simply answering her or trying to make it true. Getting married did seem like the right thing to do. But was Rafael the right person for me to marry? That was a whole different question, one that I began to ask myself so much that by the time we went for my final gown fitting, I was completely overcome by anxiety.

To hell with all the soul-searching, I decided. This was just a stage, one every bride goes through. *Wedding jitters,* I told myself as I pulled sheets of white netting over my face and reveled in their anonymity, their secrecy, knowing I could go through with anything as long as I had enough veils to hide the doubt in my eyes.

13

My shoes! Where are my shoes?"

Timothy tossed them along the floor and they tripped and stumbled toward me as if my clumsy feet were already in them, hurtling end over end.

"Thanks. Is my lipstick too dark?"

"No, it looks fine. You look stunning, hon. Relax. Deep breaths. Here, let's do some affirmations. Start with 'I love my—' "

I laughed. "Stop it! No affirmations. Come on. I'm serious."

I got up and stood next to him, peering through the tiny window of the dressing room to the grounds below. Timothy pointed and gasped, "Oh! Look. Your groom has arrived." The adrenaline started to churn in my stomach as I watched Rafael take his place up by the minister.

"I can't do this," I said.

"It's a little late."

"No, really, Timothy, I can't do this."

"You're serious?"

"I don't know. Crap. No. Yes. Oh, God." I put my neatly coiffed bride-head into my hands for a second, then looked up at him when I heard the first strains of the music that signaled the start of the ceremony.

"You'll be fine. I'll see you up there."

I swiveled my chair around to look at myself in the mirror, if that was even who this was, this person in white and tulle and pearls facing me.

It had been just over three years since I had tossed and turned in my detox bed, crying, my tangled hair matted to my sweaty shoulders. This reflection had eyes that danced like a child's and skin that was lightly tanned and smooth, with golden tendrils landing gently on my neck. Inside the dress, under all the layers of crinoline where you couldn't see it, was a spirit that had begun to mend. Beneath the flowers and ribbons that held the veil was a mind slightly less insane. I was practically a stranger to myself.

I looked out the window again. It was a classic California November noon, a brilliant blue sky with orange-leaved maple trees lit up against silhouetted palms. I began to scan the guests. Joan stood out immediately, her white hair like chrome in the sun. Sitting on her right was Hap, and on Hap's right was James.

I hadn't known until then whether he would show up or not. He wore his sunglasses like a bad disguise, and I doubted he would stay for the reception. I wondered what he was thinking, if he was remembering the nights we had shared together three years ago or if he was just waiting for the music to start like everyone else. Or if he was, quite unlike anyone else except me, thinking about what had happened between us last week.

This doesn't feel right.

I continued to wonder if this was just stage fright, a regular case of stage fright that would go away as soon as the ceremony was over. *Or would it just get worse?*

I was staring at James like I used to, squinting, craving, wanting to find his eyes behind his sunglasses and stay there.

Fuck.

My dad came to the door then. I faked a smile and turned back toward the mirror.

"Hey, kiddo. Beautiful."

"Thanks."

"I'm proud of you, you know."

I swallowed hard. He had never said those words to me before. Ever. I turned to face him.

"I'm proud of you, too." It felt awkward but good. Like deep-down good.

"You ready?"

I doubted I was, but I nodded and pulled the crisp layers of veil over my face. Like mosquito netting in the jungle, I would need it.

We stepped outside, walking up the aisle through smiles and sighs and shutter clicks, and I took my place next to Rafael.

I hadn't told anyone about what had happened last week, not even Timothy, not Joan, and especially not Rafael. James and I had agreed to take it to our respective graves, not only to protect others from the hurt it would cause, though that was a consideration, but also out of pride ("You did *what?*") and the stubborn refusal to have to work on it yet again. It was an ego thing. We had been doing so well being just friends that we didn't want to admit our failure. Nor did we want to admit the strength of our weakness for each other.

Looking at my beaming groom, I knew he would be destroyed by the knowledge that mere days ago I had collapsed into James's arms yet again, sweaty and spent and, in a wrong sort of way, happier than I had been in months. I felt like a kleptomaniac with a purse full of department-store loot, safely past the doorway sensor alarms, smiling and sick to my stomach at the same time.

I heard the minister asking me to repeat something after him, and I did, although I had no idea what I was saying. I was too filled with guilt and remorse and random images from that afternoon to make room for anything else.

We had been at James's house, just hanging out, as friends, inno-cently, with Rafael fully aware and accepting. He trusted me. He shouldn't have.

It was on those lazy days when I didn't have classes, the weather was nice, and Rafael was working that I would study or read or doze in the sun by James's pool. We would smoke and drink iced coffee and sit together in silence, reading. We would listen to music. We would gossip, sometimes joined by Timothy or another friend or two. We had come nowhere near touching each other for over two years. Until last week.

The day had been unusually hot. Santa Ana time in Los Angeles, dry and crackly, the strong gusts of wind like tumbleweeds against our sun-and-chlorine-parched skin. Looking back, ominous. Sometimes the wind would whip the shade umbrella so fiercely it was hard to hear anything else; then it would blow gray ashes up from the ashtray and into our eyes, twin sets of blue eyes that were already red from swimming and squinting.

"What time do you have?" I asked him.

"Four o'clock."

Time always flew out by the pool, but that day more than usual. I had planned to go home and shower before my evening class, but now I didn't have time.

"You can shower here if you want," he said.

"Thanks, I think I will, if you really don't mind."

"I really don't. I'll be out here for another hour or so, and then I'm taking off, too. None of which involves showering." He flashed the smile.

I tossed my suntan oil, book, lighter, and keys into my bag, wrapped the towel around my hips, and went inside. I headed upstairs to the bathroom. It felt strangely personal to be in his shower. As I peeled off my bathing suit and turned the faucet on, I tried to recall whether or not we had showered here together, back then, and didn't think we had.

If we had, I certainly wouldn't have forgotten it.

The warm water rinsed over my body, and I tried to talk it into taking those old feelings with it, but instead I was pulled further in, as I thought of him showering right here, every day, and looked at the tiny white tiles and thought, *Right where my feet are is where his feet go. . . .*

I knew I had to get out of there.

I turned the water off and got out, ran a comb through my hair, rewrapped myself in the towel, this time from armpits to midthigh, and stepped into his room.

Where he sat.

What?

It didn't register for several seconds that he had told me he would be poolside for another hour. And that he was looking at me the way he used to. And that he was standing up and moving toward me. When the realization did finally hit me, I reached for the chair he had just vacated, fumbling to sit down, unable to look away from him.

We didn't say a word this time.

He put his index finger to his lips, and I wondered if he thought I was about to scream. Maybe I was, who knows. Then he walked over to where I sat. He pulled me to my feet, his sun-hot hands gentle on my wet shoulders. He undid the towel, let it drop, and we stood staring so strongly my eyes watered. Then he sank to his knees, kissing my ribs, my hip bones, lower, and then I was on the floor, too, my weak legs unable to hold me up any longer.

I must have looked at him with a million questions in my eyes, because he put that same index finger to my lips then, before I could form the words that might dissolve our recklessness.

So I bit his finger gently, mouthed it, toyed with it, and he closed his eyes and we forgot all about the fact that I was about to get married, forgot that we had done so well at being friends, forgot about everything but how wonderful it would be for him to be pulled deep into my body and kept there forever. Or at least for the afternoon.

When we finally slowed down enough to blink and get our bearings and stop, it was dark. I could make out his eyes and the reflective sweat on his shoulders but nothing else. We sat still and searched for clues in the darkness, but it gave us nothing more, so finally we began to speak into it, our words disappearing like smoke as we vowed not to tell any-one else, as we decided like true addicts to keep trying this idea of being friends, knowing the risks it held, knowing that the energy between us was like a land mine, the way it would explode in our tranquil field of everyday life. We laughed, saying we should develop some kind of siren, a warning system. An alarm. Because it was beyond us, it made us feel helpless and unsure—the only thing we were sure of was that we were not in love with each other and that this was not the story that ends with the wedding being called off and us running off into the night together.

We were just friends, that was all; friends, but with this other, extra *thing*.

We sat close for a long time after that, not wanting the evening to end, in case it really was the last time. It could be the last time, we told each other, wanting to both believe it and not believe it with all our hearts. I traced his collarbones and neck and jaw and cheekbones with my fingers, and he closed his eyes under my touch. The moon was starting to come out, making us aware of our nakedness, and as my hands continued to move, I knew both that I loved him and that he was not mine to love. I imagined that if everyone gets one True Love, there must also be the Truer Love that we can never have, the one on the other side of the glass, the one you long for, hands pressed against the cruel unyielding surface, never to be with, only to be aware of as you settle for whatever you got instead. Crosby, Stills & Nash sang to me again, this time reminding me that if I couldn't be with the one I love, I should love the one I'm with.

That's what I was thinking about as I said my wedding vows. That and the way the raven night looked through James's windows with their canyon view of Hollywood and the way we had lingered, holding on to every last second like lovers during wartime.

I sensed a gold ring being pushed onto my finger and was aware of pushing one onto Rafael's in return, the bands that I had thought were too wide and flashy but had lost the battle over, bands that now felt to me like the tags they put on wild animals to keep track of them. I was under House Arrest. I felt sick. When the minister turned and announced Rafael and me as man and wife for all to witness, all I heard was a muffled string of words in my ears, and I knew I had just made a giant mistake. But Rafael simply held my hand and smiled, assuming that the tears in my eyes were tears of joy.

I was right; James did not stay for the reception. It would have been too strange anyway. As the wedding party was shuffled off to the side, I looked for him in the walking crowd but couldn't find him. I tried not to spend too much time searching, because I did not want anyone to ask who I was looking for, afraid I might tell them the truth, that I wasn't so much looking for someone as I had found him and lost him. Which wouldn't have been a normal answer, it would have drawn attention, so I just stared down at my bouquet, the plumerias flown in fresh from Hawaii and already starting to brown around the edges.

Not long after Rafael and I cut the cake, Joan and Hap came to say good-bye. They were leaving for New York in the morning, and Joan said she wasn't feeling well. She looked even more tissue-pale than usual, her eyes not quite as bright. We embraced tightly, and they left.

I spent the rest of the reception circulating, hugging distant relatives and my parents' friends with that limp, don't-touch-my-gown hug that brides give. My train kept getting underfoot like a nuisance cat, and my white silk shoes were wet-brown above the soles from standing outside all day. My veil itched. I didn't like it on the back of my head, I liked it when it was over my face like a bag, a screen that I could pretend was opaque.

Rafael and I froze as perfectly poised as the porcelain cake top while the photographer fired off roll after roll of portraits. He made us look blissful, so we would always remember how happy we were on our wedding day.

But I couldn't stop thinking of James and now, even more than him, Joan. She was with me for the rest of the day. As we got into the limo, I even looked around for her but was met instead with a shower of hard white rice that made me flinch and turn away, only a white satin fore-arm and a bouquet of wilted flowers with which to shield myself.

It was after our honeymoon that Joan called. We were in the middle of painting Rafael's apartment, now our apartment. Everything was covered with clear plastic and we were speckled with white spray. The apartment managers didn't mind us painting it, but they would allow only shades of white. I had wanted to add some warmth, deep yellow maybe, or a mossy green, but they said no. I made a mental note to work on them. I couldn't do sterile white; I needed color.

I wore my oldest Levi's, the ones with the knees and half the seat ripped to strings, with one of Rafael's shirts, and he was in the striped Bermuda shorts he usually wore to wash my car. I had to scramble to find the phone under all the towels and newspaper.

"Hello, my angel. You sound busy. Is this a bad time?"

"No, no, we're painting. I'm glad for the break. You're back from New York already? I thought you were going to be gone two weeks. How was it?"

"It was New York, completely. What about your honeymoon? Was it dreamy?"

I thought about the way we had argued all the way from Monterey to Santa Cruz and how I had dreamed about James. I remembered how I had turned my back on Rafael in bed in Big Sur and how part of me had wanted to stay like that forever. The next morning, I had looked down the rocky cliffs with the pines behind me, inhaled the spruce and damp dirt and sea salt, felt the wind wrap me up in ancient Californian redwood smells, and thought, *What have I done?*

"Um . . . I wouldn't know where to start." I knew from past experience that lying to Joan didn't feel good and didn't help me in the long run, but I couldn't tell her that I had slept with James. Again. While engaged. It was just too ugly. Sleeping with him must have been my way to sabotage the AA Ken and Barbie image, to confirm that I didn't deserve to be married, to rebel against tradition, to prove I couldn't be domesticated. *Or,* I thought, *maybe it wasn't that deliberate.* Maybe it was just an accident, whoopsie, a little slipup, like some people have with drinking, and I could get back on the wife wagon. Maybe it was just a meaningless mistake and had no bearing on the future of my marriage, no connection at all. And I could just tell Joan I had a basic case of newlywed jitters, not have to face the James stuff, and work with her on how I could be less of a jerk to Rafael. I knew it wasn't entirely plausible, but I liked the "accident" part. It was a much easier pill to swallow, so to speak, than the idea that I had just committed my life to the wrong person.

"Well, we'll have our Monday night tomorrow as always. You can tell me about it then."

"Thank you."

"You're welcome. Now. I have something to tell you. Both of you. Can you put your husband on the other phone?"

"Yeah . . . is everything okay? Wait; hold on. . . ."

The apartment wasn't that big, but Rafael was painting in the bathroom with the radio on, so I had to yell for him to go pick up the kitchen phone. I told him Joan wanted to talk to both of us and watched him walk past me with a clumsy lope that even a month ago I had found endearing but that now just bothered me. What was my problem? I heard the click in my ear and him saying hi to her.

"I have something to share with you both, and I wanted to make sure you heard it together. I want you to sit down, and take a deep breath, and say a little prayer." She paused so we could, then went on. "I saw a doctor in New York. You remember we left your wedding with me feeling a bit under the weather . . . well. It persisted, and I was so miserable that Hap talked me into seeing someone there instead of waiting until we got back. They ran some tests."

I waited to hear the words *the cancer has returned.* I braced myself. I knew it was bad if she was getting us both on the phone and making us pray, so I closed my eyes and waited for it.

"It's HIV." It didn't register; it wasn't right; it wasn't what she was supposed to say. She had said cancer, right? She meant to say cancer. How could Joan be HIV positive, too? First Timothy and now her? She tried to fill my choking silence with an explanation.

"Oh, baby, I know. I know. I'm sorry. Best we can figure is, when I had my transfusion in 1983, after the lung operation, the blood was infected. You know they weren't testing it then."

I still couldn't talk. Rafael told her that I must need a few minutes, and I found my voice in time to tell him to shut up. I told him to get off the phone, so I could talk to my sponsor alone. "Go finish the bathroom," I said as he walked by. "Make yourself useful."

Joan didn't say anything for a long time. We just sat there with it, until I asked how she was feeling and she said better than a few days ago. That the doctor had said to expect some ups and downs. I asked if they knew how bad it was, and she said she would be seeing a specialist next week and he would be better able to determine that type of stuff.

"My sweet, I'm so sorry. We'll all work through it together, God and us. Hap wants to talk to you, too, so why don't you come earlier than usual tomorrow, I'll leave the two of you alone for a while, then we'll go on our walk, how does that sound?"

How does it sound? My God, I wanted to scream from a bell tower somewhere, my best friend and my sponsor are both dying, I'm not sure if I was ready to get married, I want James back (not that I ever really had him), I hate my ring, I hate this white paint, I hate it, I hate all of it. I want to drink and smoke crack and claw holes in my skin, and please remind me again why suicide is such a bad idea. But what could I say?

"Great. I'll see you around five."

She told me she loved me and made sure I'd be okay until tomorrow, relatively speaking, and we got off the phone. I lit a cigarette. Rafael waited a minute before coming, tentatively, out of the bathroom. I felt bad that I had yelled at him, and for a moment I saw the boy I had fallen in love with—simple, kind, his shiny black eyes large and childlike. He pulled a box over next to my crate, sat down on it, and pulled my head to his shoulder. I dropped the rest of my cigarette into an almost empty Coke can, hearing the hiss of the cherry as it died in the warm, flat soda. I sighed along with it.

"It's not you," I told him. "I'm sorry I keep snapping at you."

"It's okay," he said. "But I feel like you hate me. Did I do something wrong?"

I couldn't tell him that it wasn't him I hated—it was myself, but I was taking it out on him. I couldn't tell him that it wasn't him who had done anything wrong—it was me, but I couldn't tell him what I had done. Secrets upon secrets. I didn't know how to start trying to make it better, so I kissed him. "You didn't do anything wrong. Nothing. I love you. Let's just turn the radio back on and start on the bedroom."

A week later I turned twenty-one. I went to the Log Cabin meeting that morning and raised my hand as soon as it was time for open participation.

"My name is Delia, and I'm an alcoholic."

"Hi, Delia," the room yelled back at me. I smiled. It was hard to believe that I had once found that ritual embarrassing and corny. Now it was one of my favorite things in the world.

"I just had to share this. When I was in treatment, I worried so much about turning twenty-one, that I would want to drink, that I would have to drink, that my little addict voice would convince me that a 'legal' drink would be different, it would be okay, since I've never had one. And I remember my counselor looking at me calmly and saying, 'Delia, that's a long ways off. You're future-tripping. Take it one day at a time.' Well, today is my twenty-first birthday, and a drink is the last thing I want. There is nowhere I'd rather be on my twenty-first birthday than in a meeting, telling you guys that it is entirely possible to stay sober, even on a day like today, even with all the stuff that society thinks should go along with this particular birthday, it's possible. And it's not only possible—it's wonderful."

They clapped.

And the cool thing was, it was true. I was of legal drinking age and it didn't matter. I sat through the rest of the meeting listening to people share their own victories and defeats, feeling so happy to have a place to go where I can be who I am, talk about whatever I want, and be loved unconditionally. I had gone from not wanting to be an addict to feeling blessed that I *got* to be one. Because I received all kinds of gifts as a result: liberation, gratitude, fellowship, responsibility, courage, love, God. A built-in family all over the world. A tribe. My people.

14

Looking around me at the angles and movement of the sea of black fabric around me, I was reminded of umbrellas in a Parisian street—except there was no rain and this was not France: it was Pauley Pavilion in Westwood, California, and the black was the caps and gowns of UCLA's class of 1991.

The ceremony ended with five thousand of those caps being flung into the air, and I had a feeling similar to the one I had on the morning of my first AA birthday (the applause, the accomplishment), but the people around me were clearly not my tribe—they were too homogenous. That was the key thing about AA: the mix. The bikers and old ladies and soccer moms all in the same room together, nodding their heads in agreement, knowing that there were more similarities than differences inside, no matter what the outsides looked like.

Rafael, Timothy, and my parents had come to watch me walk across the stage and, when it was over, found me in the crowd. Rafael handed me a bouquet of white roses and hugged me, lifting my feet off the ground like he used to. My mom and Timothy were both crying and laughing at the same time, and my dad first clapped me on the back like a football player, then gathered me up in a hug.

Not long after graduation, I finally figured out what I wanted to be when I grew up. We were living off the meager checks from Rafael's job at the hardware store and the occasional financial gift from my parents, and it was getting to the point where I really needed to declare a career path of some kind. Then one morning at Jan's after the meeting, while Timothy and I were talking about AA—the endless chain of people all helping one another, us in the middle, helping, being helped— he asked me, "Have you ever thought about being a drug and alcohol counselor? I mean, hadn't you wished, when we were in the Unit, to talk to a therapist who had gotten clean young, someone who could relate, not just some old boozer?"

I remembered the meetings on the Unit where I had become the unofficial leader. Even as toxic as I was then, I could still make sense out of a group, help harness that wild, shapeless energy and turn it into something useful. And people had always opened up to me; that wasn't news. And it's not like I hadn't done my own personal fieldwork.

"Timothy, that is just crazy enough to work."

"I know it is, hon. I can totally see it. Full circle at its best."

I made an appointment with one of the advisors at UCLA. Between my bachelor's degree and all the extra psych credits from taking summer courses, I only needed a few more classes and an internship and I could take the state board exams and be a licensed chemical dependency counselor. I started classes a few weeks later and felt something light up inside of me. This was why. This was why I had gone through my addiction, my dad's alcoholism, my mom's enabling, the Twelve Steps, all those meetings, and why I was still sober. This was why I hadn't given up. My Achilles' heel had sprouted wings and become Hermes' sandals.

"I'm going over to Joan and Hap's. Do you want to come?"

Rafael had brought the bathroom trash can into the living room and had his bare foot resting on the rim of it while he cut his toenails.

"Earth to Rafael . . ."

"Oh, I'm sorry. What?"

"I said I'm going to see Joan. She's having some people over. We're having dinner. Would you like to come with?"

I knew he would say no. He had told me he was uncomfortable going over there, because Joan was getting sick, but he had been staying home a lot lately and refusing invitations to more than just their house. He still went to work, but I couldn't remember the last time he'd been out with me socially or to a meeting. This concerned me. What I had seen in AA is that when people stop going to meetings, they start to drink again. I had tried to talk to him about it, but he had shut me out. He wasn't into AA anymore, he said. He was fine now. Cured.

"Um, no. I have some stuff I need to do."

"What, cut your toenails? Joan's not going to be around forever. Come with me. Please?"

He looked at me and then looked back down. Cut another nail. "Maybe next time."

I got in the car and tried not to be angry. It wasn't easy, but I had gotten into the habit of exercising great self-control. I still felt horribly guilty about cheating on him the week before our wedding, but I didn't let on. I still felt like I had settled a little in the sex department, but I didn't complain. Rafael's general malaise irritated me, but I stuffed it. I had wanted a sensible, calm relationship so badly that I was willing to silence myself in order to maintain it.

The previous two years, we had gone out for dinner and exchanged cards and gifts on our "other" anniversary, the Fourth of July, the night of our first date. But that year, nothing from him. Not a card, not a note, not a kiss. Not even a mention. And I didn't say anything, either—I wanted to wait and see if he would remember. Which he didn't. By August, a norm had been established: I went out and he stayed home. I grew silently, secretly furious, and my marriage became a series of tests, tests that he failed miserably and repeatedly, the whole time unaware that I was even conducting them.

I parked in front of Joan's house and took a few deep breaths before I went in. I walked in the door and found Timothy sitting at the kitchen table with Hap, and Joan stirring a giant pot of spaghetti. She was dressed in a loose ivory pantsuit with a jade necklace, its round clear-green pendant against her bony freckly chest, matching her eyes. She sang along with Cat Stevens as she cooked, and when she stopped singing to reach for the pasta scooper, I continued the verse in my head, looking from her to Timothy and back, wanting them both to last forever, knowing they never would. I could feel myself on the verge of tears. I turned back around and walked out to the front porch.

"You got a light?"

I jumped. A disembodied voice materializing out of the dark was upsetting, even when it was a familiar one.

"Sorry," James laughed. "I didn't mean to scare you."

"That's okay," I said. "I didn't know you were here."

"I just got here." He took a cigarette from behind his ear and put it between his lips. He looked at me while I held the flame to the tip of it, then backed up, leaving a cloud of smoke between us. He looked over my shoulder toward the living room. "Where's Rafael? He didn't come with you?"

"No, he had some stuff he needed to do around the house."

James looked at me, intently. Too intently. He took a step closer, and I could feel my pulse quicken. "You're not fooling anyone, you know," he said, his voice almost a whisper.

"What is that supposed to mean?"

"I know when you're not happy."

"Oh, do you?"

"Yeah—you're a free spirit. You're happiest when you're dancing in the woods or going to swanky dinner parties with Timothy, up all night, all over town. Not this Susie Homemaker thing you've got going on with Rafael. You're bored out of your mind."

"No, I'm not. I'm content. You're right, I might not be doing as much as I used to, but that's what happens when one grows up, when one becomes an adult."

"What, one loses one's *joie de vivre?* I'm just saying—"

"Well, don't. I'm fine. But thanks for your concern."

Timothy walked outside then and looked at us. "Did I interrupt something?"

"No, James was just analyzing me," I said. James and I made faces at each other.

"Save your energy," Timothy told him. "She's a tough nut to crack."

I sat down in one of the two wicker porch chairs and Timothy sat in the other. James said that he hadn't even said hi to Joan and Hap yet, put out his cigarette, and excused himself.

"How are you, with all this?" I asked Timothy. Joan was starting to get sick, and our little group was talking a lot about our feelings on death, dying, grief, and how to handle all of it without drinking or using or going mad.

"I guess I'm okay. I didn't tell you this, though. The other day, out of nowhere, I had the biggest craving to get drunk. It wasn't the usual, *You can have just one,* It was like, *Let's get rip-roaring, tits-up drunk.* It was this overwhelming feeling that nothing mattered, that I was just going to die anyway, so what's the point?"

He had told me once that he had this secret inclination to max out his credit cards and live every day as if it were his last, as they say, those people who haven't been diagnosed with a terminal illness. "Shoes," he had told me once. "We'll buy lots and lots of shoes!" Then he'd realize he was basically okay, that he would probably be around to have to pay the bills, and that he should sort of plan for a future.

"But I haven't been sick a single day since I got my test results. What if I don't die? I mean, of this. I mean, what if I do beat the odds? Then I shouldn't drink, and I shouldn't max out my cards. I get so frustrated thinking so much about death when, maybe, there's no need to."

Maybe. Maybe not. We were pulling petals off a daisy: he'll be alive; he'll be alive not.

· · ·

Halfway through fall quarter, as my classmates worried over where to intern, I called the Unit and set up an interview.

In the elevator in my new black suit, holding a letter from my professor, I couldn't help thinking about the first time I was here. I remembered, but barely, my mom wanting to hold my hand and me twisting away from her. My nose had been lined with dried blood, I had scabs on my hands and forearms from picking and scratching, my hair was a bleachy mess, and my eyes were flat and lifeless. My ankles buckled when I walked, like a broken doll. I smelled, if not of disease and misery, then of sweat and cigarettes and the pepperminty hair-spray smell of angel dust.

Now I wore Donna Karan and smelled of salon shampoo and leather shoes, fresh air and Caswell-Massey hand lotion. The elevator doors opened, and I walked into a confident handshake with the director, who looked at me with surprise and pleasure, not having realized just how well I had gotten since the last time she saw me.

The interview took place a few offices down from where the doctor had asked me all those questions years before, and it was hard not to compare and contrast the experiences. The director said they would call me soon with a decision. I searched her face for a hint of an answer, but it offered nothing. In the elevator I fluctuated between thinking how well I did and how hard she was laughing at me after the doors closed.

I called Joan as soon as I got home, so she could remind me that the results were already in and that God had a plan for me. She told me all I needed to do now was relax and wait, an oxymoronic statement, I thought. But I didn't have to wait long. They called the next day to offer me a full-time internship. I took it. I called Timothy first. He said he'd pick me up at seven for a celebration dinner, since Rafael had to work late that night.

That night we sat out on the back patio of Caffé Luna, away from the noise and movement of Melrose Avenue, under the strings of lights, eating and laughing, sitting in full view of the giant papier-mâché moon on the roof, the gold one that smiled as if he knew what a roll we were on. I was going to intern at the hospital where I was once a patient, and Timothy had been offered a one-man show at a very chic gallery with an opening on New Year's Eve. When he had said over dessert, smiling, "Nothing can stop us now, baby!" I believed him. He believed himself. His HIV seemed like a distant memory, though it sat at the table with us, quiet in the empty chair like a very timid, very patient, very clever guest.

I fell in love with being a counselor. I struggled with the statistics— most addicts experience multiple relapses before finding long-term recovery—and I worried that I wouldn't know what to say, what to ask, what strategies to use, what approach, and whether I would ever learn how to plot the course of someone's treatment. But I had a dedication and an enthusiasm that had its roots deep in my own experience of before-and-after that kept me going, made me keep trying.

One night I looked up from my homework to tell Rafael, "My first patient graduated from the program today. I unpacked her the day she checked in and today she looks—acts—like a whole different person. She reminded me of me four and a half years ago, first so confused and hurt and pissed off, and now all gung-ho about being sober. She even signed up for Aftercare."

He was flipping channels. I watched his thumb on the remote: up, down, up, down. He cheered when he found a Bruce Willis movie.

"Did you hear me?"

He sat with zombie eyes black as marbles, staring at the screen like a sugar-high child, and cheered again when somebody shot somebody else. I went back to my textbook, shaking my head and making a mental note not to talk shop with him anymore.

In the spring of 1992, I took and passed the state board exams and the hospital offered me a full-time gig. My own office, with a name-plate on the door. Letters after my name. Sometimes the patients bolted in the middle of the night or drank right after they left treatment, but sometimes they didn't. And it was the ones who didn't—who did something as unnatural for them as it would be for a fish to breathe air—who gave me hope, who were the flames that burned to light my path. I kept them tucked into a corner of my spirit like bright and lucky Guatemalan worry dolls that came to every group with me, whispering to me the right things to say. Together, we helped a lot of people.

I dipped the tiny brush into the red lacquer, blotted it on the edge of the bottle, and brought it swiftly to Joan's pinkie finger. Three long strokes and the nail looked like a wet ruby, oval and gleaming.

I eyed my work, screwing the cap back on, finished.

"Better?" I asked her.

"Much. Are you sure you can stay for toes?"

"Of course."

"My feet are very sensitive, though. Hot and cold and prickly and probably not wanting to be touched. We can skip the rub and go straight for the paint."

Joan sat by the open window, letting the cool air in, because the fumes made her nauseous. She wore silk thermal underwear from Eddie Bauer, leggings and a long-sleeved top that hung from her bones with a slinky ease. She said they were the only things her skin could tolerate on days like these, days when her skin hurt, when it itched and burned and couldn't be touched any firmer than a whisper. Even her drapey dresses were too much, so they just hung in her closet, ignored, as days like these became more frequent. She said she was glad to have only Birkenstocks, she couldn't imagine any other shoe. Sometimes she couldn't wear even those.

The manicures had begun in the fall, when Joan went in for her first CAT scan. The medications made her hands shake enough that putting on nail polish became difficult, if not impossible, and Joan was a woman to whom dignity meant everything; slopping red onto her cuticles was not acceptable, nor were naked fingernails. Her nails had been the same shade of Revlon red for decades. She had called me the day before her appointment and asked me to please come paint them for her, promising a perfect pot of tea and good conversation in return, and we'd been doing it ever since, every Monday just like we used to.

On that day with a ribbon of tissue paper woven between Joan's toes as her polish dried, we sat reclined on thickly padded chairs in her living room, feet up on ottomans, and she said to me, "Darling. I'm not doing so well."

I looked at her, her beautiful angel hair sparse against her hollowed cheekbone.

"How not-well?"

"My T-cell count has dropped below a hundred. There are still more good days than bad, but . . ." Her voice trailed off before she could add that soon that would reverse, until comfort was a memory, pain the norm.

She told me we'd spend a lot of time together, but I knew it wouldn't be enough; it never would. I didn't want a new sponsor, I didn't want to imagine my life without Joan, and I didn't want her to go away. I was being a petulant child; I knew that.

She asked if we could pray together and took both of my hands in hers. I was familiar with those hands now, with their bluish veins behind the golden freckles of her translucent skin. I knew which knuckles got sore and how her rings now spun on her fingers. Her palms were white and smooth, dry like paper, the red of her nails a beautiful shock at the tip of each finger. And then, in her voice that was magic to me, the purr of old-time movie stars, she began to talk to God like they were old friends.

· · ·

I called Timothy as soon as I got home.

"Hon!" He was always excited to hear from me. From anyone, really.

"Do you have a minute?" I asked.

"For you, I have all the time in the world. I was just going to call you anyway. I have major scoopage. But you go first."

"No, you. Mine's not breaking news; I just wanted to talk to you about Joanie. She's not doing very well. I was just over there, and it was almost like she wanted to say her good-byes. I mean, not literally, but I've never seen her like this."

"She's really sick? I was just over there this weekend and she was fine. I mean, not fine, but not dying."

"She's not sick, like coughing, but her count's under a hundred. She just seemed really frail and even closer to God than usual. Anyway. What's your dish?"

"You're never going to believe who called me."

"Matt."

"No! But I haven't heard from him in ages. Is he still in Nevada?"

"Arizona. Come on—who called you?"

"Zodiac."

"You're joking. I figured she was dead by now. Where is she? Where has she been? Why did she call you? Is she okay?"

"What are you, Barbara Walters? Easy on the questions, toots."

"When was the last time we saw her? Like three years ago? Four? Does she know I'm married? And working at the Unit? Did that totally blow her mind?"

"You're doing it again. Yes, I told her everything. She went to that halfway house and promptly got arrested for a multitude of offenses. Selling, prostitution, theft. She stole a car! Our little Miss Z, in the pokey for Grand Theft Auto. Anyway, she's living in Hollywood with a woman she met in jail. Zodiac got them both jobs at The Seventh Veil."

"Really? Well, there's a shock."

"And she wants to see us tonight."

"Are we going?"

"Sure, I told her we'd pick her up at work, and then have dinner at Butterfield's. My treat. This is clearly cause for celebration," he said.

When Timothy and I walked into the club, heads turned. Even though they say you can't tell just by looking at someone, Timothy radiated "gay," in big pink letters, all the way from his button-down Ralph Lauren shirt down to his penny loafers, which even he himself said he was a little light in. And I was wearing a gray turtleneck sweater and black pants, the only female in the building not exposing 99 percent of my epidermis. Also, I wore no makeup. I never did. But most of the women there had put theirs on with a trowel.

I looked around the room and saw Zodiac, leaning on the bar, talking to the bartender, waiting to cash out for the night. She looked like a statue, warm like coffee and smooth like polished wood, with deep brown-black nipples that looked primitive. Her hair was loose and curly like little spirals, chin-length and healthy. She looked good, relatively speaking.

She spotted us and smiled and waved, then signaled that it would be just a few more minutes. I thought, *No, it won't, it will be a lifetime, and you won't even realize it until you look up one day and you're forty and still a whore, a forty-year-old ex-stripper, half your life gone, and the rest of us run on ahead, leaving you leaning on a sticky bar in a dark room on Sunset Boulevard wearing a ridiculously tiny pair of gold lamé hot pants.* But I only smiled back, signaled *okay,* making my index finger and thumb into an *o* as perfectly empty as her life.

Zodiac called me a few weeks later, just after Timothy's opening. She hadn't shown up. Which didn't surprise me, though Timothy kept looking toward the door for her. Even as we rang in 1993 surrounded by walls of Timothy's work, in a room full of beautiful people and wine we didn't drink and us dressed to the nines, he looked toward the door, as if she would have remembered. As if New Year's weren't a big tip night for her. As if she cared about him the way he cared about her.

I figured we wouldn't hear from her for a while again, but then my phone rang, changing my up-until-that-moment normal day.

"Hello?"

"I'm pregnant."

I hated when she did this to me. No *Hi, how are you, do you have a sec, are you sitting down, I have some news, we need to talk.* No, just *I'm pregnant.* I sighed. I rubbed my forehead.

"I just found out twenty minutes ago. Damn! Can you believe it?"

Yeah, actually I could.

"You want me to go with you?"

"Go with me? Where?"

"I don't know, my doctor, your doctor, a clinic, Planned Parenthood? Tijuana? There are still lots of places, even places without picketers and protesters. When James and I went——"

She cut me off, laughing. "No, no——I'm keeping it. I didn't call to talk to you about getting an abortion, for Christ's sake! I called to tell you I'm gonna be a mommy!"

Great.

I closed my eyes and counted to ten. I exhaled. "Have you thought about this? At all? You know, a child will change everything."

"I know. And I think it would be good for me. I'll have to behave. The baby would keep me in line." She sounded excited now. Confident. Hopeful, even.

"That's not why we have babies. They aren't supposed to raise you; you're supposed to raise them. What, the baby will keep you clean? Give you morals?"

"Well, no, but I'll want to do better now that I'll have a little one to look after. I'll want to be responsible. I'll have to think about somebody other than myself."

This was a new concept for her, that other people mattered. I got the feeling that she thought other people existed only for her own personal use. I couldn't imagine her making sure somebody else was fed and clothed——two things she rarely did even for herself.

"And where do you plan to live, in that hellhole of an apartment?"

"It's not a hellhole. The manager said as long as I can pay the rent, it's mine."

"And how do you plan to do that? How long can you strip when you're pregnant? Three months, if you're lucky? Unemployment won't cover it. And I don't want to hear you're turning tricks pregnant. That's just nasty."

"I would never do that."

Right. I didn't say anything.

"I wouldn't!"

"You still have time to think about this."

"I've made up my mind."

"It won't work."

"It will."

"Zodiac. Sweetheart. I'm not saying that someday you wouldn't make a great mom. Stranger things have happened. But now's not the time. You can barely take care of yourself. When was the last time you ate a decent meal? Did laundry? Saw fresh fruit in person? Went more than a week without getting loaded? Or arrested? Do you at least plan to quit smoking?"

I could hear her taking a drag as I asked. Blowing it out so she could answer.

"I already have."

"Bullshit, you're smoking right now."

"Well, but I've cut back, since I found out."

"You found out twenty minutes ago!"

"And this is the only cigarette I've had since then. I'll quit. Don't worry."

I was afraid for her unborn child, for her, for all of us. Timothy would be more accepting, more willing to believe that this would turn her life around, but he would also get stuck babysitting every time she wanted to go out, and she would forget to pick up the baby, and Timothy and I would have to go find her. I could picture it: the phone calls, the asking if we could babysit for just a few more minutes, hours, days, years. I wished she could see what a Jerry Springer guest she was, but she was too far into her broken life and her childish ideas of how great everything would be once she had the magic baby.

"I think it's a boy."

"I think it's a big fat mistake."

"It's not! I swear—this'll be the best thing that ever happened to me."

I didn't even know what to say to her anymore. "Who's the father, do you know?"

"What do you mean, do I know? Of course I know."

"So who is it?"

She was quiet for a second and then said, "The manager of our apartment building."

Ah, I get it. "That's how you're paying the rent?"

"God, you're so blunt," she laughed. She actually laughed in the middle of all this.

I wished my call waiting would beep through. "You know what? I've got to go. Have you told Timothy yet?"

"I left him a message, but he hasn't called me back. If you talk to him before I do, don't say anything. I want it to be a surprise."

Oh, it will be. "Whatever. I'll talk to you later." I started to hang up.

"Delia?"

"What?"

"Aren't you even going to say congratulations?"

"Congratulations."

I couldn't move for a good ten minutes, thinking of the teeny polly-wog of a baby floating around in her as she smoked and drank and sold her body, as she danced naked and slept in the day like a vampire in that stale Hollywood apartment, as she dreamed of white wicker bassinets and Peter Rabbit wallpaper, imagining herself in a plush terry robe, rocking with a sleeping infant on her shoulder as the mobile tinked out "All the Pretty Little Horses."

15

I came out of group and walked down the hall to my office, which faced the opposite direction of the room I'd had as a patient, creating a constant state of déjà vu and plenty of opportunities to reflect on my before-and-after.

As I approached my desk, I saw several messages impaled on my While You Were Out spike, the top one with the word *Urgent!* scrawled across it in red marker. I pulled them all off and read them from the top down. Hap had called five times in the past two hours. *Joan is unconscious,* one of the messages read. *Come over ASAP.*

I lifted the phone from its cradle with a shaking hand. Their answering machine picked up. I hung up, grabbed my purse, and walked to the nurses' station.

"Did you get your messages?" the receptionist asked.

"Yeah, but I can't get ahold of him." I turned to one of the other counselors. "I'm going over there. Will you cover my afternoon lecture?"

She said of course she would. All my coworkers knew that Joan was sick and that we were in the pins-and-needles stage of her illness. I pushed the elevator button repeatedly, like that would make it come any faster, and when it did, I got in and pushed the *close door* button in the same manner. I prayed all the way down, memories of Joan in rapid succession: sitting in the shade at the Ivy Restaurant, her wearing silk and drinking Pellegrino with lemon; talking in her West Hollywood living room with our feet on ottomans, her in the Eddie Bauer underwear, me having just painted her nails; cleaning out my room with me the day I left this very hospital; the smell of her Princessa Borghese skin cream; her gauzy skirts; her elegance.

Arriving at their house, I said another prayer and knocked on the front door. I looked around me, at the way Joan's touch showed in the handkerchief-draped tables on the front porch, with their oil lamps and teapots and bonsai trees.

When Hap opened the door, he held his arms wide and I fell into them. I could smell coffee brewing in the kitchen and the detergent scent of Hap's shirt as we hugged.

We let go, and I saw that his eyes behind his glasses were red rimmed, watery. I started to ask, but as my mouth opened, he took both of my hands firmly in his. I think that was when I knew what he was going to say next.

"She's gone."

I hoped I had misheard him. "She's *gone* gone?" I asked.

"Yes."

I walked in and sat down on the couch, hard. It can't have happened this way. I put my head in my hands, pushing on my temples, and looked up at him. I knew what he was thinking; it was the same thing I was thinking: how could I have missed her by that much? I wondered why I hadn't just taken the day, the week, off of work, how I could have not been here, how I could have not known it was coming. I wondered where the justice was in her leaving me so suddenly.

Hap sat down next to me, his hand on my knee. I opened my mouth. No words came. None could. Shock has no voice.

I tried again. It came out a whisper. "She's really gone?"

He eyed me over the rims of his glasses just like she used to and wiped the first tear from my cheek, then kissed my forehead. There was no other word but *disbelief*. Did I really not get to say good-bye? To thank her? Nothing? My recovery, my life, was what it was because of Joan. Timothy, too, of course, but she was the one who had really shaped me, helped me make the right decisions or deal with the wrong ones, the one who guided me, who forced me to write and grow and pray and dig. She was my protector, my mentor. My fairy godmother, my teacher, my coach, my nanny, my sister. And now, my guardian angel.

"Can I see her?"

"Of course. She's in bed." He nodded his head toward the bedroom. I marveled at his groundedness, his calm. I wondered if it was denial, but on him it just looked like acceptance.

"Okay," I said, my voice cracking as the tears really started, "I'm going to go see her."

I walked down the hall, already seeing her in my mind, lying on her side with her hands in prayer position under her cheek like a child, her men's pajamas white against the even whiter sheet that draped around her waist. I could see the room with its candles and old black typewriter, her straw hat on a chair in the corner. I knew her eyes were closed, and Hap had tucked that stray piece of hair behind her ear, the one that would have fallen over her face.

I opened the door carefully, as if to not wake her. I looked around and saw that it was what I had imagined, down to the hat in the chair. Daylight was filtered by an eggplant-colored linen panel that made the whole room lilac, all shade and shadows and sleep. Her hands made that perfect prayer-shaped pillow, like wings between her cheek and the bed. The brilliant white of her hair and pajamas and sheets gave her an ethereal glow. Anything I may have previously thought about what death looked like, this wasn't it. The energy around her was so angelic and alive that I expected to see her eyes flicker as if she were dreaming. That she did not move at all but was still so vibrant took my breath for a moment. Her tranquillity made me feel loud and big and clumsy in comparison.

I hadn't seen many dead people in my life, at least not this close up, and certainly no one I had loved this much. A few distant relatives, caked with makeup and lying in caskets, but nothing that elicited the response that ran through my body—it was like cool water was poured into me, like my feet were nailed to the floor. I forgot how to breathe, how to blink. I was afraid and in awe and had no idea what to do or say.

Eventually I was able to move, and I pulled a chair up to her bedside. I held her hand and said thank you about a million times and cried and told her that she had saved my life, that without her guidance, who knows what would have become of me. I vowed to make the rest of my life a testament to her work with me: no matter what happened, I would stay sober; I would keep my integrity and speak my truth; I would retain my power; I would help others. Her not being around to check up on me would be no excuse to slack off. If anything, it would be the opposite. I would make her proud.

When I came back out, Hap was sitting in one of the wicker chairs on the front porch. It was April, warm enough for short sleeves. While I was in with Joan, he had put on a Paul Simon record and picked a few of the neighbor's camellias that were coming through the fence. He twirled them between his fingers and gazed into the distance.

I reached for my cigarettes, lit one, and blew a long stream of smoke up toward the sky.

"Have you called anyone yet?"

He blinked, startled, as if waking up. "Just you, and I left messages for Timothy and James. I didn't have a number for Rafael at work, or for Zodiac."

"I'll call them. What about . . . the authorities? Don't we need to tell someone?"

"Yeah, eventually," he said, looking down at the ground. "There are all sorts of people who deal with the formalities—death certificates and cremation, urns and funeral homes—but you know that as soon as I call them, it's going to be a circus around here. I wanted some time for all of us to just be with her." I wondered what it had been like when his first wife overdosed: police, ambulances, questions.

The phone rang, and he got up to answer it. I stubbed out my cigarette and closed my eyes, listening to Paul Simon singing about Grace-land. He's going to Graceland, Graceland, Memphis, Tennessee, and I'm sitting here talking cremation with Hap. *Not fair,* I thought, *not fair at all.*

"That was Timothy; he's on his way over. Do you want to call your husband?"

Hap handed me the phone, and I called Rafael's work. We started arguing right away.

"What do you mean you're not going to be able to make it?" I asked him.

"I'm the only manager, I can't leave the floor."

I sighed. Loudly. My Joanie's death, and this is the support I get. "Fine. If you can't leave, you can't leave. But I'm staying the night. I'll call you later."

I turned to Hap and shook my head. "What a jerk," I said, immediately feeling like a jerk myself that I was complaining at a time like that. Hap raised his eyebrows. He opened his mouth to speak but stopped when we spotted Timothy coming up the street. He wore a denim shirt and khakis and was swinging a picnic basket gently from its handle as he walked.

"I brought us a little care package, courtesy of Gelson's Market," he said, setting it on one of the tables as we stood up. He gave Hap a huge hug, and they stood like that for a long time, long enough for me to wonder what this was like for Timothy. He had tested positive before Joan, and she was gone already. Survivor's guilt? Wondering how long till we're all gathered around, mourning him?

When we went inside, I called the phone number Zodiac had given me that last time we talked. A loud *beep,* then: *The number you have reached is not in service at this time. . . .*

I hung up, and as I did, there was a light tap at the door. I got up to answer it and was faced with James, standing on the porch, holding a giant bunch of irises wrapped in cellophane and tissue paper, tied with a purple ribbon.

"I just got Hap's message. I got here as soon as I could."

I nodded and opened the door wider and told him to come on in. Hap and Timothy came out from the kitchen as soon as they heard us talking. We all just sort of stood there for a moment, silent, timid, unsure of what to say to one another. Finally Timothy took the flowers and went to find a vase, and James turned to Hap.

"I'm so sorry about Joan," he said, hugging Hap. Then, keeping one hand on his shoulder, James turned to me and asked, "Were you with her?"

"No, I just missed her. By—what did you say, about twenty minutes?"

"If that," Hap answered. "I should have asked them to pull you out of group, but I really thought she'd hang on for a few more hours. It went so fast."

"I got to spend time with her over the weekend," I offered, as if that made it okay that I hadn't gotten to say good-bye to her. At least, not really. Every time I left her in the weeks before her death I was aware that it could be the last time I saw her, but I had always imagined that she would fade slowly, that we would have more notice, that we would all gather around her bed, like a page out of *Little Women*. I was glad that Hap was with her when she went but selfishly disappointed that I was not.

James must have seen my eyes glaze over. He put his arms around me and held me for long enough that I started to get that old flippy pit-of-the-stomach thing. Our bodies touched completely from shoulder to knee, and for a brief moment I held him just a little tighter, just a little harder, just to see if the energy was still there.

When we parted, we looked at each other sideways, assessing the risk.

"Thanks," I said, playing up the supportive co-mourning-friend piece of the hug.

"Anytime," he answered, leaving me to wonder if that was an invitation.

· · ·

In the late afternoon, we made the phone calls and Joan was taken from the house. She would come back the next day, in an urn. Hap promised me a pinch of her. We laughed, at him offering me a pinch of Joan, and knew Joan would have laughed, too. Rather, was laughing, somewhere.

Well after midnight, after looking through three of Joan's photo albums, I went out to the porch to find Hap sitting in one of the wicker chairs, reading. James was going through the picnic basket. Timothy was sketching by the light of the moon, brighter than I had ever seen it. We all looked at one another, then shrugged, like, *What else can you do?*

"We're going to be a mess without her, aren't we?" Hap asked.

"Looks like," I answered.

We sat out there until about four and then decided to give sleep a try. I woke up about an hour later. I had been dreaming I was flying, holding the hand of a little girl, her pudgy kid-fingers tight around mine as we soared over blue water and low hills. I heard Joan's voice, clear as a bell, telling me she loved me, and I smiled and the little girl smiled and then, even louder, like an amplified harp, was Joan's laughter. I laughed, too, then the girl did, and I opened my eyes, still hearing the echo of Joan's laughter in the room. But there was no one there, of course, except for a few moonbeams as bright as patio lights and the outlines of three sleeping men.

At dawn I drove down to the beach. I took a towel out of my trunk, walked across the sand, and stood ankle-deep in the water. I looked around. The neighbors were too far away to see and probably still asleep. I took my clothes off quickly and dived underneath the foaming white where the waves broke.

I swam quite a ways out and went under, plunging down silent with my eyes open and burning with salt. I could see flecks of sand turning and shimmering in slow motion and tiny fish like tadpoles darting in a hundred different directions. My hair moved like gold ribbons rippling in a drowsy breeze. I could hardly feel the water, although, womblike, it held me, had me contained like a splinter suspended in a piece of amber. It was the only thing connecting me to the earth while my soul tried to find Joan. Underwater, I looked for her white hair and high cheeks, her sage green eyes, her red nails or silver Birkenstocks, but saw only my starfish hands and the bubbles from my own nose. I dived deeper and touched the bottom: lumpy packed sand, but no sign of her.

When I finally came up it took me a minute to realize I was crying because the sea salt mingled with my tears, and it all tasted the same. I thought I could see Joan for a second in the fiery points of light that were the sunrise hitting the surface before I turned my face to a sky that was deep blue like vintage cobalt glass.

I swam back to the shore and wrapped myself in the towel, shook my hair out, and dropped my dress over my head. It was a hand-me-down from my mom's hippie days, thousands of tiny flowers on threadbare brown cotton, and it laced up the back like a peasant-girl dress. Its softness reminded me of Joan's hankies, of India and hotel sheets. My shoulders were bare to the new sun and sandy.

I toweled my hair a little more and started to walk up the alley to my old house, to catch my parents before my dad left for work and tell them that Joan was gone and show them that I was okay, that I could get through the pain without taking a drink, and that Joan had done a good job with me, and tell them that they had done a good job releasing me to her.

Joan didn't want a traditional funeral or a traditional burial. She wanted a party instead of a memorial service and a tree instead of a gravestone. She had told Hap all the details, and he explained it to me a few nights later, after the party, when everyone had gone home and we were cleaning up.

"So, we need to find a tree," Hap said. "She said it has to be 'strong, self-sustaining, and good-looking.'" He smiled. "Sound like anyone we know?"

"Absolutely."

"Want to come with me to find it?"

"Of course."

The next morning he and I drove to a nursery out in Malibu. The man who worked there looked about two hundred years old, with hands as black and gnarled as the skinny tree trunk he held. He had a fog to one eye and one of the kindest smiles I have ever seen. One thing I can say about having had Joan in my life is that now I see angels everywhere.

Hap told him what we were looking for, and the man returned a few minutes later with a tree. Hap held two of its branches out as one holds a woman before a dance, in a let-me-see-you gesture that was both fond and scrutinizing. They were about the same height. Hap grinned, raised his eyebrows, then walked a slow circle around it and turned toward me. I nodded my approval.

Lignum Vitae. I looked it up in my encyclopedia when I got home and confirmed that we had picked the perfect tree: *After the initial watering until the roots catch, it completely nurtures itself. It's a hard ironwood, in some cases literally harder than the metal itself, nearly impossible to carve, mar, or abrade. Its sweet-smelling resin has been used in folk medicine for centuries. It thrives in heat, survives hurricanes. It blossoms violet-blue in spring and sum-mer, has tiny orange pods in fall, and is otherwise a bright green. Its nickname is the "tree of life."* Strong, self-sustaining, and good-looking indeed.

That evening, we picked up Timothy and James and the four of us drove to Topanga Canyon. Hap carried the tree up a hill and we fol-lowed, James with four shovels, Timothy with one of Joan's watering cans, and me with what was left of her ashes after Hap and I had taken our pinches. I looked around when we got to the top and saw the beach and the ocean below and the horizon far away, almost invisible in the near darkness. It felt like a Joan-place. I knew she had spent a lot of time up here, not only because Hap had told me but also because I could still sense her presence. She was a scent that hung in the air, a footprint not yet leveled by the wind.

Hap walked around for a minute or two, then took a shovel and twisted its tip around in the dirt. "How about right here?"

We all nodded. I picked up a shovel. The metal of its handle felt smooth and cold in my hand. I didn't want to set her ashes down, but I did, because now it was time to work. To dig.

The tree looked proud and elegant when we took it out of its bucket and newspaper and righted it in the hole. As Joan wanted, we sprinkled her ashes among the roots. They looked like coarse sand, with larger pieces like coral that I didn't really want to think about.

We stood back, hypnotized by the waxy leaves that picked up the moonlight and held it out for us to see. The bark was as smooth as if it had been polished, no splinters or sap or bugs to spoil the perfect umber surface. Each limb danced to the rhythms of the wind. We stood together in silence, and I wondered who was going to remind us to pray, now that she was gone.

In the days and weeks that followed, I was a wreck. I kept my bedside promise to her—I didn't drink; I kept up my meetings; I reached out to newcomers; I tried to carry her grace with me into every action—but inside I was devastated. I had Timothy to hang out with and my work to keep me focused, but clearly there was a Joan-shaped hole in my life, a hole that could never be filled with anything or anyone else.

I had become so accustomed to dialing her number whenever I was overwhelmed or confused by my emotions that several times during that period I actually picked up the phone to call her. Eventually those half-dialed calls became drives up to Topanga Canyon. I would take my journal and walk up that hill, sit myself down under that tree, and write letters to her. Sometimes I would read them out loud, but sometimes I would just keep them in my journal, closing it and talking to her off the cuff.

More than once I wished I could join her in there, the grief not something I thought I could bear, especially not when I thought about how it would come around again when Timothy died. Some days it took everything I had just to stay on the planet, but then her sweet, sweet voice would come to me from somewhere, from the wind as it caught the dancing leaves of the tree, from the purple petals that were already budding along the tips of the branches, from the earth itself, under my feet, holding me up, whispering that I would be okay. I would hurt, and I would cry, and I would always miss my Joanie, but I would be okay. I really would.

16

I watched Hap tape up the last box of Joan's belongings. It had been two months since she had passed away, and he was finally ready to bundle her up. I still slept with a sweater of hers that he had given me— unwashed, it smelled like her—but he was already letting go.

"I won't be staying here," he said. He sighed and sat on the couch.

He put the roll of tape down, and I sat down next to him. I looked around and nodded my understanding. This little bungalow was so her. "That makes sense."

My mild response prompted him to clarify. "I mean, I'm going away. Far away. Florida."

"Florida?" I gawked. "You can't move to Florida. What about us? We can't lose you and Joan all at once. That's not even funny."

"You'll be fine."

"But why Florida?"

"I'm old. I'm a widower, twice over now. That's where we go." He grinned. "But more important, it's for Joan. It's something we had talked about before she died. There's a house there on Fisher Island, not far from Miami, a big old plantation-style house that has been in her family for generations. You remember us going down there for vacations, don't you?"

He paused, and I stared at him. I must have nodded, because he continued.

"She left it to me. And she was very specific; you know how she could be—I'm to live there, not just visit. That way she'll know the house is in good hands and I can get out of this city and relax, start over. It's a beautiful property, surrounded by banana trees and water, and there's a boathouse and a boat, and . . . and it's going to be my new home. But you can always fly down and see me. There's more than enough room for guests. Delia? Are you okay?"

My head was in my hands. I looked up and scanned his face, all his wrinkles and stray eyebrow hairs. He looked peaceful, confident. "You're sure about this?"

He opened a drawer in the coffee table and took out a plane ticket. "I leave next week."

"You are sure about this." I let it sink in. "I'm going to miss you something awful."

"I know. Me, too. You've been like the daughter I never had. Timothy, Rafael, and James, too—all you kids have been like the family I never had. But it's too hard being here without Joan." He blinked a few times and then added, "Can I ask you a question before I go?"

"Of course. You know you can ask me anything."

"You and Rafael. Are you doing all right?"

It was the nudge that I needed. I broke down and told him everything, from the doubt that began after we got engaged, to sleeping with James the week before the wedding, to the guilt I'd been lugging around ever since. I told Hap that I hadn't wanted to burden Joan with my discontent while she was sick and I hadn't wanted to disappoint her or my parents by not having the perfect marriage.

"But now," I added, "I'm ready."

"Ready to work things out, or ready to call it quits?"

"I don't know. Either. Just anything different from what we have now."

He looked at me with his Cowardly Lion face, wise and sad and soft all at the same time. "If there's one thing I've learned, it's that life's too short. Life's too short to put up with bullshit, and it's too short to waste time. Talk to him. Sooner rather than later. Because—"

We said it together: "Life's too short."

With those words, my cage door opened and I flew out.

That night Rafael and I sat in the tiny dining room with a pizza between us, me staring out the window at our view of the cement wall and the neighbor's weeping willow, him feeding slice after slice of pizza into his mouth.

The room was undersized; the whole apartment was like a scaled-down version of a real apartment. The walls were paper-thin and everything seemed fake. The kitchen drawers rolled way too fast on new ball-bearing tracks and the mirrored sliding doors on the closet wiggled and warped us into funhouse characters. For Rafael, it represented independence. But for me, raised in an old house in a hippie neighborhood, a house with original tile work and crown moldings, sun flooding through nine-pane windows onto hardwood floors, it was like some weird form of punishment. I stared at the white halogen cone that hung over the table and took a deep breath.

"So . . . I've been doing some thinking. I don't know where to start, but I think we need to do something different. About us. It doesn't feel like the same relationship it used to, and I'm not happy in it like I used to be. There's no—" I laced my fingers together and apart, trying to communicate the concept of togetherness. "You know?"

He got up from the table and began breaking down the pizza box so it would fit in the trash. He folded it over one knee and then pulled a knife from his pocket, flicked it open on his jeans, and tore into the cardboard. I watched, silent and a little worried, as he slashed, the silver blade glinting in the fluorescent light. It was just a Domino's box, and he was killing it. I felt his rage large in the little kitchen and saw what a time bomb he was. He flicked the knife shut and slipped it back into his pocket. Then he smiled and looked at me and I felt cold.

"What do you mean?" he asked.

"I told you what I mean. I am not happy. Something needs to change."

"But I love you."

I sighed. "I love you, too. But we're in a rut. Can't you feel it?"

"We could move," he said.

"Move?"

"Sure. It's obvious that you can't stand this place. And that would be a change, right?"

"I meant more like a change between you and me, not like a change of address."

He just stared at me.

I had been patient till then, but the way he looked in that moment—blank—spoke volumes. I could feel my nostrils flare out, my heart quicken.

"Forget it. Excuse me," I said, and walked past him out the door.

I went downstairs and stood in the driveway. I wondered if this was what he'd had in mind when he proposed: a finish line instead of a starting gate. I lit a cigarette and leaned against the rough cement wall. I looked at the sky, this California sky I had known since I was born, with its low smog and high clouds, but I was having a hard time seeing anything familiar in it. I felt blind. I needed Joan. I wanted to be a million ashes mingling with hers, this time not because I wanted to join her like I had when the grief was sharper but just so I could ask her what I was supposed to do. Because something about planting her tree by the light of the moon and swimming naked in the ocean made me intolerant of a husband whose idea of self-care started and stopped at eating Funyuns and ordering pay-per-view movies.

I dropped my cigarette on the driveway, twisted the toe of my shoe on it, and heard her voice inside me, telling me to pray. So I did. I prayed for hope and strength and change, and that alone made it possible for me to walk back upstairs and talk to Rafael about this moving idea. Maybe that was our answer. Maybe it would be enough. Maybe it would be our salvation.

A few weeks later, we came home from a movie and saw our neighbor across the street sitting on the porch of his pink Spanish-style duplex, alone and smoking.

"Let's go say hi," I said.

Rafael looked down.

"What?" I hissed; I spit. "What? What's wrong with saying hi? Come on."

I had pulled into our underground parking space and turned off the car. Rafael stayed in his seat like a poky child, whining and dawdling, picking at his nails.

"Maybe we should call first. We shouldn't bother him."

"Bother! We're not bothering. We're visiting. Are you coming with me? What is your problem? Can you please get out of the car?"

He pulled himself out of the car and walked a few paces behind me up the driveway. I stopped and waited for him so we could walk across the street together.

We walked up the stone path that led to the porch. Magenta bougainvillea dripped from the Spanish-tiled roof, papery and vibrant against the pink stucco. The three arched windows upstairs were wide open, letting the night in. The steps were trimmed in hand-painted blue tiles, the same tiles as the address numbers over the mailboxes. On the house's right stood a tall, skinny eucalyptus, and the lawn was perfectly manicured, all ferns and irises and Japanese anemones.

"Hey, Simon," I called.

"Hey, you two," he called back, and his eyes slanted as he smiled. I could see them under the porch light. He was a little older than we were, handsome, angular, with a jester face, a sliver-moon face. "What's going on?"

"Nothin', just came to say hi, pay a neighborly visit." I smiled and squeezed Rafael's hand so he would smile, too.

"Well, then have a seat."

I sat on the low wall and Rafael sat on a large rock that was part of the landscaping. I remember so well the way Simon looked under that porch light, the tilt of his eyes, his smile, the way his hands moved as he talked, his forearms strong with dark hair and a tan. I remember the easy shape his long legs made when he crossed them at the ankles, leaned back on his elbows, and asked if we had a few minutes to talk.

"I've been doing some thinking. Are you sure you guys can stay for a while?"

I said yes, of course we could, before Rafael could refuse.

"Well, I'm trying to figure out what to do about the house. It's too big and too expensive for me. I've either got to rent half of it to someone else or . . . I don't know."

He looked dejected. I jumped down off the wall. They both stared at me.

"Us!"

"What?"

"We'll rent it! This is perfect!"

Rafael's air left him as if he had been socked in the stomach. Simon and I grinned at each other.

"Are you serious? I didn't even know you guys were thinking of moving."

"Well, we are. Aren't we, dear?" I called Rafael "dear" only when I was being sarcastic. He knew that and scowled. He toed the ground and mumbled that sure, we'd been thinking about it. I ignored him and smiled at Simon. "I have always loved this building," I said.

"But you haven't even seen the upstairs. That's the half I'd rent out, and it needs some work. So before you get too excited, why don't you take a look and see if you even want it."

"Can we look now?" I didn't want to seem overly anxious, but I didn't want him to change his mind, either.

Simon unlocked the front door, and we walked up the stairs to the second floor. The staircase was all wood and the walls were caked with years of white paint and chipped along earthquake cracks. There were no right angles. I fell in love.

I ran my hand along the banister. "What year?"

"Nineteen twenty-six."

I nodded.

"Go ahead and look around."

I was already moving toward the first bedroom, the one with three sets of French windows, one so close to the eucalyptus tree you could stick your hand out and feel the velvety-white bark. Its sharp, sweet medicine smell filled the room, like a sauna at a day spa. The floor bowed and dipped after so many years of settling and shifting, and it made me wonder who had been born in this room, who grew up here, died here. I never got that feeling across the street. There was no history there. There was nothing there.

I went into the bathroom next. The floor was thousands of white hexagon tiles with dark grout between them. I knelt and traced their pattern with the tip of my finger, all the little lines, every six tiles making a flower, then stood and looked in the mirror in the door of the built-in medicine cabinet. Its silver peeled around the edges and the latch was ancient. The claw-foot tub sat large and old and white in one corner, the pedestal sink in the other. I leaned my forehead on the wall and inhaled the scent of old plaster. I had to live here.

Rafael looked around in a different way—he just sort of stuck his head into each room to verify that it existed. I could hear him making small talk in the kitchen with Simon. I walked down the hall to the other bedroom and flipped on the light. The walls were lined with shelves. I could see my books filling them. In my mind it became my library. My sanctuary.

I opened the back door and stepped onto a covered deck, looking down onto a giant willow, a fig tree, an olive tree, and a stone path from the house to the garage. Ivy crawled up the wall next to me, coating the whole north side of the building in green vines. The backyard was as rustic and bohemian as the front yard was magazine-perfect.

I reentered the house through the other door, the laundry room door. Even the laundry room was charming, with its wall-mounted ironing board and a deep basin for hand-wash garments. It made me want to use wooden clothespins and wear an apron and yellow rubber gloves, put my hair in a red bandanna. It was not a present-day room. Neither was the kitchen, which was dominated by a 1940s O'Keefe & Merritt stove that sat like a classic car, all chrome and white iron. It had a clock, a griddle; its stance was firm. It looked as if it could cook the hell out of anything and not flinch. It was a real stove, a manly stove. Regal. The tile work in the kitchen was original, too, white with black trim. A black-and-white checked floor. A row of six miniature windows over the sink. The cabinets in here had the same feel as in the bathroom, paint-thick and held shut only by being wedged together. There was a built-in with chicken wire panels that reminded me of my grandparents, of the South, of the past.

I didn't realize that Rafael and Simon had stopped talking and were looking at me.

"What do you think?" Simon asked, and I just stood there, grinning like a fool. "I think she likes it," he said to Rafael, who said nothing.

I looked over his shoulder at the dining room and to the living room beyond that, the triple arch of the front windows, the fir floors, the moldings and windowpanes. Both rooms had their original light fixtures and old radiators. The amount of glass and the feeling of expansiveness seduced me after having been boxed up across the street. "We'll take it."

Behind me, Rafael choked on something.

I spun, and we stared each other down.

Simon said he'd leave us alone to talk it over, that he'd be downstairs with the door open and we could come on down whenever we were ready. I hadn't blinked. Neither had Rafael. I waited until I heard Simon's footsteps on the stairs before I lunged into Rafael, my eyes narrow.

"What's the matter with you? This is an amazing opportunity! Please don't say you need more time to think about it. It's perfect. Are you insane?"

He had on his whipping-boy look, but now with a slight jut of his chin, which meant I had really offended him. His pride. His machismo.

"Am *I* insane?" he asked. "You can't make decisions without me. Marriage is a two-way street, you know."

I counted to ten and lowered my own stuck-out jaw and looked into his eyes. I knew I had to be calm, unthreatening, the way you approach a wounded animal. I didn't want to blow my chances of us getting this place. I took a breath and started again.

"You're right. I shouldn't make decisions without you. But this is such a great place for us. It would be a fresh start. And I think we could be happy here." I put my arms around his waist and leaned back, putting on my best "please" face.

"But we don't even know what the rent is."

AA had given me faith and courage; it had taught me that it was safe to take risks; it had given me the belief that things would work out and that it was okay to dream. By dropping out of the program, Rafael had made his world very small. This is what they mean when they say AA has more to do with starting living than it does with stopping drinking.

"It doesn't matter. We both have stable, well-paying jobs. The car is paid for, my work covers health insurance for both of us . . . we can easily afford to pay more rent than we do now. We could pay double what we're paying across the street and still be fine."

He looked at me, a wild deer sniffing the hand with the oats in it.

I nodded and said, "Really," trying to assure him. But I'm sure all he saw in my eyes was the determination that meant I was willing to do this all night until I got my way. When I was a child, I believed that if I thought something hard enough and stared at someone long enough, I could make them do what I wanted. I looked at Rafael in this way now, willing him to say yes.

His eyes filled with resentment—he knew he would be worn down. He knew that when I wanted something so bad I could taste it I would get it. He knew that I had stamina and he did not. That I was smarter. That I would not give up.

"What do you think?" I asked him. "Can we?"

After a long silence, he spoke. "Okay. Let's go down and talk to Simon."

I threw my arms around his neck and kissed him, thanking him, laughing.

We walked down the staircase, me fondling the banister and smiling at that grand front door and smelling the age of the walls, him merely descending, abiding by the law of gravity, right foot after left.

I was the one to tell Simon it was a go, and though he looked at the two of us for a moment as if to discern whether or not this was a mutual decision, it was a moment that passed quickly and gave way to us talking about how great this was for all of us, how fun it would be, how perfect. Rafael's silence in this conversation did not go unnoticed—nor did it change anything. We looked at the calendar and circled October 1. We talked about appliance deliveries, repairs, and painters' schedules. Rafael deferred to me on the paint, said he trusted my judgment. What he really meant was that he couldn't care less what color anything was anymore, but saying even that aloud would have been too expressive for him. Then Rafael and I walked across the street to the building that looked even less like home to me than it had before.

When we got upstairs, I wanted to talk, but he started yawning and went to bed. In the dark, as Rafael lay snoring, I thought about the house across the street, the pink house with its old windows open, letting the night in. I thought about Joan and the way she had slept for keeps in her lilac-tinted bedroom and Hap telling me that life's too short and me standing in the driveway, praying. And I knew it all fit together, that something major was happening, the thing that could really save our marriage and maybe even bring some joy to Poor Rafael, which is how I had begun to think of him: Poor Rafael. Surely it would make me happier, and Simon could keep his house and have two built-in friends right upstairs.

I was busy the next few weeks. I became ruthless with what we could keep and what would be thrown away. My requirement was that a thing had to be either useful or beautiful, or it went away. I took days off from work to drive to the dump, hauling away the white wall unit and the framed lobby-art Rafael had brought home from the hardware store's home décor department. There would be no particleboard anything, nothing that required home assembly or pegs. When he asked why we couldn't keep the chrome-and-glass end table, I just looked at him with what may have been pity or disbelief and said, "Uh, two words? *Chrome,* and *glass?*"

When I went over to talk about colors with Simon and the painter, Timothy came with me, and we found a warm white for the hall, bedrooms, living room, and dining room that would put the house in perpetual four o'clock sunglow and for the trim a pale green-gray like sand dollars that would show off the moldings and windowpanes and door frames without being too high-contrast. Joan had said that kitchens and bathrooms should *always* be white. Not yellow or green or, God forbid, *beige.* No. Absolutely not. So those two rooms were painted white. Add in the bleached ceramic tiles and constant sunlight, and they glowed the same way she had.

I explained all of this to Rafael. I talked to him about design and style and color. I used the words *feng shui* and marveled at how gracefully they sailed over his head. When it was done, he said he liked it. When our twin chests of drawers were delivered, mission-style with brass ring pulls, he nodded like a student.

Our dining room faced the apartment building next door. With only about fifteen feet between us, when our curtains were open and their curtains were open we were practically in the same room. It was even more pronounced at night, lights blazing as if we were on display for each other. The other building was a 1950s flagstone with little asteroids orbiting the address. From our place, I could see the sparkly cottage-cheese ceiling, the plain pine cabinets—and a huge collection of gowns, hanging from racks, on mannequins, draped over the couch.

Looking closely at the flashy, almost garish, dresses, I began to wonder who lived there. Blind old ladies? Showgirls? A prom queen from Fontana? Around the living room were yards of shiny fabrics in dazzling colors, boxes of beads, jars of sequins like fish scales, feathers, sheer veil-like nylon, and oversize rhinestones. *Who on earth would wear this stuff?* I thought.

And then I met Momma.

She was getting ready to go out. It was a hot night, so all of our windows were open. I could hear disco playing in the background. When she saw me looking, she smiled and twirled and yelled, "So? What do you think?"

She stopped dancing long enough to pose in her new dress, a taffeta strapless the color of fresh tangerines with a matching boa. She had a wig like spun silk done up in a pale apricot chignon. Her eyebrows arched high enough onto her forehead to allow for inch-long curled eyelashes and plenty of gold eye shadow. Her cheeks shimmered; her fingernails looked like ten little Sunkist Popsicles. She was all rhinestones and bugle beads, with orange stilettos the size of gunboats and fake jewels glinting from her earlobes and wrists as clear and bright as rock candy.

Momma's real name was Dave. She was six-foot-five, an ex-linebacker resplendent in her brand-new wig and glittering gown.

I grinned.

"Well?" she pressed, clamping one giant hand on her hip, batting those eyelashes.

I yelled back that she looked fabulous, thinking how glad I was to have moved, how much I liked our new neighbor.

She flicked her boa over her shoulder and said, "Then I guess it's time to go. Can't be late; I'm going to the ball!" She winked. "Tonight I meet my prince." She smiled and turned and walked a runway model's walk to the door. I moved to the front windows and watched as she got into her car, slowly, careful to tuck in her gown and her hair. As she drove off, her boa escaped, a flame in the night leaving a trail of orange feathers that whirled up and burned out like the spray of sparks that hangs, spinning, over a campfire.

Momma was my secret. Rafael always seemed to miss her, and Simon had yet to meet her. Momma and I never exchanged more than a few sentences, but she became a talisman to me, her sheer presence speaking volumes to me about being who you've just got to be, about not holding back, about life in all its glory.

The meeting was packed, which always happens around the holidays. Between the already sober wanting to stay that way through family gatherings, work parties, and reminders of disasters past, and all the New Year's resolutions made by problem drinkers, AA swelled between November and January. I was scanning the room for an empty seat when I saw Zodiac, sitting in a chair off to the side, next to James. He was holding back the quilted fabric of the sling that crossed her chest, making cooing faces at a baby. Her baby. Before I could decide whether to walk over there or slip out unnoticed, Zodiac looked up.

She shrieked in excitement, waking the baby. "Delia! Get your ass over here!"

I walked across the room and sat down on her other side. The baby wailed while Zodiac felt around in her jacket pocket for his pacifier. She pulled out a wadded-up Kleenex and a lighter, the latter of which apparently inspired her to have a cigarette before the meeting started.

She hugged me, then stood up. "We'll catch up in a minute. Who wants to hold him while I go smoke?" She looked at me first, then James.

"I will," I said, taking the baby from her. He felt so tiny in my arms. "How old is he?"

She was already at the door, so James answered. "Almost three months."

"What's his name?"

"Elijah."

I rocked him gently as he cried. He smelled like cigarettes and his diaper was heavy.

"How's she doing?" I asked James.

He shrugged. "She says she's been clean ever since she found out she was pregnant."

"Do you believe her?"

He shrugged again. "She's here. Who knows."

She walked back in just as Elijah dozed off, his cheek on my shoulder.

"Thanks," she said, smiling. She took him from my arms and sat back down and put him in the sling. She turned to me. "I heard about Joan. That sucks."

"I tried to call you, but your phone was disconnected."

"Damn phone company. How's everything else? How's Rafael?"

"He's okay," I said. On her other side, James looked away, and I swore he rolled his eyes. I started to ask him what that was about, but then the meeting started, leaving us to listen to the speaker, who smiled at the sleeping Elijah and picked rebirth as a topic.

Rafael and I had started arguing. Over nothing. Over little things that became big things. Over things that, had I been in a place of love and forgiveness, would not have been a big deal. After talking with Hap and hoping that the move would turn over the new leaf we so needed and chanting to myself that life was too short, I found myself critical of Rafael. I was poised, ready to lunge.

I didn't want a CD rack or a television in the living room. I liked to have music in the house, but he wanted to look at the stereo itself. I didn't feel a television should be the centerpiece of a living room; he did. He wanted to display his electronics like trophies; I wanted a civilized, attractive living room. "Which," I told him, "does not include LED readouts or black plastic."

And then I came home from work one night, set my briefcase down, and saw it as soon as I turned the corner to the living room. Hell, I probably could have seen it from across the street, from across town, from fucking France.

On the main wall where I had hung Timothy's new painting was a big-screen television, the biggest television I have ever seen. It was the size of our bed, the size of the movie screen in the small theater at the mall. It was in a wood cabinet with magnet-close glass doors under-neath, and it was covering the bottom three inches of the canvas. Cov-ering it. It was the worst piece of . . . what do you even call that? Home entertainment? I was not entertained in the least.

Rafael sat, again the sugar-high child, this time with a remote con-trol the size of a scuba fin clutched tightly in both hands. He looked up at me standing there glaring and went back to watching his new toy.

"Hi," he said. "You're not mad, are you? I know we hadn't really fin-ished talking about it, but there was a sale at Circuit City, and I had the day off, so I figured . . ."

He figured. He was playing dumb. My purse slid off my shoulder and dropped to the floor. My keys fell out of my hand. On the screen was a very big Tom Brokaw, miles larger than a real person, reciting the evening news. I took deep breaths.

"Check it out though," Rafael said, still not moving, staring straight ahead. "It has picture-in-picture."

I could feel a scream bubbling in the far reaches of my throat.

He pushed a button on the giant remote with his thumb, and a tiny square of football appeared in the corner of the news. He smiled.

"Now watch this," he said, pushing the button again: big football, tiny news. And again: tiny football, big news.

My throat burned; my eyes watered; my hands went numb. "You are un. Fucking. Believable."

I was livid. I wanted to put my boot through the glass and watch the shards of news and sports lie dying on the floor. Maybe cut his remote-hand with one while I was at it, maybe a really important artery or his

thumb, the opposable digit that separated man from the rest of the animal kingdom, the digit Rafael apparently did not deserve. I stormed
into our bedroom and locked the door. I flew out a few minutes later
with a book and stomped down the hall, locking myself in the library.
Not that he was capable of extracting himself from the couch and seek-
ing me out.

After a while, when I was able to breathe normally and see without
the peripheral red, I went out to the deck. The fresh air extinguished
any residual rage I may have had. I inhaled it deeply, the way I used to
suck on the pipe. I heard Simon below me on his patio and leaned over.

"Hey down there," I called.

"Hey up there! What's going on?"

"Nothing. Everything. Have you seen it?"

"The TV?"

"Mmm. Did you see its *size?*"

"Yeah, I was here when it was delivered. I take it you two hadn't
agreed on it yet?"

I made a face and waved my hand like I couldn't even talk about it.
Which I couldn't. "Is that a cappuccino?" I nodded to the cup in his hand.

"Yep. Can I make you one?"

"I would *love* one."

"Want me to bring it up?"

"No. No, I'm coming down."

I grabbed my smokes and walked down the outside stairs to the
yard, to his back door. Each unit had the same floor plan. They were
fraternal twins: the same structure but in different colors and with different features. Being a photographer, Simon had turned his breakfast
nook into a darkroom and his red-lit kitchen always had damp prints
clipped to the clothesline that stretched across the counter. His front
bedroom was his studio; the back was where he slept.

I leaned against the counter as he poured the syrupy espresso from
a stainless-steel shot glass into a clear mug, added sugar, then steamed

the milk and spooned it into the mug. It was nectar. It was mother's milk. I closed my eyes. "Thank you."

Simon smiled. "You're welcome." He was still smiling. "You have a mustache." We laughed as I wiped it with the back of my hand.

That night, we sat in his studio while he hand-tinted a photograph of a marketplace in Mexico. In the three months since Rafael and I had moved in, there had been many nights after work when I went to Simon's door before my own and others that I went downstairs after dinner and stayed until midnight. We had cappuccino together every day before I went to work. We swam laps every Tuesday at the public pool. And so it happened that I grew closer to Simon in inverse proportion to how far I grew away from Rafael. In my mind it was like a teeter-totter: one side went up as the other went down.

After a while, it was like having Timothy there. When it was too late to call Timothy or when he was out of town, I went downstairs. When Rafael was irritating me, I went downstairs. When I needed a friend, I went downstairs. It was like gravity pulled me there.

Because there is nothing logical about smelling plaster or placing your palm flat against a eucalyptus trunk thirty feet in the air, nothing logical about the times in your life when you let invisible beings pull you out of your home and down into the darkroom of a neighbor. It is times like those that we drop quietly to our knees and trace the shape of honeycomb tiles with our fingers, we smile at windowpanes and empty bookshelves, we don orange boas, we laugh with milk mustaches and dream of flying, we hear the voices of dead women clear as bells and swim naked in the ocean, because the pull is like the tide, like a child's hand, tiny but so very strong, insistent, pulling, dragging, *c'mon*—and all we can do is throw our heads back and laugh and drop to our knees again, this time crying with joy and wonder, our involuntary soul-voice pushing the words from our lips: *Thank you; thank you.*

17

I found myself eyeing Simon as he sliced through the water like a manta ray, all smooth angles and taut wet muscle, each hand like a fin, each breath like a wave. Sometimes I thought I caught him looking at me, too—with my face down between breaths I saw him behind me, slowing, but maybe he was just hanging back out of courtesy and to avoid my wake.

We always walked home Tuesday nights after our workout, towels around our necks like camp kids, twirling our goggles, and we always stopped at the little café on the corner for baskets of battered fish and shoestring fries.

"The hunger that comes after swimming is like no other," he said to me one night as we sat there with our wet hair and big smiles, greasy hands and sleepy bellies.

"None?" I asked.

Simon leaned close to my ear, as if about to tell me a secret. "None," he whispered slyly, and leaned back, dipping a fry into the tartar sauce and popping it into his mouth.

I didn't know whether it was his intention or not, but my mind went straight to sex, and I was amused in places that had not laughed for months.

After that, I began to look at Simon differently. Every cappuccino, every talk, every friendly "howdy, neighbor" from the deck down or the backyard up had almost taken on the feel of a courtship. I even blushed on occasion, and he averted his eyes and kept moving, like a boxer. But we didn't try to spend less time together.

A few weeks later, we sat on the beach, his camera around his neck, sand gathering in the cables of my fisherman's sweater. "So, this is your spot?" Simon asked me, looking around.

"This is it. I can't tell you how many days I spent down here as a kid. My house is right up that street." I pointed, and his eyes followed my finger. "After I got out of treatment, I came down here a lot just to think and to get centered." I thought for a moment. "But you know what's weird? All the times we were over at my parents' house, I never once brought Rafael here."

"How come?"

"Good question. It's such a special place to me. Sacred even. You'd think it would have been one of the first things I'd want to share with someone I was going to marry."

I looked out at the waves, pounding against the sand, rhythmic, reliable. I was lost in my thoughts and in the sound of their roar when Simon said my name.

"Delia."

I turned to look at him over my shoulder, and he snapped a picture of me.

I've heard it said since that the photograph reveals as much about its photographer as it does about its subject, like some sort of psychic projection, and that the relationship between the photographer and their subject is in the picture, too, that the image reflects the energy in the space between them. In the snapshot that Simon took that day, there was mostly an ease and a simplicity—but underneath that was a faint shadow of something flirtatious, something secret. When I saw the photograph a few days later hanging on a clip in his darkroom, I stopped, amused and appalled and curious. I went upstairs and picked up the phone.

"Mom? I have a question for you." Ever since I'd moved out, I'd called her periodically with miscellaneous questions, mostly house-keeping questions, day-to-day living questions. For the heart questions, the boy questions, I had always gone to Joan. But Joan was gone. So when the Simon/Rafael teeter-totter began to seriously tilt, I called my mom.

"What is it, honey?"

"Well. You and Dad. Marriage."

"Can you be more specific?"

I sighed. "I don't know. I mean—you've been married for, like, ever, right? And it hasn't always been good, but you stuck it out. How do you know when it's worth it and when it's not?"

"Well." A long pause. "I think marriage is about give-and-take. I knew it wouldn't all be smooth sailing with your father, but I signed up for the whole ride. Why do you ask?"

"No reason." I couldn't tell her that I was wondering how long I was supposed to wait for it to get better with Rafael and what I was sup-posed to do when I found myself feeling more intimate with and at-tracted to Simon than my own husband.

"Is this about you and Rafael? Are you having problems? He's not drinking, is he?"

"No, he's not drinking, but he hasn't been to a meeting in forever—"

"Like your father."

"Yes, exactly. Dad still hasn't gone to a meeting?"

"Not since he was in treatment. You know he never liked AA. But you're changing the subject. What's going on with you and Rafael?"

"Nothing's going on—that's the problem. I mean, I love Rafael, and we get along. Mostly. But when we got married, it was like all the magic went away. And if I'm going to be with him for all of eternity, it would be nice if I felt like I had a soul mate instead of a roommate. It's flat. We fizzed. Is fizzing normal?" As I said those words, I realized we hadn't just fizzed: our relationship had gone sour the week before the wedding, when I slept with James.

"I think some degree of fizzing is normal. Married life isn't always as exciting as single life, but it's richer in other ways, more fulfilling. It's commitment; it's longevity; it's building a history. It's waiting out the hard times because you know the good times will come again."

And there was my double-edged sword. I had been given incredible staying power in AA. Endurance. I was taught to hang in there when things weren't perfect: *don't drink or use no matter what; don't leave five minutes before the miracle; this, too, shall pass.* Slogans upon slogans about patience, acceptance, and stamina. But did they apply to a marriage that was doomed from the gate? I asked my mom this question. She didn't have an answer. Neither did I.

Not long after that, an earthquake ripped and rocked its way through Los Angeles, tossing cars and breaking freeways and toppling buildings as it went. It woke us in the middle of the night not long before dawn, the three of us then awake and huddling in the still-shaking dark, a night polluted by aftershocks and sirens and nervous neighbors, news reports and phone calls. When the sun came up, Rafael left to help clean up the store and Simon and I sat on his couch watching the all-day every-station coverage of the debris, the dead, the gas line explosions, and the live power lines that slid and snapped like snakes through Valley streets. We sat close together, amazed that the duplex had not sustained more damage. It had creaked and groaned under the sway of the quake, throwing windows open, emptying shelves, cupboards, the fridge. But we were okay. The house was okay.

Late that afternoon, as the three of us sat in the front yard, I asked Rafael about his "earthquake weather" theory. It had been dark when the quake hit, I told him, and cold, with the faintest breeze, not even a hint of the Santa Anas. He looked north up our street, toward the hills, and said that sometimes these things just happened, with no warning. Sometimes, he said, they just come and take everyone by surprise. Then he turned, looked right at me, and said I should have seen the store, how much broken glass there was, how much damage had been done. He said that I wouldn't have believed the wreckage. And then he repeated, "Sometimes, you know, these things just happen, with no warning." As if I needed to hear it again. I looked away. *Yes, Rafael,* I wanted to tell him, *I do know. More than you could ever imagine, I know.*

That night when Rafael went back to the store, I called Timothy.

"We have a situation."

"What is it, hon?"

"Can you come over?"

"I'll be right there."

I went downstairs and waited for him. Sirens overlapped in eerie harmonies in the distance as they had since minutes after the earthquake. Timothy pulled up just as I was thinking that they sounded like cats in heat.

"Looks like it survived," Timothy said, nodding toward the duplex.

"It did. Yours?"

"It's fine. A few broken vases, nothing major." He cocked his head, a look of concern on his face, and sat down on the low wall next to me. "What's up? Are you okay?"

I closed my eyes. Deep breath. "It's over. The whole marriage thing, it's over. I'm out."

The words hung there for a minute.

"Does Rafael know yet?"

"No. But I'm going to talk to him. Soon."

"What made you finally decide to call it quits? Did something happen?"

"No, nothing in particular, but—"

Simon's door opened then, and he stepped onto the porch. We visited for a while, and when he went back inside, I was met with Timothy's eyebrow.

"What?"

"Oh, don't 'what' me, missy. You and Simon is what."

I opened my mouth to argue but closed it just as fast. And smiled in confession.

"Spill it. What's going on?"

"There's nothing going on," I said. Timothy just stared at me. "No—he's not why I'm leaving Rafael. Nothing's happened . . . yet. It might, though. I mean, it could. It totally could."

"So what's the connection, then, if you're not running away with Simon? Is there one?"

"No." But then I thought about it. Of course there was. "Yes. Simon woke me up. He has shown me that there are creative, sensitive men who aren't gay, no offense; that there are sexy men who aren't swine; and that there are steady men who aren't boring. He's the best of you, James, and Rafael all rolled into one." I laughed. "And I keep thinking back to what Hap said, about life being too short. Well, Simon . . . enlightened me? Reminded me? Life is too short to settle for good enough, when amazing might be out there somewhere."

"Or right in front of your very eyes," Timothy added.

"Or right in your very downstairs."

"And hello? Can you say sparks, boys and girls? Could there be more energy between the two of you? I could practically see it with my naked eyes."

So could I—I could see it; I could feel it; I could hear it. It sounded like the hum electric wires make when it rains after a long dry spell and felt like sparklers white-hot against a backyard sky, jumping out to poke my skin with dots of fire that tickled instead of burned. It was like my inner hearing aid was cranked all the way up and I was hearing what happens when flint rubs against flint in midair, in that space between two people that, at a certain point, is a very alive, very filled space, not to be taken lightly and not to be ignored, though some people miss it entirely. But not me. There were times that it seemed it was the only thing in the room, times that it filled my head with its crackles, times that it was so real I squinted to see what it looked like. I imagined it as hot and sudden as the Mojave lightning bolts Ansel Adams had lassoed in his desert photographs, only smaller, and much brighter.

I told myself we were just taking some pictures, but it was during the time between when I had recognized my crush on Simon but had not yet talked to Rafael. Marital purgatory. There was no "just"—everything Simon and I did in those days held an undercurrent, an unspoken want. The nights we swam together were charged with such electricity that I was afraid to be near water, let alone submerged in it, let alone with him so close to me and with both of us wet, almost naked, breathing hard, floating, diving, closing our eyes and going under.

"Let's try one with you in the sheet." He handed me a white sheet that he often used as a backdrop, and then he hummed off to his darkroom. I undressed, and he came back in after I had figured out how to wear it so my back was bare but my front was covered. I sat very still and listened to him adjust the lights and fire off a few shots; then he took the camera off the tripod and began to walk around, finding the angles he wanted. There were a few moments when he moved my shoulder or tipped my chin and I shivered, but I played it off and said it was because I was cold. I didn't notice that the studio lights were so hot he was sweating.

We tried a pose with me lying on my stomach on the bench with the sheet draped over my hips and my arms tucked in close to my ribs to cover the sides of my breasts, but then I raised up a little bit while he was still behind me, and even though he couldn't see much, something in his studio changed. It was that tornado-air, that loud silence that whirred with pressure and static electricity and stray thoughts that danced in circles like funnel clouds. I held still and heard him take a single photograph; then his arm slowly dropped to his side, and he cradled the camera as though he had forgotten about it in that moment. His eyes took the next few shots. I didn't breathe. I didn't dare turn around, either, not until the moment broke and he turned away, looking for his light meter. I swiveled to sit up, clutching the sheet around me the way the swimming-lesson girls at the pool hold their towels, tight against their tiny, cold, wet bodies, little chins quivering, shifting from one foot to the other. I wasn't quite as vibratory, but just about. I held the sheet as if it could anchor me. *It is cotton percale,* I reminded myself. *Two hundred count. It is not Kevlar.*

"I'm going upstairs to get a pack of smokes. I'll be right back," I said, and I shuffled out the door, holding the yards of white bedding around me. I ran up the stairs holding the sheet up around my knees like a grape stomper and stood in the dining room, catching my breath.

I looked out the window.

"Momma!"

"Darling!" She paused and squinted at me. "Darling, good Lord, what are you wearing? It's so . . . Greek!"

I laughed and told her Simon and I were downstairs taking pictures.

"Pictures! I love taking pictures! You think our little shutterbug would want to take a few of me? Someone certainly should!"

She was right. She looked like a peacock, all teal and feathers, with her smooth chest thrust out and arrogant. Her dress was silk organza in a pale aquamarine, with an aura of sheer fabric floating around it that sparkled iridescent with beads and sequins, making her ripple when she moved, like a starlit waterfall, and it was trimmed with deep green feathers, the blue-green of Timothy's satin Hong Kong pajamas. Her shoes somehow matched the dress—each giant high heel was its own swirling, glittering galaxy, the pearl blue of my grandfather's bowling ball or the Earth as seen from space. Her eyelids looked like sapphires. Her wig was a blond Marilyn.

"You're absolutely right. Come over. I'll meet you on the porch."

I ran downstairs and waited in my sheet, my very Greek sheet, watching her strut the thirty feet of sidewalk. She was a parade float all by herself.

I pushed his door open. "Simon!" I called. "We have a special guest!"

He came from his studio and stopped at the sight of this giant drag queen filling his doorway, this beautiful drag queen with her hand linked in my elbow, me looking like a very small pile of laundry next to her.

"Simon, meet Momma. Momma, Simon." I smiled. They had never met formally, I was the one who had the view to her apartment. He had heard me talk about her, but now she stood taking up half his living room as I asked if we could take some pictures of her. He'd love to, he said. He smiled wide. And switched to color film.

She was almost too much for the studio to contain.

Simon snapped shot after shot, saying "yes" and "more" and laughing with pure delight. I sat on a stool by the door and watched, hypnotized by her flashing color, the delicate dancer's grace of her movements—tons of grace, despite the fact that she was bigger than Simon and me put together—as she posed and preened and he filled two rolls with her wondrous blue landscape.

And as suddenly as she had appeared, she left. She was expected at a nightclub in Long Beach, and she'd better hustle, traffic was a bitch this time of the month, she said; then she laughed again, moving through the house and out into the night. She was like our very own moon, all pale shimmer under the streetlights.

We watched her from the living room as she folded herself into her car. I realized that I was still in the sheet. I had become used to holding it to my chest and feeling it trail behind me, trailing like little girls playing dress-up and I was the bride. I asked Simon for a cigarette.

"Sure," he said, pulling out two. I watched the way his lips clamped the tan paper gently as he lit them both and let one out while keeping the other in. I watched his hands in the fading light, the way they moved like a movie star's hands.

"Didn't you get yours?"

"My what?"

"Smokes. Isn't that why you went upstairs?"

"Huh? Oh yeah!" *No,* I wanted to say, *I went upstairs because the energy between us was freaking me out and I didn't want to accidentally run over and kiss you, at least I don't think I do, at least not now, not yet, so I ran home and came back with a large blue drag queen to distract us, ta-da!*

Instead I told him that I forgot about the cigs once I saw Momma and ran back downstairs before I remembered why I'd gone upstairs in the first place. I smiled weakly.

"You can take your sheet off."

It took me a second to realize that he just meant I could go ahead and change back into my clothes.

I went into his studio to get dressed and thought about the way you can still see the misspelled words you've typed even after you go over them with the corrector ribbon, the white indents on white paper, so small, invisible if you aren't paying attention, but so clear and obvious if you are. I knew this room would look no different to Rafael or to Momma, maybe not even to Timothy, but to me—and, I wondered, to Simon?—it was not the same room it had been this morning. Because typed in white corrector ribbon on white plaster were tiny words like hieroglyphs in the shapes of eyes and hands and hearts and a camera and nervous laughter, tiny words that were either invisible or obvious, depending on how intently one looked at them.

I walked back into the living room, said good night to Simon, and went upstairs. I curled up in the chair in the library but couldn't concentrate on the book I was reading. The words looked like ants marching in neat rows, little ants marching away from me, teasing me. I got up and went to bed, thinking about the way Simon had molded me into new positions, turning my head, my jaw, the way his hand cupped my shoulder and felt warm and firm and made me want to let the sheet drop off to swim around me on the floor like a puddle.

But I felt silly with my thoughts. I knew he wasn't down there thinking the same things. He was threading film into spools and dunking them in chemicals, flipping switches and spilling bright light onto emerging images, clipping some to a wire above his sink, stirring others in dishpans like fabric in dye vats. That night I dreamed of the sound of the shutter and the feel of Simon's hands, the drape of the sheet and my body so vulnerable and electric beneath, the smell of the bleachy chemicals and the peal of Momma's laugh. All of these things flashed behind my closed lids as my husband slid into bed next to me.

A few nights later, Simon called. "You have got to come down here."

"What's up?"

"I have something to show you. The pictures. From the other day."

"I'll be right down."

Simon met me at the door and we sat down on the couch. I could feel my heart pounding too hard for my chest, which I told myself was just from running down the stairs too fast. Shouldn't take them two at a time.

He began handing me pictures, first the ones of Momma. In one, her hands were on her hips, her giant manicured hands with the costume-jewelry rings, and her elbows stuck way out, her broad shoulders angled, her hips tipped forward. She was smiling a wild snarl of a smile, her teeth a perfect row of Chiclets, her lips a glossy wet red, her eyes with the whites showing on the top. The color was so brilliant and the focus so sharp that it almost looked 3-D.

I laughed. "That's fabulous. Can I have it?"

"Sure. Do you want to see the other one I enlarged for you?"

He handed it over quietly, gently.

It took a few seconds to realize it was a photograph of me, of my back. The sheet was gathered forward, exposing first a long curve of spine and then the place where my waist narrowed and my hips flared out. The tones were pewter and platinum and a deep graphite black. It was France and Munich and dark hotel rooms and the 1930s.

I looked up at him. He was waiting patiently, watching me. He pressed his lips together and the corners turned upward to a slight smile.

"You like it," he said. It wasn't a question.

"It's amazing. How did you . . . ?"

He started talking about lighting and positioning and angles and infrared film, and then he touched my shoulder the way he had that day and said, "See, just that slight movement changes this whole line here. . . ." He ran his index finger down my back.

I shuddered. I sat bolt-upright fast because of all the chills and closed my eyes. I inhaled sharply on the way up and held it, I held my breath and realized I was now sitting next to him straight as a board with my eyes closed, quivering.

I opened my eyes very slowly.

He was looking at me.

My mouth moved a little, but I couldn't speak. I finally breathed. Then I stammered, "I . . . sorry, it . . . just, when. I mean, you . . . you know—"

He continued looking at me, kindly, tenderly, the way you would a crazy person or a stuttering child, and I said I had to go. Now.

I took the photographs and headed for the door. He stood up and followed me.

"Delia!"

I couldn't answer.

"Delia, what is it?"

I looked up at him. We weren't even a foot apart, closer than we usually stand. I was wishing that he could read my mind so I wouldn't have to say it. I stared at him hard, hoping my thoughts were reaching him. I tried to will them out of my pores.

"What's the matter?" He reached down and grabbed my hands.

I twisted out of them. "It's *that*." I pointed at his hands with my eyes. I couldn't believe I was saying it, but it came out in a river of words, fast and unbroken. "It's that being around you lately . . . it feels different than it used to and it scares me and I didn't want to say anything and . . . when you touch me I . . . just feel so—*God!*—forget it, I've said too much, and I'll probably never be able to look at you again, and you know what, I'm going to go now; can you please move?" I turned away from him and faced the still-closed door. My breath came fast and shallow.

Just as my hand touched the doorknob he said, "Me, too."

I turned around, shocked. My eyes widened, then narrowed. "Really?"

"Well, yeah."

"For how long?"

He looked down. "A while. A month, a few months, I don't know. You couldn't tell?"

"Not at all. I just thought we were friends."

"We are."

"You're serious?"

"Yeah."

"So what do we do?" I asked him.

"I don't know."

"You're my landlord."

"I know."

"I'm married."

"I know."

"I may as well not be."

"I know."

Not three feet away, on the other side of the door, we heard Rafael coming home, his tired walk, the rattly clink of his wad of keys. Simon and I both looked at the door. We held our breath; we didn't move. I put a finger to my lips, thinking, *Let's let him go home; let's just forget about him. Forever.* We listened as his work boots first clomped up the stairs and then zigzagged back and forth overhead. He was probably looking for the remote, since I had taken to hiding it just for my own personal amusement, just to watch him walk around with sweat beads on his forehead, frantic that his magic wand had vanished.

"What about him?" Simon asked.

I sighed. "I had already made up my mind to leave him, but I hadn't told him yet." I realized that sounded like a line. I rubbed my head. "It's very complicated."

"Yes."

"So what do we do?" I asked.

"I have no idea. Sleep on it, and we'll talk in the morning?"

"Okay," I said. I imagined I wouldn't sleep.

"So good night then."

"Good night."

We both stood by the door, not moving. Nobody even reached for the doorknob. I'm still not sure who leaned forward first, because it all happened so fast, but somehow, we kissed, a small perfect meeting of eyes and then lips, at first gentle, then prolonged, intense, and I felt my knees start to give. I put my forehead on his chest because I needed to lean on something, and I felt his heart slamming away as fast as my own. I touched it through his shirt and looked back up at him. We kissed again, longer this time, with his hands under my elbows, then sliding to grip my hands and push us apart. We were both shaking.

His voice was almost a whisper. "You'd better go."

"Yeah. I'd better."

But I didn't. We stood there for another ten minutes with me trying to leave and us having just one more kiss, and one more kiss, and another, until finally I found the doorknob with a sweaty palm and stepped outside.

"Okay, bye then," I said.

"Bye. See you in the morning?"

The morning. Coffee. More kisses? "Of course. See you in the morning."

Simon closed his door, and I turned and opened ours, quietly, still shaking, hoping Rafael was already asleep and not wanting to wake him if he was. Would he know? Of course not. I tiptoed up, pleased to see the lights in our bedroom off and his heaving shape under the blankets.

I couldn't sleep right away. I sat alone in the dark at the dining room table, replaying the conversation, the kiss, all the kisses, looking at the photograph Simon took of me, marveling at this bizarre turn of events. I wondered if he was awake, too, sitting underneath me, as anxious, as guilty, as excited, smoking at his dining room table in the dark. I wanted to tap the floor to see if he would reply with his broomstick, if we could flirt in Morse code, if I could lie down naked on the floor and he could float to his ceiling and we could be together through the beams and lathing and pink insulation. In the other room, Rafael snored.

Simon was grinding coffee beans when I went downstairs the next morning. I walked in his open front door and stood to the side of the kitchen doorway and watched him, his face, his shoulders, the length of his body. His arms. I swallowed as he looked up. He let the machine stop and looked at me for a long second.

"Good morning," he said, almost hesitantly, almost a question, and went back to the coffee, tamping it into the double-shot basket, turning the handle, flipping the switch. The espresso came out like oil, slow and dark. The smell was intoxicating. He steamed the milk and ladled some into each of the two clear glass mugs. He turned and held one out to me.

It was the same simple gesture as every morning, but on that day I wondered if it was like a white flag, severance pay, a promise ring—or if it was still just a cup of fancy coffee. I wondered if I had broken some part of our lease agreement, some no-kissing-the-landlord clause. We walked to his dining room table and sat down, and I swirled my espresso and lit a cigarette.

"Did you talk to him last night?"

"He was asleep."

But that wasn't the only reason I hadn't talked to him. I was scared, and I felt guilty—aside from the original James-guilt, I now had Simon-guilt, but more than that, I was ashamed for not feeling worse about my actions than I did and I was ashamed for my growing excitement at the prospect of a Rafael-free life.

That night I told Rafael that I had been neither happy nor honest with him lately, that I'd been trying to hang in there, trying to keep up appearances, but I couldn't do it anymore.

"I thought things were better since we moved."

"Well, no," I said, thinking that things were certainly more interesting but not "better" in the way he meant it. "I mean, it's better than living across the street. I love this place. But it hasn't helped our marriage, at least not for me."

He looked back at me, a stranger's face.

I wished for the Rafael he'd been when we first met, the open, curious one, the one I took to meet my parents, the boy with the shiny black hair and shiny black eyes, amethyst pendant shining at the base of his throat like a good-luck charm as he struggled back from living on the streets. I wished for the newly proud Rafael who held my hand and led me to the front door of his very own apartment. The one who lowered himself to one bony brown knee and offered me a single diamond on a band of gold, eyes filled to overflowing with how much he loved me, proposing in English, then whispering to me in Spanish, later, in bed. I wished for the Rafael who was my buddy. But he was gone.

The man who faced me was heavier, both physically and otherwise. He was like those flowers that close up in the sun, opening only in the dark. His eyes were permanently glazed now, and he seemed to always stare at the television, even when it was off. He was stuck, imploding, alone in his world, checking in boxes of light fixtures, flipping channels, eating junk food.

I took a deep breath. "We need to separate."

His eyes closed; then he looked up. At first I thought he hadn't heard me. He sighed. "Okay."

"Excuse me?"

"Okay. If that's what you want."

I was amazed. *Okay,* he had said. "Okay? That's your fucking answer? Do you even want to talk about it?"

"It sounds like you've made up your mind. I know how you get when you make up your mind." He smiled sadly. "I'm gonna go to bed now."

And he got up and walked away.

I would have had a million questions; I would have been yelling and crying. But him? He was going to go put his head down and get some shut-eye. Amazing. I took the phone out to the deck and called Timothy. We talked until well after midnight, and afterward I curled up in the big chair in the library and opened my AA book and read the passage on acceptance, underlining this sentence: *When I stopped living in the problem and began living in the answer, the problem went away.* I dozed off reading it over and over like a mantra and was awakened five hours later by the light and a raging headache. I had slept sitting up, with my head flopped down to my chest and my contact lenses in. The book had fallen to the floor and lay at my feet fanned and wrinkled, facedown. I went into the bathroom, took out my contacts, brushed my teeth, then got in the shower. It felt like jet lag, the dry itchy eyes and the need for hot water and steam and caffeine. In the shower, I thought of how Rafael had so lamely given up. Had done nothing, not one thing, hadn't stood up for himself, hadn't even offered an argument. Nothing. In effect: *Yes, dear.* Tail between his legs.

I got out of the shower, dressed, and woke him up. We had two hours until we had to be at work and I wanted some answers, something. A discussion, a plan, a fight, anything. I sat down at the foot of the bed and shook his ankle. "Wake up."

He opened his eyes, groggy and slow, and looked at my very tucked-in side of the bed. "What?"

"We're going to talk is what. You went to bed last night, instead of talking. So now, we're talking."

"About what?"

"About what? About us. About our marriage. Or lack thereof. Ring a bell? Did you think I was just having PMS? Making small talk? Come on; get up."

"I can talk from here."

I glared at him and walked out, went into the kitchen and made some coffee, poured two cups, and walked into the living room. When I got there he was sitting on the edge of the couch with his forearms on his knees and his head hanging. I sat down next to him.

He looked up.

"So," I started, trying to be gentle even though my patience was waning. "It's over."

"Yeah, I guess it is."

All I wanted was for him to react to me, something with some life to it. He was like a wet rag, a limp handshake. I took a deep breath and counted to ten. I could feel my fingers wanting to reach out to grab him and shake him. I sat on my hands just in case. "Can you give me some kind of reaction? Anything? Are you going to even ask if we should try marriage counseling?" I would have been disappointed if he had said yes.

"You can try marriage counseling," he offered.

Tears burned behind my eyes, but they were tears of frustration and anger, not hurt. "I can? By myself? Fuck you."

I picked up my cup, poured the now-lukewarm coffee down my throat in one shot, and put it back down on the table, loud but not quite hard enough to break the glass. He watched me but said nothing.

I stood up and walked into the bathroom. I stood in front of the sink. My eyes were red, and my hands shook with rage and adrenaline. I cranked the hot knob as far as it would go, the water spattering out onto the tile. I didn't care; I soaked my face in it, letting it wet my hairline like blood from a skull injury. I turned the water off and looked in the mirror. I could see the fight blazing in my eyes. My resentment, having fermented this long, was overwhelming.

Then the thought came, with a lovely and sudden relief. It didn't matter if he understood, if we talked about it, if he gave me a reaction. None of it mattered anymore. The word *divorce* felt perfect as I said it to myself. I walked back into the living room.

"I'd like you to move out," I told him. "I'm going to file for divorce. I'm sorry."

He didn't utter a word then, not a single sound. But as I walked to the car, I heard a strange howl coming from inside. He was crying. Finally, a show of emotion. Unfortunately, it was too little too late and too easy to walk away from.

When I told my parents over lunch the next Saturday, they were not surprised, especially not my mom, after the conversation we'd had.

"Honey, we only want you to be happy," she said, laying her hand on top of mine. "You haven't seemed happy with him for a long time. You'd lost your sparkle. And you know what? I think it's back already. She's glowing, isn't she?" She turned to my dad.

"I just hope he doesn't think he's going to stick you with all the bills," he said, upbeat as usual. "Do you have a good lawyer? Are you going to be all right financially?"

"I'll be fine."

"Well, if you need any help, you just let us know."

"I won't need anything," I said, and it was true—I had everything I needed.

I found myself saying this line from the AA book a lot, either aloud or in my head: *Unless I accept life completely on life's terms, I cannot be happy.* And I prayed for patience and integrity—because although one minor infraction had already been committed, I wanted to stop there. So in those long weeks between the night of the kiss and when Rafael moved out, Simon and I exchanged a lot of longing glances—glances that literally buckled my knees and set the hair on my neck on end—but no more kisses. Not a single one. We waited, like virgins, like a young couple on an old-fashioned wedding day, discovering what most people nowadays never learn: there is something incredibly erotic about the waiting, the dance, the anticipation, the denial, the holding back.

I stayed at Timothy's house the weekend Rafael moved out. I couldn't imagine anywhere safer than that building, for those two days. We went to the art museum and for a long drive up the coast, and we stayed up late doing runes and tarot and the I Ching. We asked the I Ching about my decision, and it agreed. We asked the tarot deck about my future, and it looked bright. We asked the runes about Rafael, and they said run away as fast and as far as you can, except in more spiritual terms.

Timothy and I talked about what it would be like living on my own. I was scared. I had never done this before. I had gone straight from my parents' house to living with Rafael, and now, I told Timothy, I was alone. He reminded me that I'd never be alone as long as he was around.

We were eating miniature Hostess doughnuts and getting powdered sugar all over his Indian blanket.

"What do you think will happen to Rafael?" I asked him.

"Good question. I'm sure you think he'll self-destruct, but you never know. He might use this as a turning point, a catalyst for change."

"Does that sound at all like Rafael to you? To use this as a catalyst for change?"

"Well, no. But you know me, hon: I like to be surprised."

"I know you do. But that's because you're gullible."

"It's not gullible. It's hopeful."

"Well, whatever it is, you have more of it than I do. Anyway, you're right. I do think he'll self-destruct. One can only watch so much cable. Or order so much pizza."

"He could change, though."

"Yeah, right, him and Zodiac both."

Timothy frowned at me. "Hey, that's not nice . . . she's doing much better. Did I tell you she left that guy and got a real job?"

"Which guy? Never mind. What job?"

"She's bussing tables at Mel's Diner out in Van Nuys."

"Great. Who's watching Elijah?"

"The lady in the next apartment. Zodiac puts him to bed and works from nine to two, so he doesn't even know she's gone. And it's good money."

"He doesn't know? Bullshit, he doesn't know. Oh, forget it. I'm hungry."

Timothy looked at his watch. It was almost eleven. Plus, we'd had all those miniature doughnuts. "You're joking."

"Sweet Lady Jane's is still open." I smiled.

We sped his Volvo the half mile to the bakery, parked, dashed inside, and let the sugary scent seduce us for a minute before we decided on two lemon bars, a chocolate-pecan torte, and a napoleon; then we sped back to his house and climbed back onto his bed with our take.

We talked until two, and then Timothy stood and said we should get some sleep, that we had big plans in the morning.

And what big plans they were. The House of Blues Sunday Morning Gospel Brunch. We sat up in the balcony and ate fruit-smothered waffles, griddle cakes, flannel hash, and buttered grits, followed by giant sticky buns. On the stage below us, twenty-five big-voiced black women belted it out, and the room clapped and sang and stomped along with them, and Timothy and I got up out of our seats, clapping and swaying, too, laughing, full of food and joy and song, full of the moment and all the people around us, of the soloist's big wide voice, her dark heavy arms, her gospel version of "Take Me to the River."

On the way back to the duplex, the now-mine apartment, Timothy and I sang it together, *washing me down, washing me,* and I felt like we were on a cliff head, me peering over into the unknown, him behind me holding my shirttail.

I walked up the staircase, lingering again on the wood banister as I had that first night, and found the house exactly as I had expected to find it, virtually empty. I had told Rafael to take the television, the couch, and every single electronic toy he had accumulated: the Nintendo games, the stereo, the camcorder. I told him to leave the wedding china, just because I liked the way that sounded: final. He took the towels and pots and Tupperware; I got the kilim rug. In other words, he got the useful stuff; I got the beautiful stuff. The place was stripped to the bone except for my few loved possessions, but it was wonderful to me. It was quiet. No infomercials yelling, no game shows dinging, no movies erupting in gunshots and profanity beneath Timothy's painting. The divorce proceedings were completely uneventful. Rafael and I split our small savings and the credit-card debt down the middle. It all seemed even, except the part where Rafael was alone and I drifted down the back stairs late that first night, my hair still damp from the bath, my skin powdered and scented, my feet bare, into Simon's open back door, the one he was leaving open just for me, the one we closed immediately after I stepped in.

18

The news of the separation made its way around AA quickly, as I talked openly about my newfound independence. Other young people asked me about what it was like to live on my own, and some older people, too. It wasn't long before James called to ask if I'd speak at the morning meeting. My story would be inspiring, he said.

"Inspiring how? I'm twenty-four and getting divorced—that's what you call inspiring?"

"You're twenty-four and getting divorced without having to get drunk over it. That's inspiring. You work at one of the best hospitals in the state, the very same one at which you were a patient, you've been clean and sober seven years this month, and you're nothing like you were when you got here. Trust me; I remember." I could tell he was smiling. "You're a goddamn miracle. And you're speaking tomorrow morning."

I started my talk by reading this passage:

" *'We are going to know a new freedom and a new happiness. We will not regret the past nor wish to shut the door on it. We will comprehend the word serenity and we will know peace. No matter how far down the scale we have gone, we will see how our experience can benefit others. That feeling of uselessness and self-pity will disappear. We will lose interest in selfish things and gain interest in our fellows. Self-seeking will slip away. Our whole attitude and outlook upon life will change. Fear of people and of economic insecurity will leave us. We will intuitively know how to handle situations which used to baffle us. We will suddenly realize that God is doing for us what we could not do for ourselves.'* "

These were called "The Promises," and I'll be damned if every single one of them hadn't come true for me. My fear was gone. It had been replaced with faith. I told the meeting that morning that after going through an abortion, my best friend being diagnosed with HIV, the death of my sponsor, and now being in the middle of a divorce and starting a new relationship with a "normie"—that's what we called the nonaddicts, the normal people—and going through those things sober, there was nothing I couldn't handle. That there was no curveball life could throw me. AA had taught me not only how to catch them but also how to throw them back.

I was in my kitchen late one night when Momma appeared across the way looking like an astronaut. Her dress was silver lamé; her necklace was made of oversize ball bearings; her earrings were bright hubcap disks of metal. Everything about her was shiny chrome. She looked like a cross between an Airstream trailer and Carmen Miranda, like platinum on display in the giant picture window.

I wanted everything to freeze, it was finally where I wanted it, and I whispered to my empty dining room, "Nobody move." Timothy was healthy, my dad was still sober, I had good friends, I was in love, my work as a counselor was so rewarding, but above all of that, I had a drag queen who strutted through my life, always at just the right time, teaching me that there is glitter in the darkness if only you remember to look in the right places.

I began to spend nearly every night in Simon's half of the duplex, sometimes only going up to my half to check messages, swap clothes, get a book, and go back down. My fridge was empty, my bathroom stuff was in his cabinet, and my bed remained made. My address may still have been that of the upstairs apartment, but that was only a technicality, a post office detail that had absolutely nothing to do with where I really lived. Which was why the discussions began to take place, discussions that at first were only theoretical musings about living together but eventually became real questions: Which half would we live in? What would we do with the other half? We didn't want tenants. Ultimately, we decided the duplex was storing too much energy, too much Rafael, to be a viable choice for the two of us to begin our cohabitation with the honor that it deserved, so we decided to just move out altogether.

Within days of a *For Sale* sign being placed in front of the duplex, we found ourselves at the beginning of a ninety-day escrow. As the real-estate agent pulled away with our future in her attaché case, I leaned against the old pink stucco and looked at Simon. I wondered what would happen to me if I really did leave Los Angeles. Who would I be if I wasn't contained by the boundaries of the Pacific to the west and the ghettos to the east? Who would I be far from my family, my friends, everyone who has seen all the scary, triumphant, awkward moments I experienced as I grew from infant to woman in this phony, flashy, selfish city? Simon turned to me, and I looked away as if I had been caught staring, which I had been.

"What are you thinking about?" he asked me.

I looked up at the cement-colored sky. "That we could go anywhere. That we don't have to stay in West Hollywood, or even Los Angeles. Or even California."

The words sounded bizarre to me. I had always assumed that I needed the voice of this city to echo my own, that I required her brown hills and *E. coli* taco stands and beautiful plastic people to define me, that I was woven so deeply into her old bridges and five-lane highways and the art deco shapes of the burned-down Pan Pacific Theatre that it would be a betrayal to ever leave. But maybe I had been wrong. Maybe it was time to go.

Joan had told me a story once about some elephants in captivity somewhere, how as babies they were put into ankle cuffs with chains that were attached to spikes driven into the ground, which they couldn't pull out. They stopped trying within their first years, because it was frustrating and pointless, so they grew up believing the spikes were stronger than they were. Apparently it never occurred to them to try again later when they were giant adult elephants perfectly capable of yanking the spikes out without even exerting much effort and running free into the jungle, so they wound up staying put next to these tiny little spikes that were now ridiculously weak in comparison to their powerful legs. Joan said we were like that, too. She said we humans often remained bound by old beliefs that had no real power aside from that which we placed upon them. She said our fears were the little tiny spikes we were still seeing from the vantage point of the baby elephants, but now, my darling, she had told me, now we were mighty beasts who could uproot the spike any old time we were ready.

But I had stayed put, loyal to my hometown. Indigenous. Because I had never stopped to challenge myself to leave. Because I worshipped it like I would an abusive lover, needing its approval, loving it even as it burst into flames and cracked wide open along its fault lines, as it slid muddy into the ocean and rioted and shot at tourists and, as its final insult, ignored me, its own offspring.

But now I was big enough. I could run. I could be a stampede all by myself, trumpeting off into the jungle on thick gray legs with a pair of sharp white tusks; I could swat my tail at flies and spew water in an arc high over a lagoon and leave my spike lying small and silver in an impotent master's backyard if I wanted to.

With that in mind, Simon and I ignored the *LA Weekly* on the table between us at Canter's Deli. It was open to the rentals page, yet we talked as if we were spinning a globe with one finger extended, bouncing, trailing along its surface, waiting for it to stop so we could shout out potential destinations.

"La Paz?"

"Mexico? No way."

"I guess not. What about Boston?"

"Napa."

"Hmm."

Then we'd glance at the *Weekly* and scan Houses for Rent in the area bordered by Third, Sunset, Robertson, and Highland. Those were streets we knew. We didn't know what they would call their streets in Napa or La Paz.

But, we reminded each other, that was exactly the point. We were challenging each other; we were growing; we were reaching beyond the safe borders of those Los Angeles streets and into the world; we were taking a risk and taking it together, proving our love for each other and our strength as humans to go beyond our comfort zone. Right, okay. Back to the globe.

"Look for a sign," I said.

Our actor/waiter appeared then to take our order. His name tag read: *Dallas.* Simon and I saw it at the same time, looked at each other, and smirked.

"No."

"Absolutely not."

So maybe that wasn't the sign we were waiting for, but when we got home and Simon's machine was blinking impatiently with a new message . . . well, there it was, right there, easy as pie. No question about it. I love it when there is no doubt about the next move, when all indicators sweep my hand powerless as if it were on a big Ouija board, when my arm is pulled nearly out of its socket by the force and the clarity of truth and fate and there's no room for anything even remotely resembling self-doubt or hesitation.

"Hi, Simon, this is Neil Perkins from the U. Call me when you have a minute. You have my number here in Seattle. I'll be in the office till late tonight."

The machine beeped and clicked and we looked at each other.

"Well, there you go."

"You think so?"

"I don't know. Call him."

While Simon dialed, I lit a cigarette. He motioned for me to light him one as he listened with creased brow, and I did. Then I went into the other room, walked to the window, and looked up. For some reason I thought seeing Momma would answer the questions swirling in my head, like, Were we going to be moving to a city I had never even visited? Would I really be okay out of my birthright area code? Or would I hit the California-Oregon border and evaporate? Would the rain erode me, rust me—or would it make me flourish, turning my dry brown leaves to a rich green? What about AA up there? What was it like? It was my lifeline, and it would no doubt be different from West Hollywood AA. What if it was like that convention in Yosemite? That would simply not do. I craned my neck to see if I could catch a glimpse of gold lamé, but from down here all I could see was the cottage-cheese ceiling and one floor lamp, neither of which told me a thing, neither of which had any of whatever it was that Momma kept stored like a magic trick in the tip of her perfectly painted pinkie toenail.

I was still looking when Simon came to find me. He was wringing his hands and he was smiling, but with his eyebrows lifted up in the center, like James Dean's, like apostrophes, hovering. Worried and excited all at once.

"Well?"

"Neil offered me a position as head of the University of Washington photo department. You want to move to Seattle?"

I smiled. What a question. And what a difference, as the song goes, a day makes. Who was I now, this person saying yes? It felt crazy at first, impulsive and whimsical, but then completely logical. *Why, of course.* Of course we would move to Seattle. I threw off one garment and pulled the next over my head. I was saying yes, I would love to live under the frozen lights of stars I had yet to learn the names of, yes, I would toss everything I own onto a truck and migrate north with him like whales in summertime, yes, I would leave them all: my friends, my family, my streets, and my hundred million grains of sand that lay outside my childhood home begging me to hold them once more, to watch their crystalline grit slide weightless through the spaces between my fingers. I would leave the beachglass and cold seaweed pods and rusty cans and laughing seagulls of the Santa Monica Bay to roam upward on the map to a region called Puget Sound. A visual named for an audial. Was I crazy or courageous? What was the other thing Joan had told me? That breakdowns and breakthroughs often look the same? As I laughed and said yes through my fat, round teardrops, I finally understood what she had meant.

Later that afternoon, I sat in the chair by the window and picked up the phone.

"Mom?" I started to cry. Then laugh. Crying and laughing at the same time, again.

"Honey? Are you okay?"

"Yeah." My throat tightened as I tried to say, *We're moving to Seattle.* The words didn't want to come out. They held on to the insides of my teeth, kicking, being dragged out unwillingly like agoraphobics on field trip day. Excited as I was to be going on an adventure, happy to be with Simon, looking forward to making a new home in a new place, deep down I was ripped in two to be leaving. I wondered if on moving day I would hold on as tight as those words did coming out of my mouth, if I would leave fingernail marks that would recede out of Los Angeles County like the wide freeway that shrank and narrowed to its vanishing point as it sped out to the horizon.

Through tears and laughter, mine and hers, I finally got the story told and then excused myself so she could talk to my dad and they could digest the news and I could call Timothy. As we talked about living beyond walking distance from each other, I started a crying jag that didn't stop until he hung up and appeared at my doorstep five minutes later.

"Oh, hon," he said as I ran downstairs and into his arms.

We went out and sat on the back deck, looking through the trees at the streetlights with their dewy halos and the grid of lights that spread so far out to the horizon that they eventually blended up with the stars. I already felt the separation, and I wondered if his absence would itch the way Gabriel's had, that same amputee's-missing-limb itch that no one ever really gets used to. You keep sticking your tongue in the hole where the tooth was, and though the voice that at first screams, *Where's the tooth?* gets quieter and quieter, it never stops asking the question.

James and I met at DuPar's the week before I left. I wondered what we looked like to the other diners, if we looked like a first date, like siblings, like coworkers, like newlyweds or cousins or friends. There was no way anyone could guess our history, could tell by looking at us what it had taken for us to get to the point where we could just sit here like friends and laugh as he dabbed meringue onto my nose.

I thought about the growing up we had done together. The growing up that most people do intuitively, but since we had apparently missed receiving the Instruction Book of Life, we were left to figure out on our own—on our own but with the help of a mutt-family of old junkies, elegant alcoholics, crack whores, therapists, drag queens, and a God we hadn't planned on ever believing in until we realized that it wasn't us doing this growing all by ourselves, it wasn't us laying so flawlessly the mosaic of our lives, and it wasn't us who mustered the strength to go through all of it—the good, the bad, and the ugly, as it were—and not drink. We had not autonomously kept ourselves sober all these years. Healing us addicts took a group effort. And James and I, mad physical attraction or no, had been a part of each other's group effort.

I thought of mentioning this to him, but I didn't. He knew. He knew, and I'd have bet he was having the same thoughts, that he was in awe at his own changes and his own mosaic, at the way he was able to sit here with a woman he had seen grow from a girl, a girl who had invaded and haunted his last years as a teenager and now sat across from him as a friend. He was thinking about this moment and not the rest of it. Not about the nights in his bedroom or car, not about the driving with the headlights off nor what a perfect metaphor that was for who we were, then.

We walked slowly through the Farmers Market, me already growing nostalgic for my old-LA heritage, wanting to hold on to the market-smells of coffee and dried fruit and cinnamon doughnuts as long as I could, wanting to remember the view up Fairfax to the Hollywood Hills, crystal-clear and with a sky the color of his eyes and a crisp wind that reminded me of the way his wool coat had snapped at his calves in Jan's parking lot that night so long ago. We walked to our cars and promised to keep in touch. I gave him my new address, the one with the street that was a number instead of a word and the zip code that looked almost European in its unfamiliarity. He looked at it and folded it in half and stuffed it deep in the pocket of his khakis. I wondered if he would remember it was in there before he threw them in the laundry.

Zodiac had become nearly impossible to track down. She had been embroiled in some sort of court thing, and even though she was supposed to stay put, she tended to lose pagers, get evicted, change jobs. *The courts were trying to take her son,* was all I heard. Even Timothy only talked to her when she really needed something and had run out of people to use. But I wanted to see her before I left, so we met at the Denny's on Sunset, me the only nonmusician, nonstripper in the place, her knowing every person who walked in, every leather-pants-wearing rocker, every waify heroin hooker, every old biker and street kid lit ugly under the flickering greenish fluorescent light.

The sticky fake-wood table between us may well have been a whole ocean. She was fragile but loud, inconsistently put together, a collage of arrogance and ruin. Her front tooth was still broken, after how long? I thought about her trembling in her ice blue sequined thong that night and wondered if she even stripped anymore or had gone into full-time streetwalking.

She said she was happy for me and then told me in her expert voice that I seemed like the type of person who would like living in Seattle. I frowned and she explained, "You know, serious, responsible . . . so not LA." And I thought, *I am more LA than you will ever understand. I am LA. You don't know me.* By *serious* I knew she meant old. By *responsible* she meant boring. She saw me as a goody-goody. And had the gall to look down on me while lying flat on her back in the gutter. While I stayed clean and got a degree and a career and fell in love, she got arrested and pregnant and beaten. I got a life; she got chlamydia. She was burned-out and dirty; I was boring. Fine. I'll take boring.

As we ordered, I knew it would be my treat, and I knew she would take most of it home in a Styrofoam box for Elijah.

"How's court going?"

She rolled her eyes and held up her hand. "They say I'm an unfit mother. Can you believe that shit?"

I didn't answer. I didn't think I was supposed to.

She kept on talking, ranting, calling the social worker a bitch and a whore and worse, and said that the social worker, the state's attorney, a court-appointed child psychologist, and even her own probation officer—"My own PO!" she said in disbelief of his betrayal, her voice rising—wanted to take Elijah away from her. "I mean, damn. Does a boy not belong with his mother?"

She talked with her hands and her neck and her chin, and by the time she was done I was nearly convinced she was right. She could do that.

It was almost one in the morning when we finished talking.

She said, "I'll write you," and we both laughed at that, knowing she wouldn't. We hugged. She felt so scrawny in my arms. I made sure she had the Styrofoam box of leftovers.

"Good luck with Elijah," I said, and we both held up crossed fingers.

She turned and walked east on Sunset, and I watched until she got so far up the street I couldn't see her, until I had to stand on my tiptoes to make out her shape in the night. I turned away before she leaned into the car that was pulling over.

I didn't want to call Rafael at all, but Timothy convinced me to, something about closure: just a phone call, not lunch or an engraved invitation to come over on moving day. "You two were married once," he said, and I rolled my eyes and said, "Don't remind me."

As Rafael's phone rang, I hoped for his machine, but I got him instead.

"Hey," I said. "How have you been?"

"Good, you?"

"Great. Look, I just wanted to tell you," I said, trying to sound as swift and offhand as possible, "that we're moving. To Seattle."

"Who's 'we'?"

Fine. He was going to be weird. Who did he think I meant? Or did he think I was speaking in the royal "we" the way Joan used to? He knew Simon and I were together. I told him to take care and good luck. I had no idea what to say. Good-bye had already been covered.

I went to the Log Cabin meeting the morning before we left, as I did nearly every morning, but on that day I stopped on my way in the door and looked down at the porch, remembering; then I took my usual seat and looked around the room. The faces were ones I had known for almost eight years, some regulars, some strangers, some men, some women, a few still drinking, most not, some toxic, some saintly and spiritual. AA truly was a microcosm of the world. We were all there, all of us.

Before the meeting ended, I raised my hand and talked about my fear of the unknown, my trepidation about Seattle AA, and my gratitude for that meeting having been there to help put me back together. We closed the meeting by everyone holding hands and saying the Serenity Prayer, and I was taken back to the Unit, to that first New Year's Eve, to holding Joan's hands. I wondered which of the three I would need most on my journey: serenity, courage, or wisdom. I guessed courage. Then I remembered the prayer doesn't say *Or* the wisdom to know the difference, it says *And* the wisdom to know the difference, implying that I could ask for all three.

On my last night in LA, Timothy and my parents came over for dinner. We gathered upstairs, since Simon's downstairs had become the resting place for all of our boxes.

Simon and I showed them the picture of the house that the relocation people at UW had found for us. It was a Craftsman bungalow painted the color of putty, with deep plum-colored trim and a porch with a porch swing, and it was near a lake—everything there was near a lake. They told us that there was a gardenlike traffic circle at the corner instead of a stop sign. They said that all the residential intersections up there were like that: no stop signs, just these low-curbed circles with plants inside that you had to slow down for. We laughed at that, aggressive drivers that we were, people after whom the phrase *California Stop* was coined.

"Plants," my dad said, shaking his head like it was the dumbest thing he'd ever heard.

"How many bedrooms does the house have?" My mom asked.

"Two. Plus a loft, which I'll line with books in an attempt to reproduce the library here."

She smirked.

"What? What's that look about?"

She handed the picture back to me. "It'll be the nursery."

"Yeah, right," I said, looking down, embarrassed.

Simon found my feet under the table and nudged them with his. I looked back up. He was smiling at me, and there was a twinkle in his eye, like he was in baby-cahoots with my mom.

"Knock it off, you two," I laughed. But I could picture it. With Rafael I could never, but with Simon I could. And a city where people slow down for a circle of plants might be an all right place to have a baby. At least better than here, where we find them in Dumpsters so often it doesn't even make the evening news anymore.

Timothy stood then and raised his glass of sparkling cider. "To Delia, and Simon, and their new life. To showing the rest of us that it's not just somewhere over the rainbow that dreams really do come true, thank you, Judy Garland. To friendship. To sobriety. To living life to its fullest. To finding true love." He paused. "May the road rise up to meet you and may the wind be always at your back." He looked at Simon. "Take care of her. She's precious cargo."

In the candlelight, my mom's face shone with tears, and I even saw a few in my dad's eyes. Simon blew me a kiss, and I put my hand over my heart. And then we all touched glasses, and the chime of that moment was pure, like angels' harps, like Joan's laughter, like perfection.

The moving truck chugged away the next afternoon, holding in its belly the whole of our belongings, and I stood staring up through the haze at the tall hills that were laden with houses and engraved with streets whose names I would never forget. They rolled off my tongue like a rosary, a chant. Thresher Lane. Apollo Way. Eerie Terrace.

I sighed and walked across the lawn to the front door, the grass itchy and warm and firm against my soles. Bare feet in March. I thought nothing of it. I would think it exotic the following March as I scraped ice off my windshield, and as I scraped I would remember the way I had looked up at the hills while wearing a thin white T-shirt and capri pants and no shoes and was not cold, and the way I was tan and the sun cut through the smog at that magical angle that lit up all the dust and made the city air look both dirty and sparkly at the same time.

19

I dipped the washcloth into the pitcher of ice water, wrung it out, and draped it across Timothy's forehead. I leaned over and studied his face, trying to memorize it. He had finally started to look gaunt, not himself, so I closed my eyes and tried to picture the Timothy I had left behind when I'd moved to Seattle, the one who had made that toast to us, who had shone as pure and bright as the candles on the table. That man was already gone.

I got up and sat in the chair by the Mickey phone. I knew I should call Zodiac, Hap, try to find Matt—like sending up flares, I needed them to know that it was getting close. Instead I dialed my home phone number.

After three rings there was a silence and a scrambling and then Clara's voice, straight into my heart, making it both soar and crumple at the same time: "Hi, Mama!"

"Hi, little pea! How did you know it was me calling?"

Silence again and some shuffling. "Daddy got caller ID."

I laughed. I loved when her toddler voice said grown-up things.

"I miss you so much," I told her. Understatement of the year. Hard to believe I had only been away three weeks.

"I miss you, too, Mama," she said, and she started jabbering away. She was very excited, wanting to tell me everything that had happened since our last phone call, earlier that same day.

The call waiting beeped through, and I asked Clara to hold on. It was James, asking if he could stop by after work, bring Chinese food, hang out. I said yes and clicked back to Clara, who was patiently waiting.

"Mama, when are you coming home?"

"Oh, sweetie, I don't know. Soon, I think." I looked at Timothy. "Can I talk to Daddy?"

Simon got on the phone. "Hey, you. How's it going?"

"Oh, it's . . . going. You know what, I hate to cut this short, but I should get off the phone and clean up a little. An old friend is coming for dinner."

"Oh, fun. Anyone I know?" he asked.

"Um, no. Just an old friend from AA." Not exactly a lie. But Simon knew enough about my history with James that I didn't want to make waves. Not now.

"Okay, well, don't wear Timothy out. I'll talk to you tomorrow."

"Of course. I love you. Give that little goose lots of kisses for me."

"I will. I love you, too."

Timothy woke up. He pushed himself to a sitting position while I turned on the lamp. I sat down next to him. "James called while you were asleep. He's coming over in a little while. With Chinese food."

His face brightened. "Cool. That sounds perfect."

And even though Timothy's breathing sounded horrible and we ate sitting around the bed, it really did seem to perk him up. We sat around afterward, reading our fortunes.

"What does yours say?" James asked me first.

" 'May your wondrous journey be full of happy and friends.' Nice grammar."

"Illiteracy runs rampant. What does yours say?"

Timothy turned his fortune right side up. " 'Good forces will always with you always.' Who wrote these? The blind? The food was good, but Jesus. I'm afraid to ask what yours is."

I watched as James cracked open his cookie with his teeth and took half of it in his mouth, slipping the fortune out of the other half, slowly, with his fingertips.

He laughed. " 'The world at your feet many successes for you has.' Swear to God." He held it up for us to see.

Timothy looked at it. "Well, they do get their point across."

"I'm going to write the company."

"And what, James? Circle the typos and mail them back?"

"Maybe."

Timothy started to laugh, but that kicked off a new coughing fit, this one turning him the deep dark red of cranberry juice, watering his eyes, making him flap his hands from both strain and trying to signal me to get his inhaler. James sat back out of the way as I swooped in with the inhaler and helped get Timothy into a better position. I held him up by the back and chest and steadied him as he pumped the inhaler, his bony rib cage between my palms like a paper lantern. He took a deep breath, then another; then we were quiet for a minute.

"Okay. No more laughing," I said. "It makes you cough too much."

"Listen to you! No more laughing! You forget who you're talking to? I will not give up laughing. Ever. That's why we have these handy little things." He waved the inhaler. "So no, I won't stop. And neither will you. Missy. I didn't ask you to come down here so you could rain on my parade."

"Is that what this is? Your parade?"

"Yes, and I'll be damned if it's going to be all serious. As a matter of fact, we should have been working on floats this whole time, I can't believe we haven't been. Of course, mums are so passé."

I just stared at him and shook my head.

James asked if we ever heard from any of the old gang and who had been over. We began to take roll. Timothy held his fingers out for each one.

"Well," he said, thumb extended, "Zodiac is in New York. She's doing well."

I rolled my eyes, and he stopped.

"What?" he asked.

"Nothing; go on."

"No, you rolled your eyes—I want to hear it."

"Well, we have very different definitions of *fine,* you and I. I want her to fly out here so I can see for myself how well she's doing. When is she coming, anyway?"

"She's not sure. She'll be here soon, maybe next week or the week after. She said there was some stuff at work going on that she had to stay and take care of."

"What, greasing the poles? Give me her number. I'll call her in the morning."

"Anyway." Timothy sneered at me and looked back at James. "She's working as a receptionist at Elektra Records. She moved back East . . . two years ago?"

"Three," I said. "I was already gone, remember? She left a few months later, after she was awarded custody of her son. James, you want to take some of this home?"

He held his hand up and made a face. I knew he wouldn't do leftovers, but I also knew it would go to waste here. Between the sores in Timothy's mouth and my emotion-based lack of appetite, there wasn't a lot of eating happening in this house.

I took the containers and our dishes into the kitchen and started blasting the garbage disposal, washing forks and plates, compacting trash in the trash can. It was lovely to have such ordinary stuff to do. Grounding, in a way, to rinse and dry and stack, to make noise, to know that Timothy was not alone and I could close my eyes for a minute, Palmolive running between my fingers, hot water scalding my knuckles, only the sound of running water in my ears and a light steam heating my face.

I came back to find them still talking and laughing and just in time to catch another storm of coughs from Timothy, so I dived in again with the inhaler, the steadying hands, the assurance. When it was over, I announced bedtime.

"You can stay if you want," I said to James, then looked at Timothy. "But you, Mary, are going to bed."

James said good night to Timothy and walked out toward the living room.

Timothy needed help now to get his pills out and counted and swallowed, to unscrew the toothpaste cap, to button his buttons. Something about neuropathy and numb fingertips. We brushed our teeth, put on our matching green pajamas, and then I washed both of our faces with hot rags and Lancôme cleanser. I rubbed lotion into our hands and under our eyes, massaging Timothy's temples as I did so, memorizing his pores and the scar along his hairline. I had him rinse with his throat stuff and left him alone for a few minutes. He came out of the bathroom and sat on the edge of his bed, as if considering prayer. *If I should die before I wake,* I thought.

He swung his legs over and got under the sheet. I pulled the big Indian blanket up to his chest, the one he would kick off in a few hours. We sat and stared at each other, then said good night. I closed the door and walked out toward the kitchen to find James.

I didn't see him right away, so I started the water for tea. I had never been a big tea person until Timothy, but now I was hooked, fully believing all the stuff on the side of the Celestial Seasonings box. The teapot was a big Michael Graves number, all angles and chrome, and as I looked at my reflection in its side, warped and strange, I decided it was closer to how I felt than whatever face a mirror would reflect.

I got two mugs, two tea bags, and the sugar, put them on a tray, grabbed the kettle before it blew too loud, and walked out to the living room. James was on the far balcony. I watched the silhouetted motion of his hand bringing his cigarette up to his lips and back down, as he leaned back, looking at the sky. I stood for a minute, watching him. He turned and our eyes locked briefly. I looked down and started to walk

again while he made room for the tray. I set it down and we busied ourselves with our mugs.

We were quiet for a long time, a pause during which I again wanted
to snatch up his Camels, this time maybe just cram them all into my
mouth, chew them up, and swallow them down with a gulp of tea.
Maybe that would work.

"Are you okay?" he asked me.

No, I thought, *I am far from okay.* I should not even be here. I should
be at home with Simon and Clara, James should be across town, and
Timothy should be healthy and painting something. I shouldn't be
wearing my set of our matching pajamas out on the balcony while he
sleeps, restless and sweaty, my radar picking up on every sound his
lungs make, every movement and wince, and I shouldn't be sitting so
close to James that I can smell the sweet-and-sour plum sauce still on
his fingertips. No. Not okay.

He responded to my silence. "Stupid question, I guess."

I nodded and looked again at his Camels. He saw me looking, asked
if they bothered me. "I'm sorry," he said. "I keep forgetting that you
quit."

"Me, too."

I got up to pace, realized that I was in pajamas, and suddenly felt
self-conscious. I sat down. Except I sat down too close to James, so I
sprang back up again as if I'd sat on a tack and walked over to the far
railing, where I was partially hidden in darkness, where I could look
down at the traffic and the trees on San Vicente Boulevard. I knew Seattle was soon to be a symphony of color, that our neighbor's maple
would look like flames, that the birches along the lake were brilliant
yellow, that our street was dappled brown and golden and orange.
These trees below me here were glossy green, not dying. *Dying.* I heard
the word in my head. I gripped the railing as if it were the only thing
saving me from going over.

I felt James come stand next to me and, inside, I panicked. Simon's
presence was always like a cloak around me, surrounding me, but now

I felt it drop away, James growing too close in, invading, spreading over me like ink or fire or those Santa Anas that had chapped my lips my whole life. His Jack Purcells stayed in the same spot on the concrete, yet his heat was on my skin; his dry, warm, always-clean smell was in my nose; his hands were in my periphery as golden doves, gliding back and forth as if to smooth the railing, to make sure it was even. My sense of Simon was blowing out into the night air, out and away from me. I wanted to reach for it but knew my fingers would close on themselves, into an empty fist.

I reminded myself to breathe. That I was probably imagining this. I was tired, I told myself, emotionally tapped, and James was just being a friend. This wasn't a dozen years ago and we weren't kids, and I was imagining the feel of his hands, the weight of his arm around my waist, the sensation of our chests pressing together as I nearly collapsed on him. I closed my eyes and squeezed them shut hard enough to see the pop-art floaters that spun behind my eyes. I pushed the heels of my hands into my eye sockets so the floaters would become brighter and spin faster, these dazzling geometric shapes hanging in the blackness of my mind.

Then I realized that the weight I had imagined was real. James's arm really was on my waist, and he was asking if I needed to sit down. I could hear him, the way his voice came from a distance like the message he had left on that New Year's so long ago, as if he were very small or very far away. I couldn't answer. I had removed my hands from my eyes and still saw the floaters, now red and black, clockwise, bouncing. I tried to shake them away, but the darkness flooded in as a deeper, more serious red, as if I were seeing the world through a brain bleed. With another few breaths and blinks, I was able to see and hear. Both of his arms circled me, and I leaned forward against him, unable to stand on my own, my arms hanging limp at my sides.

He pulled me back and put his hands on my shoulders. The warmth from them through the cotton pajamas was a memory as old and famil-iar as the yellowed light of Los Angeles, the parching winds, the salty dirty ocean with the silver glints of dead fish, the poppies that dot the hills, the sage that grows wild and sweet on the fringes of the Mojave. He moved his hands to my neck, my jaw. I remembered those hands; I had been trying to fight off the memory of them since the first time they had touched my teenage body. I was convinced he was holding me up, that if he let go I would fall to the floor or disappear altogether.

I opened my eyes but was afraid to look into his. I fixed them instead on the place above the neck of his T-shirt, the place where his collarbones met within an inch of each other. I did not blink. He was saying my name, insistently now, and I finally forced myself to look up.

His eyes were locked on me. I thought back to the nights in his room that first winter. He said I was white as a ghost and brought me closer to him, looked so deep into my eyes that I wondered if he could see the evidence of my fading swirls, if he could feel how afraid I was. I thought back to Jan's parking lot. Our foreheads were almost touching. I thought back to the week before I married Rafael. James tucked a strand of fallen hair behind my ear, wiped under my eyes with the soft pads of his thumbs, and walked me back to the couch, his arm still tight around me, my steps feeling rubbery and unreliable.

We sat down, but again, we sat too close, and I started to get up.

"Don't," he said, and held my wrist, firmly but not forcefully.

We stared at each other.

In that moment, I knew we could so easily lean into a kiss, one that would last all night and that we could blame on grief and stress. We could blame it on Timothy this time. People would understand. James's hand was on my jaw again and mine was up near his temple, my palm flat on the side of his face, along his sculpted cheekbone, next to the shocking color of his eyes, blue as the cold interior of a flame, blue like the little lights along the runway. My thumb started to touch his lips, and it was then that I knew.

This was the other good-bye I had come for. Not just Timothy, not just the idea of home or origins or the past, but James, too. I knew that he had been living in me all this time, as a secret wish, the same wish I had had before on that lonely December afternoon when I called Joan: *someday.* As committed as I was to Simon, to Clara, to my own sanity, I had harbored the dream of an unexpected knock on my door breaking the quiet of a rainy Seattle morning and James and me disappearing forever into the fog like fugitives. These thoughts were nearly invisible, silent, silly, girlish thoughts far back in my mind, but they had existed. And as I sat there I could feel them fading as I admitted them to myself. They slipped away, embarrassed.

I looked hard at James and let my hand fall back to my lap. We would get through the next few days or weeks or months or however long I was here, but when I went home, I would not be taking him with me.

"I can't do this," I said. I moved to the other end of the couch. "I really can't."

He wasn't used to no, especially not from me, and I could see his ego falter and then get up and dust itself off.

"It's still there, though, isn't it?"

"James, it will probably always be there." *But,* I thought, *I won't. This is it.*

He left a little while later, after we had talked enough to fade the freshness of my near-fainting spell and the close call of us with our hands on each other. I walked him to his car and as he got in he gave me the sign language for "call me," his pinkie and thumb making a little phone that he held up to his ear. I nodded. Of course we would talk the next day and the next and the one after, but as I watched his car shrink toward the end of the block, pause, and vanish, I let go of him. I had to. As much as I thought we could put it all behind us, our magnets would always be there. They were sewn into our skins.

So, I thought, when I leave here, it will just have to be a bigger good-bye than I had originally imagined. I will get in Timothy's car and head north, returning to a life that was both incredibly full and strangely empty. I would come home holding a piece of Timothy's spirit, a ragged square like from a quilt, that I could hold tight and then sew to my own, as a patch. A patch over the place that would be hollow without him.

. . .

The nurse called with the new T-cell count the next morning. Twenty-seven. It was like watching the clock hands from the opening sequence of *The Twilight Zone* spinning quickly backward and then flying off into space. I would have to tell Timothy. He would react better to the results than I did, because he had reached some sort of agreement with his body and his God. Timothy, in fact, seemed ready to go at any time. I was not ready to let him do such a thing.

I was sitting outside the bathroom, my head down and the heels of my hands again pressed into my eye sockets, trying not to think about the night before or the number the nurse gave me. It wasn't working. All I could see was James, and all I could think was, *Twenty-seven*. The water shut off and I could hear Timothy moving around, getting a towel, humming, opening and closing the cabinet doors.

"Hon?" I called through the door. "Are you decent?"

"Mostly. Entréz-vous."

He had one towel around his waist and another on his head like a turban. He spun and referred to it with one hand and said, "Well? What do you think?"

I smiled, then laughed. Timothy. My best friend. So pleased with his turban, as if he had invented it himself. "It's fabulous."

He was so thin that I wanted to keep my eyes turned up toward that turban and away from his body. So many ribs and vertebrae, such boy hips, so concave. I flashed back to that exam when I had first checked into the Unit, my big knees and birdlike frame, the way the doctor had tried not to grimace. Timothy read my thoughts, put his hands on his hips, and pinched the extra skin he had where other men his age have sizable love handles. He made a face.

"Pretty bad, huh? I look bad."

"No, no, not bad per se . . ." I stopped talking and started chewing on a cuticle. I made it halfway around one whole nail, spit out the skin, and said, ". . . just . . . slim." I tried to smile.

"All those years of work to stay in size thirty-two jeans, and now I need a belt to keep twenty-nines on. I look like a stick." His shoulders slumped.

He was facing himself in the mirror, and I was sitting on the closed toilet seat lid behind him. His back did look too bony to be real, two flat shoulder blades like some sort of plates, and knobs all the way down the center like a string of pearls, like the ultrasounds we saw of Clara in utero. Sideways he was only a few inches thick.

"But this." He motioned again, elegantly, to his head. "This I call 'The Urban Turban,' and I shall wear it all day." He smiled, looking at it. A string dropped down over his left eyebrow. He brushed it aside as if it were bangs.

"Timothy."

"I'm joking."

"I know. But I have to tell you something."

"What?"

"The nurse called with your new T-cell count while you were in the shower."

He turned toward me. "And? How bad?"

"Twenty-seven."

"Damn." He sounded like Zodiac when he said that, which reminded me that I was going to call her today. He started rummaging through his bathroom drawer. "Let me finish up in here; then you can make us breakfast and I'll read us the paper."

I nodded and went to put the water on for tea. I grabbed our mugs, the same ones he'd had as long as I'd known him, the same ones that witnessed the scene on the balcony last night, and got Zodiac's new work number from Timothy's address book.

I picked up the kitchen phone.

"Elektra Records, how may I direct your call?"

"Oh my God, he wasn't kidding."

"Delia? Holy crap, is that you?"

"It is. How are you?"

"I'm doing great. Fantastic. I'm really busy, though. Whoops—hang on."

She put me on hold and came back. "You'd never believe how crazy this place is. Freakin' people callin' all day long, wantin' shit—"

"I can imagine. So let me just give you a heads-up, and we can talk later. I know Timothy called you the other day, so you know he's sick. But he may try to downplay it, so don't listen to him—listen to me. He's really not well. Like 'get your ass out here' not well."

"Shit. Hang on."

She put me on hold and came back again. The teakettle started to whistle.

"This is silly," I said. "We'll call you back in the next couple days when you're not at work. But you might want to get your vacation request in and look at booking a flight."

"Get the pills out of your eyes," I said to Timothy. It was a few days later, and I was getting his meds counted and sorted and writing out a list of questions for the doctor. Timothy had a Zithromax in each eye socket and his arms out straight like Frankenstein.

"Grrr," was his answer.

"Timothy. The doctor will be here soon. What, pray tell, are you doing?"

He dropped his head forward and caught the pills in his hand. "What I am doing is something you have apparently forgotten, Nurse Ratchet. Does the name Norman Cousins ring a bell? Laughter is the best medicine?"

"Okay, you're right. And don't call me Nurse Ratchet."

"Then don't act like her."

The doorbell rang. "Oh! It's the doc. I'd better put these back in—"

The doctor was here to get some blood, drop off some morphine, and give us the latest lab results. He told us that Timothy, despite his moments of levity, had only fourteen T cells left and a great deal of fluid building around his lungs.

The doctor put a catheter into Timothy's chest to drain some of the fluid. I was supposed to remove it in an hour. Timothy watched with curiosity as the doctor showed me how to slip it out, holding two or three gloved fingers over the site, applying pressure as I pulled, then dabbing it with alcohol after and putting a gauze pad over it. I was supposed to tape the gauze in place, throw the tubes away, throw my gloves away, then wash my hands with antibacterial soap and the hottest water I could stand, finally dousing them with rubbing alcohol as well. I realized we were going to smell like alcohol all the time and that my hands would dry out, that I should pick up a good lotion the next time I was at Rexall. Lubriderm, maybe, or Eucerin.

The doctor made me practice using the syringe while he was there, going into the kitchen and coming out with an orange, a slightly over-ripe orange that I shot water into until he was convinced I could, in a pinch, inject Timothy's morphine. Then he left.

My mind wandered again to safe thoughts, thoughts about lotion, about buying colored Band-Aids to make Timothy laugh, maybe the Sesame Street ones Clara loves so much. I could hear him as he bounced: "I want the Elmo one! I want the Elmo one!" like her. His big brown eyes and her big brown eyes started to blend together, and I sat down, hard, in the chair next to Mickey. I needed to call home. I needed to hear that little girl; I ached with needing to hear her voice. Simon's assurance and comfort couldn't hurt, either. As I reached for the phone, it rang. It was him. I almost cried with relief. I made him put Clara on immediately, at which point I did cry. I missed her so badly, but the sweet longing was discolored by a horrible thought, a thought that was fleeting but real enough to guilt me into a moment of self-loathing: *I wish Timothy would hurry up and do this so I could get back home to my baby.*

We stayed on the phone for forty minutes while Timothy dozed. I watched him while we talked, watched the way his features were lit by the dim lamp and fading dusk, the way his skinny arm came out from the sheets and over his head like a ballet dancer. When we hung up, I refilled the water pitcher and replaced the washcloths with new ones. I folded the blanket at the foot of his bed and counted pills. I smiled when he mumbled in his sleep. I cried when I thought about him having only fourteen T cells left.

When an hour had passed, I woke him up and told him to bear with me as I yanked the catheter out of him. I told him I was sure I was better at just dispensing pills, that I couldn't imagine sticking things in and out of him, but he just half-smiled, for my benefit, and told me to go for it. He did say that his lungs felt better, at least for now, all cleared out and opened up.

After I had successfully removed the catheter and night had swallowed the house in its big dark hands, we turned on the television and watched *Jeopardy,* answering every question out loud and laughing at the contestants' childish penmanship on their screens. The answers I didn't know Timothy always did, and vice versa, which made me want to start crying all over again.

On the first commercial break I made us a big bowl of popcorn, the only food either of us wanted, mostly because we liked having the big bowl between us on the blankets and we liked having something to throw at Alex Trebek when he said things that annoyed us. Until we found out that even the act of throwing popcorn hurt Timothy's chest.

After Timothy fell asleep, I paced, I watched him sleep, I finished the cold spongy popcorn, and I finally went out to sit on the balcony while the sun came up. And I prayed. I prayed harder than I had ever prayed before. I prayed that I had the courage to remain present for this; I prayed not to go insane; I prayed not to inject his morphine into my own arm, even though it looked so lovely in its ampoules, under my control, in my care. Most of all though, running through every prayer like a multicolored silk ribbon from a long-ago dream, was a loud, true, passionate prayer, prayer more like begging, that Timothy would not suffer. *Please, God,* on my knees in the early hours of a quiet West Hollywood morning. *Please, if you have to take him, do it without pain. Please. No regrets, no fear, nothing but peace.* Hands and knees now. *Please. Let him out nicely.* Beating the concrete with my fists. *Please, God, please. Please.* My forehead on the ground. *Please.*

20

Timothy's breath was coming in short wheezes, a low rumble more solid than not, like he was percolating coffee in there. Often he looked at me the way a dog that's been hit by a car looks at the vet. It was a plaintive look, all big eyes and question marks.

I sat next to him and dabbed at his forehead with the washcloth, helped him take his pills, changed the gauze pads taped to his arms, and occasionally injected him with the morphine. He was trying not to use it, trying to be brave, but he said that some days his whole body felt as if it were in flames and those were the days that required more than just aromatherapy and affirmations. I asked him if he still loved his spleen and he whispered, "More than ever, hon, more than ever," and even in this weakened state he managed a wink.

Dr. Vincent came over again and talked to me about viral loads as Timothy slept. Timothy's T-cell count was officially zero. That quick. I could see the grim reaper snapping his long white fingers, like *that*. I could hear the pop.

We talked about the catheter and how I could begin installing and removing it myself. He said Timothy would need it twice a day, an hour each time. He said it wasn't that different from the syringe and I didn't even have to find a vein, so it was actually easier. Easier. I almost said it out loud. Yeah, there's nothing easier than plunging a catheter into your best friend's chest.

There was no fight anymore against the virus. There was only delay. A *pause* button in the form of a tube sunk in next to Timothy's heart, taped down and emptying his bird lungs of the rattly fluid, not all of it, but enough to make both of us more comfortable. We didn't need a sound track of phlegm and fluid. This was bad enough without all that.

When Timothy opened his eyes before dawn on Friday, I knew he wanted to speak, but I also knew his throat was too dry to work. I handed him a cup of water, which he held awkwardly and sipped through a bendy-straw. The plaintive look was back, a child lost. The question marks overflowed. I started to apologize for not being able to answer, to relieve, to cure, to soothe, to rewrite history, but he stopped me with one finger, held up. *Ah-ah-ah,* he would have said if his throat weren't covered in bleeding ulcers, *none of that.* We still took turns alleviating each other's pains.

After another sip of water, he whispered, "Let's go sit in the hammock." It was a hoarse voice, almost silent, more like lips moving and bites of wheeze slipping out.

The hammock. We hadn't been in the hammock in ages. When his balcony was remodeled, the hammock had been put away and forgotten. "Do you still have it?" I pictured its rope grid fraying, sagging, breaking.

"It's on the other balcony all folded up." More lips moving, hands pointing, folding, then our sign for "help me up."

I swung his long legs around so they dropped off the side of the bed and sat next to him. He put his arm around my shoulder. We stood up at the same time, and he used me for balance. We were used to this maneuver by now; we had been doing it for a couple weeks, every time he had to go to the bathroom or just wanted to move around. Sometimes late at night we took very slow walks outside, when the air was still and we couldn't sleep and Timothy felt restless. Sometimes he just wanted to stand outside and see the sidewalk and the palms and the cacti neat in their southwestern pots. He would touch their points and say, "Ow," and we would laugh because he did this every single time, acting surprised by their sharpness. Sometimes he wanted to watch the sun set or rise, and I knew without him having to tell me that he was wondering how many he had left. We both guessed it was in the single digits now.

And so we walked to the other balcony, a slow shuffle of a dance, me with an injured football player, a drunken sailor, draped around my body, leaning, feeling so small. We got outside and I sat him down and ran back to get a blanket, since it was cool and his pajamas were damp with sweat. I sat him in one of the patio chairs, stretched the hammock from one wall to the other, picked him up by his armpits and eased him down into the knots, put the blanket over him, then balanced my way in, not wanting to flip him out the other side. We wiggled in together, all elbows and hip bones, swinging slowly, back and forth like a pendulum, hanging together above the earth, above the city, above time, suspended.

We didn't say much of anything. And I didn't comment when I saw a tear slide down his cheek. What could I say? I let my head fall over onto his shoulder and felt his body move with fresh tears.

We sat and let the newborn sun wash over us, stared at it until our eyes watered and the crying tears mixed with the bright warm pain of looking directly at the sun. We sat with our bodies under the blanket and our wet faces turned to the sky until the phone rang. I had clipped the cordless to my pajamas so when it rang, it came from under the blanket, making us jump and laugh and wipe our eyes.

It was Dr. Vincent calling to check up on us. He told me to get Timothy back inside as soon as we were done with the sunrise. He was coming over at seven to examine Timothy and take blood and collect the container of fluid.

I got up and told Timothy we had to go back in, and he put his arms out for me to pick him up, like Clara does. I half-expected him to start chanting *up up up,* the way she says it with such urgent need. I hoisted him from the hammock and draped him around me, and he turned and looked at the sky one more time before we began the long walk back to his room.

The doctor spent about a half hour with Timothy first, alone, talking more than anything. He may have drawn blood, but we were in the what's-the-point stage now—what was he going to find, one new T cell that had been hiding during the last test? He gave Timothy the good news that the dementia was most likely not coming, that there would be no brain lesions, and that he would probably just have basic respiratory failure and not months of crazed ugly pain. Under the circumstances, we called that good news. He gave Timothy a shot of morphine and then came and found me in the kitchen.

He sat down at the table across from me. "Did you get his temperature last night?"

Inside, I kicked myself. "No."

"That's okay. It's just that sometimes with Pneumocystis pneumonia the final stage is characterized by a very high fever. His is a hundred and three now. He wasn't hot watching the sun rise?"

"No, he seemed fine."

"Well. Take his temperature every hour, and call me if it hits a hundred and four. There are a few things that might help him feel more comfortable, but chances are that this is going to be a scorcher."

He asked me about Timothy's breathing. I got out my Timothy notebook and flipped to the pages where I had written down his respirations, his pulse, and his temp. I had also kept count of the number of times we had used the inhalers, how many inhalers we had gone through, how many times we had hooked him to the catheter. I had written down things Timothy had said in his sleep, the funny mumbly things as well as the semilucid spiritual things. I wrote down the hours he slept and when and what he ate and his medication schedule. In the margins and between sections I had doodled and journaled my own feelings, written down the things we talked about, who called and came over.

The doctor looked over the numbers and frowned. He looked at some of the comments and smiled but stopped when he realized he was bordering on snooping. He closed it and took off his glasses.

"You know this may be it."

"I know."

"You know it may be a matter of days."

"I know."

After the doctor left, I tried to stay busy while Timothy continued his morphine sleep. It was a different sleep from his hot, dreamless sleep. It was heavy, guaranteed—and I couldn't help but envy it. The voice in my head was louder after he'd been given an injection, especially if I was the one handling the needles and vials, even though I had never been an IV drug user; it just looked really, really good. Sleeping like that would give me a break from my own pain, the way it gave Timothy a break from his. I would be, as the song went, comfortably numb.

I could hear the sound of children squealing on the playground outside, reminding me, in the most blatant way possible, that life goes on and we are each merely a thread in a tapestry that is bigger than the sky, older than dirt, and more beautiful than most of us are able to comprehend. But frankly, when I watched Timothy sleep, I didn't care about the big picture. I didn't care if we are a part of a tapestry or if everything happens for a reason. I cared only about the world contained in the space between him and me and the fact that soon that space would be opening up so wide that it wouldn't even exist anymore.

.   .   .

I called Ian and Bill and told them everything the doctor said. They said they'd be over later. I hung up and called Zodiac at work again but made her get someone to cover the phone so we could have a real conversation.

"He doesn't have any T cells left. His count is zero," I said, learning that *zero* is a difficult word to get out when it applies to the amount of ammunition your best friend has left to battle a respiratory infection that will take his life with it when it leaves.

"What do you mean?"

"I mean, it could literally be any day now," I told her, amazed at how calm my voice sounded as it spoke such unspeakable words. "The doctor said it could be days, but it could be hours. It won't be more than a week. Zodiac, Timothy is dying. Please try to get here in time."

"I'll do my best."

I said, "Okay," and hung up, even though I didn't know, nowadays, what *okay* even meant.

James came over straight from work again and offered to go out and get subs from the deli. While he was gone, Timothy drifted in and out of consciousness. He could be completely present and almost energetic; then his head would sink into the pillow, way off to one side. I asked if having people over was going to be too much for him, but he sat up higher in bed and said it would be great. He even leaned forward so I could fluff his pillows.

The phone rang.

"I'm flying standby on Monday," Zodiac said. "It's the best I could do with the money I have, and with trying to get child care and everything figured out. Can I talk to him?"

I handed the phone to Timothy, but he could talk for only a few minutes before he started coughing. I took the phone from him, told her we'd see her when she got here, and clicked the phone off. I pumped the inhaler, but the inhaler was useless. I tossed it aside, too,

298 ♦ Wendy Blackburn

and got him to breathe into a hot washcloth, and for some reason that worked.

"We'll have to do the catheter again," I said, and he made a face, the oh-but-we're-having-company face. I got my supplies from his night-stand and got him started and me cleaned up. I was getting good at this, and that thought saddened me beyond anything else. I had never wanted to become *good at this*. Then I took his temperature. A hundred and three. I watched as the container filled and Timothy looked around the room trying to get a deep breath.

James came back in the middle of all this and froze in the doorway. I motioned for him to come in. He put the sandwich bag down and stood next to the bed, tentatively, then sat on it, behind me. He looked at the tube.

"Does it hurt?"

Timothy smiled and shook his head no, but I saw the pain in his eyes.

We always knew when we could ask only yes or no questions, and this was one of those times, his throat left raw after the coughing, the coughs having ruptured all the ulcers. I asked if he wanted a shot of morphine, and he nodded yes. He looked as if he hurt all over, his bony chest, his fevered head. I swabbed the inside of his elbow, so bruised and scarred now. I poked the needle into the vial and filled it, tapped it, slid it into his vein, pushed the plunger down, and watched his eyes soften and close. James watched me silently.

Ian and Bill came then, and they, joined by James, ate their subs while Timothy dozed. His sat snug and untouched in its wax paper wrapper right next to mine.

While Timothy slept, Ian turned on the evening news and James and Bill and I sat on my futon talking about the details: making sure all the legal stuff was done, figuring out who we would need to call other than friends and family. Timothy was a member of everything: the county art museum, a book club, the Gay Pride Parade committee, the Shanti Foundation, artists' organizations that I couldn't remember all the names of, a poetry group that had been meeting since the seventies. We talked about the house and health insurance and life insurance, and Bill made sure I had signed and notarized the Power of Attorney forms.

Ian was watching the lead story, about another foreign earthquake, one in Turkey and one in Taiwan, and now another, and another, and he turned to us and asked if we thought it was the beginning of the apocalypse. I said it probably was. I said I didn't care. I put my head on my knees and stayed silent until Timothy woke up a half hour later.

He came to in wide-awake mode, cough- and pain-free. At his request, we got out Trivial Pursuit and played one game, all of us on and around his bed, rolling dice and moving our pie pieces around the board. Even after the morphine, even as sick as he was, Timothy dominated. He knew that *BVD* stood for *Bradley, Voorhees and Day;* he knew that Marilyn Monroe's birth and death years were mirror images of each other ('26 and '62); he knew that *taxi* is spelled the same way in eleven languages. He knew everything. I watched him as hard as I could.

For a while, it felt like a regular Friday night, hanging out with friends, talking, laughing, telling stories, eating. Except Timothy was in his pajamas and I walked him in and out of the bathroom and Bill left me with a notarized copy of Timothy's Last Will and Testament and James stayed until the wee hours, helping me dispose of the container and sterilize my scissors and tweezers, then holding me as I cried in his lap when Timothy was finally asleep again.

Other than that, though, it was just like a regular Friday night.

That weekend, James stayed at the house and Ian and Bill came and went in shifts. The house was starting to feel like a hospice, even though that was the last thing Timothy wanted. Everyone bustled around helping, feeding, cleaning, making him and one another comfortable. I did as little as possible that took me away from him. I didn't cook. I had stopped answering the door. Instead we just left it unlocked, and I had affixed to it a note that read: *Come in—we're upstairs.* I did a lot of dabbing and injecting and holding. Sometimes I just lay across his body until he reminded me that his lungs couldn't really deal with the weight of me on them. At night, everyone slept on couches, mats, my futon. I never gave up my place next to Timothy in his bed.

I was the first one awake on Sunday morning. Timothy had some morphine at eleven, and though his breathing was labored and rattly, it hadn't interrupted his sleep. His pajamas were soaked with sweat, so I took off his top and bundled him up. Then I felt his forehead and stuck the thermometer under his arm—he slept through all this—and pulled it out. The mercury stopped right at 104. I called Dr. Vincent, who told me to wake Timothy up, give him ice in whatever form he could handle it—ice water, cold compresses, anything—and call him back in an hour. So I woke Timothy up and gave him some ice chips to chew on, melted cubes on his wrists and neck, and put some in the washcloth and laid it across his forehead.

When I called the doctor back an hour later I was pleased to tell him we were down to 102. He reminded me not to relax too much, that it could spike again at any time. But good job, he said, good job, and that made me want to cry again. But I couldn't cry, not now.

James put on a pot of coffee and brought us the Sunday paper. I took it and went and sat next to Timothy, our knees up, the paper on them. After our slumber parties, Timothy and I had always done the *Times* crossword together and then gone out to breakfast, so that morning, the one we suspected but did not know for sure would be our last Sunday together, we got out our pens (never pencils) and began filling in the squares with letters, making words across and down, filling in the puzzle until it was so dense that it was mostly ink with only a few blanks, my letters all lowercase, his all capitals. James watched us like people watch twins who speak their own secret language.

Sunday continued all over town like usual. People went to church, knelt in pews, held their mouths open to receive tiny crackers that were supposed to mean something. I knew they meant nothing. Timothy meant something, and he was disappearing. He was being stolen. But the people lined up anyway, drank wine from a giant silver goblet, sang songs with their children about sheep and shepherds and sunbeams, and later they would go to matinees, to garage sales, to dinner at their in-laws' homes where they would sit around a table extended with both leaves and eat meat loaf and rump roast and casseroles and apple pie. The kids would fight over toys, the women would do the dishes, the men would doze off in recliners, all of them storing up, in their ways, for the new workweek, for regular life.

Meanwhile I thought of Greta Garbo's response to the quote attributed to her: "I never said I wanted to be alone. I said I wanted to be left alone. There's a difference." And I wanted to be left alone with Timothy. I tried to think of all the things I hadn't yet told him, all the things I'd always wanted to ask him, to know about him, everything I've held back or forgotten. I wondered if we had covered everything. I didn't want to think of something later and pick up the phone only to have to set it back down. I wanted us to be complete, to get it all neat and tidy, but what I've learned is that there is no neat and tidy, there is no normal, even when it looks like people are singing about what a nice guy Jesus is, they are really begging for their secrets and sins to be forgiven, that everyone has their very own unthinkable pain, and that no one makes it through this life without one or two huge scars and about a million little ones you can't even see.

Monday morning I woke up next to Timothy, but he was very still. I whispered his name, then held his shoulder and shook it. He didn't move. I shook it harder. Nothing. I grabbed it and really shook him and practically yelled (*shrill* is the word that comes to mind) his name. He startled awake and looked at me with a wild panic in his eyes.

"What!"

"Sorry. You didn't wake up."

"Yes, I did."

"Not at first."

"What time is it? What's going on?"

"It's six. Nothing's going on. I woke up, and . . . never mind."

He didn't look right. His eyes wandered aimlessly; his mouth seemed to move as if it wanted water or to speak, but it was just him trying to get a good breath. It reminded me of a fish and I looked away.

"Are you in pain?"

"No, I'm all right," he said, but I wondered if that was only because he didn't want any more drugs. He said he didn't like the way they knocked him out. It was great for the pains that spread around his body like gypsies, settling in for a few days here, a few days there, then taking off again; the vise-grip headaches that came from the fevers; the bone ache from the pneumonia, but he hated the coma that came with the relief.

He told me that he didn't have real high hopes he'd last even another week, and I told him what I had been thinking earlier, that I worried we hadn't said everything there was to say. He smiled and said he had assumed that was one of those Zen things: we had said it all, and yet we could never say it all even if we both lived another hundred years.

For me, the collected moments of that day and the days around it are like photographs from *Life* magazine, images seared unforgettably into my mind like that shot of Tiananmen Square. Except now I was the Chinese student standing in front of the tanks. The virus was the tanks. In my head the shutter clicked every few minutes as Timothy slept, coughed, woke; as we sat, paced, cried; as the clock hands spun wildly away; as it grew light, dark, light. The shutter captured James's golden hands over Timothy's pale thin ones, my bitten fingernails. It saw the damp washcloths, the bloody gauze, the swabs, the sharps container, the way Timothy would call for one of us, whispering with a voice that would never come back to the volume it had before, a voice that would first be faint, then fall silent altogether.

Tuesday I woke up thinking of Joan. I wondered if she was watching us, if she was visiting Timothy in his sleep to prepare him for what was coming. Like a tour guide. I sometimes asked him if she came to him, but he remembered only about half of his dreams now, and though he said sometimes she was in them, he could never recall anything specific she may have told him. He said she was speaking to his spirit self. I was still struggling to accept the fact that his spirit self was the stronger part of him now.

I wish I had better memory of that day. I wish the human brain were more effective. All I'm sure of is that it was warm and that there was sun outside, out in that world that I couldn't pay attention to. I know Zodiac had called to say she hadn't been able to get a flight yet, and I know James left for a while but came back afterward. I called home several times that day. The calls were getting shorter but more frequent—I needed quick fixes of them but did not want to be away from Timothy, who slept and woke, slept and woke. He and I talked in between sleeps, and I told him over and over that I loved him and asked him if there was anything I could get him, bring him, anything I could do to make him more comfortable. He just smiled and shook his head no, told me in his wheezy quiet whisper that I was doing it, and held my hand tight as proof that I was all he needed right then.

Ian and Bill came over that night and took me aside to tell me he wouldn't make it much longer. They had been there when Paul died. They knew the signs. It was, they said, just like this in his last days. I nodded as if trying to remember directions or a recipe without writing it down. *It was just like this.* I see. Nothing was like this. Ever. *Ever.* I didn't understand.

· · ·

Wednesday morning we all sat perfectly still and watched Timothy sleep, so soundly he barely moved. James was in the wingback and Ian and Bill sat on the love seat we had brought in from the living room at some point this week. I couldn't recall actually having moved it, though Ian thanked me for rearranging. He also asked me, with a smile to let me know he didn't bite, if I ever planned on changing clothes. I looked down and saw that I was wearing Timothy's pajama top and my cut-off Levi's and couldn't remember the last time I'd worn anything other than that. Days? More than a week? Did I care? Did it matter? No, I told him, I didn't. I sat Indian-style at the end of Timothy's bed, holding his feet through the blanket, my eyes trained on the rise and fall of his breath, a movement faint as clouds moving on a windless day.

His breath was my mantra. My breath followed his; the movement was a part of me. I had nearly convinced myself that we were linked, that as long as I breathed he would breathe, but just after ten I watched his chest as it moved first up and then down and then stayed down. It was that simple. There was just no next breath. No up after the down. I kept waiting for it. I said his name. I said it louder. He didn't answer. He was done. My wild imaginings of harps and operettas and the air parting for God's large hand to come and take Timothy's tiny one never did happen. There was no gasping, no bright light, no angels, no *Evita*-like balcony scene.

It was just us as we had been all week, except Timothy's heart was done beating, his eyes done moving, his voice done speaking and laughing and singing, his legs done walking and dancing, his hands done painting. His eyes were closed, lashes on his cheeks like a child's. I couldn't blink. I kept watching him, waiting for the inhale, waiting like during a break in a song, waiting for the drum to slam back on, the guitar to cry back in, the singer's voice to fill the silence. I watched and waited and my eyes dried out from staring. Finally James touched my arm, and I knew the song really was over.

. . .

When I try now to recall that day, I find parts missing—my brain didn't record it all. I remember James's hand on my arm, the finality like a guillotine chopping off my reality, the weight of it sending me spiraling deeper and deeper into a silent cry of *no* and a held-back, unscreamed noise that was my first lashing out to God, the first sign that I wasn't nearly as accepting of this as I had pretended I was going to be. I remember the way my face scrunched up as I tilted my chin down as far as it would go, hiding in my collarbones the way ducks burrow into their own feathers for protection against cold and danger. I remember Ian straightening the blankets, Bill flipping open his cell phone and walking into the other room, and James remaining stock-still at my side like a splint. I remember Timothy continuing to not move, not hopping up to declare the joke over, just lying there holding his breath, fever gone forever, spirit already on its way up and out into the sky, a morning sky that was the palest, most innocent shade of blue I had ever seen. I remember wondering if Joan was with him already or if he was exploring solo, if he could see us or if that came later. And I remember picking up the phone and calling home and breaking down as soon as I heard Simon's voice.

"He's gone," I finally choked out.

Simon was quiet. Then, "When? Were you with him?"

"It was just a few minutes ago. I was with him. He was asleep, and then he just . . . stopped." I tried to explain it all to him, but I mostly just cried and he consoled.

"Do you want me to tell Clara?" he offered.

I hesitated, even though I had been thinking about this. It would be her first death. I wanted to tell her in person, but I didn't want to wait for the funeral. And I didn't want Simon to do it. So I had resigned myself to telling her over the phone. "No," I said, "I will. Put her on."

"Mama!"

"Hi, sweetie pea. How are you?"

"I miss you," she said. I swear her voice was more grown-up every time we talked.

"I miss you, too, but we're going to see each other in just a couple days," I said. "Clara? Remember we told you that Uncle Timothy was sick? Sweetie, he went to Heaven this morning."

"He died?"

"Yes, he did. He's gone."

"Aw-gone?" She sounded more curious than grief stricken. Oh, to be two years old again.

"Yes, all gone."

And then the words that would stay with me forever: "So he's a angel now?"

After I talked to Simon for a while longer, I called my mom and then Dr. Vincent. Then I let the bright yellow receiver dangle while I put my face in my hands and Ian took the phone and finished the conversation for me.

I was acutely aware that someone at some point took Timothy away, after I had thrown myself across the hull of his earth-body in one last attempt to hold on to him, feeling how strange it was without all the life in it, then feeling someone remove me from him.

I was aware of Bill taking over a lot of the technical stuff that I was supposed to be helping with, so I pulled myself together long enough to call the realtor and the bank, this time finishing conversations and allowing people to offer condolences. It was my first practice with the *I'm sorrys* I would grow to hate. I learned to smile and say, "Thank you," but my insides raged and shrieked and slammed fists against them and their smug ignorant happiness. They were sorry, they said. Right. They didn't know one fucking thing about sorrow.

Thursday morning I sat down in front of Mickey. I would call Hap. I would find a new listing for Matt. I had no idea how to get in touch with Zodiac—she hadn't told me which airport she was flying out of, I didn't have her cell or home numbers, and she hadn't called since Friday. I got out my address book and started with the *A*'s and went from there. I rehearsed and tried to keep my voice strong and somewhat normal, but every time I tried to say the word *dead* or *died* or *funeral* it broke and squeaked like a pubescent boy's. So I got up and stood in front of the mirror and said the words over and over until they sounded like nothing. I said it until the association with Timothy and his affirmations was gone, until my own reflection was only a two-dimensional image and not a real person, until I felt like I could safely dial the phone without cracking up, without shattering.

I started with people I didn't really know. Timothy's old friends, his poetry group, art-world acquaintances. Later, when I felt able to start on the people I did know, I dialed Hap's number in Florida, praying not to get a machine—what do you do in that case? Leave a message? Saying what? Or do you hang up? Why was there not some sort of postdeath etiquette book? Luckily, he answered.

"Hap?" Like I had to ask; he sounded exactly the same.

There was a pause, and then, "Delia? Is that you?"

"It is."

"What's happened?"

He knew I wasn't calling to make small talk. After he had moved to Florida, we hadn't done a great job staying in touch. He had immersed himself in his new life and new friends, and it had been easy for me to let him, because there was so much Joan there: every time I talked to him I was reminded of her, and it hurt. So we sent each other Christmas cards, maybe, and birthday cards for our sobriety birthdays, but not a lot else.

"It's Timothy. He's gone. He . . . died. Yesterday morning. I was with him, and James was here, and we were going to call you earlier, but . . . you know how it is. The funeral's on Saturday. I know it's short notice, but I wanted to invite you. I'd love to see you, and I know Timothy would have wanted you there."

"Oh, boy." He was quiet for a long second. "Timothy."

He said it like it was a stranger's name, a name from a time and a place too long ago and too far away to ever come back to.

Another long silence, and then, "I'm not going to be able to make it." He didn't get into a "money" thing, an "other commitments" thing, or a "short notice" thing. If he was respectful enough to not lie and kind enough to not start making excuses, I would be considerate enough to not press him for reasons. He had moved on. It was that simple, and I had to accept it.

"I understand."

We talked for a while longer, swapping stories about my new life and his new life. There was a sadness as the old comfortable ease of talking to him came back, and I realized it wasn't just Hap who had moved on—we all had. We were all in different states, living different lives. I was nearly in tears again by the time we hung up, torn between memories of my early sobriety and the reality of the present, seeing just how big the space between those times was.

I dragged myself across the room to Timothy's desk, and after a few minutes on his computer, I found a new listing for Matt. It was a "Mr. and Mrs." listing, which intrigued me and again reminded me of how much we all didn't know about one another. I wrote the number down and went into the kitchen to make some more tea, caffeinated this time, to keep me going for Round Two of the phone calls. As the water was boiling, I started crying again: it was when the kettle started to whistle and I thought of Clara, one hand on her hip, the other in the air palm up, stark naked, singing, "When I get all steamed up, hear me shout, just tip! me over and pour me out." I leaned on the counter with my tears dripping onto the tiles, tears like raindrops, full and round. She's a little teapot and her mama's a basket case and her Unca Tim is, as she said, aw-gone. I picked up the kettle, humming her song and crying, and filled my mug.

I made the rest of the calls and fell asleep sometime after midnight. It was a black and silent sleep for which I was deeply grateful: I didn't want to recall Timothy's death, I didn't want him to visit me in my sleep, I didn't want to dream of him alive and wake up to that wonderful split second of denial, the one that would be followed by the crashing realization that he was not in the bed with me. Sleep like unconsciousness was perfect.

21

The funeral was held at Forest Lawn on the backside of the Holly-wood Hills on a glorious Saturday afternoon in early October, though it could have still been summer for all I knew, or winter even. I cared nothing for weather. I walked around with my arms limp and my eyes shiny wet, my head spun like a hurricane.

I was waiting outside for the florist. I felt the beginnings of the hot breath of those Santa Ana winds that had followed me throughout my life and shivered. I knew they would come full force right after I left, come and alter the ions in the air, make people uneasy, tint the sky that uncanny yellow color, blow every leaf from every tree, fan Malibu fires from the Ventura Freeway all the way down to the beach.

As if on cue, with the next gust of wind, James's car pulled into the lot and parked next to the Volvo. I watched him walk toward me. He didn't see me. I was in the shadows and the sun was too bright. I watched as he looked up at the hillside speckled with white marble squares, stopped walking, took his sunglasses off, blinked several times, and reset his jaw. By the time he reached the covered walkway where I stood, he was composed.

He was there early to help organize guests and get a list of who to invite back to the house afterward, but mostly he was there early so I wouldn't be alone. Simon and Clara wouldn't arrive until the last minute, Zodiac had called to tell me about some freak storm that had caused a bunch of delays but claimed she would make it in time for the services, Matt was driving in from Arizona, and Ian and Bill were having a prefuneral gathering with some old friends—friends who were dwindling in number, watching their community get ravaged by this illness, but who were always there to light one more candle, make one more toast, stand up one more time: whatever it took to not allow the gone to be forgotten.

James stood at my side as the clouds overhead changed colors, from a pale orangey-white to a deep pink, almost fuchsia. I turned to him and looked into his eyes, the hundred shades of blue that glinted like seawater.

"Thank you," I said.

"For?"

"I don't know." I looked away. "For all of it. For sitting up with me, for bringing Chinese food, for just being there. I mean, I hate that we have to go through this, but I'm glad we went through it together."

"Me, too."

I saw him start to reach out for my hand. *Don't touch me,* I thought. *I am done with you.* He let his hand drop against his pants, as if he could hear my thoughts.

The feeling that ran through me at that moment was the same feeling as the last day of summer camp or senior year, the finality, the loss, the relief all mingling together. The promises of staying in touch were only made to ease the sadness of good-bye, not to be fulfilled: *"see you later," "we'll keep in touch," "call me,"* we say, when what we really mean is, *This is it.* And when it is it, you know, and I knew outside Forest Lawn that day as James and I stared up at the headstone-dotted hill and, in our own way, without saying the words directly, let each other go. All the other false starts and stops, all the declarations of things we should or shouldn't be doing, none of that had been true. This was true. No more crying wolf.

The funeral director arrived then, and I told James I'd better go talk with him. I didn't look at James when I said this, nor did I turn back as I walked away. More cars started to pull in, and suddenly I was part of a bustling crowd of kisses and hugs and handshakes.

I had walked down to the chapel and was looking inside, counting pews, when I heard the slap of tiny footsteps followed by the unmistakable squealing, screaming, "Mama!" of my daughter as she broke from Simon, making a beeline for me. She was wearing her dressy dress and the black patent-leather Mary Janes she called her slippery shoes, and her hair was a million dark ringlets. She threw herself against my legs and held on, and before I could reach down to pick her up, she was chanting, "Up up up," with her tiny arms stretched over her head. I thought of Timothy on the balcony. I squatted down and wrapped her in my arms, her twenty-five pounds feeling so alive, so solid, so perfect to me. She was wiggly. She choked me with a hug, saying, "Mama," over and over as she buried her face in my collar. There was something in her hand, but I didn't get a chance to look at it or ask her what it was.

Simon came over and put his arms around both of us and kissed first the top of my head and then the tears that had managed to slip out of my eyes onto my cheeks. Eventually we parted, so he could go in and sit down and I could go about my duties, holding Clara the whole time. I wouldn't let go of her, nor she me. I answered questions and helped people to their seats. I looked at my watch and wondered where the hell Matt and Zodiac were.

AIDS funerals are strange.

The crowds are diverse and large—Timothy's was standing room only; there had to be two, three hundred people—and made up of this great combination of stiff homophobic relatives from the Midwest and screaming queens crying into designer hankies. The priest never quite knows what to say or how to say it unless he's had enough experience with this particular sort of funeral to be at ease. Most haven't and talk all around the truth, generalizing about lives cut short but conspicuously not mentioning what they were cut short by. Sometimes there are a number of nervous recent lovers. And sometimes an aunt or cousin won't believe until that very day that it wasn't "just pneumonia." If there was a partner and he is HIV negative, there is his survivor's guilt, and anger from the Midwest Sector. But if the lover is dying, too, the sadness takes on a different angle, say, the romantic doom of Romeo and Juliet. Usually the florals are extravagant, the eulogies are heartbreaking yet witty, and there is a huge party thrown afterward with disco and drinks for everyone, to celebrate life and try to forget how many have already been taken.

Timothy's was not too far from that. Except for the drinks.

There was indeed the gaping chasm between his friends and his family. Nebraska is not a state notorious for its Gay Pride, and that is where his family lived, what was left of them. His mother flown in from Africa, an aunt and uncle, and one estranged sister, none of whom had accepted him in life and who now sat with a defensive and judgmental posture off to the side, in a corner, grim. They wanted to be back home, not here. They wanted to be invisible. They hoped this didn't go on all day. Their long, narrow farming faces were apathetic atop slumped shoulders. This was rubbing their very limited social hairs the wrong way. I smiled, watching them eye the most flamboyant of our friends—Carl in a red suit, David in tight satin pants—and I knew Timothy would have enjoyed their dismay.

Moments later, our golden boy Matt pulled into the parking lot in a convertible, his curls bouncing in the wind. His wife sat next to him, looking as if she could have been his sister. She was a slender blonde with the same hazel eyes and athletic build, tan, tall. He had been coaching tennis, working in a marketing firm, and had about six years sober. They looked like something from an Abercrombie & Fitch catalog.

When we had talked on the phone on Thursday, I could hear in his voice that he was kicking himself for not coming to visit more when Timothy was still healthy.

"Matt, don't be so hard on yourself. Besides, you were there in spirit—we did a lot of reminiscing, as you can imagine. It's so weird, the way some of us changed and some of us didn't. Speaking of, Zodiac is supposed to be coming. She couldn't make it to see him, either, but I've talked with her a few times in these past few weeks, and allegedly she'll be at the service."

"Allegedly?"

"Well, she sounds great over the phone, but her acting was always good; you know that. She has a job in a record studio in New York and she got her kid back. Timothy said she's been clean for a while. But I'll believe it when I see it."

"Is Hap coming?"

"No, he's still in Florida. He couldn't make it."

We had hung up with Matt promising to see me at the funeral, and now I was watching him pull in as Zodiac walked up from the other direction.

I almost wouldn't have recognized her. She had gotten her tooth fixed, and she was wearing a straight black shift and a single strand of pearls, with her hair clipped short again like it was when we met, neat miniature loops close to her head. I had never seen her eyes so clear. They were like glass, deep nut-colored irises against a bright white, framed by long black lashes. Her skin was flawless, vibrant. I was stunned.

At her side was a small boy in a suit, with glossy dark hair and a row of tiny teeth just like her pearls. He held her hand and looked around at all the fancy people and the long black car, and as he looked my way I saw his eyes. They were hers. Elijah. He was beautiful. I counted in my head. He had just turned six.

I watched her walk, I watched Matt get out of his car, I looked back and forth between them and down at myself, and for a second I saw who we had all been twelve years ago—a threesome of young addicts with dull skin and flat eyes, crazy minds and very bleak futures—and who we were now: radiant, fully formed, adult. I stood there in my grown-up clothes and blinked with eyes that saw the whole thing then till now. We had turned into who we were supposed to become if things turned out right. And mostly they had, except for the reason we were here, which still didn't seem right to me at all.

I watched Zodiac's confidence. I thought back to the times that Timothy had had to bail her out, to the night we went to her work to sneak her away from her boss, to the court battle that almost lost her her son. To that first dinner party. To Denny's. I felt like Timothy must have felt all those years. I wanted to applaud; I wanted everyone to see how different she was and how wrong I'd been. Timothy would have been proud. It was his turn for an I-told-you-so, and he was missing it. And it wasn't just her physical looks. There was an aura around her. I wanted to run to her, and yet I wanted to watch her for another minute longer.

I looked over at Matt, who had also just spotted her, and saw the amazement on his face as well. The last time he had seen her was about eight years ago, the night she showed up at a meeting while he was in town for a visit. She was high and asking for money and had offered him the only thing she had left to give in exchange for a twenty, and he had walked away, blinking back tears. She had been slurry that night, with clothes she'd worn for two weeks straight and nappy hair that hadn't been washed for at least that. Now, on the steps of Forest Lawn, he walked over to her, his wife hanging back.

I deliberately slowed my walk, letting my charcoal skirt brush my ankles, its long pleats like an accordion. My black jacket and crisp white shirt were probably too warm for today, but I had woken up cold and stayed cold. Under my cuffs were both that aging strand of pearls Joan had given me and the friendship bracelet Timothy and I had bought together, its colors still brilliant, its knot still strong. Clara was still on my hip, her arms tight around my neck.

Also around my neck was the necklace Timothy had given me on my eighteenth birthday, the silver one with the big hunk of beachglass and the tiny colored beads. I reached up and rubbed it, this shard of glass with the soft edges. With each tumble in the waves it had been brought closer to what it was now, and I thought about the day Timothy gave it to me and everything that had happened since then, all the things that I had joked would "build character," and realized that they really had. My sharp, cutting edges were softer. I was less brittle. Life had tossed me around and covered me with battle scars and dents and imperfections, and I had washed up on another shore a wonderful little piece of art. Broken, yes, in the sense that I was no longer the whole bottle, so to speak. But better the way I had emerged: unique, strong, with a story to tell. Something that stops beachcombers in their tracks and makes them take a second look, makes them think about the power of time and transformation.

I began to walk over to Matt and Zodiac and saw them look at me the same way I had looked at them. I guess we all got it, in those few moments: we had turned out all right. And we would get through this, too, because we could get through anything—and wash up on shore more beautiful for it. It was one of those moments that, as a memory, becomes slow-motion; it wraps itself in tissue as it's happening, to be pressed between pages and visited over and over again into old age. We couldn't not stare at one another, beaming with pride and shock and nostalgia. Mostly pride. I set Clara down and the three of us fell into an embrace, put our foreheads together, and said nothing. Some moments don't get any words; they don't need any.

I picked Clara back up and we turned to walk inside. We all walked up the wide center aisle together, stopping at the front pew. I introduced Simon to Zodiac and Matt. Matt introduced us to his wife. Elijah and Clara had already begun making faces at each other, giggling. Zodiac and I watched our children play together. Just as I looked at her to see if she saw, she looked at me. We were mothers and our children have met. Around us people mingled, and we stood there until we heard soft music coming from what seemed like the walls or the air and knew that was our cue, that it was about to begin.

·   ·   ·

Everyone sat down when the priest arrived at the altar. Father John was a friend of Ian and Bill's, a Jesuit priest, a genius, and loving even beyond what one expects from a guru. His wide-set eyes emanated compassion and kindness, and his smile was more luminous than the rows and rows of candles that glowed golden beside the pews. His laugh was genuine and deep, his words wise. Most everyone who met him instantly wanted nothing more than to shrink and curl up into his soft palm, to be cradled by the pure tenderness of his touch. One look at him standing there with that quiet smile on his lips was all it took for my tears to spring to life, poised behind my eyelids like sprinters at the starting blocks, ready to go if I blinked.

But there was a box, a seven- or eight- or whatever-foot box between him and me, a horizontal polished box of burled mahogany with subtle brushed-steel hardware, an attractive box, sure, but its lid was open and in it was Timothy, looking just as he had for the past several weeks, thin and asleep. My mind did not want to digest this.

He's in there.

Father John began to speak, slowly, gently. He addressed the group as "Dearly Beloved," said a few religious things, then put down the book he was holding and took off his glasses.

In the box. Timothy is in the box.

I wanted to scream, to tell whoever was in charge that there had been a mistake, that Timothy was not supposed to be in there. Someone else, anyone, I didn't care, just not him.

I could almost see him, if I leaned forward, safe against the white satin folds. From his sweaty vitamin-smell sheets that were constantly coming untucked to reveal the slippery blue mattress underneath, to this, the bed of a king. It smelled of citrus and clover and looked like a cloud, cool and silvery. It would be a good bed to dream in, the kind of dreams that took you out-of-body and far above the rooftops. The kind of dreams Timothy had lived for.

The priest continued to talk, but I wasn't listening. Clara sat on my lap, and I finally looked to see what it was she was clutching in her hands. It was the card Timothy had painted her for her second birthday just a few months ago, a multicolored "2" with spirals and hearts and moons around it. She held it tight to her tiny chest, mouthing one corner of it, her wide-open espresso-brown eyes trained on Father John, listening to him, sitting perfectly still.

He asked us to join him in a moment of silent meditation, and as the room quieted, it was as if they all peeked in—Joan, Timothy, Gabriel, my almost-baby—little ghosts smiling through the pews, floating milky in front of the jewel-toned stained-glass light. Around me, people's eyes were closed, their heads bowed or tipped heavenward, their hands crumpled neatly in their laps. If I strained, I could hear voices, I knew I could, under the wind that blew outside. Whether it was those little ghosts or my imagination I'm not sure, but I heard them. I just couldn't make out the words.

After Father John's talk, I stood to begin the procession past Timothy's coffin. I was supposed to go first, but when I set Clara on Simon's lap and rose from the dark wooden bench my legs felt noodly, and I didn't trust that they would actually support my body. Somehow I managed to straighten myself up and take a few steps forward. I had to grit my teeth to make my chin stop its jackhammer rattle. My eyelids were allergic raw puffs at half mast, and it seemed as if I had done nothing but cry since Wednesday, since August. I had actually grown accustomed to the heavy lump in my throat that came every time I began to say Timothy's name and the shaking inside my chest that came when I remembered he was really dead and this wasn't just a nightmare.

I made it to the front of the room but was at first unable to look at the Timothy in the box that looked like a mannequin. I thought of the people in the Wax Museum. I took a deep breath, cleared my throat, and put my hands on the edge of his coffin. I looked at him for a long time, and finally I leaned down and kissed him gently on the forehead, stroking his hair. He was cold. It startled me. I was so used to him being hot.

I whispered to him, "Get some rest, hon. It's all over now."

A teardrop fell onto his suit, disappearing instantly on the dark fabric, soaking in and fading out of sight, just as the soft twang of guitar chords began.

"Sweet Baby James." Of course. I went back to my seat and put my forehead on my knees. Ian and Bill had been right—there was hardly a dry eye in the room. Anyone who looked at Clara teared up. She was the youngest mourner, not yet three, one tiny starfish hand holding tight her souvenir of her Unca Tim, the other on her mama's back, trying to soothe. I didn't dare look at her, my beautiful daughter so sweet and brave, comprehending but not.

22

Two mornings later I packed the Volvo with my bags and the things Timothy wanted me to have. In the trunk were three small paintings, Timothy's two best turtle boxes—a glass one from Mexico and a wood one from Egypt—and a crate of books. He had arranged for the old wingback chair to be shipped to me after I got home. There were a few more things in a box that I kept next to me on the passenger seat, things that I cherished deeply: the picture from my eighteenth birthday party, his watch, his paintbrushes, Mickey, the teakettle and the two mugs, his Indian blanket, both of our sets of pajamas, and six full sketch pads. I had stayed up late after the funeral, after everyone had left and Simon and Clara were asleep, sitting on the foldout, poring over those sketch pads. Page after page of pencil drawings, some that made it to canvas and some that did not, some very rough, some so beautiful on their own that I knew I would frame them as soon as I got home.

Everything had been taken care of ahead of time. Timothy already had a realtor to list the house, and it was in his will for the money to be split among several friends and charities, the majority of it going to AIDS research. His belongings were either predetermined for certain people or donated. A local gallery was given a few paintings and his friends got the rest. It was all very organized and responsible, very reasonable. There were no squabbles, no worries, no questions. He'd taken care of it down to the last pair of moccasins. Those were mine.

I made sure the lights were off and the doors were locked. I left the key under the cactus pot for the realtor to pick up later that day. I stood in the driveway for at least ten minutes, just standing, looking at the building, as it all played behind my eyes like an old movie, a movie I had seen a million times but couldn't get enough of. I had memorized its dialogue and knew every detail of its set, every word to the sound track; I knew the actors and their motivations; I had my favorite scenes and scenes for which I covered my face.

I saw the Unit's bedrooms, the elevator, the nurses with their flashlights, and the terrifying helicopters just on the other side of the shatterproof windows; I saw Timothy and me late at night, Matt and his playing cards; I saw Joan's ruby smile and her hair as white and exact as a sheet of paper, her green eyes, her Birkenstocks. Hap was grinning and James was looking at me over his shoulder as he walked away. Rafael stood at an altar, then there was an earthquake, and he was gone. There were birthday parties, drives over hills and through canyons and into the mountains far away; there were strippers and a hundred million AA meetings. The backdrop was this building and Jan's and that little log cabin a few blocks away, it was the duplex and a tiny Venice bungalow, it was the Bodhi Tree and a man opening his door naked and smiling a crooked smile and a drag queen so big and so beautiful that when she walked across the screen everything but the music stopped, in fact it grew louder, and of course it was Gloria Gaynor, and of course she was singing that she would survive. *That* was what I had to remember, as I put my hand on the old chrome handle and opened the driver's side door. I would survive.

I let the music fade and the screen go black, and I slid into the seat. The whole car smelled like Timothy, and I closed the door quickly behind me and made sure to keep the windows up, so I could hang on to that smell as long as I could.

Two days later I was getting off the freeway and driving past clapboard houses with kayaks leaning in their driveways and little brick Tudors from the turn of the century lined with rhododendron trees just as old. There were storm clouds so far in the distance I couldn't yet see their coal black weight, but I was beginning to sense them, like I could sense the pending arrival of the Santa Anas. Most of the streets in Seattle are only one lane each way, and the cars are modest with bumper stickers about windsurfing and saving the salmon and the rain forests.

My inner *chola* snickered, and I told her to go away. *I'm home now,* I told her, and she said, *No, you are not.* She always thinks she knows better. I told her, *Go back to Mexico, to Venice, to Alvarado Street, get out of my head.* She said I'd be going south someday for good, and I said I didn't think so. *Cierre su boca,* I told her: shut your mouth.

As the street petered out, nearing the lake, I took a deep breath. Only a few blocks away now, and I couldn't help but remember the way Timothy had come leaping out of his house the day I had arrived in LA. I hoped Simon and Clara would stay inside. I hoped I was earlier than they expected and I could catch them off-guard. I didn't want them bounding out the front door like puppies, like Timothy.

Just as I was about to knock, Clara's face appeared in the sidelight window and she squealed—more like a scream—and I could hear her feet doing some sort of tap dance like Snoopy, her legs a blur of happiness as she jumped up and down, calling, "Daddy! Come let Mama in! *Now! Pleeease!*" I heard him unlocking the door; then she burst out like from a cannon and threw her body around my legs, knocking me backward a couple of steps. Simon took me in his arms and walked me inside. Clara was latched onto my hip like a monkey, with her hands on my face. I was home.

I sat down on the cool sand on the shore of Lake Washington. I had been home for three days, and this was the first time I had allowed myself to be alone. Solitude made me anxious, as if in its silence I might think a thought I hadn't had yet, and it would be the one thought that would slice through me and leave me screaming blind into the morning, leave me catatonic and shaking, leave me rocking myself and drooling as the whitecoats came to haul me away while the neighbors shook their heads in wonder. *She had seemed so together,* they would say, their freshly washed faces confused atop their fleece pullovers.

So I tried to think in a careful manner, letting words and images in one at a time as if through a turnstile in my frontal lobe. *One at a time, please,* I told them, *no pushing or shoving.*

I looked across the lake at the houses on the other side and the pinking-shear edge of snow where the mountains met the nearly kohl sky and thought of Echo Park, so different. Echo Park is downtown LA's most perfectly ugly beauty, a ring of tall skinny bending palms around a lake full of pigeons and half-dressed Mexican children brown from dirt and sun, their jet-black hair shining blue in the stale heat. Years ago, they drained the lake and people went scavenging in the muck, coming back with old coins, bottles from the forties, single shoes, costume jewelry. Even as an adult, when I drive past that lake I don't see the water; I see my childhood memory of it, crowded with people all the way out to the middle, their jeans rolled up and their eyes bright, their heads keenly sweeping back and forth like metal detectors, arms full of soggy treasure, late sun striping them with the shadows of the palm trees that circle the park like prison bars.

No palm trees here. No *Lignum Vitae,* either. Around me were pines, dogwoods, cedars, cherries. Northwestern trees. Timothy had told me once that he had always wanted to be in Paris in the wintertime, snow falling as he stood on the Champs-Elysées, cherry trees shedding pink blossoms at his feet, and we had argued about the timing: I told him cherry trees bloom and molt only in April, and he had refused to listen. Now I was glad he had held on to his vision and annoyed with myself for trying to inflict reality upon it. Let him have his Christmastime cherry trees with their pink popcorn fluff swirling together with the snowflakes.

I looked down and saw that I was sifting.

My hand was like a child's, like Clara's starfish hands. The sand that fell through it was coarser and grittier than my dusty hometown sand, but it slid through in the same way, leaning with the wind like four tiny waterfalls. I drew patterns in it and repeated a figure eight over and over like a racetrack, my fingers curving with each turn. It hypnotized me. I picked up the few rocks that lay tossed around me, collected them all in one hand, and counted them like you would count foreign money, palm arched back and full of small curious denominations, looking at each one carefully, holding them up for inspection.

I knew my grief for Timothy would never fade entirely. There would be no methodical tapering of feelings, no regularity to the amount of sadness I would feel on any given day, no mathematical process with a formula making it easier as time went on. Already today there had been rough moments sandwiched between peaceful ones, like lunatics carefully swaddled in straitjackets, and it wasn't even noon yet. Driving home I had felt strong and this morning I had felt weak. Less than a year from now I would have to face anniversaries daily for weeks, as I relived the dates between when he called and when he died. I knew that October would never again pass quietly, and I would always think how he hadn't lived quite long enough to have one more birthday, or one more Halloween. I would not want to dress up. The candy would remind me of pills. The happy scary carved pumpkin faces would haunt me, and I would look away in teary disbelief that my best friend was really gone.

But I would hope that in this comparatively conservative northern town, at least on Halloween I might somewhere spot a man dressed as a woman and be reminded of Momma, of the way she always came to me like a vision, reminding me that we do go on, we do survive, and that even when we don't feel like doing anything other than sitting on the couch, we get up, we get dressed, we put on our makeup, we paint our toenails the campiest Pepto-Bismol pink we can find, and we smile, wide, because life is just too short to feel bad for too long. She would tell me with a single bat of her inch-long eyelashes that pain is no reason not to live. Her fingernails would click like maracas; she would

sweep an arc overhead with her huge hand, snap her fingers, and tell
me to get my bony ass out of bed and go dancing.

As I pulled another trickling moving handful of sand up out of the
beach and into the air in front of my face and watched the millions of
grains pour out in quadruple streams, I glimpsed a piece of beachglass.
It fell through almost unnoticed, but I dropped the rest of my handful
to retrieve it.

It was pale green like Joan's eyes and shaped like one of Timothy's
guitar picks. I remembered what Timothy had told me when he gave
me the necklace, the thing about survival and not only surviving but
thriving and how, as alcoholics, that's what we did. *We took a lickin', and
kept on tickin', hon.* I rolled and stroked it yet another layer smoother; I
spun it between my fingers like a lucky charm; I closed my eyes and felt
its satin edges.

It was beautiful not despite but because of the friction it has had to
endure. It had been thrashed around, but instead of being destroyed, it
was improved with every scratch and scrape, sculpted. In fact, the
scuffs themselves are what gave it its quiet splendor; they are responsible for turning a simple piece of glass (which could have just as easily
been trash) into a gem. It wouldn't be the same without the wear and
tear; it wouldn't be something pretty enough to be turned into jewelry
if it hadn't been damn near broken. I closed my fist around this tear-
shaped gem and thought about my own uneven edges, my own abra-
sions, the things I have endured that have, instead of breaking me,
completed me, prepared me for the next tumble. Its odd beauty was
hard-won. It came from reinventing itself. From having risen to the top
of the discard pile. Like a phoenix, from victim to victor.

In that moment, all my blurry musings about why this had to happen came into focus. I still thought it extreme that it took losing my
best friend, but, as the old AA saying goes, *it takes what it takes.* And for
me, it took losing Timothy to make me stop and take stock of my life
up until that point. To see my own metamorphosis. To reflect back on
my recovery and realize that yes: I have gotten better. And yes: I can

get through anything—even this, even the next thing, and the thing after that—because each prepares me for the next. Ironic that the disease
that almost killed me provided me with the recovery that makes it possible for me to live—and live fully and abundantly and completely,
without getting drunk over anything. Not even this. I heard once that
when a broken bone heals, it is strongest in the place where it was broken. Well, so was I.

I held the piece of beachglass up to the weak sunlight. From that angle I could see through it. Its scar tissue had left it nearly impenetrable,
but not entirely. I could still see the light through it, and the world, in
a whole new way. I stood up and put it in my pocket.

I felt like an explorer coming home from a long expedition—yes, *a
dig,* thank you, Joan—where I sat facing a carved-out hillside and either
unearthed or interred the characters who had once upon a time played
the main roles in my life. I have sorted them into their proper phyla and
genera and species; I have labeled their remains and packed them in
gauze and vials or brought them with me as tiny shamans. I've wrapped
Rafael in a sheet and placed him in the ground; I've kissed James's
cheekbone and set him far away on top of the mountain like a god. I
had been prepared to leave Zodiac in a cave, but she ran out into the
sunlight at the last minute and sits naked on my shoulder like Nefertiti.
Matt remains beyond the horizon but otherwise close by and brushed
free from dirt, where I know he is safe but have no need to disturb him
unless there's another emergency. Hap is on the shoulder opposite Zodiac, storytelling like a tribal elder, looking up over the wire rims of his
glasses.

And there are two others who are where they've been since the moment we met: woven into the fabric of my very being. Joan has her
pure-white place secure in my soul, a place of silver Birkenstocks and
secret smiles, a place from which I am guided on a daily basis. And
Timothy is right next to her in his paint-thick overalls and suede moccasins, holding on to my heart. We talk all the time in my dreams, and

I see his face as a constellation when I am alone in our backyard, lying flat to the ground so I don't get sucked into space.

As I walked home that afternoon, I knew that Joan had been right, that I had what I needed inside me all along. They were all there. Where else would they be? And now I have a new family to walk home to, a man who knows that when I tip my head a certain way I am listening to things that not everyone can hear, and a shiny-eyed angel-girl who will grow up wondering who Unca Tim was and why he was so important to her mama.

I will try to explain to her that without him, she wouldn't exist, that without him, her mama might never have made it all the way through to this side of it, that without him, everything would have been so different, so unfull, so just a shell of what it is now. She will tip her head in the same way, as if trying to hear that secret swirl of ghost voices that I do, and she will ask again to see the pictures. I will open a scrapbook of photographs, a notebook of sketches, a journal of stories. She will stare at one picture, taken on a long-ago birthday at a moment when the whole world was perfect, on fire but perfect. As I watch her eyes widen and her chest fill with giggles that escape through her smile like a song, I will finally understand that it is always perfect, that when you have a whole mountainside of people inside you and a lucky charm of beachglass in your pocket and a life made complete as much by the pain as by the joy, you've done something right. I'll watch the flames reflect in her eyes and be reminded of birthday candles never blown out by Gabriel, of desert campfire ashes and orange feather boas sparking into the sky, and I will know that only in the hottest fire lies the brightest light.

Acknowledgments

Writing and publishing this book would not have been possible without the help of the following people:

First, Charlotte Gusay—agent, guide, advisor, friend: Thank you for it all. For finding the gem that was buried under all those extra words and never giving up on making me dig for it, for understanding why this story needed to get out there, for connecting me with exactly the right people, and for walking me through every step of the process. Also, thank you to Marta Peimer for insisting that Charlotte read it.

Diane Reverand: An extra-special thank-you for your savvy, your expertise, for treating my book with such good care, and for "getting it" in a way that few others did. And to the rest of the team at St. Martin's Press—namely Regina Scarpa, for patiently answering all zillion of my questions.

Marti Kanna, upon whose doorstep I arrived one long-ago summer evening. I plunked a very unwieldy 688 pages down on her coffee table and asked her if she thought there was hope. She said she did, and it was her initial edit that got that big shaggy manuscript into a manageable size and shape. Marti, I thank you for wrangling my raw work into something coherent.

For the final polish and utterly brilliant mind: Debra Ginsberg, editor extraordinaire. Without your hand in this, I honestly doubt that my work would have ever found its way into publication. I mean that. Thank you in the grandest way possible.

For reading some or all of early and later drafts, I thank the following people—fellow writers, teachers, wordsmiths, grammar police, friends, cheering section: Trina Burke, Dolores Carney, Sean Carroll, Alev Croutier, Alison Leon, Daniel Matlock, Roy Ngan, Ray Rhamey, Gary Schmechel, Mark Sivertsen, Wendy Tokunaga, and Jan Wright. Thank you for your passion for the written word, your trust in the process, your encouragement, and your candid critiques. A nod of recognition also to Suzanne Murray and the Writing Circles writing group, the Richard Hugo House, and Seattle Writergrrls.org.

Maybe a little less directly, but certainly no less important, the following people have had a hand in the creation of this story simply through their fabulous presence in my life:

My colleagues in the chemical dependency field: I treasure the spirit of solidarity we have as we fight the disease of addiction together, and the camaraderie shared regardless of victory or defeat; specifically to the team at Residence XII, I feel fortunate to work with such skilled clinicians, such wisdom, such integrity. To my clients past, present, and future, it's an honor to be a part of your early days of recovery. To the people of AA worldwide, I thank and applaud you for always being there to save the next life; and to the people of AA in Los Angeles, I thank and applaud you for saving mine.

My longtime friends, whom I thank for making my world such a rich and wonderful place to be: Cindy Victorín Ortiz and Vicki Musenga for being like sisters to me for as far back as I can remember. I cherish our childhood and the way we have held on through the years—it's rare, and it's a beautiful thing. Jennifer Werndorf, for the sound of your laughter as we have gone from summer camp and braces to motherhood and mortgages. Your unflagging friendship is invaluable to me, and I look forward to growing old with you. Kori Shintaku Brown, whose confidence in me was often much greater than my own, for always telling me that I was going to write a book when I grew up (you were right!). Galen Kawaguchi, for nearly a decade of babies, long days at the beach, and all-around good times. Rick Cronin, for hanging in there with me in the very beginning, for seeing the good in absolutely everything, and for making me laugh when I thought I couldn't anymore. Also: Ricardo Bracho, without whom I may not have survived junior high school. Dana Alatorre, Lisa Lierley, Nash Perkins, and Peggy Pahl: strong women, good friends.

And finally, my most profound expression of gratitude is to my family: My parents, Mike and Linda Harrington, for their unconditional love, for all the stuff they taught me, and for being far better parents than the ones in this story. My husband, Jerry Blackburn, whose persistent optimism and boundless energy are the perfect antidote for my creative angst. I am so glad we found each other in this big world, and I love you more than anything. Ted Witus, for the various permutations of our relationship and the ease with which we've moved into each new phase. Lindsey Witus, my magical little girl, for delighting and amazing me every single day. You're the best daughter a mom could have ever dreamed up and the light of my life. And to the tiniest one still in my tummy as I write this page, you've already brought me so much joy, and you're not even here yet! You all mean so much to me, and I know that without each of you I would never have had the inspiration, the strength, the time, or the reason to sit myself down and actually go through with this, one of my biggest—and I thought most unattainable—dreams. Words, for once, fail me. So a simple "thank you" will have to do for now.

Garrett's popcorn